MURDER
BY
MOONRISE

Kensington Books by Patrice McDonough:

Murder by Lamplight

A Slash of Emerald

Murder by Moonrise

PATRICE
McDONOUGH

kensingtonbooks.com

KENSINGTON BOOKS are published by

Kensington Publishing Corp.
900 Third Ave.
New York, NY 10022

All Kensington titles, imprints, and distributed lines are available at special quantity discounts for bulk purchases for sales promotion, premiums, fund-raising, educational, or institutional use. Special book excerpts or customized printings can also be created to fit specific needs. For details, write or phone the office of the Kensington Special Sales Manager: Attn. Special Sales Department. Kensington Publishing Corp., 900 Third Ave., New York, NY 10022. Phone: 1-800-221-2647.

Library of Congress Control Number: On file

KENSINGTON and the K with book logo Reg. US Pat & TM Off.

ISBN: 978-1-4967-4642-9
First Kensington Hardcover Edition: March 2026

ISBN: 978-1-4967-4644-3 (ebook)

10 9 8 7 6 5 4 3 2 1

Printed in the United States of America

The authorized representative in the EU for product safety and compliance
is eucomply OU, Parnu mnt 139b-14, Apt 123
Tallinn, Berlin 11317, hello@eucompliancepartner.com

To Carol McDonough, always my first reader

At the rising of the moon, at the rising of the moon . . .
Who would follow in their footsteps at the rising of the moon?

—John Keegan Casey

MURDER
BY
MOONRISE

The tall, pole-thin man in a dark topcoat and bowler hat looked out of place.

He trailed the Moonraker's tavernkeeper through the crowded, low-ceilinged pub, shouldering past fishermen and dockers who'd labored since sunup. He ducked under a soot-blackened beam, knocking his hat and curling his nostrils at the reek of spilled beer, carp, and sweat.

"He's in the storeroom." The barman jerked his thumb at an oak door. "Downing my whisky."

The newcomer fished in his pocket and flipped the innkeeper a half crown. Then he lifted the iron latch and pushed. A man the size of a steamer trunk in a soiled tweed cap hunched over a half-empty bottle, a shot glass on the table and another in his square, meaty fist.

"Could've grown a beard, waiting for you," he growled, downing his drink.

"And look more a ruffian than you are?"

He dropped his bowler on the table and sat. Light from a hanging oil lamp glinted off hair the color and texture of straw.

His eyes were nearly as colorless, shading to light blue at the edge of his irises. He tipped whisky into the empty glass, sipped, and grimaced.

"Bilge. How do you drink this swill?"

The burly man reclaimed the bottle and poured two fingers. "What's taking you to the island?"

"Spot of bother over a girl, but I'll arrange things."

"The maggot couldn't keep his hands off her, I'm guessing."

"She'll be sorted, although he was reluctant at first. As for the shipment—"

"McGrath's sweating it, saying they know it's on the way."

The thin man cocked his head. "That's what you wanted to tell me?"

"Could be trouble at the port."

Pale eyes flashed. He grabbed his companion's wrist, sending a jet of amber liquid across the table. "Don't go sour on us now, boy-o."

"Bleeding hell." He broke the man's iron grip and rubbed his hand.

"Plenty of sweets for all the kiddies when it's done and dusted." The thin man retrieved his bowler and stood. "Hate to break up the party, but the last steamer leaves for the island in an hour."

Outside, he raised pale eyes to the night sky. A waning crescent moon shone dimly through a bank of thin clouds. He brushed the crown of his bowler, flipped it, and tugged it on by the back of the brim. Then he patted his scowling companion on the shoulder.

"You worry too much," the thin man said, raising his voice over the rattle and screech of a passing train. "No loose ends . . . that's my motto."

He whistled, strolling away, heading toward Southampton's docks and the last ferry to the Isle of Wight.

CHAPTER 1

October 1867

Dr. Julia Lewis flinched as a spray of saltwater slapped her face.

She braced herself on the heaving deck as the steamer's bow rose and fell, the ship plunging toward the Isle of Wight. At that moment, she'd happily exchange her lot for London's clammy fogs, solid pavements, and a line of patients queuing at her clinic.

Kate Connelly's right hand anchored her straw bonnet. She took Julia's arm with her left. "Come away from the rail, Doctor Julie," her maid said. "You're looking all green, you are."

Julia shook her head and tightened her grip. "I'll disgrace myself on the deck if I look away."

"'Tis mind over matter, they say."

"More like my head over the rail in another minute."

Julia dragged her eyes to where sea and sky met and tried to fix her gaze on the line. It wasn't easy as the paddle-wheeled vessel pitched and churned. She was never a happy sailor. Julia's trip across the Atlantic to medical school in America had been a voyage of prolonged torture. As for the steamer to the Isle of Wight, there were many days when the strait that separated the island from Britain's south coast was in a placid mood. That afternoon, it kicked and scowled.

Things went from bad to worse when word spread among the ship's passengers that their route had changed.

"Shoals, miss," the first mate said. "They've formed across the approach to the landing at Cowes Harbor, so we'll swing farther east."

Julia groaned. "How much longer?"

"Nothing to speak of," he said. "Quarter of an hour, maybe."

The sightseers and seasoned sailors with iron stomachs didn't seem to mind. They crowded the rails and craned their necks: the eastern route afforded a distant glimpse of Osborne House, the queen's residence in East Cowes.

"The royal standard isn't flying," a passenger said, peering through field glasses. "Her Majesty must be away."

Someone whistled. "Look at the size of that yacht at anchor. Belongs to the Prince of Wales. Wonder what Bertie's doing at Osborne without the queen?"

A third man elbowed his friend and winked. "While the cat's away."

Twenty miserable minutes later, the steamship slipped into the protected waters of Cowes Harbor.

Kate said, "You're looking less green already."

Julia smiled wanly. "I may live after all."

"'Tis just what the doctor ordered, if you don't mind me saying. New sights and fresh air to breathe."

"You and I could do with both. Speaking of sights . . ." Julia peered over the rail, scanning the crowd on the quay. "I don't see—"

"There they are. Over to the left." Kate streamed her handkerchief. "'Tis Doctor Lewis and your great-aunt, waiting by a four-wheeler."

Julia's grandfather lifted his hat and waved it, his snowy hair catching the early afternoon sunlight. Then he pointed them out to his sister, Lady Aldridge.

Kate left Julia with her doctor's case and carpetbag and searched for a porter to carry the rest of their luggage. A half hour later, they rolled up to the white, ivy-covered hotel only steps from the seawall. Julia climbed down from the carriage and looked up at the castle-like façade of the Marine Hotel.

"Grandfather, you've booked us into a palace by the sea."

Dr. Lewis took Julia's arm. "Fit for a future king. Fit for my granddaughter. I'm told the Prince of Wales is a regular guest during the yachting season."

"How grand."

"A party of young men in his set is staying here now," Aunt Caroline said. "Laying up their boats for the winter. Or putting them down. I can't remember which they said."

"Odd that the prince takes rooms here," Julia said. "Why not stay at Osborne House with the queen?"

"Oh, he stays at Osborne when Her Majesty is away." Dr. Lewis chuckled. "Keeping out of his mother's sight affords Prince Bertie, ah . . ."

"More scope for mischief," his sister said.

"He's there, now. Kate and I saw his yacht at anchor." Julia turned her face to the light breeze. "You were right about the soft air and sunshine, Aunt. On land, at least."

"The Isle of Wight is just the tonic you need, my dear. But first, a rest is in order." Lady Aldridge handed Kate the room keys. "After that, join me downstairs for tea."

"With pleasure." Julia kissed her aunt on the cheek and followed Kate up the stairs. *Six weeks away from London, and she's longing for the news,* Julia guessed. *And she'll want to hear about Richard.*

Julia was Scotland Yard's first female medical examiner and had worked two cases with Detective Inspector Richard Tennant. After a rocky start, their uneasy alliance evolved into a respectful partnership and friendship. *And something more?*

Lady Aldridge would ask about his hunt for the man who'd slipped the net on their last case. But nearly a month of silence followed Julia's last letter. Aunt Caroline would want to know the state of the chase *and* her niece's heart.

If only I had answers.

Lizzie Dowling sped down the path from Osborne House. Her lithe way of moving made her seem girlish, but when she smiled, fine, radial lines etched lightly from the corners of her green eyes. She wasn't a child but a woman in her late twenties and lovely enough to turn heads.

The queen's parlor maid had spent the morning of her half day changing sheets at Osborne House. Just before two o'clock, Lizzie passed through the gate, peering down York Street, afraid she'd missed the omnibus. She pined for the solace of her secret place. If the 'bus had gone, it would be another week until her next free afternoon.

Lizzie pulled a letter from her pocket and hesitated at the pillar box by Osborne's gate. Her hand hovered at the slot. She hadn't written to her younger sister since the summer. That was before it started up again. Lizzy sighed, thinking, *Granny always said, let sleeping dogs lie.*

But when the 'bus rounded the bend, Lizzie pushed the letter into the slot. She signaled the driver and climbed up, relieved to spot an empty seat in the crowded cabin. At least she'd avoid a windy, rocking ride aloft. As the road swung east around a curve, she watched the tall, square towers of the queen's house vanish behind a stand of gray-barked ashes.

Lizzie settled in, tucking loose strands of auburn hair under her hat. *She'll help me. She'll tell me what to do.* The girl started to make the sign of the cross, then stopped herself, looking around at the other passengers, wondering if they'd noticed.

She closed her eyes and said a silent prayer, *Hail Mary, full of grace . . .*

Warm weather lingered on the Isle of Wight, the trees showing just a trace of autumn yellow at their tops. The 'bus rumbled through green hedgerow alleys and rolled past golden fields. After a few miles, it rattled over the timbers of Wooten Creek Bridge, and her shoulder bumped the elderly rider beside her. The man smiled at her apology and looked back at his newspaper. As they passed the Old Mill Pond, its glassy surface turned gray, then blue, and gray again as clouds slid across the sun.

Nearly there.

The busman slowed and stopped just before Quarr Lane began its turn away from the sea. Lizzie hurried forward, one hand holding her bonnet in place, and handed the driver a sixpence.

"Don't forget, lass. The last 'bus of the day returns at five." He gave her a long look. "You take care in that lonely place."

But Lizzie never felt alone there, and she wouldn't be late. All the queen's servants had watches to keep them on the household's strict schedule, and she'd pinned hers underneath her shawl. Not that she needed a timepiece. As a child in Ireland, she had lived on a farm. *In the days before . . .* Lizzie closed her eyes. She wouldn't think about that. But she knew the close of day by the churr-churring of the grasshopper warbler and cooling air that felt like a caress across her cheek. She'd be waiting for the 'bus long before moonrise.

'Tis a Hunter's Moon tonight, she remembered. It would light her way on the dark walk across Osborne Park, the house towers glowing in the moonlight. Lizzie watched the omnibus disappear around the bend and stood for a moment in the sudden quiet. Then she pulled her skirts away from her boots and slipped through an opening in the hedgerow.

Across the road, a figure moved in the shadows of the trees.

* * *

Lady Aldridge and Julia sipped tea from the hotel's flowery, red-and-yellow cups. An observer might have guessed they were relatives. They sat erect in their chairs, looking taller than most women even while sitting. Lady Aldridge's hair was silver and Julia's chestnut, but she and her great-niece shared the same high cheekbones, firm chins, and faces better described as handsome than pretty. The arch of their brows was identical, but not the eyes beneath. Julia's were brown, and her aunt's a cornflower blue.

"Well, my dear . . ." Lady Aldridge returned her saucer and cup to the table, leveling her gaze.

Julia, who knew her great-aunt well, thought, *Tea, cucumber sandwiches, and interrogation.*

"I'm not sure which surprises me more," Lady Aldridge said. "That you absented yourself from the clinic for three whole weeks or that you traveled here like a lady, for once, in the company of your maid."

"I thought you'd be pleased," her niece said, smiling.

Julia had opened her clinic in Whitechapel five years earlier and was used to coming and going unchaperoned. But it was not merely the travel that worried her aunt. Lady Aldridge fretted about the long hours Julia devoted to the clinic. She thought her niece looked worn out on many evenings and told her so. Often.

"How are they managing at the clinic without you?"

"Doctor Barnes will come twice a week and every Saturday. Nurse Clemmie will send any patient needing more than routine care to the London Hospital."

"High time you had a holiday. The sea air will soon put some color in those cheeks."

"And Kate's. She needed to get away."

"Is she not well?"

"It's Finsbury Circus that's ill. The atmosphere in our neighborhood . . ."

"Atmosphere?"

Julia frowned, fiddling with her teaspoon. "It's six weeks since you and Grandfather left London."

"That's hardly a lifetime. What has changed?"

"You've missed the vicious . . ." Julia pushed away her cup and saucer. "The guilty-by-association judgments from friends Kate has known for years. Fellow servants who work in the houses around Finsbury Circus."

"I don't understand."

"The Manchester outrage in September, Aunt. You must have read about Sergeant Brett. The policeman who died in the raid. He was the cousin of a servant in Kate's circle of friends."

"But what has that to do with your maid?"

"The Irish Republican Brotherhood carried out the attack."

"Ah . . . Kate *Connolly*." Lady Aldridge nodded. "Old hatreds rekindle easily, I'm afraid."

"They've flared up with a vengeance. It's sickening." Julia picked up a tea sandwich and then dropped it, pushing away her plate. "Kate, of all people. Is there a kinder soul?"

"I think we've had enough, yes?" Lady Aldridge folded her napkin. "Come, my dear. Let's stroll along the Parade while the light still favors us. You can tell me about it."

Julia linked arms with her aunt and crossed the street to the seawall. The sun was low in the sky, spangling the strait with flashes of silver. Most boats had called it a day, captains heading to the moorings and furling their sails.

Lady Aldridge sighed. "Poor Kate. That policeman's death made the front page of *The Isle of Wight Observer*. Still, I'm not aware of any anger directed against the Irish here."

"Maybe not, but I doubt this little island has absorbed a large influx from Ireland."

"Well, not like London, to be sure."

"Aunt, there are streets and back courts in Whitechapel where nearly every resident is Irish. They want to live in peace, but they're tarred by the tiny minority who—"

"Resort to violence to break Britain's hold on Ireland," Aunt Caroline said. "Oh yes, I see."

"And with Guy Fawkes Day around the corner . . ." Julia sighed.

"Oh dear. I hadn't thought of that. In my younger days, the bonfires always ended with the Pope's effigy alight. I thought that repulsive practice had died away."

"Sergeant O'Malley says the police expect trouble in mixed neighborhoods of Irish Catholics and English Protestants."

"And how is my old friend, the sergeant?"

"He's well and asked to be remembered to you, although the sergeant isn't happy with his new inspector."

Lady Aldridge stopped. She planted the point of her ebony walking stick. With both hands gripping the knob, she turned to face her niece. "And what about his *old* inspector? What do you hear from Richard?"

Julia had expected the direct question; subtlety was as foreign to her great-aunt as Hindustani.

"Aunt Caroline, you've set a record," Julia said, smiling. "Three hours in my company, and you've only just asked about him."

"Then surely my restraint deserves to be rewarded with news."

"You *have* been patient, Aunt," she said, kissing her cheek. "I'll give you that."

"I warn you, my girl. I shan't be satisfied with a kiss."

"I never dreamed you would."

"The time you're taking to make up your mind about him . . ." Lady Aldridge shook her head. "Tortoises and glaciers are speedier."

Julia hadn't told Aunt Caroline that she'd nearly decided

months ago. But Richard was gone when she looked for him at his country house in Kent.

Julia took her arm. "Let's head back. I'll tell you about Richard's last letter at dinner."

The letter was nearly a month old. *I won't mention that either*, she thought. He'd written he was traveling to Antwerp in search of the man he hunted. Julia had delayed her departure for the clinic each morning, looking for his letter in the early post. In the evenings, she shuffled through the afternoon's correspondence in vain. Disappointment had grown into dread and the fear that something was wrong.

Lizzie Dowling's footfalls struck noiselessly on the springy path to Quarr Abbey. The bordering beeches had held on to their leaves, forming a dense, round canopy that blotted out the sun. When Lizzie rounded the bend, she startled a red squirrel that froze over a pile of nuts and then darted off in a russet streak.

The quiet pressed in on her until a sudden breeze carried the silvery sound of shivering leaves. Under the leafy vault, day seemed like dusk. Then she broke through the grove into the sunlight and stopped at the edge of a broad, green field. Quarr Abbey's ruins stood at the meadow's far end. Another stand of trees rose in the distance. Beyond was the shimmering sea, where boats with sails reefed in the steady wind tossed amid the swells.

Quarr Abbey—the Abbey of Our Lady—was nothing more than broken walls and scattered stones, remnants of religious troubles from an earlier age. Lizzie couldn't say why she sensed a holy presence amid the wreckage. She felt it more strongly than at her parish church in Cowes. She circled the field and crossed to the shattered walls, running her hand across the velvety moss that clung in patches. Then the girl stooped, gathered three flat stones, and slipped them into her pocket.

Lizzie rarely saw others at the abbey and told no one about her visits. *No one except him.* She closed her eyes. *Sweet Mary, Mother of God, forgive me, for there's nothing I can deny him.*

They'd said their goodbyes ten years earlier. Then they met again in the summer. It felt as if they'd never parted . . . at least for her. Then, one July day, he'd followed her to Quarr. He tracked her through the trees, across the field, and caught her in his arms in the sheltered glade by the holy well. *Not here,* she'd said on that still afternoon, summoning all her strength.

Lizzie's footsteps scattered leaves along the path to the well. Water bubbled and murmured from a source deep underground. Someone had surrounded the spring with a stone wall and hacked a primitive bench out of the trunk of an ancient oak. Lizzie sat and fumbled in her pocket, extracting a single stone. She closed her eyes and rubbed her thumb in circles across its flat surface. She kissed it and then crossed herself, praying, *Forgive us our trespasses*, knowing it was wrong to harbor a sinful yearning, longing for something that couldn't be. Tears soaked her lashes. She let them fall.

Lizzie sat longer than she intended. She stood in the fading light, looking for the pile of stones she'd left on her last visit. She spotted them, and her heart lifted. Sometimes, she'd find them knocked away, but they were there, a good sign, perhaps. Then she performed the ritual as her grandmother taught her. She fell to her knees, praying, "Hail holy Queen, Mother of mercy . . ." Lizzie moved three times around the well, stopping each time to repeat her prayer, adding a stone to the pile. For the final reverent act, she got to her feet and placed her left hand on the stone wall. She leaned forward, cupping her right to scoop water for the sign of the cross, looking down, reaching, never noticing the shadow that moved behind her.

CHAPTER 2

Susan Styles pulled gently on the reins, and her pony cart rolled to a stop at Osborne House's stables. The head groom pushed the double doors open and offered his hand to help her down from the driving platform.

"A pleasant drive, Lady Styles?" He signaled to a stable boy who led the trap away.

"Yes, thank you." She tucked back strands of fair hair loosened by the breeze. "Am I the last to return?" Susan nodded to the pair of young groomsmen watering a horse and picking out its hooves.

"Not quite. Captain Montgomery is back." He looked over her shoulder. "And here's the major."

Peter FitzGerald, equerry to Queen Victoria, dismounted, tossed the reins to a stable boy, and removed his hat, raking his dark, tangled hair. "Well met, Lady Styles, but I thought you'd been out driving with Princess Louise."

"Her head ached, so I dropped her at the house."

"Shall we walk there together?"

"Of course."

Susan had been surprised to find Peter at Osborne House while Her Majesty was absent. But he had stayed behind to supervise the renovation of the queen's stables, returning for a final inspection. For her part, Lady Styles had arrived at Osborne with the Prince and Princess of Wales. As Princess Alexandra's "lady of the wardrobe," Susan was her senior lady in waiting. Some in the royal household thought her twenty-nine years made her too young for the job. Mature duchesses usually held such posts. But the princess liked her, and the formal role had warmed into a friendship.

"Princess Alexandra tells me you are leaving us," Susan said.

"Next week," FitzGerald said, rolling his eyes. "For the delightful trip to Balmoral and back."

Susan smiled in sympathy; few of the queen's courtiers relished the five-hundred-mile journey to her castle in Scotland.

The head groom asked, "Any last instructions, Major?"

He frowned, stroking the scar that ran from his right ear to his chin. It was a Crimean War "souvenir," he'd once told her, "courtesy of a Russian saber." It hadn't made him less attractive, and time had tamped its fire to dusty pink. Susan first traced its line years ago, her breath coming quicker.

"I spotted a decayed section of fencing in the north paddock," FitzGerald told the head groom. "Get Merriweather and Sons to do the fence repairs."

"Not Gibney's? They built the original paddock."

"The house steward thinks they're padding the bills." FitzGerald shrugged. "But Michael Bolger might be wrong, so the less said, the better."

"I'll see to it, Major."

"Good man." FitzGerald nodded to an empty stall. "I see the grooms haven't stabled the prince's mount."

Susan, too, had noticed the vacant stall for the horse belonging to the Prince of Wales.

"Still out and about," the groom said. "Fine afternoon for a gallop."

FitzGerald looked at the darkening sky. "He shouldn't leave it too late. Night falls earlier these days."

"Hunter's Moon tonight, Major. That will light his way."

Three hours later, Susan fiddled with the brooch pinned to her bodice as she walked along the Grand Corridor of Osborne House, looking for a mirror. She found one and checked to see that the jewel was secure, sighing at her reflection. Susan had worn the black silk gown once too often. Widowhood had required an entirely new mourning wardrobe, followed by "half-mourning" dresses in mauves and grays. Both were expenses she could ill afford.

Susan turned left at the hallway's end, passing the dining hall and surprising a pair of whispering, white-gloved servants setting the table.

"Her half day off, and Lizzie's not back."

"There'll be hell to— "

The second footman broke off when he spotted Lady Styles. The pair bowed stiffly and returned to setting out the wineglasses.

After dinner, Dr. Lewis asked his granddaughter, "Shall we walk along the Parade, you and I? Your aunt isn't overly fond of my pipe."

"It's bedtime for me at any rate," Lady Aldridge said as she gathered her things.

Julia and her grandfather crossed the road and stopped at the harbor wall. The wind had shifted, and a light breeze from land to sea barely rippled the sea's surface. Dr. Lewis cupped his hand around his pipe bowl. After three puffs, the tobacco took his match and glowed.

Julia hooked her arm around his and rested her head on his shoulder. "Thank you."

He tossed the match over the seawall and looked down at her. "Thank you for what?"

"For persuading me to come. For three uninterrupted weeks with my grandfather." She squeezed his arm. "I feel like a schoolgirl, books packed away, and taken on holiday."

"Well, Aunt Caroline said I mustn't take no for an answer." He swept his pipe across the harbor view. "And I ordered up this perfect evening. Just for you."

The full moon had painted a silvery highway, splitting the dark water from horizon to shore.

Julia said, "It's one of those nights when you could walk the Parade without a lantern to guide you."

"A Hunter's Moon, my dear," he said. "The second full moon of autumn."

"Beautiful . . . but I've always found something menacing in the name."

"The origin is American, I believe. The time to go hunting, when the birds and animals have stored up energy for the winter."

"Fattened and ready for the kill."

"And what about Richard's hunt?" Dr. Lewis said, releasing her arm and turning toward her. "Four months scouring Europe, and the man eludes him still."

Julia bent for a loose stone. She tossed it into the water and watched the spreading rings. "There was some . . . confusion over aliases that slowed the chase. It turns out his real name is Edgar Romilly."

"My dear . . . is it time for the inspector to give up and come home?"

Julia lifted her shoulders. "I don't know. He has two months left of his leave from Scotland Yard. I doubt he'll return until it runs out or he tracks Romilly down."

"Murderous scoundrel. Well, success or failure, Richard hunts for justice." He reclaimed her arm, giving it a shake. "Now, what say you? Shall we go on a hunt of our own? I propose we wake with the birds, explore the eastern shore, and discover the island's beauties."

"Yes, please. So long as we travel by carriage, not by boat."

At breakfast the following morning, Julia said warily, "A *floating* bridge, Grandfather?"

"I know you said, 'not by boat,' but it's the only way across the river to East Cowes unless you travel ten miles downstream to Newport."

"I'm not picturing—"

"It's a steam barge. Horse-powered chains dragged an earlier vessel across the river. This one is large enough to carry carriages, carts, and passengers."

"This modern world of ours," Lady Aldridge said. "You two enjoy yourselves. I intend to stroll to the Green, read in the shade of the umbrella tree, and rest after luncheon."

A hotel servant strapped a wicker basket with a picnic lunch to the back of their hired carriage. Fifteen minutes later, Julia and her grandfather joined the queue at the ferry dock.

"Here she comes, Julie."

She looked east, shielding her eyes from the morning sun. The approaching barge belched steam from its squat funnel and juddered to a stop. Two long seating sheds ran the length of its sides with a center space for carriages and wagons. Julia and her grandfather boarded and made the short crossing. When they reached the other side, they resumed their carriage seats and rumbled down the exit gangway.

Their coachman turned right on York Avenue, passing a man standing by a carriage with the VR cipher for Victoria Regina on its door. Dr. Lewis rapped the roof with his walking stick. The driver slowed and pulled to the side of the road.

Dr. Lewis unlatched and lowered the window. "Charles?"

A thin, stooping man with gray muttonchops turned. He shifted his medical bag to his left hand and offered his right through the carriage window.

"Andrew, my dear fellow. This is a surprise. Where are you staying?"

"The Marine Hotel."

"A long visit?"

"We'll be here a few more weeks."

The gentleman glanced over his shoulder at the royal carriage. "Forgive me for hurrying off, but I'm expected at Osborne House. May I call on you tomorrow?"

"Of course. Delighted."

The gentleman tipped his hat and climbed into the royal coach.

"Who was that, Grandfather?"

"Sir Charles Locock. We were at medical school together. He's the queen's physician. Delivered all nine of her children."

They followed the doctor's carriage until it turned at the entrance to Osborne Park. Julia said, "If the queen is away, I wonder why the doctor is in a hurry."

Dr. Lewis shrugged. "Attending the Prince or Princess of Wales? Princess Louise is in residence, too." He patted her hand. "Now, my dear, let's get down to the business of pleasure. I propose we explore as far as the island's easternmost point."

On Culver Downs, Julia left her grandfather and a fellow bird enthusiast discussing peregrine falcons and trekked to the edge of the cliff. The chalk precipice curved away, gleaming above the midnight blue of the channel's waters. Julia dragged some wind-whipped strands from her eyes and thought of Dover's white cliffs. In early summer, she'd gazed across the channel to France, wondering about Richard and where he was. *And here it is, October.*

He'd finally written a month after he left England. After four silent weeks, he wrote from Paris to say he'd collect his letters at the Bureau de Poste on the Rue du Louvre. Julia took that as an invitation and sent three letters in as many months. She believed Richard would get his man. As for the two of them . . .

Aunt Caroline had dismissed Julia's early hesitations, saying, "Yes, there will be challenges to face. But, my dear, you've never lacked courage or imagination. Why allow them to fail you now?"

It had taken Julia many months to imagine a shared life: one with room for a doctor and a detective. Last June, she'd been on the brink of commitment. She had appeared, uninvited, on his doorstep in Kent with an overnight case in her hand, only to find he'd decamped for the Continent. He'd left without saying goodbye, knowing he'd likely be away for months. His abrupt disappearance and weeks of silence confused her. At other times, she felt angry. Was his regard so slight that he thought a few letters at lengthy intervals were sufficient? He shared details of the chase but gave no hint of his feelings, no sign that he was impatient to be home. *Did I nearly make a fool of myself that day in Kent?*

Still, Julia missed him. The rare leisure hours in her busy life seemed emptier than before. *Were his?* Julia sighed and turned away from the sea, the push and pull of her contradictory feelings as continual as the tides. She retraced her steps, her mind and heart as restless and unsettled as ever.

It had turned twilight by the time Julia and her grandfather arrived at their hotel.

"Well, well," Dr. Lewis said as the carriage wheels crunched to a stop on the gravel. "Sir Charles Locock is on the porch with your aunt. I'm flattered by his alacrity. He said he'd visit tomorrow."

Dr. Lewis handed Julia down and hailed his old friend.

Sir Charles rose stiffly from the bench, his expression grave as they shook hands. "Good evening, Andrew."

"This is my granddaughter, Doctor Julia Lewis."

The queen's doctor bowed. "The very person I want to consult."

A surprised Julia said, "Indeed, Sir Charles? I'm honored."

The doctor drew together his bushy, white brows. A deep furrow creased the space between them, and his long, thin fingers worried his watch chain. "I sorely need your professional services . . . and your discretion."

Two laughing young men burst through the hotel doors and stopped to light cigars. Andrew Lewis drew Sir Charles aside. "What is it, my friend?"

"The police found the body of a young woman at the Quarr Abbey ruins. She'd been missing since last evening."

"Good heavens," Dr. Lewis murmured.

Sir Charles rubbed his forehead. "A local doctor usually handles postmortems, but he's on the other side of the island, assisting at a difficult birth."

Julia said, "You want me to examine the body?"

"Yes. Yes, I do. My eyes are no longer up to the demands of a postmortem. I'd planned to ask your grandfather, but Lady Aldridge suggested you."

"I explained you had retired, Andrew, but that Julia served as a medical examiner for Scotland Yard."

The queen's physician took Julia's hand. "Will you come with me now?"

"Of course, Sir Charles. I'm at your service."

"Thank you, Doctor. It's a sensitive case. The victim's name is Lizzie Dowling, and she was one of the queen's household servants."

At sunset, Susan Styles returned from her walk. Two hours earlier, Sir Charles Locock had reappeared after his morning visit, carrying the news that Lizzie Dowling was dead. Then he drove away, leaving behind shock, a tonic for the Princess of Wales, and Princess Louise in tears. For the past six months, Lizzie had been the only servant in attendance on the independent but emotionally fragile Louise. Susan had left the princesses resting before seeking the solitude of the outdoors and some fresh air.

I should go inside and find Princess Louise, Lady Styles thought. *And Alix may be awake and wanting me.* Susan had fallen into the habit of thinking of Princess Alexandra as "Alix," the royal family's pet name for the Princess of Wales.

Alix had a duo of young maids of honor whose duty was to attend royalty at any hour. But Lady Styles was the lady-in-waiting who was her chief support. At twenty-nine, she felt ancient next to the younger attendants who'd only recently left their governesses behind. While Susan's duties weren't taxing, often, they felt unrelenting. She looked up at the tower looming over the entryway and felt the three sides of the courtyard press in on her. Susan thought, *Another quarter of an hour.* She backed away and turned, her boots crunching on the pebbled drive.

Susan strode away rapidly until she reached the parterre's flower beds. There she slowed, trailing her hand, brushing the pink globes of the tall, massed amaranth, hearty survivors until the first frost. She walked on, entering the still-leafy glade at the south end of the house where a break in the trees opened a view across the emerald lawn that sloped to the sea. The sinking light caught the distant water. It glittered like a blue, undulating blanket flecked with diamonds.

Susan found her bench—she'd begun to think of it as hers—and thought, *Other people's houses.*

The grander they were, the less they felt like home. Marlborough House in London, Sandringham, the country estate of the

Prince and Princess of Wales, visits to the queen's palaces and castles: Susan lived her life in a succession of apartments and rooms, none of them hers. Still, it was the lot of a lady-in-waiting, and she was honest enough to admit her luck.

Her husband's death nearly three years earlier had left her a young widow with limited means. His cousin inherited the title, the estate, and the town house in London. Susan was grateful for the royal accommodations during two three-month assignments each year and the 300 pounds she earned for "waiting" on the princess. It spared her the indignity of living year-round in her childhood home by her brother's "grace and favor." She knew her sister-in-law didn't welcome the intrusion. Susan readily agreed to Alix's request that she extend her waiting by another three months to the end of January. She was grateful for the extra money.

Susan looked at the cedar of Lebanon tree at the grove's edge and envied its rootedness.

I must get up, she thought, forcing herself to her feet, feeling twice her age. Two days hence, she would attend the inquest into Lizzy's death at the request of the Princess of Wales.

Susan headed back to the house, thinking, *Other people's houses. Other people's tragedies . . . and secrets.*

Julia's carriage slowed and stopped at the corner of Birmingham and Mill Streets. The police station's blue lantern illuminated a trim man in a Wellington hat pacing in front of the doorway.

Marching guard, Julia thought. She asked Sir Charles, "Is the coroner expecting a female doctor?"

"I sent a note informing Mister Milgram that your grandfather was unavailable, but Doctor Julia Lewis had offered her services and would perform the autopsy."

"Hmm . . . a Hobson's choice," Julia said, smiling. "Take her or take her."

Sir Charles chuckled and took her arm. "Come, I'll introduce you."

The queen's physician performed the pleasantries. Mr. Milgram's granite face cracked into a scowl at the end of the introduction. "I think this is highly irregular, Sir Charles. And a grave error."

"What is?"

He jerked his head at Julia. "The autopsy results will be scrutinized by the palace, the government, the press. By everyone. Having some . . . some *chit* of a girl perform the procedure is a mistake."

"Milgram, I call that damned offensive and—"

Julia touched the doctor's arm. "I've weathered insults far worse than 'chit.' Mister Milgram, you'll find me on the medical register. I've lost count of the number of autopsies I've performed, and I've never had my findings questioned. Doubtless, Scotland Yard can supply the exact figures."

Milgram glared. Then he dropped his crossed arms and tipped his head at the door. "This way, madam."

"You have everything *Doctor* Lewis will need?" Sir Charles said. The coroner nodded. "Then I'll leave her to get on with it."

Milgram blinked behind his steel-rimmed spectacles. "You're not staying to supervise, Sir Charles?"

"No need. Good evening to you." He walked off, leaving the coroner hesitating at the entrance.

"Come along, Mister Milgram," Julia said, opening the door. "I'm not a dose of castor oil. I know my job and will be easy to swallow. I promise."

Julia's first glimpse of the body jolted her. The girl's auburn hair, the spray of light freckles across her cheeks, her death by drowning reminded her of Helen, her medical school classmate. Julia still struggled with her failure to prevent her friend's suicide. But she no longer dreamed about it; those nightmares had faded, even though the memories hadn't. Julia had found a measure of peace, accepting that Helen would always be a part of her and her death a deep regret.

At the autopsy's end, the doctor took a last look at Elizabeth Dowling. *Lizzy.* Underneath her pallor and blue-tinged lips, Julia glimpsed the lovely young woman she'd been. She drew the sheet over the girl's face. Julia hated that moment more than any other in the postmortem process. The Y-incision from collarbone to pelvis, the removal and examination of internal organs: those gruesome procedures were part of her medical training. But the act of covering Lizzie's face—of shrouding a young woman who might have been sleeping but would never wake—filled her with sadness and pity.

Julia washed her hands at the sink, lowered the flames on the two hanging lamps, and closed the door quietly behind her. Mr. Milgram and Chief Constable Phillips of the Cowes Constabulary awaited her preliminary report. Phillips was a big, bluff, square-chinned man with a thick crop of steel-gray hair and a walrus mustache. Julia judged him to be closer to retirement than the beginning of his career.

"I'll have my written conclusions for you tomorrow," Julia said, "but I can tell you now that Lizzie Dowling drowned. Water filled her lungs."

Phillips asked, "Suicide, accident, or murder?"

"I cannot say with certainty, Chief Constable."

"Well, that's torn it," Milgram said savagely. "A damnable waste of time."

Julia ignored the coroner and addressed the policeman. "Suicide is least likely, given the state of her fingernails. Still, those who decide to end their lives sometimes change their minds. She may have tried and failed to claw her way to safety."

"Good Lord," the chief constable muttered.

"It's also possible that she overbalanced and fell in accidentally," Julia said. "It's equally likely that someone tipped her in and held her underwater. Perhaps by her ankles. Her leather boots would leave no trace of bruising from an assailant's finger-marks."

Chief Constable Phillips asked, "Were there any other signs of violence on her body?"

"Abrasions on her right forehead and cheek. An attack would explain it, but so would thrashing against the stone wall of the well, trying to save herself."

Milgram scowled. "Not very helpful."

"My report will record that she was pregnant. I'd estimate she was about four months gone."

The following morning at breakfast, Lady Aldridge said, "That poor girl. Alone, perhaps abandoned in her trouble, now to be a victim again. This time, of gossip and speculation."

"Violent death affords no private place," Dr. Lewis said. "Her tragedy becomes public property at the coroner's inquest. When do you give your evidence, Julie?"

"Tomorrow."

"Quarr Abbey . . . I visited it once," he said. "Such a strange and lonely place to die."

"An omnibus driver said she visited often, according to Chief Constable Phillips."

"Thank you, Kate," Dr. Lewis said as Julia's maid removed his empty plate. "They found no evidence at the scene?"

"The chief constable said nothing, except . . ." Julia frowned. "It's strange, but the police found two piles of flat stones on the well's wall."

Kate dropped a teaspoon that clattered across the parquet floor. She bent to retrieve it and rose, pink in the face. "Mother of God, is it a holy well, this water at Quarr Abbey?"

Dr. Lewis looked at Julia. She lifted her shoulders and said, "I don't know, Kate."

"Sure, it must be if the girl left piles of stones behind. All my old aunts in Ireland did the same to ward off illness or beg a blessing. What sort of abbey are we talking about?"

"They're just ruins, now," Dr. Lewis said. "But it was the Abbey of Saint Mary and—"

"Praying to the Virgin at a holy well? Sure, she'll not be taking her life in such a place. 'Tis a mortal sin, and to do such a terrible deed after asking for a blessing? Never."

"I can't be certain," Julia said. "Suicide is one possibility. It may have been an accident or—"

"'Twas no accident if she knew the place and prayed there often." Kate picked up the tray of plates. "They should be looking for the maggot who got her in the family way."

Doctor Lewis stood and held the door so the maid could pass through. He closed it and said, "We know where Kate stands. If not suicide or accident . . ."

Julia nodded. "That leaves murder."

At the inquest the following morning, the omnibus driver testified to Lizzie Dowling's unaccompanied journey to Quarr Abbey, and a local constable described the discovery of the body by hikers. Then the court clerk called Dr. "Julius" Lewis to the stand.

"If only it were true," she murmured to her grandfather, standing. "Mister Milgram would be much happier."

The clerk blinked at her approach. Julia raised her right hand and swore the oath, correcting her name. Near the end of her medical testimony, a low hum buzzed across the room at the news of the girl's pregnancy. Silence greeted Julia's inconclusive determination of the cause of death. The coroner's jury shuffled out, deliberated for ten minutes, and returned with an open verdict. The stone-faced coroner gaveled the proceedings to a close.

"A suspicious death but no certainty," Doctor Lewis said, taking his granddaughter's arm. "Still, no other conclusion was possible beyond a reasonable doubt."

Julia murmured, "The coroner doesn't look happy."

Mr. Milgram approached her on the courthouse steps. Without a word, he counted out four crowns and six shillings, handed them to Julia, and stalked off.

"One of the world's charmers," Dr. Lewis muttered. "I wager he'd be civil enough if Sir Charles had performed the autopsy."

"Never mind. Your friend foisted me on him, and Mister Milgram just paid for the privilege." Julia jingled the coins. "Although it's half the going rate for an autopsy and expert testimony in London."

Her grandfather said, "Between your clinic work and medical examiner fees—"

"I'll never get rich." Julia's gaze drifted away from Milgram and down to the courtyard. "That woman . . . the one speaking to Sir Charles. She's striking."

Her grandfather turned. "Yes, I noticed her in the courtroom. A young widow, by the look of her."

The tall, fair woman wore a gown of mauve and gray, her collar and cuffs trimmed with narrow ribbons of black silk. She glanced their way and then laid a hand on Sir Charles's sleeve. He said a few words to the lady and mounted the steps. At the top, he tipped his hat to Julia.

"Doctor Lewis, can you spare a moment to speak with Lady Styles? She is a lady-in-waiting to the Princess of Wales and would like a word."

"Of course."

"I'll bring her to you." Sir Charles smiled. "Then, unless I take my leave, I'll be late for a celebratory luncheon. We're welcoming a new grandson into the family."

"A happy occasion, Sir Charles," Julia said.

"Thank you, my dear. The boy is called Henry Locock, named for my father."

As she waited for Sir Charles to return with Lady Styles, Julia overheard two elderly ladies whispering behind her.

"Married three months, and the young Lococks are adopting a child? Why, they've hardly had time."

"Mark my words," the second lady said. "There's a family connection. Some 'by-blow' of one of Sir Charles's sons and a servant girl."

"Could it be Captain Locock's own child? He's always been the wildest of the brothers."

"That might explain why Frederick and Mary would take a strange child into the family. It seems distinctly odd for a newly married couple."

Julia shook off her distaste at the gossip. She smiled when Sir Charles introduced Lady Styles and then excused himself.

"Thank you for seeing me, Doctor. I attended the proceedings at the Princess of Wales's request, but an open verdict leaves many questions. I suppose you can't say—"

"Which possibility is most likely?" Julia shook her head. "I'm sorry."

"Princess Alexandra's concern . . ." Lady Styles sighed. "I suppose some at the palace will fear scandal, but her heart breaks for the girl. How alone she must have felt. You said she was four months pregnant? Of that, you are sure?"

"An autopsy allows one to make a reasonably accurate assessment."

"I see."

Julia thought she did. The lady could do the simple subtraction. *And remember, perhaps, who was at Osborne House in the summer.* "Did you know Lizzie Dowling well, Lady Styles?"

"Not really. She was part of the queen's household, not the Wales's establishment. The prince avoids his . . ." Lady Styles dimpled a charming smile. "Waiting on the princess has taught me that family conflicts are the same everywhere. The only difference is that the combatants have royal titles."

"They seem like exotic creatures to mere mortals."

"The two princesses, Alexandra and Louise, will be fascinated by *you*, a lady doctor. Do you practice in London?"

"At our house in Finsbury and my clinic in Whitechapel." Julia reached into her medical bag and produced a card with her particulars. "Seeing is believing, so they say. Evidence to convince a skeptical world."

"Proof positive of a female physician." Lady Styles waved it like a prize. "Thank you, Doctor."

Julia watched her walk to her carriage, thinking, *I'd like to know her better.*

An hour after luncheon, Lady Styles retreated to the quiet of her favorite Osborne grove and sat on her bench. She had informed the Princess of Wales about the inquest's findings. When she ended with the news that Lizzie had been pregnant, Alix's face matched the white tablecloth.

Susan retrieved the card from her pocket and tapped it against her palm. She turned it over. DR. JULIA R. LEWIS, 17 FINSBURY CIRCUS, LONDON. It also listed the location of her clinic on Fieldgate Street in Whitechapel.

A woman doctor . . . I wonder.

Susan looked up on hearing her name called and sighed at the imminent interruption. Peter FitzGerald and Captain Oliver Montgomery crossed the grounds from the direction of the stables. They made a dashing pair: the queen's tall, dark, clean-shaven equerry and Montgomery, matching Major FitzGerald in height but with sandy hair and a neat military mustache. Oliver Montgomery was an equerry to the Prince of Wales. *And Alix's faithful swain*, Susan thought.

The captain had been in Cowes for the past week, riding with the prince and Peter FitzGerald. But he hadn't turned up for tea with the Princess of Wales until that day. It had surprised Susan because it was plain to everyone that he adored Alix. *Obvious to everyone except the princess.* Montgomery stood guard over his love like the Sphinx: lionlike in his strong attachment, rooted, mute, and immutable.

A pity her husband isn't as devoted. No, that wasn't entirely true, Susan thought. *Bertie is devoted . . . he just isn't faithful.*

Captain Montgomery clicked his heels and bent over Susan's hand. She couldn't put her finger on it, but there was something in his manner. *Overdone?* He charmed Alix, but his gallantry left Susan untouched.

"Lady Styles, sitting in a bower, grave and lovely as ever. I haven't had the pleasure of seeing you since . . . when?"

"Last July and then the yachting in August."

"Of course."

Susan thought, *If the queen only knew.* She had left early for Balmoral. And from her distant Scottish retreat, Her Majesty had no idea Bertie had filled her beloved Osborne House with friends she deplored. The newspapers had dubbed the prince's circle the "Marlborough House set." The queen called them "rogues, roués, and hangers-on."

Captain Montgomery's smile vanished. "And now this tragedy. I know Peter is eager for news."

"Are you staying for dinner?" Susan asked.

"Thank you, no. I'm meeting the chaps at the Yacht Club. If you'll excuse me, I'll find the princess." Montgomery bowed and headed toward the house.

When the captain was out of earshot, FitzGerald said, "Well? What happened?"

"The jury returned an open verdict. It's a suspicious death, but its cause is unknown. And she was pregnant."

"Worse and worse. No resolution, just endless speculation. Well." FitzGerald lifted his shoulders. "It will probably come to nothing. The police won't trouble themselves over—"

"A pregnant Irish girl," she said sharply. "Not even a maidservant of the queen?" Susan had thought the same thing, but that shrug rankled.

"I suppose they'll go through the motions."

"After the inquest, I pressed Doctor Lewis about the cause of death, but she—"

"She?"

"Yes. Doctor Julia Lewis examined the body and testified before the coroner's jury."

"Good Lord, a woman doctor. What next?"

"I had no idea such a person existed," Susan said, looking down at the card. "I asked if I might consult her."

FitzGerald hesitated. Then he said, "I trust you are not unwell."

"Quite well, thank you."

"Then . . . it's not about Princess Louise?"

"No. Of course not."

"Good. I understood from Sir Charles that she has recovered her spirits, and her headaches are less frequent." When Susan didn't reply, the major said, "Wouldn't you agree?"

"It seems so." *But you haven't heard Louise weeping in her bedroom.* Susan tucked away the card. "Princess Louise had made a pet of Lizzie. She's deeply distressed. At a loss."

"Yes. I imagine she is."

"Do you know if the queen's private secretary has written to the girl's family?"

FitzGerald looked surprised. "The housekeeper said her parents are dead, and she had no other family in England."

"There's a younger sister in Ireland. Brigid Dowling. She's in service with a family somewhere in County Cork."

"How do you know that?"

"Princess Louise remembered but couldn't recall the town's name. She said Lizzie was very protective of her sister." Susan stood, brushing the folds from her dress. "I'll look into finding her address."

"Lady Styles . . . Susan."

"Yes?"

He shook his head. "Nothing."

Nothing, Susan thought. There was a time when a word from him meant everything.

"The prince and the two princesses leave for London on Monday," she said. "Are you traveling with the royal party?"

FitzGerald shook his head. "Montgomery will join you, but I must leave tomorrow for Scotland."

"A sudden change of plan?"

"A telegram from the home secretary arrived while you were at the inquest. The government got wind of an Irish plan to kidnap the queen at Balmoral and—"

"Good God!"

FitzGerald flicked his hand. "Tempest in a teacup. Or a pint glass, as so many Irish plots start in pubs. These so-called 'Fenian patriots' can't get out of their way."

"What's being done?"

"The Scottish police swarmed the castle grounds." FitzGerald chuckled. "They found nothing, but they irritated the life out of Her Majesty."

"Five assassination attempts, and—"

"Six, as it happens. Victoria has almost as many lives as a cat."

"It's not a joke," Susan said. "The queen is too careless of her safety."

"These Irish . . . What do they expect from us, for God's sake?"

She raised her eyebrow and said, "Their land back?"

"Do they think we'll just hand it over to them?"

"This from you, Peter FitzGerald? An Irishman with family estates in Kildare?"

"Anglo-Irish, my lady, and British to the core. We landowners prefer to hold on to our property. At least, the little my junior branch of the family has left."

FitzGerald's glance drifted over Susan's shoulder. She turned to see Princess Louise striding toward the stables.

"By the time you return from Balmoral with the queen, Louise will be gone. She travels to London with us for an extended stay at Marlborough House."

"Good," he said. "The princess could use time away from her mother."

The queen had little patience with illness, real or imagined, or with prolonged emotional distress. *All but her own,* Susan thought.

"Louise asked me to try to trace Lizzie's sister. I'll write to the authorities in Dublin. They may know where to find Brigid Dowling."

FitzGerald frowned. "Do you think it's necessary to— "

"Wouldn't you like to know if your sister were dead?"

He started to say something and then looked away. "I must pack." The major bowed.

Susan watched him stride across the lawn. *A little stiff in the back?* She dragged off her bonnet, unclasped the black mourning brooch pinned at her throat, and dropped them on the bench. Then she walked to the grove's edge and faced the sea, undoing the hook-and-eye fastening at the top of her bodice. She opened the black-trimmed fabric at her neck and lifted her face to the breeze, dragging strands of her fair hair away from her face.

Brigid Dowling, where are you? After a moment, Susan thought, *Louise . . . I wonder.* A map might jog the princess's memory. Susan strode back to the house, re-hooking her bodice and thinking, *An atlas. That's what I need.* She would look for one in Osborne's well-stocked library and show it to Louise. Then she could send a letter to the officials at Dublin Castle, mentioning the name of a town.

Another letter—a dead girl's letter—had traveled from the pillar box near Osborne House's gate and by steamer across the strait to Southampton. From there, it went by train to Bristol and by boat across the Irish Sea. From the city of Cork, it bumped along in a pony cart to Clonakilty village, and then traveled in a postman's pack to Lansdowne Hall. There, a housekeeper set it aside to await the return from Dublin of the mistress of the house and her maid, Brigid Dowling.

CHAPTER 3

In November, Julia and her family returned to a still-simmering London. Anger lingered through the autumn. By December, little had changed. Headlines shouted, Irish protesters filled the parks, and editorials demanded harsh measures to quell the unrest.

Dr. Lewis looked up from *The Times*. "The prime minister has banned all demonstrations."

Julia swallowed a last bite of scrambled egg. "Has he the power to do that?"

"The opposition will challenge it." Her grandfather folded the morning paper. "Seven hundred years," he said, shaking his head. "It's seven centuries since we first invaded Ireland, and we're no closer to a 'united' kingdom."

"No one likes to be tied to another by force." Julia stood and planted a kiss on her grandfather's head.

"You're off then? A busy day?"

"Lots of respiratory ailments this week, but we'll see."

Julia sorted through several medical journals, waiting for the morning's mail. It had been nearly two months since she'd had a letter from Richard. There were endless explanations: if only she could think of one that satisfied her. *Surely Sergeant O'Malley would tell me if something had happened to him?*

Julia gave up and descended the town house steps. She spotted the postman rounding Finsbury Circus's curving pavement and waited. But the morning post brought only bills and letters for her grandfather.

For months, Inspector Richard Tennant tracked Edgar Romilly across the Continent. From Paris to Berlin and on to Antwerp, the distance between them grew. He'd come full circle, back to the City of Light, and was as much in the dark as ever. Then, with only weeks left of leave, came a glimmer. A note from Lt. Jules Picard of France's criminal bureau brought the inspector to a Paris café near the train station that served Lyon. He'd instructed the inspector to pack an overnight bag.

Tennant spotted Picard at a small streetside table, smiling at a dark-eyed waitress who swiped a slow circle around the marble top. She laughed at something he said and sauntered away. Picard eyed the sway of the girl's hips as she slipped between tables.

"You haven't changed, Jules."

"Richard." Picard stood and greeted his English friend in the French fashion, gripping his upper arms and leaning in for a quick brush to each cheek.

Tennant glanced at the retreating waitress. "Madame Picard is well?"

"She enjoys the country air and rarely visits Paris, so everything arranges itself." Picard double-twitched the arched eyebrows that made him look perpetually amused.

"Nearly twelve years since the Crimea." Tennant dropped his carpetbag and sat.

"From war to peace. From the army to the police for us both." The Frenchman poured two glasses of red wine. "To our survival." He sipped, eyeing Tennant over the rim of his glass. "How are you, my friend?"

Jules Picard would understand. Still, Tennant kept to himself the dizzying bouts of disorientation, the suffocating fear of enclosed spaces, the nightmares, and night sweats that left him shivering. He had survived a bombardment and a live burial in the Crimea. He doubted the memory would ever leave him.

"A little stiffness in my leg," Tennant said. "Especially on cold, foggy days."

"Are there any other kinds in London?"

Tennant smiled. "A handful in August. And you, Jules?"

"Well enough. What is it you Britishers say? Mustn't grumble." Picard set his glass aside. "*Alors* . . . down to business. I have news about this villain, Romilly, and his latest venture."

"Which is?"

"Running guns out of Lyon."

"What sort of weapons are we talking about?"

"Stolen ones from our arms factory at Saint-Étienne. Five thousand of our very latest bolt-action rifles, to be precise."

Tennant sighed. "The man is nothing if not resourceful. In London, it was kidnapping, prostitution, and pornography. Have the guns changed hands?"

"We hope to prevent that in Lyon."

"You said to pack a bag for overnight. What is the plan?"

"The army will supply a force of heavily armed gendarmes to seize the weapons. The soldiers get their guns back, the Paris police arrest the criminals, and you—"

"I want Romilly."

"I regret that won't be possible. I offer a chance to be 'in at the kill,' as the hunters say, but we retain custody of the fox." Picard tapped the table. "An arrest on French soil requires a trial in a French court."

"Romilly is an Englishman. He must face a—"

"Trial by an English jury? That, my friend, is always unpredictable. No, Monsieur Romilly will enjoy a long, unhappy stay on Devil's Island. Many 'guests' of our emperor never leave."

"You have a point." Tennant hesitated. "Very well, Jules."

"The train leaves Paris in thirty minutes." Picard stood and clapped Tennant's shoulder. "Cheer up, Richard. Ten years in a disease-ridden penal colony in the French tropics? An English hanging might be preferable."

The gendarmes parted company with Tennant, Picard, and his officers at the station in Lyon, the soldiers heading for a warehouse outside the city. The policemen left for Lyon's central square, La Place du Change, and a rendezvous with the local police.

When they arrived at the plaza, Picard asked Duclos, the sergeant in charge, "Where is our pigeon?"

"Romilly is at the café opposite. At a table under the striped awning," Duclos said. "His wiry drinking companion is Jacques Morin. A villain with fingers in every dirty pot."

"*Très bien,*" Picard said. The lieutenant tapped an officer on the shoulder. "*Vous allez.*" The Paris copper sauntered across the plaza, joining two of Picard's men loitering on Saint-Jean Cathedral's steps.

Morin threw some bills on the café table and tapped Romilly on the shoulder. The two men crossed the plaza at a rapid pace and headed down the Rue Saint-Jean.

"*Merde*," Duclos said. "He's spotted your officers."

"No matter," Picard said. "I have four men posted at the turning to the river." The lieutenant signaled his remaining two officers. "Follow me."

Duclos grabbed Tennant's elbow. "Let them go, Inspector." He tipped his head. "This way."

Tennant eyed Picard's progress. Then he joined the Lyon coppers heading in the opposite direction.

"I told him not to fill the square with his men," Duclos growled. "But these Paris *flics* think they're God almighty."

"Where are we going?"

"At least three *traboules* lead to the quay. Our prey will slip through one and vanish before Picard reaches the river."

"*Traboules*?" Tennant said, hurrying to keep pace, wincing when his boot twisted on an uneven cobble.

Duclos smiled. "Hidden passageways connecting streets. Shortcuts known to every Lyonnaise in a hurry. Lyon is like a honeycomb riddled with them."

As they exited the plaza, Duclos and his officers broke into a run. *Local knowledge*, Tennant thought, scrambling after them. *Trust it every time.*

At the river, Duclos turned right. He pointed to an oak door that looked like an entrance to a house. "We will remain here. My officers will cover the other two exits. The wait won't be long."

Duclos was right. Tennant pulled back as the heavy door swung open. Jacques Morin emerged and turned right, straight into the grasp of the French sergeant. Romilly turned left and spotted Tennant. The man spun and darted back into the dim, curving tunnel.

Tennant entered the maw of his nightmares. The dark stone corridor swallowed him, and invisible bands tightened around his chest. He reached for his revolver and followed the sounds of pounding boot leather. When the tunnel turned left, Tennant stopped. He was about to round the corner when Romilly darted out of the darkness. He lunged at Tennant, his knife slashing the inspector's upper left arm. Romilly struck again. This time, Tennant parried the thrust and felt the searing pain of a defensive wound slice across his right hand. But he kept his grip on his revolver, and when Romilly came at him a third time, Tennant fired.

The shot cracked like a hammer against granite, but Tennant hadn't missed at that close range. Edgar Romilly staggered and collapsed on his back, a crimson stain spreading across his white shirtfront.

Tennant fell against the tunnel wall. His gun slipped, clattering across the stone floor. He pulled a handkerchief from his pocket and wrapped his hand, securing the makeshift bandage as tightly as he could manage. Then he watched the red patch bloom.

Two days later, Tennant was back in Paris, walking along the right bank of the Seine, his right hand bandaged and his arm in a sling. He headed for a meeting set up by Jules Picard.

Was the pursuit worth it? Tennant hadn't intended to become Romilly's executioner; others with powerful friends were beyond his reach, never to be held to account. Tennant would leave for England the following morning to resume his life. But what would that mean?

Tennant stopped at the entrance to the Invalides Bridge and leaned against the balustrade, propping himself on his left forearm. On that late Sunday afternoon, Paris was a study in December gray: the sky, the leafless willows, and the pewter surface of the Seine looked like a pencil sketch. Even the golden dome over Napoleon's tomb had lost its luster.

Julia . . . They'd met just over a year ago. *Is that all it is?* He looked from the bridge into the dark Seine. The memory rushed back: the cold shock of the canal water, reaching for her, and how close Julia came to drowning. After empty nights in Paris, he understood more deeply what her loss would have meant to him. He'd walked the boulevards as a stranger, passing café tables, watching couples lean in, laugh, and smile at a lingering caress.

But what had he done in London all those months ago? Tennant remembered that, too. He'd left without saying goodbye, dashing off a short note in Kent before sailing for France. Julia's first letter was decidedly cool. The last was warmer. More cheerful. *Friendly, damn it. Well, what did I expect?* But the silence had stretched well beyond a month. Tennant pushed away from the balustrade and turned his back on the river. *Christ,* he thought. Paris was the worst place in the world to be alone and longing for someone. There was nothing to do but return to London and pick up the threads.

Dropping things and picking them up again—or not—had come easy to him before he met Julia. Part of it was temperament; some of it was circumstance. Unlike Julia, Tennant hadn't grown up in a loving family. And a broken engagement had walled him off for a while. Later, after he'd changed careers, he'd lost touch with army friends. Two he'd left behind in Crimean graves. His colleagues at Scotland Yard regarded him with suspicion. He was a "toff," not one of the lads. And to make matters worse, he was the commissioner's godson. The old boy network damned him in their eyes. In fairness, he'd made little effort to change their opinion.

Tennant pulled out his pocket watch. He crossed the bridge and waited near the left bank entrance. What did a General Staff officer in the French Army want with him? The usually communicative Jules Picard had shrugged in a way that might have meant anything from "I haven't a clue" to "Don't ask."

After a ten-minute wait, a scarlet-tasseled peacock—his midnight blue uniform crisscrossed in gold brocade—strode toward him, brilliant in the city's monochrome twilight. He spotted Tennant, shifted a hinged leather case to his left hand, and extended his right.

"Ah," Colonel Chabert said, withdrawing it when Tennant raised his bandaged fist. "I hope I haven't kept you waiting. You return to London immediately. It is true?"

"I take the train to Calais tomorrow morning."

"If you will be so good, it is the wish of the General Staff that you deliver this case to Sir Richard Mayne at Scotland Yard." He passed it to Tennant. "Here is the key."

Tennant pocketed it. "May I know the contents?"

"Intelligence gathered about the Irish Republican Brotherhood."

"The Fenians?" Tennant said. "What is the French government's interest in Irish independence?"

"We recovered the bulk of our rifles from the Lyon warehouse, but a thousand are missing. An informant tells us that Romilly sold them to a 'man in square-toed boots.' An Irishman."

"The guns are heading for Ireland?"

"England. We believe they are steaming toward Southampton. We want our rifles back. In return, the case in your hand includes lists of names; prominent among them is Patrick McGrath. He moves between Ireland, England, and France like a phantom."

"And McGrath is . . ."

"The agent who bought the guns. The documents in the case provide information about American funding for the Irish Republican Brotherhood and the Fenian plans to—"

"Overthrow British authority in Ireland?" Tennant shook his head. "It's been tried, and it's failed many times."

"Something new is afoot. Not pitched battles by soldiers but a stealthy campaign of terror."

"A war from the shadows?"

"Precisely. The targets will be high and low. A police station or a train station bombed. As for your royals . . ." Chabert held Tennant's eye. "Queen Victoria has survived—what is it—five, six attempts on her life?"

"Are you saying—"

"We have no specific intelligence that points to the queen. Still, such a horror would be a coup."

"But one difficult to pull off," Tennant said. "Since Victoria's widowhood, she rarely appears in public."

"Ah, she must emerge sometime," Chabert said. "One cannot grieve in private for a lifetime. Not when one is the queen. And from what I've read, criticism of Her Majesty's isolation is growing."

"True enough," the inspector said. "When is this 'campaign of terror' to begin?"

Chabert looked at him, surprised. "You have not heard about Friday's bombing? It has begun."

Julia had left early for the clinic on Friday morning. Her coachman threaded the carriage through Bishopsgate's morning crowds, slowing the horses to a stop on Duke Street. Mr. Ogilvie waited for a funeral procession of black-hatted men to exit the Great Synagogue and turn off the road before flicking the reins. Julia opened a medical journal, resigning herself to one of those endless drives to Whitechapel.

She was wrong. When they turned left at Whitechapel High Street, it felt like they'd traveled from a circus into a tomb.

Julia counted on one hand the carriages and carts that passed in the opposite direction. It was midmorning, yet there was little foot traffic along the usually crowded pavements between Irish Court and Half Moon Passage. They rolled past the White Swan public house, its shutters down. Most mornings, Julia would see early drinkers queuing up for their first pints. She spotted a woman clutching a net sack in her left fist and a child's hand in her right. She hurried, head down, keeping close to the buildings' walls, vanishing into Plough Court.

It was a mixed neighborhood of English Protestants and Irish Catholics. *Perhaps they sense trouble*, she thought. *They took the prime minister's ban on crowds to heart and are staying indoors.*

Traffic on foot and by wheel picked up after Commercial Street. Julia's coachman had to wait for a break in the stream of pedestrians to turn right onto Fieldgate Street. He stopped the carriage on the other side of Plummer's Row, where the road was wide enough to turn the carriage. The coachman jumped down to open the carriage door.

Julia said, "All seems as usual here, Mister Ogilvie."

"Aye, but it was a strange ride. You'll be all right?"

"Of course."

But her coachman looked doubtful as he glanced back and drove away. Julia paused before walking on, listening to deep, resonating bongs as someone sounded a newly cast bell at the Whitechapel Bell Foundry.

At first, Julia had found most of the neighborhood's sounds, sights, and scents alien. A clanging ironmonger occupied a soot-stained building with peeling paint. Next to him, a carcass butcher's headless pigs hung from a line like pink washing. But five years after Julia signed her lease, her neighbors were like old wallpaper in an often-used hallway. Julia walked past the shops without a glance.

The doctor crossed the street and entered her clinic through its front door. She stood and listened. The quiet told a story: the night had been peaceful. A woman with dark, graying hair as streaked as the wings of a black-and-white magpie emerged from the men's ward with a basin of soiled bandages in her hands. Somehow, Nurse Clemmie's white cap always looked as clean and starched at the end of the day as it did in the morning.

"You're early, Doctor," the head nurse said.

"No private patients on my books today."

So Julia inventoried the drugs cabinet instead. She'd shelved the last bottles of carbolic solution when Kate Connelly knocked on the door and entered the office.

Her maid held up two letters and passed them to Julia. "They came in the morning post. Doctor Andrew sent me along, thinking you'd want to read them straightaway."

"Bless him. And you, Kate."

The top one was postmarked BERLIN. Cancellation stamps tattooed the envelope, telling a story of delay. Tennant had sent the second from Paris a week earlier. The misdirected Berlin letter explained the long silence, but it would tell her nothing about his present circumstances. She hoped the Paris note would be more informative.

"You'll be getting on with your reading," Julia's maid said, backing away.

"Stay a minute, Kate, and I'll send a brief reply. You can drop it in the pillar box on Whitechapel Road."

Julia fished around in her top drawer for a letter opener, her head snapping up when the clinic's front door banged, and shouts erupted.

Nurse Clemmie opened the office door. "It's Sergeant O'Malley with two ambulance wagons of patients injured in a prison explosion."

The big policeman filled the doorway. "We're hoping you have some empty beds, Doctor."

"Who have you brought us?"

"Four men, two women, and a little lad. The worst of the injured went to St. Barts and the London Hospital. Doctor Franklin is hoping you can take these patients unless—"

"We'll manage."

"He'd be sending Doctor Barnes to you, but the London is swamped. And they'll be needing the young doctor there tomorrow, so he'll be missing his usual Saturday."

"No matter. I'll be here."

Constables carried in bloodied victims on stretchers, starting with the women and the child.

"Take them to the women's ward," Julia said. "Jackie?" She looked around for Jackie Archer, the clinic's young orderly. "Bring up cots from the storeroom. Put one in the women's ward for the boy and another four in the fever room."

O'Malley waved over a copper who turned away from a stretcher, looking white in the face. "Help the lad with the beds."

Kate touched Julia's arm. "What can I do?"

"Will you take the carriage home and tell my grandfather I need his help?"

"Mister Ogilvie can do that. I'll send him along with your message."

"All right, Kate. We'll need bedding for seven extra beds. Use the cart by the door. Nurse Emily will show you what to do."

Julia bent over the young boy's stretcher. The child stared up at Julia as she cut away his bloody shirt. She was relieved to see the boy's wounds were largely superficial, with one deeper gash producing most of the blood.

She smiled at him. "What's your name?"

"Willie, miss," he whispered. "Willie Abbott." He tried to raise his head. "My little sister, Minnie . . ."

"Minnie isn't here, Willie, but we'll try to find out where she is. You lie back now. We'll move you to a bed, and Nurse Emily will look after you."

"Careful now, lads," O'Malley said to the stretcher-bearers as they shifted the boy to the cot.

Julia asked him, "Why are children among the injured? I thought this was a prison explosion."

"A barrel of gunpowder blew a fifty-foot hole in the Clerkenwell Prison wall, destroying the house opposite and damaging others on Corporation Row."

"Good God. Do we know who was responsible?"

"Not yet," O'Malley said grimly. "I'm hearing the Irish brotherhood was behind it. But I'm praying it isn't so."

Amen to that, Julia thought, moving to a female patient's bedside.

Kate caught the doctor by her elbow. "What can I do after the beds?"

Julia looked around the waiting room, where anxious family

members had started to arrive. "Can you greet the visitors as they come in? Take their names, seat them, and try to calm them with cups of tea."

An hour later, Julia emerged from the women's ward and greeted her grandfather in the hallway. "Thank goodness," she said, and brushed his cheek with a kiss. "Can you assist Clemmie in the fever room? We put the men in there."

"Of course." He stopped at the door and looked at his granddaughter. "I passed a newsstand and saw an early headline. It said, 'Fenian Outrage at Clerkenwell Prison,' although it's soon to be certain who is behind it."

She thought, *Just what this neighborhood doesn't need.*

Julia jumped when the front door's handle cracked against the wall. A man entered, dressed in gaiters, heavy hob-nailed boots, and a soot-smeared canvas smock. He dragged off his dustman's cap and looked around wildly.

Kate approached him. "Begging your pardon, sir. Can you tell me your name and who you're seeking?"

His head whipped around. "Irish, is it?" He prodded her shoulder with a stubby finger and followed her as she backed away. "Another of those murdering bogtrotters. You and your kind are halfway to making orphans of my sister's children." His last words came out with a sob, and he shoved Kate aside.

Julia called, "Sergeant O'Malley?" He appeared at the men's ward door. "Can you help me with this gentleman?"

The dustman ignored Julia. "Oh, so it's Sergeant *O'Malley*, is it?"

The man was a head shorter and two stones lighter than the policeman, but he tried to bump chests with the sergeant, glaring up at O'Malley's face. The sergeant put his hand on the man's shoulder, forcing him back a pace.

"How can we help you?"

"O'Malley." The man shrugged out of the sergeant's grip. "They're sending the likes of *you* after the bleeding bombers?"

The dustman snorted. "No wonder the Irish bastards who killed that Manchester copper are still in the wind."

The man tried to shove past the sergeant, but O'Malley's bulk blocked the dustman. "Who are you looking for, sir?"

The man jutted his chin. "My sister."

"If she's here, you can rest easy," O'Malley said gently. "They sent the less injured to this clinic. What's your poor sister's name?"

The man's belligerence collapsed. "Alice Jennings. A nurse at the hospital, she . . . she told me they brought Alice here."

"We'll be making allowance for your troubles, but that lass at the front door had nothing to do with them. Now, follow me, and we'll find your sister."

Julia blessed the sergeant, thinking, *We'll need an army of O'Malleys to keep us from each other's throats.*

Hours later, an exhausted Julia finally opened Tennant's first letter.

Lady Styles circled Marlborough House's front lawn twice, thinking about a letter she intended to write. Then the clouds rolled across the sun, and a chilly December wind sent her indoors. Susan walked through the Blenheim Saloon, her favorite room. She loved the ceiling fresco, an appreciation she shared with Princess Louise. She found the princess looking at *An Allegory of Peace and the Arts Under the English Crown*. Her finger pointed up, and she was counting.

"I make it twenty-five, Susan. That's twenty-five female personifications of everything imaginable. "Look." The princess gestured. "Do you see 'Sculpture' in that corner, carving a head?" She sighed. "Think of that."

Poor Louise, Susan thought. *It's what she imagines for herself.* A string of tutors had told her she was talented enough for professional training. Painting flowers or portraits was one thing; the queen herself was an accomplished watercolorist. But chiseling in marble? The queen thought it had "something of the stonemason about it" and was inappropriate for a female royal.

"Princess Alexandra is resting," Susan said. "Is there anything I can do for you?"

Louise shook her head, still gazing at the ceiling.

"I'll be in my room for the next hour, writing letters for the Princess of Wales."

In theory, "waiting" on the royal sisters-in-law was twice the work they'd hired Susan to perform. If by "work," one meant waiting for Princess Alexandra or Princess Louise to decide if the day was fine enough for a walk, waiting to be summoned for a carriage ride, or waiting hours for a request that never came. By her second day of employment, Susan understood that "lady-in-waiting" described her job perfectly. But Lady Styles hid her amusement at the occasional absurdity and boredom of it all, aware that London's toiling women would laugh at the word *work*.

With all that waiting and little to do, Susan had feared her royal service would throw Peter FitzGerald into her company. But their paths seldom crossed. Peter was the queen's equerry, and the Prince of Wales gave his mother a wide berth. Besides, eight years was a long time. *A lifetime.*

They had married others. Peter wed the heiress of Josiah Cuthbert, "the Marmalade King." Harriet's money had rescued him, a second cousin of the Duke of Leinster. The fortunes of Peter's family branch had faded two generations earlier. His wife's settlement allowed the major to live like "an officer and a gentleman" of the Royal Irish Dragoons. And in a neat bargain, her father added his son-in-law's silver-and-red coat of arms to the company's jam jars.

Susan had married a baronet but paid a price for the title "Lady Styles."

She realized her mistake on the wedding trip. And after four years that passed like four decades, the marriage ended suddenly and violently. Sir Augustus Styles spent his last night on earth whoring, gambling, and drinking to excess. In the morning, he'd roused himself for a foxhunt, downed two glasses of champagne, and broke his neck when his horse hesitated at a hedge, throwing him to his death.

My third year of widowhood. Susan had spent the time wearing hypocrisy literally on her sleeve. She dressed in deep black for the first two years, transitioning to "half-mourning" gray and mauve in the third. But the queen, still bereft six years after her husband's death, was a stickler about the formalities of sorrow. So, Lady Styles swallowed her self-disgust and performed a charade of grief.

That afternoon, Susan sat at her writing table and set to work. *That word again*, she thought with a shake of her head. She had four letters to write: one to Alix's dressmaker, another to the milliner, and a third "duty" missive to her brother.

Susan pulled a fourth piece of stationery toward her. But over the last letter, she hesitated. Then she penned a few swift lines to confirm an appointment for Monday, addressed the envelope, and sealed it. *Done.*

A servant tapped on her door and entered at Susan's invitation. "Pardon me, my lady, but the Princess of Wales asks if you would wait on her. She is in her sitting room."

Susan hid a smile. "Please tell Her Royal Highness I will attend her in ten minutes."

Lady Styles pinned her mourning brooch in place and checked her hair and dress in the mirror. Then she gathered her letters to carry downstairs for a servant to post. But as soon as Susan handed them to the footman, she regretted the last one she'd written. She nearly called him back to retrieve the note she'd written to Dr. Julia Lewis, confirming an appointment.

Was it Susan's business to interfere? And what if her worst

fears were true? *If so, there is nothing to be done.* In the end, she let the letter go out with the afternoon post. *Monday it is.*

Susan stopped on the stairs at the sound of insistent knocking. The footman opened the front door to a pair of constables and a captain in the Queen's Guards. He asked for the Prince of Wales.

"He's not in," Susan called, descending the staircase.

The captain said, "I have urgent orders to locate His Royal Highness."

Susan glanced at the clock. "I expect he's . . . making a late-afternoon call." Almost certainly, the prince was pursuing his latest conquest. They would find him with the twenty-year-old wife of an aging baronet. "His private secretary will help you. If you'll follow me."

The secretary scribbled the London address of Sir Charles and Lady Mordaunt and said, "Number six Chesham Place is just off Belgrave Square."

"Thank you." The captain handed the paper to one of the two constables. "Escort His Royal Highness back to Marlborough House."

Susan asked the officer, "Can you tell us what has happened?"

"A bombing at Clerkenwell Prison, probably by the Irish Brotherhood. It destroyed half a block of houses."

"Good God. Are there many injuries?"

"Hospitals are filling. We're mounting additional guards at all government buildings and royal residences. I must inspect all doors and windows on the ground floor."

"Of course," she said.

"First, may I see the Princess of Wales?"

They made their way up the staircase. From the landing's window, Susan spotted soldiers fanning across the front lawn, rifles at the ready.

* * *

Just after seven, Nurse Clemmie shifted an empty plate, teacup, and saucer from Julia's desk to a tray. Her head nurse insisted that she eat something before her last round.

"All quiet and resting more or less comfortably," Julia said, returning to her office. She deposited some soiled bandages in the bin by her door.

Clemmie nodded to Julia's coat rack. "Then there's no need to stay any longer. I'll send Jackie to the corner to whistle up a cab."

Julia, bone-weary, nodded. She stretched and flexed her fingers. "Thank goodness my grandfather and Kate pitched in." Then Julia groaned at a rumbling commotion outside the clinic. "So much for quiet." She called to their orderly, "Jackie, see what's happening."

Jackie Archer parked a rolling cart of bedding by the wall and tossed the daily paper he'd tucked under his arm onto a bench. Before he reached the door, a constable opened it and stood back. Two men staggered through the entrance, supporting an unconscious man whose heels scraped across the stone floor. There were no free beds, so Nurse Clemmie grabbed a blanket from the cart and unfurled it with a snap.

"Lay him down here."

"My bag, Clemmie," Julia said, sinking to her knees. She folded back the man's ragged corduroy jacket, uncovering a shirt saturated in blood. He made no sound, and his fixed, blue-green eyes looked lifeless. Julia felt for a pulse in his neck. Clemmie handed her the stethoscope from her medical bag. She listened. Then she sat back on her heels, looked up at her nurse, and shook her head.

A man in a white barman's apron said, "There was some high talk in the pub about the bombing. Someone spotted two Irishmen walking by the window, and the room emptied."

The second man dragged off his rough tweed cap. "I knew

him. Kevin Leary was a warehouseman and a Paddy, all right. But a good fellow and all."

"'An eye for an eye for Clerkenwell,' some bloke shouted," the barman said.

"And we all end up blind." Clemmie closed the dead man's lids, brushed his cheek with the back of her fingers, and pulled a sheet over his body.

Jackie extended his hand, and Julia hauled herself up. She dropped onto the bench where the young orderly had tossed his newspaper. *The Whitechapel Evening Chronicle* had rushed to print with a one-word headline in two-inch type: OUTRAGE! A short editorial set in a box called for "utmost measures to protect the British public from Irish murderers."

Julia looked at the spreading stain where the sheet covered Kevin Leary's once-beating heart. She thought, *Who will protect the Irish from us?*

CHAPTER 4

Princess Alexandra nearly canceled Saturday's ball. She'd thought it callous to hold the entertainment the day after the Clerkenwell Prison explosion. But in the end, Alix relented. Bertie wanted to dance, and she wouldn't deny her husband his pleasure.

Susan stood at the top of the grand staircase, watching a rising stream of ladies lift yards of peach, periwinkle, and golden tulle away from their slippers. Mostly, they kept their backs straight and their eyes forward. But occasionally, a lady glanced at the left-hand wall and its large-as-life battlefield picture. The supine corpse and dead face of the Duke of Marlborough's aide-de-camp stared back. Susan smiled in sympathy as one young woman nearly missed her footing.

"Could be worse," someone drawled in her ear. "Chap in the picture had his head blown off by a cannonball."

Susan turned. A tall, spare, dark-haired gentleman in his middle thirties, wearing a black tailcoat and white tie, looked at her with an amused glint. "The painting is dreadful enough without adding that detail."

"Good evening, Sir Lionel."

He raised her hand to his lips. "Lady Styles." His smile spread slowly. "The truth . . . not quite the thing to hang on one's wall."

"I would draw the line."

People called Sir Lionel Dermott "an amusing fellow" who did "something at the Home Office." Susan wondered if that meant they didn't know or chose not to disclose his role there.

"When the dancing begins, would you honor me with the first waltz, Lady Styles?"

"Delighted, Sir Lionel."

He leaned forward. "The lovely Alix is looking your way. I'll leave you to the evening's greetings. But promise you won't forget me." He bowed and walked away.

A footman announced the guests as they reached the landing. Susan's job was to prompt Princess Alexandra by repeating the name, speaking clearly and distinctly. Hearing loss plagued Alix, although she was only twenty-three, a problem that had grown worse in the past few months. When the flow of arrivals trickled to an end, Susan followed the prince and princess into the ballroom. Princess Alexandra, aided by a walking stick and her husband's arm, made her way slowly to a chair. The Prince of Wales bowed and walked away.

Seeking companions more entertaining than a lame, deaf wife, Susan thought. Since the winter, Alix had been ill with a list of strange symptoms; the most persistent and debilitating was a swollen knee that made movement painful and difficult. Bertie's response was to absent himself from the domestic scene as often as possible.

Lady Styles shivered near a chilly window. The outside world looked black on the moonless, mid-December night. She wondered how many additional soldiers and policemen ringed the residence. Inside, the ballroom blazed, lit by bronze chandeliers and wall torchiers that had turned the rose-and-cream room golden. Officers in scarlet, Scots in black velvet and tartan, and gentlemen in ebony tailcoats and snowy ties twirled their partners around the room.

After a difficult autumn, Susan was happy to see Princess Louise in better spirits. The queen's prettiest daughter looked stunning in a silvery, avant-garde "aesthetic" gown. The unfussy lines of the dress suited her. She held the white-gloved hand of a scarlet-coated colonel, leading the company through the opening quadrille. *Time away from Her Majesty is better than a tonic,* Susan thought. Most of the queen's children masked their frustration with the queen's incessant demands and gave in. Louise fought back.

The evening marked Susan's first ballroom appearance in half-mourning mauve. After two years and more of widowhood, etiquette's stringent rules finally allowed her to dance. She had enjoyed waltzing and sparring with Sir Lionel Dermott in the past, so she smiled when he claimed her hand for the second set. Susan suspected her partner's air of arch amusement was a pose. *But what does it mask?* She wasn't sure.

For all his languor, Lionel waltzed beautifully. But that evening, her usually chatty companion made only glancing stabs at conversation, spending much of the time scanning the room.

Mildly miffed, Susan asked, "Have you lost something?"

He said without a trace of chagrin, "Unforgivable bad manners, Lady Styles. Let me think . . . Shall I mention the excellence of the orchestra? What about the weather?"

"If you must."

"Perhaps a comment about the dancers will do. Princess Louise looks radiant this evening on the arm of her handsome colonel."

"You never wear your uniform, Sir Lionel. May I ask why?"

His smile faded. "I'm afraid my glory days are behind me. I left them in the Crimea."

There was an undertone, a hint of something in his voice like a spice one tasted but could not place. *Is it bitterness?* Susan asked, "What were you searching for over my shoulder?"

"I'm on the lookout for old G-H," Sir Lionel said, referring to the home secretary.

"Mister Gathorne-Hardy? Why?"

"Tedious business, m'dear. Too sleep-inducing to talk about."

"It seems oddly energetic of you," Susan said with a smile. "Mixing work and pleasure."

"Energetic?" His eyes widened in horror, and he looked left and right. "Don't let *that* rumor get about." His catlike smile spread. "I aim to keep expectations low. The bottom rail on the fence is all I'll jump."

"You're not a show pony, I know. But eager matrons with eligible daughters long to put you through your paces." Susan tipped her head. "Look."

He glanced to his right. "Ah . . . but one becomes so distracted by the whistling sound."

"Whistling?"

"Nothing from ear to ear. Now you, Lady Styles. With you, I have the opposite fear. All that gray matter behind eyes that put me on my mettle."

When the waltz ended, Sir Lionel said, "I see the lovely Alix has attracted half the Marlborough House set."

"Marlborough House set? You read the illustrated weeklies, Sir Lionel?"

"Avidly. One must be *au courant* in everything. Shall we join the entourage?"

Susan wasn't surprised to find the ever-faithful Oliver Montgomery among Alix's courtiers. Captain Frederick Locock, the doctor's son, was there as well. Both men wore the blue uniforms of the Royal Horse Guards. Major FitzGerald blazed in the scarlet tunic and gold shamrock lace of the 4th Royal Irish Dragoon Guards. His wife, Harriet, was there, too, chatting with the seated princess. *But looking over Alix's head at Princess Louise,* Susan thought, amused.

Harriet FitzGerald and Princess Louise shared the same abundant fair hair. Lately, Peter's wife wore it long and loose in imitation of the princess. That night, she seemed to be eyeing Louise's dress. *Harriet will visit her dressmaker on Monday.*

"Lady Styles." Susan turned and took Peter's offered hand.

"Major FitzGerald, you know Sir Lionel Dermott, I believe."

"Oh, FitzGerald and I are old friends and adversaries," Lionel said. "We pitted our yachts in sail-to-sail combat last summer at Cowes."

The major smiled. "I believe you had the better of me that day."

"A lucky shift in the wind." Lionel turned and clapped Oliver Montgomery on the shoulder. "Ollie, old man, how are you? And Trev." He extended his hand to George Trevor. "How was the shooting?"

Peter drew Susan aside. "I haven't seen you since . . . Any news from the Isle of Wight about that business over the girl?"

"Nothing from the Cowes Constabulary," Susan said. "But the officials at Dublin Castle— "

Lionel turned around. "Dublin Castle? That lot makes my sleepy corner of the Home Office look sprightly. What do you want with them?"

"Information about a murdered girl's family," Susan said. For once, she blessed Alix's hearing difficulties as Captain Montgomery lowered his voice and explained the tragedy to Lionel.

"You'd be better off applying directly to the efficient Dublin police," Dermott said. "Although their plate is full just now."

"Dublin Castle's officials were helpful, as it happens," Susan said. "They provided the address once I knew the town's name and the family that employed the girl," Susan said.

"How did you discover that?" FitzGerald asked.

"Princess Louise and I sat with a map of Ireland, and it spurred her recollection. Then I exchanged notes with Brigid Dowling. A last letter from her sister had arrived in the post, and she—"

"After all this time?" FitzGerald said.

"Miss Dowling had been in Dublin. When the family returned to their country house, she found a note from her dead sister and my letter." Susan frowned. "She wrote, asking to come to London to speak to me."

"Seems odd," Captain Montgomery said.

Susan frowned. "Something is bothering her."

FitzGerald asked, "Did she explain her concern?"

"I'll find out on Tuesday. She's coming to see me after luncheon."

Lionel asked, "Coming from where?"

"County Cork. I suggested lodgings at the Chapter House near St. Paul's."

"A modest, respectable hostelry," Lionel said. "Your concern does you credit, Lady Styles. Now, if you'll excuse me?" He bowed and walked away.

Susan watched Lionel cross the room. He took the elbow of a balding man with the sagging face of a Labrador and steered him to one side. Mister Gathorne-Hardy listened, smoothing his wispy side whiskers. Then he nodded and returned to his wife.

Next, Lionel threaded his way through the knot of men around the Prince of Wales. Each year, the ever-stouter Bertie was easier to find in a crowd, and Lionel and the prince made an amusing contrast. *The pencil and the powder keg*, Susan thought. Lionel had Bertie's ear, holding his attention while he spoke. Bertie nodded when he finished, and Lionel bowed and slipped away.

"Funny chap."

Susan started. She hadn't realized Captain Locock stood behind her. Oliver Montgomery had watched Lionel, too.

"Can't help liking him," Locock said, "though half the time, I think he's laughing at me."

"And he seems to know everyone . . . and everything." Captain Montgomery narrowed his eyes. "He's privy to more secrets than a Roman Catholic confessor."

"Still, he's an amusing chap," Locock said. "Livens up a dull evening."

Susan arched an eyebrow. "Like this one?" When he started to protest, she said, "Perhaps you're just missing Mrs. Locock tonight."

"My wife hovers when the baby fusses. She'll drive the nursery maid mad if she keeps it up." Locock shook his head. "Mary sends worried telegrams to my father every other day."

"New mothers. It's quite understandable."

"Thank God we're leaving for Cowes next week. Then she'll have my father and his medical advice on the spot." Locock lowered his voice. "Mary and I feel grateful and blessed. Adoption was likely her only chance at motherhood, but you know the whole story, Susan."

George Trevor claimed Lady Styles for the next set, and they followed Princess Louise and Frederick Locock to the floor. By the time Susan finished dancing and talking politics with the well-informed Mr. Trevor, the story had circled the room.

On Monday, the Prince of Wales would visit the Clerkenwell survivors at St. Barts Hospital.

Many guests planned to dance until dawn, but the frail, ailing Princess of Wales left with Lady Styles just after midnight. Alix winced with every step.

Two footmen waited at the end of the hallway with an invalid chair. They carried her up the stairs and wheeled her to her chamber. Susan opened the bedroom door, and a footman rolled her across the threshold.

"Thank you, Wilfred," Lady Styles said. "That will be all for this evening."

Susan closed the door and turned up the gas lamps on the center table. Family portraits and religious paintings crowded the walls, and a nearly life-sized figure of the crucified Christ loomed over the canopied bed. Susan often wondered what the Prince of Wales made of it. *Four pregnancies in five years. Bertie mustn't find it too off-putting.*

The princess eased herself into the chair at her dressing table. She slipped the catch on her pearl choker necklace and laid it aside.

"Shall I ring for your maid?" Susan asked, reaching for the bell pull. The princess didn't answer. "Your Royal Highness?"

"This appointment you have with Doctor Lewis . . . when do you see her?"

"She suggested Monday morning at her clinic."

"How shall we . . ." Alexandra's hand went to her throat, her fingers worrying the small scar on her neck. "How will it be managed?"

"I'll suggest to the doctor that we visit her at Finsbury Circus on Friday, if convenient. Princess Louise has a drawing lesson that morning." Susan touched Alexandra's shoulder. "And no one will know it's not a social call," she said gently.

The princess sighed. "Very well." Her hand slipped from her throat and fell to her lap. "I must do something."

On Monday morning, Kate surprised Julia. Her maid waited at the front door, dressed in a hat, gloves, and a coat. She had a wool throw draped over her arm.

"Mrs. Ogilvie is after giving me the whole day, so I'll be going to the clinic to help out."

Julia was touched. "Mondays are your half days, Kate. You don't have to— "

"The nurses looked tired out, and an extra pair of hands

will be welcome to change the linens at least." Kate shook her head. "The work of a clinic . . . it's not only fixing broken bones, is it?"

"No, but after that business on Friday . . . this is kind of you."

"'Tis over and done, and the world could use a little kindness just now, I'm thinking."

"Amen to that," Julia said, pulling on her gloves.

Kate climbed into the coach behind Julia and held up the wrap. "The cold's come on us something fierce, so Mrs. Ogilvie sent this along. Are you needing it?"

"I don't think so. You take it."

Kate tucked it around her. "We're all happy to hear the inspector will soon be home from his travels."

A post office telegram marked "Handed in: Lyon, France" had arrived for Julia on Saturday. Then, a second sent from Paris came at breakfast that morning.

"He should be back in London on Thursday."

"He nearly got you drowned, but there's much to be said for a man who sends you hothouse roses after he fishes you out of the water."

Julia laughed. "That's one way of looking at it."

She had spent considerable time "looking at" the inspector's imminent return from every vantage. Relief flowed, her first emotion. After that came the familiar to-and-fro of her complicated, contradictory feelings.

Julia's morning filled with Monday's typical duties and patients. With winter setting in, many of the ill were respiratory cases. She examined the Clerkenwell victims, pronouncing two fit for release. Young Willie Abbott had gone home with his aunt on Saturday, but the little sister he'd been looking for was dead. Minnie Abbott, just eight years old, died when her house on Corporation Lane collapsed, the bombing's youngest victim. The remaining injured patients required several more days of attentive nursing to avoid the danger of infection.

The grim tally from the attack was a dozen dead and 120 wounded. The final reckoning was anyone's guess as newspapers filled with animus against the Irish and vitriol against the police. Editorials in some Sunday papers called for a Parliamentary inquiry into Scotland Yard, and many demanded Sir Richard Mayne's head.

Kate dispensed cups of tea and attended to the extra piles of bedding, relieving the nursing staff of distracting housekeeping chores. At one o'clock, she tapped and opened the office door.

"Lady Styles is here, Doctor Julie."

The doctor rounded her desk and offered her hand. "It's a pleasure to see you again." Julia patted the chair's armrest. "You found us without difficulty?"

Susan sat, smoothing her skirts. "London cabbies seem to know every cranny of the city. When I gave the address of your clinic, the driver rattled off the names of the nearest public house and the corner draper's shop where we turned."

"It's a varied neighborhood, to say the least. Lady Styles, I've wondered . . . Before we begin, have you heard anything more about that sad business on the Isle of Wight?"

"Nothing from the police, but Lizzie Dowling's sister is traveling from County Cork to see me. She'll be here tomorrow, as it happens."

"That's a long trip."

"Yes. I have little to tell her, but the girl has something to tell me. I'll know more tomorrow afternoon."

Julia's visitor looked grave but composed. The mauve lace at her throat relieved the gray of her fitted jacket, adding color to her cheeks.

"Well, you *look* perfectly healthy, Lady Styles. Blooming, in fact," Julia said. "So, what brings you here today?"

"I'm quite well, but . . ." Susan peered at the ornate lettering on Julia's medical diploma affixed to the wall. "Does that say Philadelphia? You traveled far to become a doctor."

Julia knew a delaying tactic when she heard one. "Yes. Parliament opened a back door for females by adding foreign doctors to the medical register. They either forgot or didn't know that some women hold medical degrees from abroad." Julia smiled. "My money's on 'didn't know,' or they would have slammed that door shut."

"You're probably right." Lady Styles played with the buttons on her dove-gray gloves.

Julia leaned forward. "Confiding in a stranger is difficult, but you can rely on my skill and discretion. For me, a consulting room has the seal of a confessional."

"Thank you for that reassurance. I hesitate because the matter is delicate, and it's about Alix. Princess Alexandra."

"The Princess of Wales must have . . . surely, she's under a doctor's care?"

"Her Royal Highness sees all too many doctors," Susan said dryly. "And they provide detailed reports about her condition to the Prince of Wales and Her Majesty."

"To the queen?"

"Not all doctors share your belief in the privacy of a medical consultation. But the princess has begun to wonder . . ."

Julia waited while Lady Styles wrestled. Finally, she sighed and said, "Princess Alexandra would like an independent opinion. She made up her mind when I told her about you, a lady doctor."

"I would be honored, Lady Styles. May I suggest Her Royal Highness visit me at my consulting rooms at Finsbury Circus?"

"Friday morning would be convenient for the princess if it suits your schedule."

"Friday it is . . . at ten o'clock?" When Lady Styles nodded, Julia made a note.

Susan stood. "There's no point in my being here unless I'm frank with you. I know what Alix fears. The princess is loyal, but she's not a fool. She understands that the Prince of Wales . . ." She held Julia's gaze. "Princess Alexandra is afraid she may have contracted an illness from her husband."

"I see," Julia said.

"I'm sure you do, Doctor. She hasn't put a name to it, but I will. Princess Alexandra is afraid she may have syphilis."

Shortly before two o'clock on Tuesday, a tall, thin man with a wiry abundance of ginger facial hair and pale blue eyes hailed a hackney cab on Ivy Lane.

"Where to, guv?" the cabbie asked.

"The Chapter House on St. Paul's Alley. We'll be waiting for a lady, but I'll make it worth your while if she's delayed."

"Right you are."

Promptly at two, a young woman came through the front door, stopped on the pavement, and looked around. The ginger-bearded man approached her and touched the brim of his bowler.

"Miss Dowling?"

She pulled a paper from her pocket. "You'll be the one sending me this note?"

"That's right. Lady Styles didn't want you to lose your way." He opened the carriage door. "You brought the letter with you?"

She reached into her handbag and took it out.

"Excellent, excellent. Hold on to it for now." He handed the girl into the cabin. "Drive to Upper Thames Street, cabbie, and turn left. I'll knock when I want you to stop."

The driver nosed his horse through the traffic around St. Paul's Cathedral and headed toward the river. Shortly after he turned onto Upper Thames Street, his passenger pounded on the hackney's roof. The man leaned out the window and shouted, "Stop the coach."

The driver slowed his horse and stopped. "Guvnor?"

"Turn right into Trig Lane. And pull up at the entrance to the wharf."

The cabbie drove as instructed, and the hackney rattled to a stop at the end of the lane.

The passenger stepped out of the cabin. "Driver, can you assist me? The lady seems overcome."

The cabbie climbed down and peered inside the cabin, eyeing the crumpled figure in the corner. He ducked inside and leaned over the girl. At a tap on his shoulder, he twisted around.

The driver's brain registered a searing pain under his chin a split second before oblivion.

Lady Styles waited all Tuesday afternoon for Brigid Dowling to appear. She'd told the footmen to expect a visitor and thought to warn the kitchen staff that a girl might present herself at the servants' entrance, asking for her. *Has she changed her mind?* Susan wondered. *Or lost her way?*

She spent part of the time reading the newspaper coverage of the prince's visit to St. Bart's. Both *The Times* and *The Daily Telegraph* praised the Prince of Wales for comforting the Clerkenwell victims, their criticism of the absent Victoria implied rather than stated.

The queen complains of Bertie's idleness but gives him nothing to do, Susan thought, putting the newspapers aside. *And he's good at this sort of thing.* Perhaps that was the problem. Victoria refused to take the stage but guarded it jealously, denying her heir the limelight.

On Wednesday morning, Susan sent a note to the Chapter House and asked the second footman who carried it to wait for a reply. An hour later, the servant returned.

"Brigid Dowling paid for two nights and left yesterday afternoon, my lady."

"And she never returned?"

"The desk clerk hasn't seen her since. Said he was holding her carpetbag and wondering what to do with it."

On Thursday morning, Sergeant O'Malley arrived early at Scotland Yard. He found his new inspector's office empty, his desk cleared out, and a message from Chief Inspector Clark. The chief wanted to see him.

Clark sat at his littered desk, reading a letter. His scowling bulldog's face made him look more combative than usual. When he dropped the note, O'Malley spotted the commissioner's heading.

"Sit."

The sergeant lowered his bulk onto the battered wooden chair and winced when it creaked. The squat, bald Clark leaned back and hooked his thumbs into his waistcoat pockets.

"I've got just the job for you, O'Malley," he said, stressing the "O" in his surname. "Some Irish servant girl has gone missing. For some reason, Marlborough House cares, so—" The chief looked over the sergeant's shoulder. "Well, well . . . Look what the cat's dragged in."

O'Malley twisted around in his seat. Tennant stood in the doorway.

"Thank you, sir," the inspector said. "It's a pleasure to be back." Tennant turned to O'Malley and smiled. "Good to see you, Sergeant."

O'Malley got to his feet, the grin underneath his bushy mustache splitting his face. He reached to shake the inspector's hand and stopped when he saw the bandage.

"Nothing much, Paddy. A flesh wound. I'll tell you about it over a pint."

"You'll put off the bloody reunion for now," Clark said. "This message from Sir Richard . . ." He snatched it up. "The commissioner wants to—let me read it—'reinstate a winning team' and put you on a case." The chief tossed it aside. "Princess Alexandra's lady-in-waiting filed a missing person's report about a servant girl."

"Indeed, sir," Tennant said, his expression impassive.

"Yes, 'indeed,' so let's not make a pig's ear out of this one." Clark handed O'Malley the file. "We'll have Marlborough

House, the palace, and half the bleeding Home Office looking over our shoulder."

"I see."

Clark waved them out of the room. "Hop it."

When they were out of earshot, O'Malley said, "You'll be noticing the chief hasn't changed."

"Charming as ever," Tennant said, opening the door to the office he'd exited nearly six months earlier.

He stood a moment with his hands on his hips. "Well, it hasn't gotten any larger since I left." He walked to the window and put his hand on the sill. "The window is just as drafty. All the same . . ." Tennant dropped Clark's report on his desk, swiveled the creaky chair, and sat.

"All the same, I'm glad you're back. And that maggot, Romilly, or whatever he's after calling himself. Good riddance."

"I'll tell you the whole story later, but Romilly was up to his neck in gunrunning. Sold weapons to the Irish Republican Brotherhood."

"Have you told the commissioner that?"

"Yes. French military intelligence asked me to convey some documents to Sir Richard about IRB activities." Tennant looked at his sergeant. "So, tell me . . . how are things at the Yard?"

"Morale's been better, and if you happen to have a name that starts with 'O' or 'Mc' 'tis a bit like having a dose of leprosy."

"I was afraid of that."

"The fella sitting at your desk for the last six months has joined a special division looking into the brotherhood threat. I wasn't invited to the party."

"I'm sorry, Paddy."

O'Malley shrugged. "Like the old music hall song says, 'No Irish Need Apply.' "

"Well, I'm glad you've held down the fort. The Yard seems under siege."

"That it is. And there was some trouble over at the doctor's clinic on the day of the bombing." O'Malley explained what happened to Kate Connelly. "'Twill all blow over soon enough, I'm thinking."

Unless Colonel Chabert is right, and it's just begun, Tennant thought. "Damned unpleasant for poor Kate."

"Have you seen the doctor?"

"Not yet, but she knows I planned to be back today. So, this missing girl. What's our first order of business?"

"I'll be looking at the daily reports from the divisional chief inspectors for anyone answering the girl's description."

The inspector picked up Clark's report. "She's described as a young woman in her middle twenties, auburn-haired, wearing a gray coat and hat."

"I'll be sending a pair of constables along to check the hospitals," O'Malley said. "A country girl from Ireland looking the wrong way? A cab may have knocked the poor lass down in the streets."

Tennant scanned Clark's report again. "Last seen at the Chapter House around the corner from St. Paul's Cathedral. A copper interviewed the desk clerk."

"St. Paul's . . . I'm remembering something about a cab going missing thereabouts." O'Malley retrieved a stack of reports from his desk and shuffled through them. "Here it is. On Tuesday night, a hackney driver never returned with his cab. His turf was Cheapside and the neighborhood around the cathedral."

"All right, Paddy. Track down the copper on that beat and talk to the Chapter House desk clerk again. I'll interview Lady Styles at Marlborough House."

A pair of young mud larks had waited until midmorning for the tide on the Thames to turn and the gray water to recede, leaving a band of slime-slickened mud. The boys had come equipped with rubber boots, rakes, and a basket. They headed down the cobbled roadbed of Trig Lane. The stone steps at the bottom of the street gave access to the oozing strand where they planned to dig for treasure. Almost anything would do. Even an old shoe could be dried out and sold for scrap.

Near the top of the lane, the sharp-eyed older lad spotted a battered tin near a broken crate.

"Empty," he said. "Might be worth a ha'penny." He dropped it in his basket. "Here, what's this?"

He squatted, retrieved a red, hairy mass, and smoothed out a false beard. The boy fitted the hooks around the ears of his younger brother. "You could do a turn at the music hall with this, Sammy. Let me try."

They took turns hooking on the beard and laughing at themselves. Then they stopped at the old warehouse near the turnoff into Trig Wharf.

"Oy, Bert. Look," the younger lad said. "Somebody's gone and smashed the lock."

"Funny, that."

They'd tried to explore the abandoned building earlier but hadn't found a way inside. That morning, they heard neighing and banging behind the door.

The broken latch and the strange sounds were irresistible.

Tennant and a constable took a hansom from Scotland Yard, driving along the Mall, keeping St. James's Park on their left. The cabbie turned right on Marlborough Road and rolled to a stop in front of a three-story brick mansion, the London residence of the Prince and Princess of Wales.

The inspector paid off the cabbie and looked up at the columned portico that sheltered the front door. Then he walked up to the entrance.

"Blimey," the young copper said. "Begging your pardon, sir, but you'll not be knocking at the front door?"

"Certainly, Constable."

The footman who answered hesitated when Tennant gave

his name and rank and asked to see Lady Styles. Then the servant led the two policemen down a short flight of marble steps to the entry hall and asked them to wait. The young copper stood rooted at the room's center; the inspector crossed the Persian carpet to examine the tapestry on the wall.

Tennant turned when someone said, "*La Primavera.*" A tall, fair woman dressed in a gray-and-black day frock stood in the doorway. "It's an exquisite woven copy of the Botticelli masterpiece."

"Lady Styles?"

"That's right, Inspector." She descended the steps and offered her hand. "There's a small drawing room in this wing where we can speak in private. The maids light a fire in the morning, and I often sit there before luncheon."

"Thank you."

She opened a door and smiled. "It feels a little less like sitting in a museum."

Tennant and his constable followed her into a bright, south-facing room with a large window that afforded a garden view. The inspector and Lady Styles sat in facing armchairs by the fireplace. The young copper stood, waiting for instructions.

The inspector held up his bandaged hand. "With your permission, my constable will take the notes for this interview."

When Susan said, "Of course," Tennant nodded to the young policeman who fished a notebook and pencil from his tunic pocket.

"Lady Styles, a constable interviewed the Charter House desk clerk. He described Brigid Dowling, reported her arrival on Monday, and said she left at two in the afternoon on Tuesday. In your own good time, tell me about the girl and Marlborough House's interest in her."

Lady Styles began at the Isle of Wight with the discovery of Lizzie Dowling's body, ending with her sister's note and failure to keep the appointment.

"We'd arranged to meet on Tuesday, Inspector, so Miss Dowling has been missing for two days."

"My detective sergeant and two constables are at work on her disappearance. You said you were concerned about the letter she sent. May I see it?"

"The last lines, Inspector." Lady Styles handed him the note.

Tennant read, *I'll be showing you Lizzie's last letter, but I'll not be easy in my mind until you're telling me it's nothing. She was always looking after me, and now that she's gone, I must do the same for her.*

The inspector said, "I'll keep this if I may. The death of the sister . . . the coroner's jury reached an open verdict?"

"Yes. I spoke with the doctor who examined the body, and she—"

"She?"

"Yes, Doctor Julia Lewis," Lady Styles said. "That must sound strange."

Tennant half smiled and said, "Not as strange as you might think. I know Doctor Lewis. Will you explain her involvement?"

"Doctor Lewis was visiting the Isle of Wight with her family. The local medical man was unavailable, so she stepped in."

"I see," Tennant said.

"Might the girl have changed her mind and returned to Ireland?" Susan asked. "Perhaps a telegram to her employer, Lady Browne at Lansdowne House, might—"

"Would she leave without her luggage? She left her carpetbag in her room."

Susan bit her lip. "I'd forgotten."

"One obvious line of inquiry is the local hospitals. Miss Dowling may have met with an accident. If not, I may need to return with more questions."

"I understand, Inspector. Is there anything else?"

"For the present, no."

"Then I'll see you out." She looked over her shoulder at a tap at the door.

"Pardon me, my lady," the footman said. "A messenger from Scotland Yard is outside with a carriage."

At the front door, Tennant said, "Thank you, Lady Styles. We'll keep Marlborough House informed." He replaced his hat and touched the brim.

A hansom and the messenger waited at the bottom of the steps. "Sir." He handed the inspector a note from Sergeant O'Malley.

The inspector read it. Then he said, "Take down this message, Constable." He dictated a brief note and an address in Whitechapel. "Take it to Doctor Julia Lewis at her clinic. I'll drop you as close as I can."

"Yes, sir."

"Then return to the Yard. Write up your report and have a summary of the interview with Lady Styles on my desk in the morning."

Tennant and the constable climbed into the coach. The inspector looked out the window as it turned from Wellington Road. It was a chilly late morning, but the bright sunshine had tempted strollers along the Mall to defy the cold. A gentleman handed a lady to a bench across from Carlton House Terrace. Tennant envied their leisure in the middle of the day. He had intended to drive to the clinic to see Julia after the interview with Lady Styles. Instead, he would summon her for a pair of postmortems.

The inspector told the constable, "Two boys found a cab and its dead driver on the wharf off Trig Lane. Sergeant O'Malley believes they also found our missing girl."

A few minutes before eleven, Nurse Clemmie looked at the watch pinned to her uniform. "Aren't you supposed to be—"

"Giving evidence at the Kevin Leary inquest," Julia said,

walking past her head nurse and into her office, dropping her medical bag on her desk. "Postponed until Saturday by a local magistrate's order. Doctor Barnes is scheduled for Saturday, so the delay is just as well."

"Unusual."

"The official used the word 'unhealthy' to describe the state of local opinion, 'necessitating a "cooling-off period."' Well, 'unhappy' describes *my* state. I had three—count them, Clemmie—three private patients I needlessly rescheduled."

"Well, that's looking up."

"Looking up? That's practically Piccadilly Circus in my waiting room," she said, dropping into her chair. "Anyone requiring attention at the start of our rounds? Our blast patients?"

"No signs of infection among them, thank goodness. We'll need to reorder carbolic solution."

Julia nodded, glancing at the wall clock. "No . . . no messages for me?"

"Were you expecting—"

"No, nothing," Julia said, standing. "Let's begin."

Richard's first day back at the Yard. Of course, he's swamped.

An hour later, a young constable with his helmet tucked under his arm appeared at the door of the men's ward. "Doctor Lewis? I have a message from Inspector Tennant."

CHAPTER 5

Tennant arrived at Trig Lane as a low layer of marine fog crept along the Thames.

At the street's end, the masts of low-slung hay boats sprouted from the water like a winter forest. Before long, the moored flotilla would vanish into the curling mist, leaving creaky rigging and slapping water the only hints they were there. Along the lane, abandoned wharf-side warehouses leaned together, sills and lintels peeling and sagging, their hoisting hooks and chains rusted from disuse.

"The constables are finishing their sweep of the wharf," O'Malley said. "They'll not be seeing the tips of their boots in another ten minutes."

Tennant nodded. "What have they found?"

"Nothing to speak of, but the lads who stumbled across the cab plucked a prize from the trash." O'Malley handed Tennant a false ginger beard.

"Well, well," he said, holding it by an ear hook. "Where are the boys now?"

"I'm after sending them with a copper to the potato peddler

on the corner. The pair of them could use something hot and filling."

Two mortuary assistants waited outside the warehouse with a wagon. A driver from the City of London Hackney Company looked downriver and frowned. "Fog's coming on something fierce, guvnor," the cabman said.

"We won't keep you long. All right, Paddy, let's have a look at our victims. Then we'll release the cab to this gentleman."

Tennant followed O'Malley across the warehouse threshold. The sergeant aimed the beam of his bull's-eye lantern into the gloom. The triangle of light illuminated a horse that had consumed most of the hay bale brought by the company driver. The animal had drained a bucket of water as well.

"Half-starved, the poor creature," the sergeant said. "With nothing to eat or drink since Tuesday."

"Point the lantern inside the cab, Paddy."

O'Malley redirected the beam, lighting the bodies of a crumpled woman in the far corner and a man face down on the cabin floor.

"Looks like bruising on the lass's neck and blood stains on the cabbie's throat and collar," the sergeant said. "I spy nothing on the seat or floor."

"No handbag? After we remove the bodies, take another look in the daylight."

"What's left of it."

"And check the young woman's pockets before they take her away for the postmortem." Tennant signaled the stretcher-bearers.

The bearers transferred the corpses to the mortuary wagon. Rigor had come and gone, and cold weather had delayed death's cloying stench, so the grim task was relatively easy. The cabman crossed himself as the bodies passed. He led the horse out of the warehouse, and O'Malley took a final look inside the hackney's cabin, finding nothing. Then the driver turned the cab around and rattled up Trig Lane's cobblestones, passing a policeman and two lads munching their last baked potato bites.

O'Malley clapped the taller, dark-haired boy on the shoulder. "Inspector Tennant, this is Bert Hawley and his brother, Sammy."

"Good work spotting that ginger beard." Tennant leaned over the boy's basket. "Anything else we should know about?"

"Sarge had a squint and said no," Bert said.

O'Malley nodded. "A tin can and a coil of copper wire."

"Might earn you a shilling or two," Tennant said. "Were you mudlarking here on Tuesday afternoon?"

Bert scratched his head under his tweed cap. "That when the blighter and the girl got done in?"

"We think so."

"Nah," the boy said. "We was 'larking over by Southwark Bridge that day."

"Think back to the last time you were here," Tennant said. "Did you see anyone hanging about? Someone who looked out of place?"

The boys exchanged glances and shook their heads. Sammy pointed to the beard in Tennant's hand. "Can we have it back?"

"I'm sorry, son." O'Malley ruffled the younger boy's sandy hair.

Tennant fished in his trouser pocket. "You boys turned over valuable evidence like loyal subjects of the queen. You deserve a reward with her face on it." He handed each boy a half crown.

"Cor blimey, two-and-six," Sammy said, staring at the coin in his palm. "Wait'll Mum sees this!"

"Aiding the Yard in our investigations," O'Malley said. "That's champion. Now, the officer will see you home and explain things to your mam."

Tennant watched the boys scamper up the lane with the constable trailing them. "Stumbling across two dead bodies . . . they don't seem worse for the experience."

O'Malley grinned. "If they're anything like my nephews, they'll be entertaining their mates with every gory detail."

"You're probably right. Did you retrieve Brigid Dowling's carpetbag from the Chapter House?"

"Yon copper's looking after it," O'Malley said, waving over a young constable.

"There's little doubt, but we'll need the Chapter House desk clerk to identify the victim as Brigid Dowling and link the body to the bag."

"I asked the fella to report to Horseferry Road at three o'clock."

"Good. That should give Doctor Lewis time to arrive." Tennant took out his pocket watch. "Let's flag a hackney before the fog swallows them all. You can brief me on the way to the mortuary."

They found a cabstand on Upper Thames Street, took their seats, and headed toward Westminster as the leading edge of the river's mist turned midafternoon to dusk.

"Let's start with Brigid Dowling's belongings," Tennant said.

O'Malley hauled the carpetbag from the floor and balanced it on his knees. It was a typical double-handled textile case in a plum-and-green flower design. It lacked a lock, but the owner had added a buckle to secure its contents. The sergeant unhooked the strap and parted the handles.

"The lass had a change of linen and stockings, a nightdress and wrap, a pair of slippers, and a net bag of toiletries."

"Anything that confirms her identity?"

"A label inside, stitched into the fabric." O'Malley pointed to the spot. "Here. 'Tis hard to see in this gloom, but it says B. Dowling and gives an address in Ireland."

"Anything else?"

"She had a telegram tucked into an inner pocket from the Chapter House, confirming her reservation."

"No letter?"

O'Malley shook his head. "You were expecting one?"

"Yes. I have the note Brigid sent to Lady Styles." He pulled it from his pocket and handed it to O'Malley. "Read the last lines.

"According to this, a letter from Lizzy Dowling should have been on her."

"Yes. Something in the sister's letter upset the girl. She intended to discuss the matter with Lady Styles."

"And I'm thinking there should be a second note as well," O'Malley said. "The desk clerk said a boy delivered a message for Brigid Dowling."

"Did the clerk know the sender or its contents?"

"Brigid read it at the desk, looking tickled pink, he said. 'A lady' was sending a carriage to pick her up at two."

"The supposed writer was Lady Styles, I'd wager." Tennant explained what he'd learned at Marlborough House about the death of Lizzie Dowling on the Isle of Wight.

"Puts the sister's death in a new light," O'Malley said. "No jury will return an open verdict on this girl's demise."

"Did the desk clerk see Brigid Dowling get into the hackney?"

"That he did not, but I was just getting 'round to someone who did. A sweeper lad with sharp eyes on him saw her get into the cab with a ginger-bearded fella."

"Well, well. Any other details?"

"Tall and thin, the lad said, and he dressed like a toff in a gent's boots and a bowler hat. Waiting in a cab at the door for a good quarter hour."

"Someone went to considerable trouble to silence a servant girl," Tennant said.

"A callous brute of a man, slaughtering the cabbie to cover his tracks. Curdles the blood, it does."

"Callous and well-informed about the girl's movements," Tennant said.

"Narrows our list of suspects, I'm thinking."

"To those who knew where to find Brigid Dowling on Tuesday afternoon."

O'Malley buckled the carpetbag. "Is it Doctor Lewis who'll be doing the postmortem?"

"I sent her a message to meet us at Horseferry Road."

Here it is, nearly Christmas, Tennant thought. *I should have called at the clinic to say goodbye.* A few more hours wouldn't have mattered to the chase, although it had seemed urgent at the time.

He regretted it now.

Julia's cab slowed to a stop in front of the Horseferry Road mortuary. She spotted Tennant pacing the pavement, his back to her.

She exited the hansom, dropping her half-crown fare. It lodged in a crevice between two cobbles. By the time she retrieved it and paid the driver, Tennant was only a few steps away. He looked thinner than she remembered and had a strained look around his eyes. *The chase has taken a toll.* Her glance fell to the sling and his bandaged right hand.

"I got in the way of Romilly's knife," Tennant said, smiling. "Nothing serious."

"By the size of that bandage, that's more than a scratch. Well, a proper handshake is out of the question, so . . ."

She brushed his cheeks in French fashion, then held her gaze steady before stepping back. "Thank goodness. Home, safe and . . ." Her voice caught. "Safe and mostly sound." She smiled and tried to keep her tone light, adding, "Although you're a shockingly bad correspondent."

"I'm sorry," Tennant said. "The post . . ."

"We were worried."

Julia hooked her arm around his left elbow, and they mounted the steps. "Your note mentioned *two* postmortems. Isn't the commissioner piling it on your first day back?"

"The two deaths entangle Marlborough House and Osborne House in murder."

Julia stopped at the top of the steps. "What do you mean?"

"Someone murdered Lizzie Dowling's sister."

"Good God." She dropped his arm and turned, searching his face. "That means Lizzie— "

"Was murdered, too."

"And the second body?"

"The cabdriver who might have identified the killer." He opened the door with his left hand. "I'll take you to Brigid Dowling's body and then find O'Malley. He's somewhere inside, trying to soothe Willie Sommers, the desk clerk who's here to identify the body. One of our few witnesses."

In the examining room, Julia removed the covering sheet and drew a breath. *So like Lizzy*, she thought. She smoothed back the sister's auburn hair, and tears stung at the waste of another young life. She spent ten minutes on initial observations and then prepared Brigid Dowling's body for identification.

O'Malley escorted a white-faced, bespectacled young man into the cramped examining room. He raked nervously at his straw-colored hair, leaving patches that stood up like a badly scythed hayfield. Julia had turned the gaslight burners up, and the clerk blinked at the brightness. The bump in his throat jumped as he looked at the shrouded figure on the table.

"There's no rush, Mister Sommers," Julia said. "Tell me when you're ready."

The young clerk swallowed hard and nodded. She drew the sheet to Brigid's chin, exposing her auburn hair and pale face, shielding the livid bruises on her neck.

Tennant asked, "Is this the young woman who registered as Brigid Dowling and left her carpetbag at the Chapter House?"

"Yes," the clerk rasped and turned away. Julia replaced the sheet and patted his arm.

Tennant said, "Thank you, Mister Sommers. Sergeant O'Malley will take you to another room and ask you to sign a statement."

"Never seen a dead body before." The clerk's hand shook as he pulled off his spectacles and wiped them with his handkerchief.

"Come along, son," O'Malley said, gripping the clerk's arm. "We'll find you a cup of tea and a quiet place to finish our business."

When the door closed behind them, Julia said, "We forget, don't we?"

Tennant regarded her curiously. "Forget what?"

"The sight of our first dead body."

"Paddy remembers. He'll see the fellow through it." Tennant pulled out his watch. "It's getting late. I must inform the commissioner and Marlborough House without delay."

"Of course," Julia said. "There is no need to stay."

"I know." He half smiled and said, "If anything, I'm in your way."

"I didn't mean that. Two postmortems will have me working well past seven. It's a long time for you to wait."

"That's a long day for you as well. I'm most interested in Brigid Dowling. May I suggest you finish her autopsy and then return tomorrow to complete the cabbie's postmortem?"

"I have an appointment in the morning that I can't postpone."

"Then Doctor MacKay or Doctor Abernathy. I'll see to it."

Julia folded the sheet to Brigid's shoulders and brushed her auburn hair from her forehead. "Nine months ago . . . we stood in this exact spot, looking down at another Irish girl who died violently. Franny Riley."

"The man who put Franny on this table will never harm another person."

"Grandfather and I are eager to hear about it."

"Then may I . . . will you permit me to drop in at Finsbury Circus later this evening? To hear your preliminary findings?"

"Of course." Julia looked at him, surprised by his stilted tone. "Barring surprises, it appears straightforward. Manual strangulation."

"I'd also like to hear about Lizzie Dowling and the events on the Isle of Wight."

"And I'd like to look at that hand," Julia said, pointing. "You may think it's nothing, but infection is always a danger. Those bandages should be changed."

He looked at the smudgy wrappings. "You're probably right."

"Come for dinner if you can manage it. If not, then something in the library on a tray."

"Thank you."

Julia remembered the last time he sat in her library. *Collapsed is a better word.* It was their last meeting before the dismaying end of the Romilly case. He'd been too exhausted to finish Mrs. Ogilvie's sandwiches. Then he disappeared for nearly six months.

The same Marlborough House footman who had admitted Tennant earlier led him into the hall to wait for Lady Styles. The only change to the foyer was the holiday pots of white chrysanthemums and holly that the staff had added since the morning. Tennant circled the room, checking the time. *Just before six. Not changing yet for dinner.* He'd just tucked away his pocket watch when Lady Styles appeared.

"Good evening, Inspector," she said, offering her hand. "Your return must mean news, good or bad."

"I'm sorry to say it's bad news, Lady Styles. Brigid Dowling is dead."

She closed her eyes. "I've been afraid of that."

"There is little we know at present, but the commissioner and I thought Marlborough House should be informed immediately."

"Thank you, Inspector. It's been a long day for you, I know."

Tennant glanced over his shoulder. The foyer opened into hallways traversed by passing servants. "May we speak somewhere more private? Perhaps the room where we sat this morning?"

"If you don't mind the chill. The servants don't light a fire there in the afternoon."

"I won't keep you long, but if you prefer to get a wrap . . ."

She shook her head, and Tennant followed her to the sitting room. They sat in the same chairs they'd occupied that morning.

"We found Brigid Dowling's body and that of her cabdriver in an abandoned warehouse near the river. He'd picked her up at two o'clock. Someone murdered them within a half mile of the Chapter House."

Susan's hand flew to her throat, clutching the mourning brooch pinned to her collar. "I thought . . ." She cleared her voice. "I thought perhaps an accident, not murder."

"Shall I ring for the footman? Some water, perhaps?"

Susan shook her head. "Just a moment, please, Inspector." She wrapped her arms and shivered in the cold room.

Tennant watched her. Her gaze dropped to the carpet. Her focus moved back and forth between two points on the patterned rug. That morning, he sensed a formidable intelligence behind her gaze. He thought, *She hasn't said she doesn't understand or asked what it means.* Lady Styles was working it out for herself.

Finally, she looked up. "Is there anything more you can tell me, Inspector?"

"We know that someone lured Miss Dowling to her death. A witness saw a tall, well-dressed man with a ginger beard waiting for her with a hackney. A false beard, as it happens."

Tennant paused, expecting a reaction or a question. When

none came, he continued. "The witness saw them enter the cab, and we recovered a costume beard near the murder site. We found no letter on her body or with her belongings."

"But the letter from her sister . . . Inspector, her note to me said she was bringing it to me."

"We didn't find it. Lady Styles, just to be clear, did you send a cab to bring her to Marlborough House."

"I did not."

"I didn't think so."

Throughout their conversation, she had watched him closely as he spoke. Tennant waited, curious about what she would say next. Lady Styles got right to the heart of the matter.

"Inspector, it seems unlikely that two ordinary Irish servant girls—sisters living their separate lives hundreds of miles apart—that their suspicious deaths are unconnected. *Unlikely* is an inadequate word."

"I agree. The open verdict in Lizzie Dowling's death must be reconsidered. That much is clear. Murder is the likely conclusion."

Lady Styles leaned her right elbow on the chair's armrest and rubbed her forehead. "My God, the queen's servant and a second murder linked to the first . . . the thought staggers."

"We know little else," Tennant said. "And I doubt Doctor Lewis's autopsy will yield surprises, but one never knows."

"Julia Lewis?"

"Yes. That is all for now, Lady Styles, unless you have a question before I leave."

When she shook her head, he stood. "The commissioner thought you might prefer to inform the Prince and Princess of Wales unless you want me to do it."

"No. I will tell them. And Princess Louise. I dread breaking the news to her even more than the Princess of Wales."

"May I ask why?"

"Princess Louise loathes being fussed over by servants, but Lizzie was the exception. The princess was very fond of her."

"Was the princess aware of Brigid Dowling's travel plans?"

"Yes, Inspector. And she was as curious as I about what the girl planned to say."

"Brigid Dowling's proposed visit to Marlborough House was generally known?"

"Yes. I don't know how this affects your investigation, but we leave tomorrow afternoon for Osborne House. Christmas with the queen on the Isle of Wight, by Her Majesty's command."

"When do you return?"

"After the new year. So, if you have additional questions . . ."

"Lady Styles, you realize the person responsible for Brigid Dowling's death not only knew the day she arrived in London but also where she stayed. That person either committed the crime or arranged it."

She held his eye. "I do realize, Inspector."

"I'll ask you to think carefully, and before you leave—"

"I'll think of little else. You'll have my list of those who knew Miss Dowling's movements before I leave for the Isle of Wight."

"Thank you, Lady Styles."

She stood but didn't move to the door. Then she turned to him. "I am a woman who lives in other people's houses. But my title and my position as a senior attendant to the princess protect me. Lizzy Dowling had no such shield. And now her sister."

Tennant hailed a hansom on Marlborough Road and gave the cabbie the address of the Lewis town house.

Tennant settled in for the ride to Finsbury Circus. *Not chilly, exactly*, Tennant thought, assessing the temperature of his first meeting with Julia. *Restrained.* But what could he expect after his abrupt departure and a nearly six-month absence? When the cab rattled to a stop at number 17, gaslight from lamps flanking the front door cast a golden glow across the house's limestone façade. He wondered if the atmosphere indoors would match its warmth.

Julia carried her medical bag into the library, glancing at the clock. She wasn't sure when Richard would arrive, but she wanted to be ready. She covered a side table with a white towel and lined up surgical scissors, wads of cotton wool, and a bandage roll. She added a bottle of carbolic solution and pulled up a chair.

Dr. Andrew Lewis twisted around in his seat. "For Richard?"

"Yes."

"And how did you find him? You know your great-aunt will quiz me tomorrow at luncheon."

"Even Aunt Caroline can't expect much from a reunion at a morgue."

"Don't be too sure about that."

"You can give her a firsthand report. That sounds like his cab now."

"I doubt it's *my* impressions she wants to hear."

Andrew Lewis was on his feet with his hand outstretched as Mrs. Ogilvie led Tennant through the library door. "Richard." Dr. Lewis turned his handshake into a pat on the upper arm. "Come, sit by the fire."

"First things first, Grandfather." Julia took Tennant's elbow and steered him to the chair by the side table. She cut away the old bandages, daubing the wound with carbolic solution and wrapping his hand with a clean covering. Then she gripped his chin lightly and turned his head to the right.

"What's this?" She touched the edge of a sticking plaster peeking from under his collar.

"Nothing. Only the result of my first attempt at shaving. Tricky with one's left hand."

"Hmm . . . did you forget they're called 'cut-throat razors' for a reason?"

"Learned my lesson and visited a barber this morning."

"Very wise." Dr. Lewis patted the armrest of a fireside chair. "Julie, a drink for the inspector."

"Whisky?" When he nodded, she poured. "Now that I think of it, you and Grandfather are just about the only clean-shaven men I know."

"Shaving was impossible in the Crimea. For two years, I dreamed of hot towels and a sharp blade scraping my cheeks. Most of us looked like shipwreck survivors when we got back to England. All of us were bearded and scrawny."

Four sentences, Julia thought. It was the most Richard had ever uttered about his experiences in the Crimea. He looked into the fire without comment and sipped his drink when her grandfather declared the war's poor provisioning had been a national disgrace. *Perhaps one day, he'll say more . . .*

Dr. Lewis said, "You've had a long first day, Richard."

"Did it begin with Chief Inspector Clark's warmest welcome?" Julia sat opposite him with her sherry. "He's always a little ray of sunshine."

Tennant smiled. "The man hasn't the wit to hide how much he resents me. And that I caught up with Romilly in the end."

Dr. Lewis said, "Tell us about the hunt."

"You had us worried," Julia said. "Nearly two months of silence. Your letter from Berlin turned up the same day as your last one from Paris."

"I'm sorry. I thought the Prussian postal service was more efficient than that."

Dr. Lewis asked, "How did it end for the scoundrel?"

Julia noticed he addressed her grandfather with only an occasional glance at her. He minimized the danger, but she wasn't fooled. Her hand shook as she set down her sherry glass, thinking how close he came to death in that narrow passageway.

"A thousand rifles making their way to England?" Andrew Lewis shook his head. "Perhaps already in the hands of a thousand Irish hotheads."

"A thousand so-called patriots." Tennant sipped his drink.

Julia said, "Men who make the lives of fifty thousand *peaceful* Irish living in London a misery of hostility and suspicion. That includes Kate."

"Paddy told me what happened at the clinic," Tennant said.

"When will it all end?" Julia asked. "*How* will it end between us?"

"With a parting of the ways, my dear," her grandfather said. "And an independent Ireland. But not before we're drained dry of tears and grow weary of the bloodshed."

Kate entered with a tray, followed by Mrs. Ogilvie with a pitcher of ale. She poured out a pint and handed Tennant a plate and napkin. "Can I bring you anything else, Inspector?"

"Thank you, Mrs. Ogilvie. This looks splendid." He helped himself to a sandwich and looked at Julia. "Now, tell me about the autopsy."

"Well, no surprises there," she said. "Brigid Dowling died of manual strangulation."

"Doctor MacKay agreed to do the cabbie's postmortem tomorrow morning. As for the first one, your examination of Lizzie Dowling. Tell me about it."

"While you eat, I'll tell you all I know."

When she finished, Tennant said, "There was no alternative to an open verdict, but now . . ."

"Kate was right all along," Dr. Lewis said. "It was murder. And her money was on the 'maggot' who got the girl pregnant."

"It's a motive and place to start," Julia said.

"It's absurdly far-fetched to suspect that a local sweetheart or a fellow servant murdered Lizzie then traveled to London to kill her sister," Tennant said. "No, these crimes needed someone with resources, mobility, and accurate knowledge about the Dowling sisters' movements."

"A gentleman with a lot at risk if Lizzie's pregnancy became known," Dr. Lewis said.

"Would it be so threatening, Grandfather? Gentlemen usually find ways to deal with the problem, short of murder."

"But Lizzie was no ordinary maid, my dear. She served in the queen's household. That might raise the stakes for someone."

"The question of timing is critical," Tennant said. "Your autopsy narrows the frame."

"Yes, someone at Osborne House last July when Lizzie became pregnant and someone on the Isle of Wight in October."

Tennant said, "Lady Styles is preparing a list."

"There may be more overlap than you think," Julia said.

"Why do you say that?"

"Bertie's yachting set treats Cowes like a private playground. The sailing season starts in the summer and stretches into autumn. Do you remember, Grandfather? His friends were staying at our hotel during our October visit."

"Remember? I heard them returning from the yacht club in the wee hours and in their cups."

Tennant asked, "Do you recall any names?"

"Captain Oliver Montgomery introduced himself." Julia shrugged. "As for the others . . . Lady Styles can tell you who else was there in October."

Nine chimes sounded from the mantel clock. Tennant drained the last of his ale and stood.

Dr. Lewis said, "Come back in a few days, Richard, and we'll change that bandage again. Ogilvie has the carriage waiting for you."

In the foyer, Julia held Tennant's coat as he shrugged into it awkwardly. "I can't wait to see the back of these bandages."

"We'll replace it soon with something easier to manage." She handed him his hat.

Tennant frowned, brushing the crown against his sleeve and tapping the brim against his knee. Julia recognized the signs. *Making up his mind about something.*

He cleared his throat. "Hannah told me . . . that is, my housekeeper said you traveled to Kent to—"

"Something of a wasted journey," Julia said with a slight smile. "Sergeant O'Malley told us you'd decided to resign from the Yard."

"That was my original plan."

"I went to Kent to talk you out of it. And there you were . . . or rather weren't. You were off, sleuthing on the Continent."

"I'm sorry."

Julia felt her smile tighten. "No harm done. I just left with a little egg on my face."

"Hannah said she offered you a bed—"

"I had a hotel reservation in Dover," she said quickly.

"I'm sorry I wasn't there to—"

"How were you to know?" She opened the door.

"Julia, I . . ." He looked over his shoulder. Mr. Ogilvie waited at the curb with the carriage. "Well, thank you for this," he said, holding up his hand before settling his hat awkwardly with his left.

"It's good to have you back," she said.

But it would be a long way back. *Back to where we left off.* She sighed as she closed the door. *Back to wherever that was.*

CHAPTER 6

A message from the commissioner awaited Tennant when he arrived at the Yard the following morning.

The inspector glanced at the wall clock over the duty sergeant's head. "Sir Richard is in his office?"

"Up this morning with the birds."

Tennant read the note on his way to his first-floor office. He found O'Malley scanning the morning reports. "Command appearance in thirty minutes, Paddy. I spoke with the commissioner late yesterday afternoon, so something's come up."

"Didn't I follow a pair of fancy suits and top hats into the building?" O'Malley said. "The looks on their faces were something brutal. 'Mister Gathorne-Hardy to see Sir Richard,' the younger fella says."

"The home secretary. Well, well." Tennant hung his overcoat on the rack and crowned it with his hat. "Has anything worth our notice come in?"

"The final report on the canvass of the wharf. The coppers found nothing to interest us. But a team is doing a door-to-door along Upper Thames just to be thorough."

"Doctor Lewis's postmortem concluded the obvious, and I doubt Doctor MacKay's will find any surprises with the cabbie. But a message from Lady Styles should arrive today with actionable information."

"The fellas who knew the whereabouts of Brigid Dowling?"

"That's right," Tennant said. "And we must inform the family she worked for in Clonakilty. Sir Hugo and Lady Browne. Lady Styles provided the name and address. I'll send a telegram to the local constabulary, asking them to break the news. They'll need to search her room for any letters."

O'Malley stroked his bushy mustache. "I'm thinking about that ginger beard. 'Tis just about the only piece of evidence we have."

"Put a pair of constables on it, Paddy. Have them check theatrical supply houses and the like. Businesses that cater to West End theaters and East End music halls."

"Someone may remember a tall fella, well-dressed, who bought a ginger beard."

Tennant reported to the commissioner at the appointed time. A dark-haired man in his middle thirties sat in an armchair across from Sir Richard, elbows on the armrests, fingers loosely laced. He turned his head at the inspector's entrance.

"Inspector Tennant, this is Sir Lionel Dermott from the Home Office."

Dermott unfolded his long legs and stood. He had dressed in the Whitehall civil servant uniform: a black, double-breasted frock coat and waistcoat, dark tie, and striped, gray trousers. Sir Lionel's one deviation from a colorless palette was the red-and-gold paisley square he'd stuffed casually into his breast pocket.

"How do you do, Sir Lionel," Tennant said, offering his hand. He looked around the commissioner's office. "I understood Mister Gathorne-Hardy was here."

"Here and gone, Inspector," Sir Lionel said, resuming his seat. "Leaving your humble servant behind."

The commissioner cleared his throat. "You're not going to like this, Richard, but you'll be accompanying Sir Lionel this afternoon to the Isle of Wight."

"Nothing personal, I trust," Sir Lionel murmured.

"You want me to leave London at the start of an investigation? Sir Richard, I— "

"Sergeant O'Malley can carry on for two days. I have orders from the Home Office. The queen wants to hear from the inspector in charge of the case."

"Before I have anything meaningful to report?"

Sir Lionel waved away the objection. "Handholding. Must be done, old boy. You say, 'Your Majesty, the investigation is running at full gallop.' That sort of humbuggery."

"A waste of police time," Tennant said.

"To be sure, but for my part, I'm jolly glad to be your travel companion. Followed your 'railway murder' derring-do in the *Illustrated Police Gazette*. 'Tennant of the Yard' and all that."

"Is that so?" Tennant looked at the commissioner and read his expression: *Fellow's an ass.*

"Happy we'll be rowing in the same boat, Inspector."

"Er, yes . . . well." Commissioner Mayne cleared his throat. "You'll travel by special train to Gosport on the coast and then to the Isle of Wight. Two days should be adequate. Back on Sunday. On the way, Sir Lionel will put you in the picture."

"Indeed, indeed. Full speed ahead. Shoulder to the wheel and whatnot."

Tennant sighed. "Where and when do I meet you?"

"Waterloo station at one o'clock." Sir Lionel sauntered to the door, spinning his hat. "By the way, the 'special train' is the queen's royal one. Traveling in style with Bertie and the princess. Cheerio." He bowed and exited.

"Young jackanapes," Sir Richard muttered. "Brief Sergeant O'Malley and return to London as soon as you can."

Tennant headed to the door, stopping when the commissioner called, "And Richard . . ."

"Sir?"

"I know it's tempting, but don't miss that train."

Outside Tennant's office, a constable handed him a note from Lady Styles. He read it and passed it to O'Malley. "The list of those who knew the details about Brigid Dowling's arrival."

"Mother of God." The sergeant whistled. "'Tis a lineup of royal equerries and other swells. Major Peter FitzGerald, Captain Oliver Montgomery, Captain Frederick Locock, the Honorable George Trevor, and a Home Office fella named—"

"Sir Lionel Dermott. He was one of the 'fancy suits' you followed into the Yard this morning."

"Everything will have double pairs of eyes on them," O'Malley said. "And decisions from on high taking three times as long."

Tennant related the details of his meeting with the commissioner.

"So, I'm on my own for two days, is it?"

"See if you can wrap it up before I return, Paddy. Bag the fellow, and we're done with it."

"I'll be doing my best. Where do you want me to start?"

"The servants at Marlborough House. Several traveled to the Isle of Wight with the Prince and Princess of Wales, including the prince's manservant."

O'Malley tapped his nose. "I'll see if I can sniff out any servant hall gossip."

"Wait until Their Royal Highnesses leave for the Isle of Wight. The staff may speak more freely once they leave the house."

"And after that?"

"Find out what you can about Sir Lionel Dermott. Drop in for a pint at the pubs around the Home Office. Chat up the junior clerks."

O'Malley grinned. "Always happy when duty mixes with pleasure.'

"Dermott's an odd duck. I'd like to know how odd."

In Julia's examining room, Lady Styles buttoned the back of Princess Alexandra's gown.

While the princess dressed, Julia considered what to say. The prince, not Alexandra, needed advice, but who would tell *him* to avoid risky partners to lessen the danger to his wife?

As Susan fastened the clasp on Alexandra's choker necklace, the princess looked at her and said in lightly accented English, "You will stay and listen to the doctor?" She turned to Julia. "That is permitted?"

"Of course." Julia gestured to the two chairs facing her desk.

Lady Styles wrapped a shawl around Alexandra's thin shoulders and sat beside her. After a moment's pause, the princess said, "Never have my male doctors made such a thorough examination. Truly, it would be most embarrassing. I think many women must prefer you, Doctor."

Julia smiled and said, "I'm afraid the opposite is also true and explains why I have no male private patients."

Princess Alexandra looked down at her gripped hands. In a quavering voice, she asked, "Can you tell me what is wrong, Doctor?"

"Your Royal Highness, I see no evidence of infection beyond the swelling confined to your knee. Something triggered a septic arthritis. Time and rest will heal it. You have nothing else to fear . . . at least right now."

"Thank God." The princess had been sitting as still and straight as a post. She sank back against the chair. "Oh, thank you, Doctor. For once, I shall sleep."

Julia saw Lady Styles register the implication of the words "right now," although she feared they were lost on the princess. "Worrying about one's health can undermine it," Julia said. "As can other worries. Two shocking deaths. One in the queen's household."

"Horrible." Alexandra pulled her wrap tighter. "Those poor girls. I pray the police will soon have an answer."

Julia's glance flickered over Alexandra's slender frame. "How is your appetite?"

The princess smiled. "Like Her Majesty, you are about to tell me I am too thin."

"A little, perhaps."

"I'll see if we can coax the princess to eat a little more," Lady Styles said. "Her Royal Highness enjoys physical activity, Doctor," Lady Styles said. "What do you advise?"

"The princess should continue to use her stick to avoid unnecessary strain on the leg. Short walks are in order, but avoid climbing stairs when you can. And rest with the knee elevated."

Susan sighed. "At the queen's command, we leave today for a month's visit to Osborne House. Her Majesty expects family and guests to . . . dance attendance."

"Lady Styles, you have your work cut out for you." Julia stood and smiled. "Thinking of ways to minimize the dancing."

Princess Alexandra and Susan followed Julia out the side door of her ground-floor office. Their carriage waited at the end of a pathway that led to a gate at the edge of the property. A cab slowed and stopped by the main walkway. Inspector Tennant got out, glanced to his left, and then away. He paid the cabbie and headed to the front door.

The princess had been fiddling with her glove buttons and hadn't noticed him. Lady Styles looked away, fixing her attention on the carriage as they walked. Twenty minutes later came a knock on her door. Julia had been expecting it.

"Come in, Richard," she called.

He held up a lightly bandaged hand. "Courtesy of your grandfather. At a pinch, I can manage a pencil." He shook his head when Julia patted a chairback in invitation. "I can't stay."

"Thank you for your discretion just now."

"Of course. I assumed it wasn't a social call."

"I don't believe the princess noticed you."

"Just as well. I'm traveling with the royal party this afternoon." Tennant explained the circumstances. "Sergeant O'Malley will make a start while I'm away."

"I see."

Tennant shifted his weight, sliding his hat brim through his fingers. "Well . . . the train leaves at one. I return on Sunday."

Julia said, "Safe journey."

After the door closed behind him, she winced at the formal awkwardness of their exchange. *How long will it take?* Julia wondered. How long before they returned to something close to normal?

At Waterloo Station, a porter with a clipboard stood by a locomotive. Iron pillars rose to a metal-and-glass honeycombed ceiling. The station was eerily deserted. The inspector's boots echoed along an empty platform that usually bustled. In the distance, a porter stood by a locomotive with a clipboard. Tennant gave the man his name and showed his warrant card.

"The first saloon car is Her Majesty's," the porter said. "As the queen is not traveling, it is unused today. The Prince and Princess of Wales will occupy the second carriage. Take your seat in the third car, sir."

Tennant walked the length of Victoria's claret-and-gold painted saloon. He caught glimpses of the luxury inside: the richly upholstered blue-and-gold seating section, sleeping compartment, and dining car. Gold-tasseled shades obscured his view of the second car, the "Prince of Wales" saloon. A standard first-class compartment followed, and two additional cars completed the string.

"In here, old man."

Sir Lionel Dermott sat on the burgundy leather seat facing the engine, legs crossed. He had the day's newspapers on his lap and a hinged leather case at his feet. He'd tossed his formal frock coat and overcoat on the seat beside him.

Sir Lionel eyed Tennant's bandaged right hand and reached for the inspector's carpetbag. "Let me relieve you of that." He lifted the case and slid it onto the metal shelf above the opposite seat. "Cheer up, old man. You'll be back in London in two days."

"Unless Mister Gathorne-Hardy has more plans for diverting my attention."

"You don't like him, do you?"

Tennant raised an eyebrow. "Why do you say that?"

"I suspect you hold the home secretary responsible for the unfortunate end of your last case."

"You're well informed, Sir Lionel."

"Information is my stock in trade." Dermott sat back, eyeing Tennant under half-closed lids. "You're wrong about my guvnor, you know."

"You'll never convince mine of that. Chief Inspector Clark sees the evils of the 'old boys club' at work, letting the well-connected escape justice."

"Your chief is wrong. Gathorne-Hardy is a moralist at heart. No, the decision not to prosecute came from higher up."

"Higher than the Home Office narrows it to—"

"Yes, Inspector. The prime minister thought it wise to avoid a lurid scandal that would taint his party." Dermott knitted his hands behind his head, stretching his legs. "That should clear the air of any suspicions you harbored."

"You're certain you know my thoughts, Sir Lionel?"

"Oh, I know quite a lot about Richard Wellesley Tennant."

Dermott ticked a list on his fingers. "Captain in the Grenadier Guards, had a bad time of it in the Crimea, overlooked—criminally—for the Victoria Cross, and things not looking up when you got home."

"You *are* well-informed. I'm flattered."

"One thing surprises me: your godfather didn't lend your services to the new Irish branch, although I suspect the commissioner thinks it's a colossal waste of time."

Tennant said dryly, "I believe he thinks I'm more useful working on routine Yard business. Now, you tell *me* something. Why do you want Sir Richard to think you're a fool?"

A slow smile spread. "A reflexive bad habit, I'm afraid."

"That doesn't answer my question."

Tennant waited, and Sir Lionel sighed. "I see I am up against that most formidable of persons, the patient man. Do you object to a pipe while I consider your question?"

"Not at all."

"I'll let in some air."

Dermott unlatched the window. Then he reached into his coat pocket and extracted a briar pipe burnished to a glossy amber. He packed the bowl with tobacco, struck a match, and passed the flame over the top layer. Then he tamped a second and a third time. With each repetition, he drew on the stem until the tobacco flamed.

Sir Lionel moved the pipe to the corner of his mouth. "The pater taught me the proper way to do it. Lighting a pipe is a bit like you, Inspector. It rewards patience."

After a few more puffs, he said, "Why do I play the fool? I've found that the English upper classes say the most extraordinary things in front of two sets of people. Servants and twits." His slow smile came again. "It's most convenient for information gathering if one is assumed to be amongst the latter."

"I must keep your method in mind," Tennant said.

"Now, those who unmask me . . ." Dermott pointed his pipe

stem at Tennant. "They intrigue me. I think my unmarried state must lower me in your catalog of suspects."

"What makes you think you're on the list?"

"Tut, tut, Inspector." He shook his head in mock disapproval. "Don't disappoint me now. I know you interviewed the lovely Lady Styles. You've done the simple sum, concluding two and three are five."

"Would you mind spelling out the arithmetic for me?"

"Gladly, despite the mixed metaphor. It was at the Marlborough House ball the night the fateful travel arrangements were disclosed. Three gentlemen who were present are married men. Two are single. In the case of a pregnant servant, a husband has more to lose than a bachelor."

"Were you on the Isle of Wight last summer and in October?"

"Yes, as it happens. Spot of yacht racing over the summer and hauling her out in the autumn."

"Were you sailing the day of the murder?"

"My last run of the season. Had the old girl taken out of the water the next day."

"The marina owners in Cowes will confirm that?"

"I belong to the Royal Victoria on Wooten Creek, worse luck."

"Why unlucky?"

"Quarr Abbey is an easy walk from the marina. So is the Fishbourne, the 'ye olde' Tudor inn where I lodged that night." Dermott smiled his slow, lazy grin. "Most unfortunate for me."

A sudden flurry announced the royal party's late arrival. Porters wheeled cases to the storage car, and household servants passed their window looking for seats in the rear carriages. Sir Lionel dangled his arm out the window, banged the tobacco from the bowl, and closed the glass panel.

"Those five men at the ball may have told others," Tennant

said. "If so, the list expands. And you've left someone off. A sixth person and a married man."

Dermott raised his eyebrows. "Oh?"

"The Prince of Wales."

A tap on the window interrupted them. A sandy-haired man with a neat mustache gestured to Sir Lionel. "Excuse me," Dermott said, opening the door and stepping down.

They spoke with their backs to the window. Sir Lionel mostly listened as his companion raked fingers through his hair and pointed to the royal car. At the sound of a whistle, the man looked over his shoulder and strode away.

Sir Lionel resumed his seat. "One of your suspects, as it happens. Oliver Montgomery."

"Equerry to the Prince of Wales."

Sir Lionel nodded. "And you'll meet another when we arrive at Osborne House. Peter FitzGerald, the queen's equerry."

"Captain Montgomery seemed agitated."

"He related the latest intelligence from the Home Office. Plans were in flux when I left Whitehall. Inspector, we aren't alone on our way to Osborne House. Some one hundred and fifty Scots Fusiliers will join us. The soldiers will bolster the usual police presence on the ground."

"What has happened?"

"The Home Office received word that an attempt will be made at Osborne on Her Majesty's life."

Three hours later, Tennant and Sir Lionel waited on the quay for the royal party to board the HMS *Black Eagle*, the royal steam yacht that would take them across the strait to Cowes.

"Three masts for canvas and a steam-driven paddlewheel," Sir Lionel said. "I like a ship that hedges its bets."

Tennant pointed out to sea. "It looks like the Royal Navy is taking no chances, either. They've dispatched half the fleet to patrol the stretch between Portsmouth and Osborne House."

"The Irish are madder than I thought," Dermott said. "Two boatloads of rabid nationalists sailing from New York plan to invade through this naval thicket? Suicidal."

"Is the queen alarmed?"

"Annoyed, I understand," Sir Lionel said.

"When is our audience with Her Majesty?"

"This evening at seven." Lionel grinned. "I thought, no mucking about. Get the tooth out right away."

Tennant and Dermott hung back, waiting for the royal party to finish boarding. Captain Montgomery trailed behind. Tennant asked, "Who are the three married gentlemen you think are on my list?"

Dermott ticked them off. "George Trevor, Freddie Locock, and Peter FitzGerald. Trev is out of the race, I think. He only returned from India in September."

"Was Frederick Locock on the island last July?"

Dermott hesitated. "Yes, as it happens. He crewed for the Prince of Wales. And before you ask, Freddie was there with the rest of us in October. Just back from his wedding trip."

"You've named the suspects. Now, handicap the horses for me. Who's your favorite?"

"Oh, Peter FitzGerald. Absolutely."

"Why?"

"Can't stand the fellow," Lionel said cheerfully. "So, I'd like it to be him."

"I suggested a fourth married man . . ."

"Bertie? I thought you were joking."

"Not the prince himself," Tennant said, "but some obliging member of the Marlborough House set . . . someone who might remove an embarrassment for him?"

Dermott threw back his head and laughed. "Have you followed the prince's dalliances in the illustrated press? London would be littered with female corpses."

The great engine began to churn, and the *Black Eagle* slipped its mooring. Sir Lionel grabbed his hat brim and removed it as the wind picked up. He leaned against the rail, looking at the horizon. Amusement had vanished from his face.

Considering the possibility? Tennant wondered. *The Prince of Wales stays on my list.*

Around the time Inspector Tennant's train left for the south coast, his surrogate, Sergeant O'Malley, sat on the bench of a long trestle table in the Marlborough House kitchen, drinking a cup of tea.

"Just poking my big nose around for the Yard to see that all is well, Mrs. MacIntosh," he'd told the cook. With all that's happening, we can't be too careful."

A century's worth of scrubbing and polishing had burnished the table's oak planks until it resembled a golden mirror. Across the room, two cast-iron ranges had replaced the open fireplaces, and glowing coals heated the oven chambers and the room. A slatted wooden box the size of a bed hung by chains from the ceiling, suspending green sage, rosemary, and baskets of foodstuffs, keeping them high and dry and away from the mice.

"Mrs. MacIntosh, 'tis a lovely warm room and a fine place to spend a winter afternoon." O'Malley breathed in. "Sure, that aroma is the bread you're baking, and no mistake."

Mrs. MacIntosh had grown gray in royal service. As with many cooks, she was a red-cheeked, stout woman, the result of a lifetime's leaning over a fire, surrounded by food—tasting, seasoning, and tasting it again. She'd pushed her sleeves back from thick wrists and square hands that had beaten more batter and shaped more dough than there were days in most people's lives.

"You're after being the queen of your kingdom, Mrs. MacIntosh."

"Most days, Sergeant. But when the royals do fancy entertaining, they bring in a Frenchman who turns my kitchen upside down. I'm happy to see the back of him."

" 'Tis hard work you're doing, and that's no lie," O'Malley said.

Mrs. MacIntosh preened. "Let me add a wee dram to your cup." She carried a bottle of whisky to the table and tipped an ounce into his tea. "A little fortification is welcome on a December afternoon."

"I'm thanking you kindly, missus." O'Malley took a sip. "Now, if I was to go into service, I'm thinking the master's manservant would be just the thing for me."

The cook sniffed. "Brushing the prince's coats and hats is about all the work he'll do. Mister Hackett farms out the bootblacking to the second footman. And he's always after the princess's seamstress to stitch up the prince's shirts."

"Sounds like the fella has landed in a tub of butter. What sort of time off does a valet like himself have?"

"*Two* half days a week to my one. On Tuesdays and Sundays, you'll see no sign of that one."

"Is Mister Hackett a pleasant fella to be around?"

Mrs. MacIntosh looked over her shoulder to see if the scullery maid was out of earshot. "The laddie fancies himself. That's clear as daylight. Travels with as much luggage as a lord, and he's always buying new hats and aping the prince."

"Seems a harmless way to waste his wages."

She lowered her voice. "Fancies other things as well. I see him looking, and I keep a close eye on the lasses."

O'Malley scratched at his side whiskers sagely. "Something of a Casanova, the creature."

* * *

The sergeant left Marlborough House to pursue the inspector's second line of requested inquiry: Sir Lionel Dermott. Some A-Division coppers had steered O'Malley to the Golden Lion pub on King Street. It was a stone's throw from the building that housed the Home Office; clerks and junior officers in government service frequented it. O'Malley recognized a few familiar faces from the Yard, as well.

The barkeep drew a pint of Guinness for the sergeant and pocketed an extra crown. He confirmed that Dermott was an occasional patron.

O'Malley said, "I heard the fella has an eye for the ladies." He took a sip, watching the barman over the rim.

"News to me, and I've heard my share of bragging. But you know how it is, Sarge." He held a glass under the spigot at a forty-five-degree angle, curled his fingers around the tap handle, and winked. "The bigger the talk, the smaller the tackle."

He pulled the handle, poured a perfect pint, and delivered it to a patron. Then he returned to O'Malley and mopped the bar top.

"I'll tell you one thing about Sir Lionel. He'll stand his juniors a pint from time to time." The barman leaned in, his elbow resting on the polished oak. "Not like some of these grand panjandrums who swan around Whitehall with poles up their arses."

On Friday, Julia's clinic treated more than the average number of daily injuries. Tired workers grew inattentive as a week of exhausting manual labor wore on. By three o'clock, Julia had set two broken bones and a half-dozen gashes deep enough to require stitches. But by the middle of the afternoon, an ebb in the flow of the sick and injured gave Julia time to think.

She glanced at the wall clock, thinking, *He's nearly at the south coast by now.* Again, Julia wondered about their awkward conversation. "What's the matter with me, anyway?" she muttered.

Julia drained her teacup and carried it to the trolley in the hallway, stopping at the open door to the women's ward. Kate was there, sitting with a patient. Nurse Clemmie joined Julia, looking over her shoulder. "She has a way with the patients, that girl."

"She does indeed."

"You're giving evidence at the Leary inquest tomorrow morning. A shame on your free Saturday."

"It won't take long. A jagged, fatal wound from a broken bottle won't be hard to explain to the coroner's jury. I haven't heard of an arrest, so 'by person or persons unknown' most likely."

Julia returned her attention to Kate. She'd been coming in two afternoons a week, and Mrs. Donohue, the patient in bed two, had her attention. The lady had merry eyes, blue and bright. In late middle age, her complexion resembled pink-and-cream porcelain with fine lines around her eyes and mouth like the crackles in an old teacup.

" 'Tis lucky we were in Black 'forty-seven," Mrs. Donohue said in a light Irish brogue. "Our family survived the famine. We had helpful relatives in Cork who worked the hop fields in England each September."

"I'm knowing many who did the same," Kate said.

"My cousins had saved a little money, so we took the steamer to Bristol and ended up in Kent. Lovely, golden days they were, and not so different from the fields of Kildare."

Kate then shared a childhood story that Julia knew well. After her parents died, she lived with a great-aunt, a retired housekeeper for a well-to-do Dublin family.

"Auntie was a fast learner," Kate said. "She worked her way up and taught me what she knew."

"Ah, I'm seeing her, now," Mrs. Donohue said. "*An téarma cuirtín lása.*"

"You're right about that." Kate laughed. "Lace-curtain Irish, she was, and proud of the label. She found me my first job in service, and after she passed, I left Ireland for London. An agency placed me with the doctor's family."

"Our lucky day," Julia called from the door.

"Luck and the Fates . . ." Mrs. Donohue yawned, her lids drooping. "I might have ended up a wren on the Curragh like the poor Murphy girls, but for my cousins from Cork."

Kate adjusted the patient's blanket and carried away her teacup.

Julia stopped Kate in the hall. "What did Mrs. Donohue mean by a wren on the Curragh?"

"They're the poor creatures who live like birds in the hedges around the Curragh. The British army camp on the great plain. The 'wrens of the Curragh,' people are calling them." Kate looked at the doctor. "Serving the soldiers, if you'll be taking my meaning."

"Yes, I see."

"They're much despised, but I'll not be throwing stones like many who've landed on a comfortable perch."

"Speaking of perches, back on the Isle of Wight, were you surprised that Lizzy Dowling found service in the queen's household?"

"Was she a kitchen skivvy?"

"No. Lady Styles told me she was a parlor maid who sometimes assisted Princess Louise as a lady's maid."

"Then I'm surprised at that. 'Tis hard enough for an Irish lass to find work in a respectable house, never mind the highest in the land."

"I thought the same thing."

"I don't know Lizzie's history, but a girl who grows up in a country cottage? She doesn't know the dainty ways of the English."

Kate wheeled the tea trolley back to the kitchen, and Julia returned to her office, thinking. *What was Lizzie's journey? There must be a story there.*

She also wondered if Tennant realized how unusual the girl's employment had been. Lizzie Dowling had traveled a great distance, measured not merely in miles. How had a young Irish girl ended up in the queen's household and serving a princess? It was something of a mystery.

Might the tragedy's roots be in Ireland?

CHAPTER 7

At ten minutes to seven, Tennant and Dermott arrived at the entry hall of Osborne House. Sir Lionel waved away a footman's offer to take their overcoats.

"Hold on to it," Dermott said. "The queen likes to keep the temperature a degree or two colder than Siberia."

When the footman was out of earshot, Tennant said, "That servant had a black armband on his sleeve. Has there been a death in the royal family?"

"My dear inspector, what a question! The armband is for Prince Albert, of course. It's a mere six years since the queen's widowhood commenced."

"Formal mourning after all this time? Extraordinary."

"The rituals are followed meticulously, especially here. Albert designed Osborne, a German prince's notion of an Italian villa."

They turned right into a long hallway and left into an audience room. They'd barely arrived when a booming voice echoed from the corridor. Tennant looked at Dermott.

"Prepare yourself for two extraordinary sights," Sir Lionel murmured. "Your Sovereign and the 'Queen's Highland Servant.' That's John Brown's official title. Princess Louise calls him 'that absurd man in a kilt.'"

A towering, broad-chested man of about forty entered with the queen. In her fifth decade, Her Majesty was nearly as wide as she was tall, but Brown dwarfed the diminutive Victoria. His calf muscles bulged beneath his tartan kilt, and a *skene-dhu,* the silver-handled knife he'd tucked in a scabbard, glinted in the cuff of his right knee sock. Brown's gray tweed jacket and waistcoat strained across his barrel chest. Ginger strands threaded his grizzled gray hair, the red more prominent in the beard that fringed his chin from ear to ear.

The queen wore widow's black from chin to toe, and when she sat and spread her skirts, she resembled a short, squat mound of coal. Only a touch of creamy lace at her wrists and neckline and a white widow's cap relieved the depressing effect of yards of black taffeta. While Tennant rejoiced that he'd kept his coat, the room wasn't cool enough for the queen. She fanned her pink face furiously, and a faint shine on her forehead and cheeks glowed in the lamplight.

A second gentleman, gray and stooping, with receding grizzled hair and a drooping walrus mustache, followed the pair into the room. Brown seated the queen, and the second man approached to shake hands with Sir Lionel.

"General, this is Detective Inspector Richard Tennant," Dermott said. "General Charles Grey, the queen's private secretary."

The general shook the inspector's hand. He returned to the queen and bent, murmuring in her ear.

Victoria inclined her head. "Pray, let Inspector Tennant approach and present his report to the queen." Her voice was a surprise: high, light, and pleasantly musical, making her sound younger than a woman in her middle years. German had been the language of her mother and governess, and traces lingered in the queen's speech.

Tennant summarized the facts as he knew them. He explained

that the sisters' deaths suggested—but did not clarify—a link between the killings. "If Your Majesty has any questions, I will endeavor to answer them."

At that point, Tennant thought she'd press him about his suppositions. Instead, she said, "The queen assures you of the household's fullest cooperation. General Grey will assist you in every way possible."

Tennant thought, *I came all this way for that?* He said, "For his part, Sir Richard Mayne assures me I will have all the Yard's resources I need, Your Majesty."

"The queen is satisfied." Victoria looked from Tennant to Dermott. "As to this deployment of soldiers. Sir Lionel, you may tell Mister Gathorne-Hardy that we have gone down this road. At Balmoral, it came to nothing."

"Your Majesty, rest assured that the Home Office is—"

She raised her hand. "We have little confidence that this so-called threat is—"

A rumbling Scots bass filled the room. "Woman, will ye not listen to the man?"

Dermott and General Grey didn't blink; only Tennant was startled by Brown's interruption.

"Yer daft to ignore the danger to yerself."

Victoria smiled. "My loyal Brown is always solicitous of his queen's safety."

"Aye, so take heed. Now come, woman, or ye'll be late dressing for dinner."

The Scotsman offered the queen his arm. Sir Lionel and the inspector bowed to Victoria as she exited.

On his way out, General Grey fished in his pocket and handed Dermott a key. "To Osborne Cottage. Make yourselves at home." He followed the queen and her Highland Servant out the door.

Tennant said, "The general looks worn down by his duties."

"He's aged since Prince Albert's death," Dermott said. "And dealing with the impossible Brown is exhausting."

"Does the fellow always speak to Her Majesty like that?"

"Yes." Dermott flipped the key and pocketed it in his waistcoat. "Makes one wonder what other liberties are permitted. The 'Queen's Stallion' is the nickname whispered among the servants."

"Surely not."

"I agree. But the court has grown terribly dull since Albert's death. Long faces and everyone draped in black. On and on for years and years. People need *something* to amuse them."

Dermott behaved as if the world were an elaborate joke organized for his enjoyment. But the man was so droll that the inspector couldn't help liking him. He would guard against it. Married or not, some men saw servants as easy prey, and Sir Lionel was on the Isle of Wight during the months in question.

Their last stop was the stables, temporary quarters for the Scots Fusiliers sent to guard the queen. The major in command was out on an inspection, but a young lieutenant explained the deployment of forces.

The officer had just begun his recital when a soldier interrupted, saluting smartly. "Telegram for Inspector Tennant, sir." He handed over the message.

"Thank you, Private." Tennant opened it.

"Developments?" Dermott said.

"From my sergeant, Patrick O'Malley."

"An able chap to leave in charge?"

"He's a first-rate copper." Tennant folded the message and pocketed it. "O'Malley adds a name to our list of suspects."

"Ah . . . the plot thickens," Dermott said. "All right, Lieutenant, carry on with your report."

"We're operating on eight-hour shifts," the officer said. He cocked his thumb at the ceiling. "A third of the company is asleep in the hayloft. Another patrols the grounds around the house and the gates, and the rest guard the pier and roads leading to Osborne. They're stopping carts and carriages traveling from East Cowes and Whippingham."

"I'd send soldiers into the towns, as well," Dermott said. "Tell them to keep a sharp eye out for men wearing square-toed boots. If they answer in an Irish or American accent, bring them in for questioning."

It was a short hike from the stables to Osborne Cottage, General Grey's grace-and-favor house on the edge of the estate. On the way, they passed the Scots Fusiliers guarding the main gate with torches blazing.

Dermott said, "Lit up like a Christmas tree."

"The lengthy perimeter of Osborne Park is mostly in darkness."

Dermott walked on. "That's the cottage ahead of us. Now, about those square-toed boots they spotted on the chap in Lyon . . ."

"You read Colonel Chabert's report."

Dermott said, "Such boots were standard issue in the American Civil War, and they've turned up on a surprising number of Irish American 'patriots' arrested by the police in Ireland."

"They should share that intelligence with the Yard."

"Oh, they have, old man, they have. But as one Irish copper told me, 'a Dublin policeman is only a policeman from Dublin.' Typical English contempt for the Irish."

"Idiotic, given their success against the brotherhood," Tennant said. "The failure of the spring rising in Kerry and Dublin was thanks to Irish police intelligence. I understand they infiltrated IRB ranks at the highest levels."

"Contempt is a contagion on this side of the Irish Sea." Dermott looked up at the sky. "Moon's waxing. Lovely evening for an invasion."

"I thought you were skeptical about the threat, like the queen."

"Oh, I am, I am." Sir Lionel opened the gate and bowed Tennant through. "But did you know that over a hundred thousand Irishmen fought in the American Civil War?"

"That's a lot of battle-hardened men in square-toed boots," the inspector said, heading up the path.

"Nail on the head, old bean." Dermott clapped Tennant's shoulder. "And most of those boot-wearing Irishmen hate our guts."

In London the following morning, Julia threaded through a muttering crowd, most with grievances etched into their Celtic faces. Hopeful men and women, once, Julia thought, who'd fixed their gaze on England as they crossed the Irish Sea. Their anger hummed like a hornet's nest.

When a constable opened the door of the King's Arms public house, a wave of stale ale and tobacco stung her eyes. The local coroner had rented the pub's back room for the inquest, a common practice in London's East End, where nearly every corner had a public house. Publicans earned a few extra pounds on mornings when drinkers were few. Julia was there to give medical evidence in the death of the Irish warehouseman, Kevin Leary.

She looked around and spotted a seat in the second row. A man with a reporter's pad stood and shifted to make space for her on the aisle. The room was nearly full when six men from the hostile crowd entered and took the last seats in the back.

The coroner called Constable Tilden to the stand. He testified that he found Leary alone and face down on the pavement outside the Prince of Hesse public house. The assailants had fled, leaving a barkeep and one customer to carry him away for medical aid. Neither man had witnessed the fight that led to Leary's death.

The coroner asked, "Are the men giving evidence this morning?"

"No, sir, as they had nothing to add."

Then Inspector Slack from Scotland Yard took the stand. He

testified that, despite a diligent canvass of the neighborhood, no witnesses came forward.

Julia was the last to give evidence. When the coroner's assistant called her name and she stood, the dozy reporter at her side sat up and blinked. Whispers and a short bark of laughter followed her across the room. She spotted Chief Inspector Clark, Tennant's superior in the detective department, standing in the rear with Inspector Slack.

Leary's death was straightforward, Julia testified. Massive blood loss resulted from a broken whisky bottle thrust into his abdomen. She'd extracted pieces from the wound.

The coroner asked if she had anything else to add.

"Yes. In my hearing, the two men who carried Mr. Leary into my clinic spoke of threats they overheard uttered by men in the pub. Threats directed at the deceased."

The six Irishmen at the back leaped from their seats and pushed out the door. The reporter scribbled furiously. With the proceedings over, a scowling Chief Inspector Clark turned on his heels and exited, followed by Slack. Julia stood at the door, waiting for the coroner to finish his business with the publican. Shouts and catcalls greeted Clark and Slack as they made their way through an angry gauntlet.

The coroner, a balding, precise little man with steel-rimmed spectacles and a thin mustache, counted out the medical examiner's standard fee: two pounds, two shillings. He handed her the coins, saying, "Well, Doctor Lewis, you certainly put the cat among the pigeons."

"That hearing was a travesty," Julia said.

"Slack should be sacked. Still, he has his uses."

"Meaning?"

The coroner pushed his spectacles up the bridge of his nose. "He's probably the Yard's least energetic officer. Call him in if you *don't* want answers."

"Slack is aptly named."

"The East End has little sympathy for an Irish victim. Slack will box up the evidence and stick it on a shelf."

"Then they'll have an Irish tinderbox on their hands," Julia said, pocketing her fee.

The same morning on the Isle of Wight, Inspector Tennant sought answers at Osborne House, holding interviews in the office of the queen's private secretary. O'Malley's telegram added Stanley Hackett to the inspector's list of promising suspects, and the prince's valet was the morning's first interview.

Hackett arrived promptly, wearing a charcoal cut-away coat that showed off a royal blue, diamond-patterned waistcoat. Tennant judged him to be in his middle thirties and more expensively suited than the typical manservant. Full muttonchop side whiskers and a fringe beard didn't altogether hide a receding chin. The valet's restless fingers fiddled with the knot in his tie. The bump in Hackett's throat jumped like a jack-in-the-box when Tennant asked him about his movements on the day Lizzie Dowling was murdered.

"It's difficult to say." Hackett pulled a silk handkerchief from his pocket and mopped his forehead. "Probably tending to the prince's wardrobe."

"Probably or definitely?"

Hackett scowled, stuffing away the pocket square. "You can't expect a fellow to remember one afternoon two months ago."

"I think the day that an Osborne House servant goes missing and then turns up dead would linger in one's memory. You don't agree?" When Hackett didn't answer, Tennant said, "No? Well, let's consider a more recent day. Last Tuesday, the day her sister, Brigid Dowling, was murdered."

"I . . ." Hackett pulled at his collar, and the stud popped and shot across the carpet.

Tennant retrieved it and handed the servant his mother-of-pearl fastener. “Tuesday is a half-day off for you, I believe. Where were you at two o’clock?”

“Walking in Hyde Park.”

“Observed?”

“I don’t know. Maybe someone saw me. I was there. That’s all I know.” Then an alert expression flared like a lighted candlewick. He lifted his chin and said, “I’d like to see you prove otherwise.”

Tennant held the man’s gaze, waiting. The manservant’s bravado proved fleeting. He dropped his eyes and grasped shaking hands behind his back. Then the inspector dismissed the valet and scribbled some awkward notes with his injured hand. He left the study looking for the queen’s secretary, General Grey. Tennant passed the household dining room and spotted the valet in agitated conversation with a tall, lean, broad-shouldered man in a dark frock coat.

The inspector found the queen’s private secretary in the library. Tennant described the servant he saw with Hackett and asked his name.

“That sounds like Michael Bolger, the house steward,” General Grey said.

“What are his duties?”

“Bolger hires the house servants and pays their wages. He orders all Osborne’s supplies. That includes everything from furniture and linens, the queen’s writing paper, to the barrels of flour used to bake our daily bread. Bolger superintends the delivery, storage, and dispersal of the lot.”

“An indispensable man,” Tennant said.

“He supplies the claret, brandy, and port that make the long evenings in royal service bearable.” General Grey smiled thinly under his drooping mustache. “Or nearly so.”

“Would he have had dealings with Lizzie Dowling?”

“Only to pay her monthly wages, as he does for the rest of the household staff. Other than that, I doubt it. The housekeeper supervised her work.”

"Thank you, General. I'll speak to the house steward next."

During his interview, Michael Bolger was as composed as the valet had been agitated. A line from Shakespeare popped into Tennant's head. Like Cassius, Bolger had "a lean and hungry look," gazing back from shrewd and calculating blue eyes. *Good-looking chap and knows it,* Tennant thought, taking in his square, cleft chin and dark, curly hair.

The inspector asked him a few routine questions about his role at Osborne House. Then Tennant shifted to his movements on the day of Lizzie Dowling's murder.

Bolger's shrug was just short of insolent. "Going about my duties, as usual, I expect."

"You knew Miss Dowling well?"

"She lined up for her monthly wages like the rest, but my duties do not include supervising the female staff."

"Just now, I saw you in earnest conversation with the prince's valet."

"Mister Hackett is a friend of mine," Bolger said. "He left his interview a little agitated. Being interviewed by the police isn't an everyday event."

"That was the only reason for your conversation?"

"That and cigars. Mister Hackett asked me to order the prince's favorite brand from the Cowes tobacconist. His Royal Highness is smoking through his supply."

"So soon? And the prince arrived only yesterday. Will Mister Hackett confirm your explanation if I ask him?"

"Certainly, Inspector." The house steward said, his blue eyes unblinking. "Why wouldn't he?"

Bolger had a military air about him. He stood before Tennant in a posture of parade ground at ease. "Are you a former army man, Mister Bolger?"

"Sergeant Bolger, sir, back in the day." His eyes flicked to Tennant's regimental tie. "Grenadier Guards?"

"That's right. Brothers-in-arms. Thank you, Mister Bolger. That will be all."

A smooth, plausible liar, Tennant thought. *But lying about what?* According to General Grey, Bolger was on the Isle of Wight the day someone in London murdered Brigid Dowling.

The middle-aged housekeeper was next. "How long have you served the queen, Mrs. Forsythe?" Tennant asked.

"I assumed my duties a year ago," she said.

"Tell me about Lizzie Dowling."

The housekeeper considered for a moment. "Lizzy was a kind young woman, Inspector. I liked her. She was thoughtful and observant about people. She noticed when things needed doing and stepped in. Quietly. Without *over*stepping, if you know what I mean."

"I think I do."

"If I thanked her, she'd say she was grateful to be here. I thought it wasn't just words. I sensed she'd seen trouble in her life and counted herself lucky."

"She gave you no hint about her trials?"

"No. I'm sorry, now. Sorry I didn't encourage her to confide in me."

Tennant asked about Lizzie's friends, but the murdered girl had lacked a confidant among the servants.

"She kept herself to herself," Mrs. Forsythe said. "But Princess Louise made a pet of the girl."

"How so?"

"Her Royal Highness moved Lizzie to a small room in the princesses' wing," the housekeeper said. "Treated her like a lady's maid rather than a parlor servant. It caused some resentment."

"How much are we talking about?"

"Bruised feelings and petty sniping, Inspector," she said. "Nothing that would lead to murder."

"You heard the findings of the medical examination?"

"Yes. And before you ask, I have no idea who the father was."

"She hadn't made friends with the male servants? Mister Bolger, for instance? He's a good-looking chap."

Mrs. Forsythe smiled. "There's a pecking order among servants, Inspector. Mister Bolger condescends to greet me if we meet in a hallway, but a house steward in a place like Osborne would take little notice of a servant girl."

"Even a very attractive one?"

"I saw no sign of it. Now, the prince's valet . . . he's another matter. He has an eye for any comely female. But as far as I know, Lizzie never looked back."

Tennant thanked her and turned his attention to the two equerries on his list, starting with Oliver Montgomery. The tall, sandy-haired captain stretched himself on a settee and began with a sardonic joke about being arrested. He crossed his legs and waved to the inspector. "Fire away," he said, looking as if he hadn't a care in the world.

Tennant asked Montgomery about his movements on the afternoon of Lizzie's death.

"No alibi to speak of. I took the floating bridge to the island's western side. Rode to Yarmouth and back."

"Did you see anyone you knew?"

The captain shrugged. "Only strangers on the roads who wouldn't know me from Adam."

"The prince and Major FitzGerald were out riding as well. Who returned first?"

"I did. A gentleman might find your line of inquiry somewhat offensive, Inspector." But Montgomery sounded more amused than affronted.

"A gentleman with something to hide might," Tennant said.

"Well, that lets me out."

"The circumstances surrounding Brigid Dowling's murder in London suggest foreknowledge of her movements. Lady Styles discussed the girl's arrival in front of you and others at the Marlborough House ball."

"Someone may have followed her from Ireland. Or a London rough might have set out to rob her."

"Overlooking the cabbie's pocket, stuffed with half crowns and shillings?"

Montgomery shrugged. "It's certainly a conundrum, Inspector. But sorting mysteries is your stock in trade, not mine."

"Were you in London on Tuesday afternoon?"

"Yes."

"Just to confirm . . . You were here on the Isle of Wight last July as well as in October. Is that correct?"

"That's right. Readying my boat for the summer races. Here again in the autumn."

"One last question. Did you see Major FitzGerald, Sir Lionel Dermott, and Frederick Locock here during those months?"

"Yes, Inspector. All of us, on the spot." Montgomery grinned. "In both meanings of the phrase." He ambled to the door with his hands in his pockets and stopped. "Bit of bad luck for Freddie Locock."

"Meaning?"

"He wasn't meant to be here in October. Just back from his wedding trip. Called down to see his father over something or other. Pity, or old Freddie would have been in the clear."

Tennant wondered: was Montgomery's nonchalance a careful pose or the sign of a clear conscience? The captain's self-possession and air of amused boredom contrasted with his next and final interview at Osborne House.

Major Peter FitzGerald's answers were terse, and his voice clipped. He'd confined his ride on the afternoon of Lizzie's murder to the estate grounds, he said, making his final inspection of Osborne Park before leaving for Balmoral. His account tallied with the recollections of the head groom, but no one had seen FitzGerald riding around the estate.

"Major, as the queen's equerry, you usually travel with her. Yet, you were here in July and again in October rather than at Balmoral."

"I remained to begin the renovations of the queen's stables and returned for a final inspection."

"Can you tell me anything about Lizzie Dowling that might aid my investigation?"

FitzGerald raised an eyebrow. "I take little notice of the comings and goings of the female servants. Is that all, Inspector?"

"For the moment. Thank you, Major."

He's not as cool as he pretends, Tennant thought. The pink scar on his left cheek had turned a darker shade of rose by the end of their conversation.

Tennant's notes didn't take long. *No witnesses and all the suspects were in the wind.* Tennant had murder sites in London and on the Isle of Wight, eighty miles apart. And at any time, the royals could pack up and leave for one of their estates in a distant corner of the country, taking his chief suspects with them.

The thing's impossible, Tennant thought, closing the study door behind him.

An hour later in Cowes, Tennant scanned the map of the Isle of Wight on Chief Constable Phillips's wall. The inspector asked him, "How far is the murder site from Osborne House?"

"Quarr Abbey is four miles along two main roads. Lizzie Dowling traveled there by omnibus."

"And if you went by horseback, wanting to avoid detection?"

"Well . . ." The burly chief smoothed his walrus mustache with his index finger and thumb. "I'd skirt the bridge over Wooten Creek and go cross-country."

"Where is the Royal Victoria Yacht Club located?"

"Here." Phillips pointed. "Just north of the bridge on the Fishbourne side of Wooten Creek. What's your interest in the Royal Victoria?"

"It's Sir Lionel Dermott's club. He sailed from there on the day of Lizzie's murder and lodged at the nearby Fishbourne Inn."

"It's an easy walk to Quarr Abbey," Phillips said, tracing the line with his forefinger.

Tennant resumed his seat. "Six men were on the Isle of Wight during the months in question. This morning, I took statements from four of them."

"Who are they?"

"Major FitzGerald, Captain Montgomery, the valet of the Prince of Wales, Stanley Hackett, and the queen's house steward, Michael Bolger."

The chief constable blew out his cheeks. "Two royal equerries and a pair of royal servants? By God, Tennant, you don't do things by half measures."

"Can you point me to a stable where I can hire a horse? I want to cover the ground to Quarr Abbey and see the murder site for myself."

"I'll do better. I'll lend you a horse and accompany you."

"Thank you," Tennant said. "Three men on my list were out riding on the afternoon of Lizzie's murder. Major FitzGerald, Captain Montgomery, and the Prince of Wales."

Phillips stared. "Is that a ruddy joke?"

"The head groom said he'd ridden to Newport and back. We cannot overlook His Royal Highness."

At eleven the following morning, the crunch of carriage wheels on a pebbled roadway announced an arrival at Osborne Cottage. Tennant parted the curtains, expecting to see the pony cart that would carry Dermott and him to the Southampton steamer dock. Instead, a carriage with a VR cipher stopped at the door.

Sir Lionel emerged from his room, combing his hair. "Is that our transport? It's early."

"No. Royal visitors." Lady Styles and two women Tennant

recognized as Princess Alexandra and Princess Louise walked up the path.

Sir Lionel pocketed his comb, opened the door, and bowed them into the hallway. "Your Royal Highnesses are out and about early. And Lady Styles. To what do I owe the honor and pleasure?"

"No church today," Princess Louise announced gaily. "Too many soldiers and roadblocks between Osborne House and Whippingham."

"Tut, tut, Princess," Dermott said. "Should you sound so pleased to be missing Sunday services?"

"It's all such nonsense," Louise said. "I don't mean church. I mean this invasion of soldiers in kilts. The queen is furious. Not even the absurd Brown can persuade Mama to take it seriously."

"Princesses, may I present Detective Inspector Tennant of Scotland Yard, the officer in charge of the Dowling case. You find the inspector and me nearly on the fly. We are taking the twelve-thirty steamer from Cowes."

"Oh," Alexandra said. "Then perhaps . . ."

"We're packed and prepared, Your Royal Highness, and have a quarter hour until the pony trap arrives."

Lionel led the princesses to seats in the sitting room. They presented a striking contrast. The Princess of Wales—thin and delicate, with dark curls pinned under a flat, angled hat—had the kind of pale skin that seemed nearly transparent. She'd dressed elegantly but conventionally in a fitted blue jacket and skirt. Princess Louise—robustly figured with fair hair cascading down her back—dropped her hat and cape in a pile on the sofa and then sat. She wore a flowing, high-waisted claret gown in a relaxed, modern style and had a touch of the bohemian about her.

Tennant stood until Princess Alexandra said, "Please sit, Inspector." Those were the last words she spoke until her farewell at the interview's end. She looked at her sister-in-law and nodded.

Princess Louise peppered Tennant with questions about the discovery of Brigid Dowling's body and the progress of the investigation, pressing him to speculate about a link between the sisters' deaths. The inspector found a convenient refuge, claiming it was too early to draw conclusions.

Louise sighed in frustration. "I suppose we shall have to be satisfied with that."

"I share your impatience, Your Royal Highness, but it is often thus at the start of an investigation."

With the aid of her cane, the Princess of Wales stood. "Thank you, Inspector." She offered her hand to Tennant, who bowed over it.

Louise tied her bonnet's ribbons with careless impatience, allowing her hat to hang down her back. She thrust her hands into her muff. Then the princess looked up, the top of her head barely reaching his chin. She held his gaze.

"Lizzie was a lovely person, Inspector. She was the only one I could stand to . . ." She turned away abruptly, but not before Tennant saw her tears.

An hour later, Sir Lionel and Tennant passed a noticeable police presence patrolling the Cowes harborside.

"I pity the poor chief constable," Sir Lionel said, signaling a porter. "So much on his plate. Irish invaders and the death of a queen's servant. A case that's wide open again. I assume you and the chief confirmed my unfortunate presence near the scene of the crime?"

"The Royal Victoria marina master and the clerk at the Fishbourne Inn were most obliging."

"Tell me, did you share your *entire* list of suspects with the chief constable?" Dermott chuckled when Tennant nodded.

"Hearing Bertie's name amongst the potential culprits made his day, I'll wager."

When they reached the top of the steamer gangway, Tennant said, "Speaking of wagers. On our railway journey, I asked you to handicap the suspects. Major FitzGerald is your favorite. How does Captain Frederick Locock rate on your racing form?"

Sir Lionel shrugged. "I have nothing against Freddie."

"That's not an answer. Assess the man's capacity for murder . . . and his motives."

"I know nothing that could help you with either."

"The Royal Victoria marina master said Locock recently purchased a yacht. An expensive hobby for a doctor's son." Tennant waited for a reply. Then he said, "Socially, Captain Locock seems an 'odd man out' in the prince's set."

"Does his social standing affect his status as a suspect?"

Once again, Dermott had deflected. "No. But it makes it harder for me to fit him into the picture frame."

"He and Ollie Montgomery were in the same regiment, the Royal Horse Guards. Locock is in the Colonial Office now."

"In a position of some confidence?"

"Not really."

"Newly married, I understand," Tennant said.

"Yes."

"Do you know his address?"

"Don't recall it offhand. I'll send it to you."

Somehow, either the loquacious Sir Lionel had grown bored with the game of coppers and culprits, or . . . *or what?*

Tennant said, "Should I have reason to suspect Major FitzGerald? Something beyond your dislike of the man."

Dermott's slow smile spread. "Now that I consider it, I can think of one reason FitzGerald might kill to cover up a dalliance."

"What is that?"

"His father-in-law's money. It cost FitzGerald a thousand pounds of the old Marmalade King's tin to jump from captain to major. It'll be thousands more to purchase the rank of colonel. And I hear Fitz covets the crown-and-star for his collar."

"Then the major has a motive for good marital behavior . . . or its appearance."

"Rumor is the old man tied his daughter's money tighter than a sailor's knot. Most of it jumps a generation, settled on the major's 'heir and spare.' "

"So, in a divorce—"

"Harriet FitzGerald's lovely lucre vanishes . . ." Dermott fished a shilling out of his pocket, palmed the coin, and then opened his empty hand. "Just like that."

CHAPTER 8

Mrs. Ogilvie had decked the halls of the Lewis town house in Christmas trimmings, but Julia felt low on holiday cheer. Inspector Tennant had dropped by briefly on his return from the Isle of Wight. But Sir Richard Mayne was impatient for the inspector's report and expected him that evening. He stayed only long enough to wish them a happy Christmas.

Dr. Lewis had asked, "Do you have plans, Richard? My sister is our only guest. You'd be most welcome to join us."

Tennant hesitated. "Thank you, sir. That's kind of you, but I spend Christmas in Kent with Hannah, our old housekeeper."

Julia accompanied the inspector to the front door. "I'm sorry to refuse your invitation," Tennant said, fiddling with the brim of his hat. "Hannah is . . . well, she's something more than a servant."

"I gathered that last June in Kent," Julia said. "Over tea, she called you 'Richard.' Not many housekeepers use the Christian names of their employers."

"The story is too long for the front door."

"Another time, then." *Blast*, Julia thought. *I sound so . . .* She tried to infuse more warmth in her voice and said, "Good night, Richard, and happy Christmas."

Julia closed the door and leaned against it, eying her look of dejection in the hall mirror. *What's wrong with me?*

When her hansom cab had pulled up on Horseferry Road, and she'd seen him for the first time in months, her heart had leaped. *Not something described in my anatomy books*, she thought wryly. And what had she done? She'd coolly brushed his cheeks when she'd wanted to wrap her arms around him. *And I call him buttoned up.* One thing she knew. *We've become too polite with each other. Perhaps . . .*

Julia nodded, smiling at the mirror's reflection. *Yes.* A healthy jolt of annoyance might shake things up. In the past, she'd been skilled at provoking it. She had an idea about a line of inquiry that needed pursuing. *Why not?* She pulled her skirts away from her ankles and bounded upstairs to her sitting room. She found the half-completed thank-you note to Lady Styles on her desk. Alexandra's lady-in-waiting had sent Christmas wishes and a twenty-pound contribution to the clinic from the princess. Lady Styles had added a postscript, writing that she hoped the doctor had room on her private patient's list for her, as well.

Room? I can add an auditorium of ladies-in-waiting to my practice.

Julia thought for a minute, added a question for Lady Styles, and sealed the letter. *There. It's done.*

In Tennant's office on Monday morning, O'Malley reported his lack of progress in the Dermott inquiry.

"Throwing money around a pub always earns praise from a barkeep," Tennant said. "We'll have to look elsewhere for information."

"'Tis early to hear back from Brigid Dowling's employers in Ireland. Something might turn up in her belongings."

Tennant asked, "Any joy over the canvass of the theatrical supply shops?"

"Nothing so far, but there's more of them than you'd think. Our coppers are still on it."

"Our only witness is that young sweep who saw Brigid entering the carriage. He said the ginger-bearded suspect was a tall fellow. So is Dermott, and an absurd disguise would appeal to his odd sense of humor."

A young policeman knocked. "Arrived by messenger, sir." He handed the inspector an envelope.

Tennant turned it over and read the flap. "Well, well. Speak of the devil." He opened it and read through the opening lines. "Sir Lionel sends us Frederick Locock's address, as promised." The inspector read the rest of the note and chuckled.

"You said the fella's something of a card. What's he saying for himself?"

"Dermott is trying his best to incriminate Major FitzGerald for Brigid Dowling's murder. Listen to this. 'I ran into Skittles on my ride in Hyde Park this morning and—' "

"Skittles, sir?"

"Catherine Walters, known as Skittles, is a high-priced courtesan, rumored to be the mistress of a long list of wealthy and important gentlemen, including the Prince of Wales."

O'Malley shook his head. "And him, a young father of three and married to the lovely princess."

"Dermott writes, 'I remembered seeing FitzGerald riding with Skittles recently. Checked my diary, and happily—' He's underlined the word for us. 'I noted an outing in the park on the morning in question, as you coppers say. So, FitzGerald was in London on the fateful day of Brigid Dowling's murder!' "

"Why happily? What's the major done to him?"

"He doesn't like the man, so it amuses Dermott to implicate him."

"Sure, it's daft since he puts himself in the frame as well."

"Sir Lionel knows that, Paddy. It speaks to his innocence or a breathtaking arrogance if he's guilty." Tennant passed the note to O'Malley. "At least we have one accurate piece of information—Captain Locock's address."

"St. James Mews. Off Cleveland Row and near Green Park, he's saying."

"It's early and a short walk. Let's see if we can catch Locock at home. We'll ask him what took him to the Isle of Wight in October."

Their trek took them past the exclusive gentlemen's clubs on Pall Mall and along Cleveland Row. The first right turn was St. James Mews. Six Georgian town houses lined the courtyard. O'Malley's knock at number three went unanswered. Tennant stopped a passing postman who said the Lococks would be away through Christmas. From the pavement, Tennant looked up at the house, jingling the coins in his overcoat pocket.

"What's your guess, Paddy? How much would the monthly rent set one back?"

"More than I earn in a year, I'm thinking."

Tennant spotted a bowler-hatted man unscrewing a discreet FOR RENT sign at number six. "Let's find out." The inspector crossed the street and tipped his hat. "Are you the agent for these properties, sir?"

"I am." The smiling, gap-toothed man stuck his screwdriver in his pocket and shifted the sign to his left hand. "What can I do for you gents?"

"I'm too late for number six, I see."

"Sorry, guv. Got to be quick if you want to rent one of these beauties. Grosvenor properties they are, the three of them." He grinned. "Folks like to brag that the Duke of Westminster is their landlord."

"What about the houses across the street?" Tennant asked.

"What rent might I expect to pay for number three, for example?"

"You'd pay nothing for that one. It's a grace-and-favor. Rent-free if you're a friend of the Prince of Wales. Chap who lives there moved in a few months ago."

"So, I'm out of luck."

The man reached into his breast pocket and pulled out his card. "Lots of other fish in the sea, guvnor. Drop by my office anytime." He tipped his bowler and walked off.

"Rent-free, royal accommodations. Captain Frederick Locock grows more interesting by the hour," Tennant said as they retraced their steps to Pall Mall.

On their way back to the Yard, they passed the columned portico of the Athenaeum Club. Tennant eyed its gilded statue of Athena, the goddess of wisdom. *I could use some just now . . . and not only for the case,* thinking of Julia.

It had been a snowy day in December when Dr. Andrew Lewis invited him to the club for a drink. *Only a year ago.* Strange how much a part of his life Julia and her grandfather had become in so short a time. *Even Lady Aldridge.* Tennant sensed a concern from her that he had never felt in his mother. *And Julia . . .* He had to find a way to gather the strands before things were beyond raveling.

The inspector and his sergeant stopped and waited for the traffic to clear at the corner of Pall Mall and Waterloo Place. Tennant's left boot slipped off the curb, and he winced.

O'Malley's gaze flicked to Tennant's leg. "You all right, sir?"

"Yes, thank you, Sergeant." *Who do I think I'm kidding? He's watched me struggle.* O'Malley had never said a word, but the sergeant was an observant copper and no fool. "Are you spending Christmas with your sister, Paddy?"

"That I am. With those two young hooligans, my nephews, and a new niece, as well. What will yourself be doing, if I may ask the question?"

"I'll spend Christmas in Kent with the woman who was like a mother to me."

O'Malley nodded. "Ah, family. Whoever they may be. There's nothing like having them around you at Christmas."

When the traffic cleared, two sweeper lads brushed a clear lane through the road's dung, and in the spirit of the season, Tennant gave each boy a shilling instead of a penny.

"All right, Paddy," Tennant said when they reached the other side. "Give me your thoughts on Locock."

"'Twas some good turn the fella did for Bertie to earn that grace-and-favor gaff."

"He's a half-pay captain, a man with a middling job in the Colonial Office, a doctor's son, the third of five. He bought himself a yacht and lives, rent-free, at an expensive address, and moves in the first social circle."

"They say there's always room at the top," O'Malley said. "But what did the fella do to climb there?"

On a crisp, clear Christmas morning, Dr. Andrew Lewis and his granddaughter attended services at All Hallows Church on the London Wall road, a short walk from the entrance to Finsbury Circus. They had lingered for the celebratory ringing of the bells. One hundred years earlier, in 1767, a new church had been built to replace the old.

"My grandfather missed the old All Hallows he knew as a boy," Dr. Lewis said. "But I'm fond of the new church. You were baptized at its font, and I married your grandmother at the altar."

"When was the old church built?"

"In the twelfth century. Parts of its foundation were older than that, constructed on the site of an older church and on the remnants of the Roman wall that ringed the city. You can spot some of the wall's remains along the road if you look for it."

"Think of that," Julia said. "Worshipers on a Christmas six hundred years ago. Workers fitting the wall stones a thousand years before that. And here we are, on the same spot."

"A blink in time's eye." He squeezed Julia's arm. "A reminder that it's fleeting, my dear."

"Yes," Julia said. She took a last look at the church tower as it disappeared behind a stand of trees.

"Pity Richard isn't joining us for dinner," her grandfather said. "Christmas in Kent. He must be fond of the place. And of Hannah, his housekeeper."

"She's something of a substitute mother, I think. Aunt Caroline told me his real one was less than maternal. Perhaps that explains his reserve."

"He just needs someone to bring him out of himself."

"Aunt Caroline proposes me for that role. I see she's recruited you in her campaign."

Her grandfather chuckled. "Well, we're both fond of the chap. Your aunt believes you are, too. If only you'd make up your mind to it."

"She tells me so. Often."

They'd reached Bloomfield Street. At the corner, Dr. Lewis pointed his walking stick at a rough, triangular remnant of the ancient wall. "Those old Romans . . . they had a saying for every occasion, my dear. *Carpe diem.*"

"I'll match your 'seize the day' with *caveat emptor,* Grandfather. 'Let the buyer beware.' "

He took her elbow. "Have it your way."

When they turned onto East Street, Julia spotted Kate exiting the side door of St. Mary's Chapel, one of the few Roman Catholic churches in central London. The maid looked right and left and then hurried across the road to the servants' entrance of their town house.

"Kate looks almost furtive, Grandfather. As if she'd done

something wrong by attending Mass on Christmas Day." Julia shook her head. "It's a little heartbreaking."

"It's not an easy time to be Irish and Roman Catholic," he said.

"These old hatreds . . . They endure like pieces of the ancient wall. It's a depressing thought."

"The other day, an old fossil at my club said there was 'something un-English' about being Roman Catholic."

"What did you say?"

"Oh, I agreed with him. As un-English as every king from William the Conqueror to Henry VII."

Julia squeezed his arm. "Good for you, Grandfather."

On the Isle of Wight, the third time between Christmas and New Year was not the charm. Nor was the queen amused. Susan Styles hid her smiles and feigned sympathy.

For a third night, shouts and flares at Osborne House disturbed Her Majesty. On two earlier occasions, it woke her from her sleep. Victoria was a great believer in the health-promoting properties of leaving windows open a crack, no matter the weather. Hadn't Miss Nightingale proved the case for fresh air in the hospital wards of the Crimea? So, there was no muting the Fenian false alarms that erupted on three nights.

John Brown was the culprit in the first instance. He had consumed a "wee dram" more than he could hold of his favorite Highland blend. Around midnight, he staggered across the terrace beneath the queen's bedroom windows. Then he tumbled into the bushes, roaring and swearing as he tried to disentangle himself. Four Scots Fusiliers ran with guns pointed and torches blazing. They led Brown away, cursing colorfully in a broad Highland dialect. In the morning, the queen's assistant dresser, a Scotswoman, giggled when she related the story to Susan.

"The queen watched from her window," the dresser said, "but she didn't understand a word, thank goodness."

Two nights later, a pair of roe deer invaded the estate grounds. They emerged from the woodlands after dark, looking for food and water. Osborne's terraced gardens and fountains provided ample supplies of both. The queen woke at the crack of a gunshot and struggled from her bed. She parted her window curtains to see a pair of kilted soldiers holding torches over a dead deer rather than an Irish intruder.

A third incident proved to be the last straw. That evening, the queen and her household ladies had lingered unusually late in the drawing room. Prince Bertie played billiards in the adjacent games room, growing jittery and impatient for a smoke. Victoria loathed the habit and forbade it in the house, a rule ignored as soon as Her Majesty retired to her bed. Frustrated by the delay, the prince slipped out a side door while his companions continued with the game.

It mattered not that it was late December. The drawing room windows stood open an inch, and Susan shivered at the piano, partway through the first set of Mendelssohn's *Songs Without Words*. Shouts interrupted. A red-faced young officer, mistaking the prince for an intruder, appeared with Bertie, his cigar extinguished.

The queen had had enough. Crimson, furious, and perspiring, she fanned herself at hummingbird speed and delivered a decree: they would stay one more night and be gone. Victoria would leave for Windsor Castle on New Year's Day; the prince and princess would return to Marlborough House a week earlier than planned.

Susan started packing.

On New Year's Eve, Julia stopped at a vendor by the cabstand on Whitechapel Road for the most recent copy of *Punch*, her grandfather's favorite illustrated magazine. She'd left the clinic early, so she was home, dressed for dinner, and in the library before her grandfather came downstairs. And for once, she'd arrived before her aunt. Lady Aldridge would stay the night with them, ringing in the first day of January. They kept the celebration small. Each December 31, they raised a glass to the dawn of another year and to Julia's grandmother. She died on New Year's Eve while Julia was in Philadelphia attending medical school.

Julia had time to spare, so she poured herself a sherry and paged through *Punch*. She had the magazine open on her lap when her grandfather entered the library with an envelope.

"This came for you in the afternoon post . . . my dear, what's wrong?"

Julia held up a page. "This cartoon. Despicable."

She exchanged *Punch* for her letter. An article on the Clerkenwell bombing included a caricature of an Irishman. He sat on a barrel of gunpowder with a lighted torch in his hand, looking like a cross between a leprechaun and an ape. A woman and a group of angelic children gathered at the foot of the keg.

Dr. Lewis read the caption, "'The Irish Guy Fawkes.'" He shook his head. "Guy Fawkes. We remember the Catholic who tried to blow up the king in Parliament two centuries ago, forgetting the thousands of Irish Catholics who fought beside Wellington at Waterloo."

"Put it away, Grandfather. Somewhere Kate won't find it."

Dr. Lewis tore out the page, crumpled it, and dropped it in the fire. Then he fished his penknife from his pocket, opened it, and passed it to Julia. "Royal correspondence from Osborne House must be read at once."

Julia sliced and extracted the letter. "I wrote to Lady Styles about a line of inquiry . . ." She scanned the note and said, "The lady agrees with me. Lizzie, a country girl from Kildare, was an oddity among the queen's servants."

"Does she explain the circumstances of the girl's employment?"

"No, but she promises to make some inquiries."

"Did Richard ask you to look into this?"

"No . . . not yet. But I'm sure he will." She smiled and passed the letter to her grandfather. "Once it occurs to him."

Early on Friday morning of the new year, a man slowed and stopped his milk wagon at the top of the road. He'd spotted a policeman passing the mason's yard halfway down Duke Street, a stone's throw from Buckingham Palace. The driver waited. A feral cat screeched from behind a collection of bins, upsetting a lid that clanged on the cobbles. A triangle of light from a bull's-eye lantern caught and froze the creature before it darted into the darkness. Then the beam swung around, and the constable and his light moved on.

The driver grinned, picturing the man who waited in the 4:00 a.m. cold, cowering amid the mason's broken stones. *And crapping himself over that copper.* He flicked the reins and then slowed the horse to a stop at the stonemason's gate. A gas lamp illuminated his cart's painted sign: DOWNEY AND SON. MILK AND CREAM.

"Hisst . . . Danny," he called in a hoarse whisper. "You there?"

Someone moved out of the yard's shadows. "Thought you'd changed your bleedin' mind," the man said. "Been freezing my arse off."

"Patience, Danny boy. Patience is the key." The driver in a dairyman cap patted the bench. "Climb aboard."

Danny hauled himself up. He twisted and looked back at the cart. "What's this milk lark about?"

"You'll find out soon enough."

The driver had pulled the peaked cap low over his pale blue eyes. A gray muffler circled his neck, covering his chin. The only thing that showed in the space between his hat and scarf was the luxuriant thatch sprouting under his nose.

"When did you have time to grow that bush on your face?"

"You don't like it?" The driver unhooked one side of the walrus mustache and grinned.

Danny jerked his thumb over his shoulder. "Odd way to travel to a meeting."

"Change of plan, old son. I'll explain on the way." He reached under the bench and pulled out a second smock. "Meanwhile, put this on."

"Thing's as stiff as a board," Danny said, shrugging into the rough cotton jacket.

"It soaked up some of the wares." The driver chuckled. "But there's no use crying over spilled milk, right?" Then he snapped the reins, and the horse clopped off, heading south toward Marlborough Road.

"So, what's this meeting about?"

"No meeting, Danny. We've a job to do."

"News to me."

"The chief kept it quiet." He tapped the side of his nose and winked. "Just his trusted lieutenants on this one. You and me."

"You and me what?"

"We're giving the heir to the throne a warm welcome home from the Isle of Wight."

"Meaning?"

"Instead of leaving Downey and Son's milk at the side door, we're spilling five-gallon cans of paraffin and setting it alight."

"Sweet suffering Jesus."

The pale-eyed man chuckled. "Hope the royal couple prayed to him before bedtime. They sleep on the same side of the house."

Danny said, "But I thought the queen was our—"

"The Osborne plot came to nothing." He shrugged. "Still, Victoria has nine children. Lots of tempting sport."

Danny's knee jumped like a piston. He drummed his boot heel against the oak platform, shifted in his seat, and scanned the pavements, side to side.

The driver shot him a look. "You're nervous as a cat, boy-o." He turned left onto Marlborough Road, pulled on the reins, and stopped the cart in the dark expanse between two pools of lamplight.

Danny looked around. "Why have we stopped?"

He cocked his thumb. "Time to slip into the back. The soldiers at the side gate expect one deliveryman, not two."

"What if one of them searches the cabin and finds me?"

"No worries, mate." He slid out a knife and returned it to the sheath hidden in his boot. "Let's go."

The driver led Danny to the wagon's rear door and unlatched it. A mustachioed man's dead eyes stared back at them.

"The unfortunate 'son' of Downey and Son," the driver said. "Let's move him aside, shall we? Make a little room for you." He shoved the body back a foot. "Careful of the four cans on the right. Mustn't spill the paraffin yet." He bolted the door behind his passenger and returned to the driver's seat. The wagon jolted forward and then rattled to a stop at the gate.

The driver let loose a rheumy, rattling cough. "Morning," he wheezed to the guardsman on duty.

"You need a hot toddy, mate," the soldier said, stepping back a pace. "You sound like death warmed over."

"Funny you should say that." The driver turned his face away, hacking. Then he jerked the reins and drove on. Another turn and the wagon rolled to a stop. The pale-eyed man's boots crunched on the gravel as he rounded the wagon to open the cart's back door.

"Right, Danny boy. Now, move two of those cans to where I can reach them."

Danny shifted the galvanized containers to the door, and

they each hauled a can down the path and up the steps to the side door of the mansion.

"Dump it so the stream runs over the doorjamb and inside the house," the driver whispered. "But be careful. Don't get any on your boots."

Danny removed the bunghole stopper, tipped the container, and stepped back. He repeated the process with the second can.

"Two more to go," the driver said, inches from his companion's ear.

Danny unloaded the last two containers from the back of the wagon.

"Stop here a minute," the driver said, halting halfway to the door.

Danny set his can down and swiped his forehead with the stiff fabric of his sleeve.

"Funny thing about that plot against the queen." The driver took off his milkman's cap and clapped on his bowler. "There never was one." A match illuminated his pale blue eyes as he applied the flame to a cloth-wrapped stick. "The chief peddled that fairy story to one person only. You."

Danny turned to run. When the driver tossed the flaming stick, Danny's paraffin-soaked smock ignited, and he lit up like a dried-out Christmas tree. The driver tipped the last can with the toe of his boot, and the stream fed the flames. Then he tossed his milkman's cap and mustache into the fire and scrambled for cover.

Ghastly shrieks brought the guardsmen running from Marlborough's gates. The driver slipped behind bushes surrounding the garden maze. The rail-thin man ripped off his jacket, exchanging his white outer smock with the overcoat he wore underneath. He made his way silently along the inner brick wall. He waited in the shadows at the side gate, listening for the coppers on the Marlborough House beat. A minute later, he heard the crunch and spray of flying gravel as they dashed through the entrance and along the carriageway.

He adjusted his bowler, slipped through the gate, and turned right on Marlborough Road. *No worries about being spotted,* he thought, walking away at an easy clip.

The sentries only had eyes for the human torch writhing in agony.

CHAPTER 9

"Wake up, Doctor Julie." Kate shook the doctor's shoulder and then dragged open the drapes.

"What time is it?" Julia said, propping herself on her elbow. She covered her eyes against the streaming light.

"It's just gone six. Sergeant O'Malley is waiting downstairs. There's been trouble at Marlborough House."

An hour later, Julia and Tennant stood over the charred remains of a corpse. A line of six constables crossed the nearby grounds, searching for evidence.

"We found the Downey and Son wagon where you see it," the inspector said. "The milkman's body is inside. A young man in his twenties, at a guess. The arsonist tied a cloth around the horse's eyes to keep it from bolting."

"Downey and Son. Singular," Julia said. "The poor father, if the dead man is his son."

"The guardsman at the gate identified him. Sergeant O'Malley is breaking the news to Mr. Downey now. The victim has a single puncture in his throat, just under the chin. It looks like the wound we found on Brigid Dowling's cabbie."

"I'll need to see Doctor MacKay's autopsy report to compare them."

"You'll have it," Tennant said. "The arsonist carried two milk cans filled with paraffin and dumped them at the side door."

A second pair of overturned cans lay nearby on the pathway. Twenty feet away, servants removed the last traces of paraffin from the steps.

"Somehow, he accidentally set fire to himself while delivering the second set of cans." Tennant shook his head. "It seems staggeringly inept. He ended up here, twenty paces into the grass."

"The impulse to run is strong. He should have fallen and rolled in the gravel, but . . ." Julia looked around. "I see nothing to run to . . . there's no fountain at this end of the garden."

"One of the guardsmen on sentry duty tried to fetch water from the house," Tennant said. "He slid on a paraffin-coated step and broke his leg, poor fellow. They took him to Westminster Hospital."

Julia looked up at the house. "Was the royal family . . ."

Tennant nodded. "In residence." He pointed to a pair of corner windows two floors above the side door. "The nursery, a footman told me."

"Good God," Julia said. She turned away, shaken.

A tall, slim gentleman dressed in gray striped trousers, a charcoal overcoat, a bowler, and a starched, stand-up collar rounded the front of the house. He hailed the inspector.

"One of our suspects," Tennant murmured to Julia as the man approached. "Doctor Julia Lewis, this is Sir Lionel Dermott, representing the Home Office."

Dermott touched the brim of his hat and offered his hand. "Doctor Lewis. Under other circumstances, I'd be charmed. But this ghastly sight . . ."

Tennant said, "It seems our channels of intelligence weren't—"

"We're a pack of fools played by knaves."

"Why 'played,' Sir Lionel?"

"We had one hundred and fifty Scots Fusiliers at Osborne House, guarding the queen against an impossible assault, while here . . ." He turned up his palms and looked around. "Who protected the heir to the throne in the heart of the capital? Pairs of guardsmen on sentry duty at the front and side gates and two sleepy bobbies patrolling the perimeter."

Tennant said, "Sir Lionel, those sentries—"

"I meant no criticism of them," Dermott said, flicking his hand. "The fault lies with their senior officers and Her Majesty's government."

"The young guardsmen at the side gate admitted a man in a dairyman's coat driving the expected milk wagon. He'd bundled up heavily about the neck and chin and below his prominent mustache. They exchanged only a few words as the man had a hacking cough."

"A mustache and a cough. Damnably clever." Sir Lionel touched his brim. "I'll let you and Doctor Lewis get on with your investigation."

Dermott walked away, kicking a stone. He headed toward the house and then changed direction, pulling a pipe from his pocket. Julia watched him drop onto a bench and light it. Lady Styles crossed the lawn and sat next to him.

"The mask has slipped," Tennant said. "You'll know what I mean when you see more of Sir Lionel Dermott."

"Where will the examinations take place? Horseferry Road?"

"Yes. As soon as that infernal police wagon arrives to transport the corpse. It's late."

"The milkman's body may tell us something. But given the state of this charred corpse, there's probably little it will reveal. Still, I'll do my best."

"I know you will. And like Sir Lionel, I wish the same were true about others." Tennant sighed. "That includes Sir Richard, but I'd say that to no one else."

Julia knew Tennant's loyalty and affection for his godfather ran deep. She touched his sleeve. "I'll speak to Lady Styles and meet you at the mortuary."

When Julia approached the bench, Sir Lionel uncrossed his long legs and got to his feet, offering the doctor his seat.

Julia nodded her thanks and sat next to Lady Styles. "How is Princess Alexandra?"

"Shaken. Appalled. Her windows overlook the garden. The man's screams woke her, and she saw the full horror. But the prince asked us not to mention the paraffin under the door. At least, not yet."

"And His Royal Highness?" Julia said.

Lady Styles looked at Dermott. "You were with him a little while ago."

"I've never seen him this furious," he said. "Bertie is a man who gives in to his appetites, but he controls his temper admirably. He has his provocations, God knows. Usually, only the absurd Scotsman, Brown, gets a rise out of him."

Julia asked, "Has the press gotten wind of this?"

"It was a small kitchen fire, quickly extinguished," Dermott said. "That's the folderol we'll peddle to the press."

Sir Lionel turned at the sound of hooves scattering gravel. A horseman trotted up the Marlborough's carriageway. He jumped from the saddle, tossed his reins to a footman, and dashed up the steps.

"The knight errant has arrived to console his princess," Sir Lionel said. "And on a white steed, no less."

Julia asked, "That gentleman is . . . ?"

"Captain Oliver Montgomery," Lady Styles said. "He is an equerry to the prince."

"And a slave to the princess." Dermott's mobile features flickered in amusement.

"Don't mock, Lionel," Susan said.

"Indeed, I don't." He turned to Julia. "Doctor, I am in awe

of Ollie's devotion. Truly. But alas, I would find his romantic self-sacrifice from afar quite . . . ah . . . *un*satisfying."

He accompanied the drawn-out word with a crooked smile, arched eyebrows, and a music-hall leer that telegraphed his meaning. Julia looked at Lady Styles, and they laughed.

"That's the spirit." He took each of their hands and kissed them in turn. "A doctor and a widow-lady. Absurd to be missish." Then he trotted along the path to Marlborough Road, waving his gloves behind him.

"Sir Lionel is an acquired taste," Lady Styles said.

"Inspector Tennant said something of the sort."

"I'm happy to see you, Doctor, despite . . . but perhaps this isn't the time to ask a favor."

"What can I do?"

"I'd planned to write to you today with a request. Princess Louise wishes to visit your clinic if she may. On some suitable day, of course."

Julia smiled wryly. "Planning an appropriate day at Whitechapel Clinic is tricky. One must forge ahead and hope for the best. So, any day that suits the princess."

"Is tomorrow morning too soon? A visit would be a welcome distraction. That's not the right word. It's not a whim on her part. You'll find that Princess Louise has a keen interest in medicine."

"A diversion after this horror isn't a bad thing."

"And you wrote to me, asking about Lizzie Dowling's employment. Princess Louise will tell you what she remembers. I questioned the housekeeper at Osborne over Christmas, but I'm afraid she wasn't much help. She arrived several years after the girl first arrived."

"Let's say tomorrow at eleven?" Julia stood and offered her hand. "The police wagon is here, so I must go."

Tennant entered the mortuary's examining room with Dr. MacKay's autopsy of Brigid's cabbie tucked under his arm.

Julia had completed the milkman's postmortem and was working on the charred corpse.

Tennant handed her Dr. MacKay's report. "Mister Downey Senior is here with Sergeant O'Malley."

"His son's body is ready for identification," she said. "A young man in the prime of life."

"Engaged to be married, Mister Downey told me."

Julia sighed. "Poor girl." She paged through the report until she found Dr. MacKay's description of the cabbie's stab wound. "I'd say the causes of death are consistent. A single thrust using a sharp, narrow blade, inserted at the top of the throat immediately under the chin."

"A piece of physical evidence links the crimes, as well. A copper thought he found a pair of damaged spectacles in the grass. The metal ear hooks match the ones on the ginger beard found by our young mud larks."

"So, this man, the arsonist . . ." Julia looked at the remains on the second table.

"Is likely the murderer of Brigid Dowling and the cabbie."

At the Yard on Saturday morning, Tennant set aside the morning paper. *A kitchen fire at Marlborough House. Sir Lionel was right about the story.*

A constable knocked. "Parcel dropped off for you with the duty sergeant, sir. By Doctor Lewis's coachman."

Tennant untied the string, and two autopsy reports slid from the paper wrapper. He started with the shorter one, the burn victim's examination, thinking, *This won't take long.*

He reached the end of the first paragraph and swore. Then he grabbed his hat and overcoat and scrambled out the door.

At 11:00 a.m., staccato knocks on Julia's door and Jackie Archer's breathless "She's here" announced the royal visitor. Her young orderly stood back to let the doctor pass through the office doorway.

Lady Styles and Princess Louise had only gotten as far as the waiting room's first bench. The princess crouched to bring her eyes level with a little girl's gaze. They opened as wide as a pair of gold sovereigns when her mother whispered, "This is Princess Louise, Sally." When the girl tried to wipe her nose with her sleeve, her mother stopped her hand.

"I had a bad cold before Christmas, just like yours," the princess said. "And I never had enough of these about me." She pulled a handkerchief from her muff and handed it to the little girl. She straightened up, saying, "I hope you feel better soon, Sally," touching her lightly under the chin.

The mother tried to return the handkerchief, but the princess shook her head. "A gift." Louise smiled as she passed two elderly men who struggled to their feet, doffing their caps. For her part, the doctor dropped a respectable curtsey and opened her office door.

Lady Styles gave Julia a card. "The photographers, Hills and Saunders, sent Her Royal Highness a box of these."

It was a carte de visite, a photograph the size of a calling card, a head-and-shoulders picture of the princess. PHOTOGRAPHERS TO THE QUEEN and the royal crest were printed on the back. Louise had signed, starting with a bold "L," the tail of the ending "e" in "Louise," extending like an underline beneath her name.

"I never know what to do with them," the princess said. "I thought perhaps your patients? A token of apology for disturbing their rest. Susan thought twenty-five was about the right number, but I could send more if they're needed."

"We have eleven patients occupying beds today. Twenty-five are enough for my staff."

"Oh, that's splendid, then."

Julia said, "Shall we begin our tour?"

They started with the two wards, the princess chatting easily with the patients bold enough to speak to her. Lady Styles trailed behind, handing out the cartes de visite. After that, Julia explained the workings of the outpatient dispensary and showed the princess their well-equipped fever room.

"Empty just now, thank heaven," Julia said. Then they returned to the doctor's office for tea. "Oh dear. I meant to add some coal to my fire."

"Please," Louise said quickly. "Not on my account."

Lady Styles smiled. "Like the queen, the princess prefers a room to feel like January, not July."

"It's true," the princess said. "It's the one thing Mama and I never quarrel about."

Louise walked to a poster illustrating the body's muscular structure. "Fascinating," she murmured. Then the princess took her seat, accepting a cup and saucer from Julia.

Lady Styles said, "Princess Louise visited Elizabeth Garrett's dispensary for women and children last year."

"She's accomplished wonders in Marylebone," Julia said. "Especially during last year's cholera outbreak."

"Oh yes," the princess said. "And Doctor Garrett told me she visited *your* dispensary before setting up hers. After that, I knew I wanted to meet you, but I wasn't able . . ." The animation vanished from Louise's face, and she looked away.

Lady Styles's gaze shifted from the princess to Julia. She set down her cup and saucer.

"One had such a sense of life amid death at that dispensary. So many fell ill with cholera and succumbed, yet the work continued, and lives were saved." She glanced back at the princess; Louise stared into her teacup. Julia wondered at the alteration in mood. Susan pressed on. "Life and death. As a physician, you must understand its mysteries better than most, Doctor Lewis."

"The cause of a life's end is sometimes clear," Julia said. "Often, it's not. For me, the greater wonder is the life force in a living being. What impels it, keeps it surging, keeps the heart beating, day after day? That's the mystery."

"Yes . . . the life force." The princess sat forward, animated once again. The 'aliveness' of living beings is something I struggle with . . . it's a challenge for a sculptor. Oh, for painters, too." She waved her teaspoon. "But to take a lump of clay, to chisel a piece of marble. To animate it, make it seem to breathe . . ."

Lady Styles smiled. "You've gathered that Her Royal Highness is an ardent student of the sculptural arts."

"If only Mama wouldn't stand in my way. The queen would prefer I paint flowers or sketch landscapes."

"I understand Her Majesty is a talented painter," Julia said.

"Yes, she is. But Mama thinks sculpture is unladylike because sculptors carve and hammer. And she doesn't like that it requires a close study of the human body. Something she deems inappropriate for females. But I will wear Mama down." The princess put her cup and saucer aside. "Now, Doctor, before I forget. You asked about poor Lizzie."

"Anything you remember might be useful."

"She came to us shortly after dearest Papa died, so I'm afraid it is no use asking the queen. That time is a blank to her. My brother doesn't remember—"

"The Prince of Wales?" Julia asked. *Good Lord.* Had her request become a general discussion?

"Yes. Bertie said if anyone knows, Alice will."

Lady Styles said, "Princess Louise's sister, Princess Alice of Hesse."

"During those black months, she relieved Mama of all domestic cares. I've written to her in Germany, but it may take some time to hear back."

"Thank you, Princess Louise."

She sighed. "It may come to nothing, but for Lizzie's sake . . ." Then Louise brightened. "You would approve of my sister, Doctor Lewis. When Hesse filled with the wounded during the late war with Prussia, she took charge of the capital's field hospitals."

Julia looked away from the princess and spotted Tennant outside her door. "Will you excuse me for a moment? I see Inspector Tennant in the foyer."

"No, no," Princess Louise said, getting to her feet. "I've taken up too much of your time. Come, Susan. We'll leave Doctor Lewis to get on with her day."

Tennant joined Julia on the doorstep as the carriage rolled away. "A hired four-wheeler, not a royal coach," he said. "I had no idea who was with you until Nurse Clemmie told me."

"Princess Louise is astonishingly unroyal," Julia said, smiling. "If that's a word."

"I thought the same thing when I met her at Osborne House."

Julia glanced at the autopsy report in his hand. "You have questions?"

"Yes. Well, one."

"Come inside, then."

He followed her into her office and looked around. "It's my first time back since—"

"Last June. Before you left for France."

Tennant sighed. "Julia, I should have tried to see you and caught a later train. I owed you an explanation, not a rushed note scribbled in Kent. You had every right to be angry."

"'Deflated' is a better word. We'd uncovered the truth together. I felt . . . dismissed as a colleague. And slighted as a friend."

"I'm sorry."

"My relief that you were safe after those silent, anxious weeks was . . ." Julia shook her head. "I know I didn't sound relieved. More like a mother who shouts at her child for nearly running under a carriage."

He took a step, closing the gap between them. "Forgive me."

Julia looked into his gray eyes framed by dark lashes. When she first knew him, Julia had called them "granite eyes." But the emotions that flickered in them were new to her. *Relief? Some-*

thing more? she wondered. Eyes that had once seemed cold looked lit from within. Seconds passed, and the office that felt chilly earlier seemed warmer.

He offered his hand, palm up. "It's a new year," he said. "Shall we begin again?"

Julia placed hers in his. Her voice caught when she said, "Yes, Richard. Please." He seemed in no hurry to take his hand away. Neither was she. Julia turned it over, traced the scar with her fingertip, and smiled. "This has healed, too."

"Yes. Mended."

Julia released his hand. "You said you had a question about the postmortem."

"It relates to the man's height."

"He was about average for an English male. Five feet, six inches."

Tennant asked, "Are you certain?"

She sat back against the edge of her desk. "Within an inch or so. All the man's bones were present, so it's not hard to ascertain. The broken teeth all along the left side of the mouth will be useful for identification. They resulted from a fight or an injury. They're not from natural wear or poor nutrition."

"Something is wrong," Tennant said.

"What is?"

"Sir Lionel called the arsonist 'damnably clever,' the way he disguised himself to gain access to the grounds. And the man who murdered Brigid and the cabbie was a cold-blooded killer, careful to an extreme."

"True."

"Yet, we're meant to believe the same man who killed them made a careful plan to torch Marlborough House but burned himself alive by mistake?"

"When you put it that way . . ."

"O'Malley located a sharp-eyed sweeper who saw a *tall* man with Brigid Dowling. Someone over six feet got into the cab with her, not a man of average height."

"So, the dead man at Marlborough House— "

"Is too short to be Brigid's killer," Tennant said.

"But her cabbie and the milkman in the back of the wagon were killed in the identical way."

Tennant nodded. "By a tall man, wielding a thin blade, thrust under the chin. He's still out there, Julia, committing murders linked to the royals. And he's added paraffin to his arsenal."

Raucous laughter erupted from the men's ward. Julia and Tennant exchanged glances and walked into the foyer.

A burly man wearing the gaiters and leather apron of a brewer said, "Look at him, Tim. Blushing like a bleedin' maiden."

Nurse Clemmie said, "You'll have to remove those trousers if the doctor is to take a look."

The sandy-haired young man gripped his waistband, scowling. "I'll ruddy well wait for him then."

"The doctor is a 'her,' so there's nothing for it." Clemmie hooked a finger under one of his braces and pulled it off his shoulder. "You best get on with it, lad."

"Come on, Freddie," the brewer said. "Drop your drawers. Someone's got to sew up that gash on your arse."

"My cue, Inspector," Julia said, smiling. "I'd best get on with it, too."

"So must I," Tennant said. "I've been summoned to a meeting at the Home Office."

CHAPTER 10

Inspector Tennant and Sergeant O'Malley were the first to arrive for the meeting with the home secretary.

Mr. Gathorne-Hardy's assistant ushered Tennant and O'Malley into a conference room. The bald and bespectacled Mr. Greaves was as starchy as his shirt's stand-up collar and looked like he'd swallowed a lemon. He pursed his lips, commanding them to wait rather than inviting them to sit.

"Frosty bugger," the sergeant muttered after the door closed.

Tennant circled the empty room, examining the portraits of past home secretaries. Minutes ticked by, and Greaves opened the door again. Mr. Gathorne-Hardy bustled in, taking the seat at the head of the mahogany table. Sir Lionel Dermott and Sir Richard Mayne followed, nodding to Tennant and O'Malley. Mister Greaves ushered a fourth gentleman to the table and closed the door. The newcomer sported a drooping mustache, lavish side whiskers, and the blue frock coat and red-striped trousers of an officer in the Cold Stream Guards.

The home secretary waved Tennant and O'Malley to chairs and nodded to Sir Lionel.

Dermott made the introductions. "Inspector Tennant, you know everyone except Colonel William Fielding. He's heading up the Fenian division. Colonel, Patrick O'Malley is the inspector's sergeant."

Gathorne-Hardy cleared his throat. "Thank you, Sir Lionel. Our subject is the outrage yesterday morning at Marlborough House. Her Majesty's government is dismayed by the incident. 'Dismayed' is a poor word to describe our reaction to the most recent debacle in a string of Yard failures."

Sir Richard scowled. "I take exception— "

"But it wasn't *exceptional,* was it?" Sir Lionel ticked off on his fingers, "A dead Manchester police sergeant, the Irish prisoners he guarded in the wind, and the Clerkenwell Prison blown to bits. Scotland Yard seems singularly out of its depth."

"The Yard got wind of both those plots from a trusted source," Colonel Fielding said. "Local police bungling is responsible for the failures on the spot."

Dermott shrugged. "Contrast that with policing in Ireland, Colonel. Over the past year, Dublin's coppers thwarted every Irish scheme without a stumble."

"Talking of plots and blunders," Tennant said. "What about the stolen rifles shipped from France? Shouldn't they have turned up by now?"

"It's too early to assume the worst," Sir Lionel said with a flicker of a smile. "But point taken, Inspector."

"These damnable Yankee Irishmen . . ." Colonel Fielding smacked the tabletop with the flat of his hand. "Why don't they stay on their side of the Atlantic?"

After a brief silence, O'Malley said, "They'll not be forgetting the famine and their starving mothers giving them the bread from their mouths. An ocean isn't wide enough for that."

The colonel's drooping mustaches wobbled. "Damn it, man, you're not in sympathy with these brotherhood bastards, are you?"

The home secretary raised his hands. “Gentleman, let us set history aside and address the present. Colonel, what about this ‘trusted source’ you mentioned?”

“Trusted?” Dermott said. “He warned of phantom attacks on the queen at Balmoral and Osborne but stayed silent about the arson at Marlborough House. Why is that, Colonel?”

Fielding scowled. “I don’t know. Our man has . . . disappeared. He left his lodgings the night of the fire and hasn’t returned.”

Tennant and O’Malley exchanged glances. The inspector asked, “Is your source a man of average height with broken teeth along his upper left jaw?”

“But how . . .” Fielding stuttered. “See here, how do you—”

Sir Lionel smiled above tented fingers. “Does that describe the charred victim at Marlborough House?”

“Yes,” Tennant said. “Someone silenced your reliable source. What was his name?”

“Boyle,” Colonel Fielding said. “Daniel Boyle.”

Sir Lionel noted the name. “Kindly send me what you have on the man, Colonel.”

“Inspector, where do we stand?” Gathorne-Hardy asked.

Tennent spent ten minutes reviewing the murder cases and tracing their linkages to the Dowling sisters’ deaths. Colonel Fielding refused to concede the connections.

“A knife wound to a cabdriver’s neck?” The colonel snorted. “That’s your evidence? Surely, it’s commonplace among the ruffians you see in your line of work, Tennant.”

“There is something singular about these throat wounds.”

“He didn’t stab the girl on the Isle of Wight,” the home secretary said.

“I think our killer wanted to mask that first murder, sir. Make the authorities believe the suicide or accident theories.”

Fielding flicked his hand as if brushing away an annoying gnat. “I say it’s thin. Irish rebels, arson, and murdered servant girls? A link is farfetched. A fiction.”

O'Malley cleared his throat. "With respect, Colonel, are you forgetting the theatrical disguises? The taxi passenger with the ginger beard and the mustachioed man driving the milk wagon."

"The wire frames are similar," Tennant said. "I'd say coincidence as an explanation is *farfetched*."

The colonel glared at the repetition of his word. "Damn it, Tennant, you're saying the queen's servant girl was—"

"Linked, somehow, to an Irish Republican Brotherhood conspiracy." Dermott smiled. "Dashed inconvenient."

"No, by God," Fielding shouted. "It's damned preposterous!"

After the meeting broke up, Dermott invited Tennant and the sergeant to his office. Sir Lionel pointed them to a pair of comfortable leather club chairs, lined three glasses on his desk, and produced two bottles from his bottom drawer.

"Scotch whisky or Irish, gentlemen? I'm making a life study of my preference. Sergeant, I'm guessing you vote for the nectar of your native heath."

"That would be grand."

Sir Lionel poured three tots of Bushmills and raised his glass. "To your very good health, and apologies about that Scotland Yard crack."

O'Malley said, "*Sláinte*," followed by Tennant's "Cheers."

Dermott sipped and settled back in his chair. "A pity Her Majesty's government didn't send Colonel Fielding to Egypt or the Sudan. So much lovely sand for head sticking."

"The colonel seems unpersuadable," Tennant said. "Not a constructive outlook for a man leading an investigation."

"May I inquire about your next steps?" Dermott waggled his eyebrows. "Or would you infer nefarious motives behind my innocent question? Chief among your suspects, as I am."

"We've had officers canvass the theatrical suppliers for the buyer of a ginger beard," Tennant said. "We'll send them back, asking about the mustache."

O'Malley said, "The dairyman drove south from Camden Town, a three-mile trip to the center of London. Coppers on the graveyard shifts along the way are questioning the early risers."

"And, like you," Tennant said, "I want to know more about this informant, Daniel Boyle." The inspector shrugged. "All this is standard police procedure. No state secrets, so no harm done . . . whatever your motives, Sir Lionel."

Dermott sighed. "If only I could convince you of my innocence. Still, I see it's hopeless, barring . . ."

"Barring what, Sir Lionel?"

"Why, the swift arrest of Peter FitzGerald, of course."

On Sunday, a tall, thin man in a bowler hat took the train from London to Windsor and arrived shortly after one o'clock. He exited the station and blinked, his pale blue eyes sensitive to the bright sunlight.

A short walk down the High Street brought him to the churchyard. Morning services had concluded, and he noticed no one about. He pretended to look at the gravestones, his head down, his pale eyes shifting left and right, confirming that no one observed him. Then he crossed St. Alban's Street, entered the woods, and settled among a grove of yews. From there, he had a clear view of a lone cottage at the edge of Windsor Great Park.

He struck a match, applied it to the bowl of his pipe, and flicked it away, waiting for the lady to take her afternoon walk. She never missed a day when the weather was favorable. And that afternoon was crisp and clear, a glorious January day for an English winter.

A few minutes after the tower bells rang twice, an elderly lady rounded the path and made her way to a bench within a quiet grove. Nothing moved: not a sigh of wind, nor a darting squirrel, nor a flutter of wings amid the branches. He knocked the remains from his pipe, circled the grove, and came upon her as if he were out for an afternoon stroll.

The man lifted his hat. "I wonder if you remember me, my lady?"

She didn't. Not at first. No surprise, as he'd heard that her memory was fading. He'd been counting on it.

"May I?" he asked, gesturing to the space beside her on the bench.

They spoke about the weather. Then he asked if she remembered the royal visit to Ireland. She had. He brought the conversation around to a young servant girl the lady had befriended.

She supplied the name without missing a beat. "Lizzie Dowling. And her sister. We saved them from the nest. Not like those other poor creatures."

Her mention of "nest" would have meant nothing to most listeners. But the man sighed. *Nothing for it,* he thought. *No loose ends.*

She smiled sweetly. "We saved them, the captain and I."

Her last remark settled the matter, so he rose from the bench. "Let me rearrange your cushion."

"Thank you, young man. Most kind."

He slipped the pillow from behind her back, pushed her down, and covered her face until she was still. Then, he propped her up, her head tipping forward, and replaced the cushion behind her back.

He retraced his steps to the station. There was no need to rush; he had ample time until his train. And a man in a hurry was a man remembered. He brushed at his sleeves, plucking a small goose feather that clung to his coat. At the station, he passed a stream of excited Eton schoolboys in wide, white collars, ears protruding from under the brims of their top hats, waving cricket bats to their friends. Harried parents followed in their wake. The beginning-of-term pandemonium was ideal for getting lost in a crowd.

That afternoon's work had been an unfortunate necessity, but the previous one had been his pleasure. So, the next would be.

And then the last.

On Monday at noon, Lady Styles slipped out of the side entrance of Marlborough House and lifted her face to the sun. There was just enough time for a walk around the grounds. The stretch of cold but clear weather continued for a sixth day into the new year, and it was a pleasure to be out of doors. Susan circled the east garden and sat on the bench on the great lawn. She opened the letter she'd received that morning and reread it, smiling.

"May I join you?" Princess Louise called, striding across the lawn. "I saw you from my window."

"Of course." Lady Styles pulled away her skirts to make room on the bench and folded her letter.

Princess Louise said, "Please, not on my account. Finish it."

"It's from my bank manager, and I've read it twice." She tucked it into her pocket. "My royal stipend and a small legacy from an elderly aunt have my affairs in order. He can put a scheme of mine in motion."

"A plan you can share, or would you prefer to wait until it's in place?"

"I'll tell you at once. My banker has reviewed the leasing arrangements for a small flat. Now, in the months I'm not waiting on Princess Alexandra, I have somewhere to go besides my brother and sister-in-law's house."

Princess Louise sighed. "How I envy you, although most would think me spoiled to say it. What care in the world could a royal princess have?"

Susan reached for her hand. "I know things are difficult. Your life isn't all you'd wish it to be. I'm sorry."

"I'm twenty this year, and Mama has begun to discuss marriage. I'm sure she plans to marry me off to some . . . some German princeling or other." Louise flicked a dismissive hand.

"Like your sisters." Susan had learned something in royal service: the queen's adult children were also Her Majesty's subjects. *And daughters are more subject than sons.*

"Those marriages were Papa's dearest wish. Alice . . . I'm not sure she's happy, but Vicky adores Fritz. It's Prussia she loathes. There she is, the Princess Royal of England, a captive in a foreign land." Louise slumped on the bench. "I cannot bear the thought of leaving my homeland. To be away from . . . everything."

A hansom cab rattled through the side gate and stopped before it reached the front entrance. Sir Lionel Dermott paid off the driver and strode across the lawn.

"Thank goodness." He bowed to the princess and took Susan's hand. "If you are out here, I'm not late for luncheon in there." He cocked his thumb at Marlborough House.

"You've arrived in good time," said Princess Louise, "and we could use a bit of cheering up."

"Ah, court jester. My favorite role. You'll permit me to join you?" Lionel extracted a large paisley handkerchief from his pocket, arranged it on the lawn, and sat cross-legged. "Now, what are we talking about?"

"Marriage, as it happens," Princess Louise said. "What is your opinion? But perhaps you're not the best judge. I notice you haven't rushed to sample its joys."

"Marriage . . ." Lionel stroked his chin. "Now that depends. If you mean matrimony in general, I approve. If you are speaking of one in particular . . . as a rule, I advise caution." He smiled. "Princess, my lady, please consult me before taking any drastic step."

Susan turned at the sound of a rider. Oliver Montgomery had entered on horseback. "Alix's last luncheon guest has arrived," she said.

Lionel sighed. "Ollie makes me quite ashamed. I really must exercise my filly more often. Can I persuade you ladies to join me for a ride sometime this week?"

"Only if you promise us a good canter," Louise said.

"Perhaps we should go in?" Susan said. "It must be nearly time."

Lionel uncrossed his legs and rose in a fluid motion. Then he swept up his handkerchief, flourished it in a circle, and stuffed it into his pocket.

"Neatly done, Sir Lionel," Louise said. "An acrobat as well as a jester."

"My dear Princess, one learns to be nimble in government service." Dermott offered his arms to the ladies. "Who else is expected at luncheon?"

"Peter FitzGerald and his wife," Louise said.

"Harriet FitzGerald . . . Do you know, I imagined I saw Your Royal Highness on Bond Street last Thursday," Lionel said. "I had prepared my best bow when I saw it wasn't the princess after all. It was Harriet."

"So, you made your second-best bow?" Susan said.

Lionel grinned. "I ducked into a doorway and avoided it altogether."

"What an odd mistake," Louise said.

"I had the same sensation at the ball," Susan said as they walked across the lawn. "It's the style of hair and manner of dress that are similar."

Lionel said, "They say imitation is flattery, Princess."

They parted briefly inside the house for the ladies to dispose of their wraps and hats and freshen up in their rooms. Ten minutes later, Susan joined Lionel at the dining room doorway.

Dermott took her elbow and drew her aside. "I hope your first experience—and the unhappy examples around you—haven't turned you against the married state."

"Whom do you mean?"

Lionel looked meaningfully at the Prince of Wales as he handed Princess Alexandra to her seat. "And Harriet Fitz-Gerald. It looks like the bloom is off *that* rose," he said softly. "She and the major seem to lead separate lives these days."

"Harriet prefers London to Windsor and Balmoral."

"A pity. The queen avoids Buckingham Palace as if it were a plague site. Still, FitzGerald manages to get away to the capital for . . . entertainments of his own."

"What are you saying, Lionel?"

Princess Louise's appearance, followed by a footman, spared him a reply.

"Excuse me, Your Royal Highness." The servant offered the princess a silver platter. "A message."

She read it and smiled at her brother. "Bertie, I'm borrowing your private secretary this afternoon. Mister Fisher is taking me to the telegraph office to send a cable."

On Monday, Sergeant O'Malley dropped a stack of reports on Inspector Tennant's desk with a grunt of disgust.

"Days of asking and still nothing from the canvass of the milkman's route. High time one of our coppers turned up something."

"I wouldn't count on it, "Tennant said. "Our murderer is a disciplined fellow. Discipline reminds me . . ." He leaned back in his desk chair and contemplated the cracks in the ceiling plaster. "The military is well represented among our suspects."

"'Tis true," O'Malley said. "We have two captains—Montgomery and Locock—and Major FitzGerald in the frame."

"Then there's Sir Lionel, who resigned his commission as captain several years ago. I need a better sense of them as men."

"Three of our pigeons belonged to the same Guards regiment."

"Yes . . . the Blues," Tennant said. "Except for Major Fitz-Gerald, who was in the 4th Royal Irish Dragoons."

O'Malley shrugged. " 'Tis a shame none of them were in the Grenadier Guards. You'd be knowing them, I'm guessing."

Tennant righted his chair. "That's a thought, Paddy. Ask around the Yard. Coppers who served in the ranks in Crimea. See if you can find someone who fought with either regiment."

"Ought to be someone. Or someone who knows someone."

"Meanwhile, I had it from the constable who walks Captain Locock's beat that he's back from the Isle of Wight. I thought of sending him a note at the Colonial Office, but I'll arrive unannounced."

"Sure, an interview with the fella is overdue," O'Malley said.

"I'll push him hard and see what turns up."

The Colonial Office was a short walk down Whitehall Road, well within the tolerance of Tennant's leg. As was true of the world, the Colonial Office building encompassed petty kingdoms and great ones, too. A walk down a long corridor brought the inspector to a distant room. With little space to spare, the door announced its occupant: ASSISTANT TO THE PERMANENT UNDERSECRETARY OF STATE FOR THE COLONIES. Smaller letters underneath informed a visitor that "Captain Frederick H. L. Locock" served as "Director of Affairs for the Crown Colony of Malta." Tennant knocked and entered at the command, "Come."

A lanky, dark-haired man pushed a pile of newspapers aside and hauled himself out of his leather chair. *Six-foot-two, if he's an inch*, Tennant thought. Locock's Monday copy of *The Times* looked pristine, but Tennant spotted the masthead of the *Sporting Gazette* peeking from under it.

Tennant removed his hat. "Detective Inspector Tennant from the Metropolitan Police. You are Captain Frederick Locock?"

The man's welcoming smile and outstretched arm froze. Then he blinked and grasped Tennant's hand as if released by some hidden spring. "That's right, Inspector." Locock gestured to the club chair in front of his desk. "Grab a pew."

"Thank you, Captain."

Captain Locock said, "I spoke with Oliver Montgomery at Christmas, so I have a general idea of why you're here."

"That saves time. I have a pair of Irish sisters murdered in London and on the Isle of Wight. Two nights ago, an Irish police informer burned to death on the grounds of Marlborough House. Physical evidence links that death to the murder of the second girl, Brigid Dowling."

"Your summary is clear but incredible, Inspector. I cannot fathom the connection."

"You just returned from the Isle of Wight. I understand that you travel back and forth and were there in July as a guest of the Prince of Wales. Is that correct?"

"Yes."

"The lady who was soon to become Mrs. Frederick Locock . . . she didn't accompany you on that trip?"

"No."

"A last fling at bachelorhood?"

"I don't know what you mean to infer, but it's damned offensive."

Tennant shrugged. "How can I offend if my inference isn't clear? Let me make my meaning plain. A gentleman spends time away with male friends shortly before his nuptials. The . . . frolics at such gatherings are well-known."

"Not to me, Inspector."

"Captain Locock, you were a guest at Osborne House in July when someone impregnated Lizzie Dowling."

Tennant waited. Locock squirmed but said nothing.

"After your wedding trip, you returned to the Isle of Wight in October. Someone murdered Lizzie Dowling in October. Someone who held her head under the water until she drowned."

"I know nothing about it. To imply I do is outrageous."

"You attended the Marlborough House ball in December and were privy to her sister's travel plans. Captain, you are one of a small fraternity I can place in all three locations at the relevant times."

Locock stared and blinked rapidly. Then he relaxed his shoulders and spread his hands. "As you say, I am *one* of a group of men. But not the right one. You must search for your killer among the others in your 'fraternity.'"

"Describe, if you will, your movements on the afternoon of Lizzie Dowling's murder. You recall the day, I presume. The murder of a queen's servant isn't an everyday affair."

"I spent the day at my father's house. He was absent, attending the royal family at Osborne House. I went for a long walk and returned for tea in the late afternoon. I cannot be more precise about time."

"You saw no one?"

He shrugged. "Some farm workers, bringing in the hay. I doubt they noticed me, either."

"And Mrs. Locock? Will she confirm your statement if asked?"

"Damn it, Inspector. I don't want her bothered. She's not strong, and she's worried about our baby just now."

"I'm sorry to hear that. And where were you Thursday night and into the early hours of Friday morning?"

"I was at my club and returned home around one. And before you ask, I let myself in with my latchkey and slept in my dressing room, not wanting to disturb my wife."

"Can a coachman or cabbie confirm the time of your return?

"I belong to the Army and Navy." Locock glanced at Tennant's regimental tie. "You know the club and my address in town?" Tennant nodded. "Then you know it's a short walk along Pall Mall to my house."

"I believe your town house is a grace-and-favor," Tennant said. "Interesting term. Tell me, what *favor* made the prince *grace* you with that expensive address?"

At last, Tennant thought he'd rattled the man. Locock licked his lips. His gaze dropped to the desktop. "Bertie . . . His Royal Highness is generous to his friends."

Tennant stood. "It's unfortunate that you can't supply an alibi for any of the days and times in question."

"That proves nothing."

"True. But it means you remain a person of interest." Tennant tugged his hat in place. "Good afternoon, Captain."

The inspector exited and glanced back at the nameplate on the closed door. He smiled. *I've rattled Captain Frederick H. L. Locock, Director of Affairs for the Crown Colony of Malta.*

Dr. Andrew Lewis folded Tuesday's *Times* and laid it beside his breakfast plate.

"Why the sigh, Grandfather?"

"At my age, one shouldn't read the death notices. It's not a week into the new year, and I just saw a familiar name."

"Someone I know?"

"Ancient history, my dear. A great beauty from the time just after Waterloo." Dr. Lewis chuckled. "One should be grateful not to find one's name on the page."

Mrs. Ogilvie entered the dining room with a fresh pot of tea and a note for Julia.

"A footman is waiting for a reply."

Julia held the letter and looked around the table. "I have jam on my knife. May I borrow yours?"

"Allow me." Dr. Lewis slit the black-bordered envelope with a clean blade and handed it back.

"From Lady Styles," Julia said. "She asks if she and Mrs. Frederick Locock could come in tomorrow morning for consultations."

"My, my. Early in the new year, and you're attracting the carriage trade. Things are starting well, my dear."

Julia smiled wryly. "No need to consult my diary to see if I'm free. Willie Oakes is coming in today and—"

"The young chap who lives at number twenty-six?"

"Yes. A sprained wrist and time for the splint to come off. But my appointment book is blank for tomorrow."

The housekeeper brought in a pen, paper, and an envelope; Julia scratched out a reply.

"Mrs. Frederick Locock . . ." Dr. Lewis mused. "Sir Charles's daughter-in-law?"

"Yes." Julia signed with a flourish. "So, I must be on my mettle." Julia sealed up the note and handed it to Mrs. Ogilvie. "For the footman."

Dr. Lewis reached across the table and squeezed Julia's hand. "Things *are* looking up, my dear."

"Lady Styles also writes that she has something to tell me . . . Let me see." Julia scanned the letter. " 'Information to impart about my inquiry,' she says."

"*Your* inquiry?"

Julia smiled. "A small matter the inspector may have overlooked."

CHAPTER 11

Mrs. Locock and her baby arrived promptly at ten on Wednesday morning. Lady Styles waited in Julia's outer room with the child's nursemaid.

Mary Locock laid the boy on Julia's examining table, peeled back two layers of blankets, and untied the strings of an outer hat, revealing a knitted cap underneath. A five-month-old with blond curls, blue eyes, and a runny nose emerged from his wrappings.

"This dreadful weather, but I bundled baby Henry up."

"A case of the sniffles, I see," Julia said.

"My husband thinks I fuss. He's a great believer in mustard plasters for colds, but I wasn't sure. What do you think, Doctor?"

"I wouldn't apply one to a baby's delicate skin. It does nothing but cause blisters. Let's have a look."

Julia performed an ear, nose, and throat examination. She listened to the baby's lungs and heart, inspected his skin, and checked for a rash under his nappy. Then she weighed him.

Julia asked, "Is he eating well?"

"Yes. My father-in-law arranged for a wet nurse. Sally, poor soul, lost her husband and only child last year. She is waiting outside with Susan."

"Henry's weight is normal for his age, so all seems well."

The mother bit her lip and looked down at the baby. "One hears so many things about wet nurses."

"Such as?"

"A relative who visited over Christmas told me . . . She said . . . Well, my cousin painted a very dark picture."

Heaven, defend us from well-meaning relations. Julia asked, "Tell me, does Sally live with you?"

"Yes, and she is a tidy and most respectable person. And so fond of my little boy."

"Then let me ease your mind. Sally is well-nourished and lives in a warm, comfortable home. You have nothing to worry about."

"Thank goodness. And little Henry . . . What is your opinion, Doctor?"

"Children catch colds, and you're right to be concerned. But I listened to his chest, and his lungs are clear. So is the discharge from his nose, a sign there's no underlying infection."

"He is so precious to us. A gift from God after I thought I'd never . . ." Mrs. Locock sighed. "I had little choice about hiring a wet nurse. Henry is adopted."

"I see."

"As a girl, I never began my monthly flow. The doctor's examination found that my womb hadn't developed properly."

"It's a rare condition. I'm sorry, Mrs. Locock."

"Frederick said it didn't matter, but I hesitated when he asked me to marry him. Then his father heard about a baby. My father-in-law said the mother was unmarried but from a good family."

Julia nodded. "I know of other such arrangements."

"Frederick and I wed last summer in some haste, in time to receive the child."

"So, marriage and motherhood all at once."

"Yes." She looked down at the baby and stroked his hair. "Henry . . . although my husband wants to call him by one of his middle names, Leicester. He thinks it sounds distinguished. I think it's a mouthful."

"Well, whatever his name, it's a happy conclusion."

"For us, certainly. But I sometimes think . . ." She bit her lip. "I wonder about the mother. Who she is. If she's at peace. Frederick says I mustn't dwell on it."

"Well, we can't always command our thoughts. It seems natural to wonder. But don't worry about your baby. He'll be fine in a few days." Julia smiled. "Whatever you decide to call him."

"Thank you, Doctor." Mrs. Locock gathered her things and stood.

Lady Styles and Julia walked Mrs. Locock and the wet nurse to their carriage. By the time they rolled away, the baby was asleep in his mother's arms.

"With the weather turning on us, she's anxious to get the baby home, Susan said. "I didn't want to make her wait for me. The fog is likely to grow worse."

"There's a cabstand a few steps away at the top of Circus Road, so you'll have no difficulty."

Lady Styles sighed. "Mary Locock is a sweet soul but a worrier."

"Not unusual with new mothers. Come inside." Julia took her arm. "And tell me what I can do for you."

"First, I have a request from the Princess of Wales." Susan smiled. "Your conversation about women patients preferring women doctors got her thinking. Could the princess call on you to treat the illnesses of her female household staff?"

"Of course. Princess Alexandra's offer is an honor."

"I explained to Alix that your afternoons are devoted to the clinic . . . but perhaps your mornings?"

"They're freer than I'd like, so yes."

"Splendid. I mentioned it to the housekeeper, hoping you'd agree." Susan smiled. "Mrs. Craddock said to put her name at the head of your list."

Julia shook her head. "This is a morning of surprises. Now, how can I help you?"

"I'm not ill, at least as far as I know. I suppose what I want is a . . . talking consultation."

"Very well." Julia gestured to a pair of chairs. "Let's sit by the fire." After Lady Styles had settled into her seat, Julia said, "Now, in your own good time, tell me your concerns."

Susan looked down at her hands. She twisted her wedding ring, frowning. "I suppose I should begin with my marriage. It wasn't a happy one. My husband died four years after our wedding."

"I've noticed your half mourning. So, you've been a widow for . . ."

"Nearly three years. I'm not naïve, Doctor. My late husband was my senior by over a decade, and one imagines men have . . . experiences that women lack."

"Generally, that's true."

"But I was unaware of the extent of my husband's profligacy. One isn't supposed to say these things, but his death was a release. Now, Alix's anxiety has made me wonder if I have reason to worry that he may have infected me."

Julia reached across and squeezed her hand. "If polite society knew how many ladies come to me with your fears. Let me see if I can relieve them."

The doctor questioned her about the range of syphilis symptoms. Happily, Lady Styles was free of them all.

"Timing is critical," Julia said. "The disease often goes through a long, latent period. And the sufferer is least infectious during the latent stage."

"So, my husband . . ."

"Either he was free of the disease, or his illness was at the stage when the disease was quiescent."

"Thank you, Doctor. You've lifted a weight. And should I ever marry again . . . Well, one wouldn't want to cause harm to another person."

"Of course." Julia wondered if she had a particular gentleman in mind.

Lady Styles opened her handbag's catch. "I also come as the bearer of news from Princess Louise. Information about Lizzie Dowling."

"The princess heard back from Germany so quickly?"

"After Princess Louise wrote to her sister, she decided the post would take too long. Her Royal Highness enlisted the prince's private secretary to help her send a cable."

"How good of her to take the trouble."

"Oh, she enjoyed it, believe me. The telegraph may become her preferred mode of communication. Princess Louise adores speed—on foot, horseback, and driving a carriage. She terrifies her sisters when she takes the reins." Lady Styles handed Julia a cable. "Princess Alice's reply."

The telegram read, ASK LADY MIDDLEBURY ABOUT HER LITTLE BIRD FROM KILDARE. WILL WRITE TODAY WITH DETAILS I REMEMBER. Julia looked up. "Who is Lady Middlebury?"

"She was the queen's lady of the bedchamber when Lizzie joined the royal household."

"Lady Middlebury's 'little bird from Kildare' . . . It's an odd phrase," Julia said. "Is the lady still in royal service?"

"She retired and lives in a grace-and-favor cottage near Windsor Castle." Susan frowned. "I'm afraid the subject of the cable came up at luncheon. Princess Louise explained its purpose and mentioned your name."

"May I ask who was lunching at the time?"

"Everyone on the inspector's list, I imagine," Susan said ruefully. "Except Captain Locock. I don't believe Princess Louise grasps the implications for her brother's circle of friends. Any novelty excites her, and the need to be discreet about the cable never occurred to her."

"What do you make of it all, Lady Styles? You are acquainted with all the—"

"Suspects? I suppose that's the word. Yes, I know them all. Some very well, making it more difficult to believe anyone is guilty."

"The first case I worked on with Inspector Tennant—and the most recent—the guilty parties were people I'd come to know."

"Are we to believe that anyone is capable of murder?"

"It's an unsettling thought."

"Lionel seems to think . . . He believes that Frederick Locock has risen to the top of the inspector's list. I'd put Captain Locock on the bottom, frankly."

"Inspector Tennant isn't the sort of policeman who fastens on a suspect and pursues one theory of a case." She held up the cable. "May I keep this? The inspector should see it."

Julia walked Lady Styles to the pavement, pointing out the cabstand just visible in the mist that crept along Circus Place. She watched Susan's cab disappear into the fog, happy she'd allayed her health questions, wondering about other suspicions the lady harbored. Susan Styles struck Julia as uncommonly intelligent. Was it as difficult as she claimed to think any one of the men was guilty? And why had she risen to the defense of Captain Locock?

Least likely, Susan thinks. I wonder who tops her list?

Tennant's hunch about army veterans at the Yard who served in the Crimea paid off.

O'Malley said, "A sergeant gave me the name of a fella in the Blues. Ted Watford. He walked a Westminster beat until the Met let him go for drunkenness on the job."

"Where do we find him?"

"He turns up from time to time at the Golden Lion. Old pals stand him a pint or two. But the man does his serious drinking near his home in Aldgate. 'Drowning his troubles,' the sergeant said."

"Do we know where, exactly?"

"The Hoop and Grapes on the High Street."

"Let's pay it a visit."

"Leads aren't thick on the ground, I'm thinking," O'Malley said, following him out the door.

After a week of clear weather, a "London particular" took hold on Wednesday, and their cab crawled from Westminster to Aldgate in the fog. At every intersection, coppers waved bull's-eye lanterns in the impenetrable gloom, trying to move the traffic along. After an hour's halting drive, their hackney stopped on the High Street in front of the only timber-and-wattle structure standing amid a row of brick houses. Gilt lettering on a black sign identified the Hoop and Grapes. It was late morning, but gaslights glowed yellow above the front door and the mullioned window.

Inside, a polished oak bar ran the length of the room. Bright, whitewashed rectangles of plaster wall shone between blackened half-timbered beams. A snowy-aproned barman with a handlebar mustache and pushed-back shirtsleeves nodded a greeting as he polished circles into the bar top.

"Your building is a survivor in the neighborhood," Tennant said. "Seventeenth century?"

"You've got that right, guvnor. The Great Fire stopped fifty yards from that door." The barman grinned. "They must have sold a pint or two that day."

"The firefighters would've had a thirst on them something fierce," O'Malley said.

"Speaking of . . . what can I get you gents?"

"Paddy?"

O'Malley smoothed his busy mustache. "'Tis a shade early, but a pint of Guinness wouldn't come amiss. And a cheese-and-pickle sandwich if there's one to be had."

"Make that two," Tennant said.

The publican drew two pints of stout, their creamy heads bulging above the rim. He set them on the bar and turned his attention to a carving board, slicing from a loaf of crusty bread. He layered on the cheddar, cracked open a new jar of chutney, spooned it on top, and delivered their plates.

"We're looking for an old colleague of ours," Tennant said. "Ted Watford."

He looked Tennant up and down. "You're coppers?"

"Detective Inspector Tennant. This is Sergeant O'Malley."

The barkeep gave him a doubtful look. "Ted's not in trouble, is he?"

"Not a bit of it," O'Malley said. "Information is what we're wanting."

The publican looked at the wall clock. "Shouldn't be long. Ted's usually here by now. Maybe this peasouper is slowing him down."

Tennant asked, "What does he usually drink?"

"Same as you."

"Slice up another sandwich. And draw a Guinness when he comes in."

The publican nodded. "He could use a meal that isn't only liquid."

Five minutes later, the door opened. "Morning, Ted," the barman said to the new arrival. "Couple of gents here to talk to you."

The inspector introduced himself and extended his hand. Warily, the man took it. Tennant noticed his tremor, bloodshot eyes, and cheeks covered in spidery veins. The barman placed a freshly poured pint and delivered a sandwich to the former copper.

Tennant said, "Join us, Mister Watford."

The man licked his dry, cracked lips. He gripped the Guinness, closed his eyes, and sank a third of the glass.

After Watford put his glass down, Tennant said, "I have a few questions about your old army days."

Ted Watford didn't know Major FitzGerald or Captain Locock, but his slack face stiffened at Oliver Montgomery's name. "That sod."

O'Malley wiped foam from his mustache. "Now, why would you be calling the captain that?"

"He commanded a firing squad they forced me to serve on. A poor, pathetic private who had frozen at the order to charge. Dropped his rifle and ran." Watford propped his elbows on the table and dropped his face in his hands. "Jesus."

Tennant said, "I'm sorry, Mister Watford."

"Cold as ice, he was. Montgomery. When it was over, he said to the burial party, 'Take him away and clean him up.' The poor blighter had crapped and pissed his trousers before we blew a hole in his chest."

Watford couldn't tell them anything else, but it had been enough. His shoulders sagged. He pulled his glass toward him, staring into the pint. Then he lifted his head and looked out through bleary eyes.

"Montgomery lied to us. Said they'd loaded most of our rifles with blanks, and we'd never know whose bullet . . . But I felt the kick against my shoulder. Feel it, still. Bastard."

Outside the pub, O'Malley said, "No wonder the drink has taken him. The fella's haunted." A few seconds ticked by. "You never talk about the Crimea, sir."

"I've spent a dozen years trying to forget it." Tennant buttoned his coat and pulled up its collar. "I'm sorry I forced Watford to remember."

O'Malley nodded. "Ours is a bloody business, sometimes.

Sorting other people's messes. Still, we've learned that Montgomery is a practiced, cold-blooded killer."

"Remotely, by command, and in the performance of his duties. I'm not sure it gets us far."

"Our murderer is another creature with ice on him. Fits the bill, the captain does."

"Montgomery is in the frame. The trouble is all of them are." Tennant looked around. "We'll never flag a cab in this murk, Paddy. Let's walk to the stand on Fenchurch Street."

When they arrived back at the Yard, the duty sergeant handed Tennant a message. "Coachman for Doctor Lewis dropped this ten minutes ago."

The inspector read it. "Doctor Lewis says she has information about Lizzie Dowling."

They climbed the stairs to Tennant's office. There, they found a constable's report on his desk and a summons from the commissioner.

"The results from the canvass of Camden Town." Tennant read it and passed it to O'Malley. "What do you make of it, Paddy?"

"So, milkman Downey stops at the same coffee vendor each morning."

"He's alive and well when he finished his cup and left for Harrington Square."

"Not for long," O'Malley said. "A driver blows past the baked potato man at the corner of Euston Road without stopping for his usual breakfast or giving a wave. Likely, he's our murderer, now."

"It's a reasonable surmise, Paddy. It's only a distance of a few hundred yards. Our killer lurked somewhere along that stretch of road, killed the driver, and tossed him in the back."

"I'll look for a likely place."

"Talk to the vendors, and then go home. It's a filthy day."

Tennant pulled out his pocket watch. "Sir Richard wants to see me at four o'clock, and I have a few questions for Lady Styles. After that, I'll take a cab to Finsbury Circus."

Eliminate, damn it, Tennant thought in the crawling cab. *Why is it so hard?*

It was a critical step in any investigation. Every murder case was like a game of skittles: knock eight pins away, and it left the killer standing. So far, the only man in the Marlborough House set that Tennant had excluded was George Trevor. He had been too busy running for Parliament to go yachting at the Isle of Wight.

He'd had a frustrating interview with Sir Richard. *For both of us.* At least he reported directly to the commissioner, leaving Chief Inspector Clark out of the loop. But Tennant's case was long on theories and short on evidence, and an arrest was nowhere in sight. Many investigations went through a similar phase. Still, Tennant feared the case was stuck.

Julia's note had asked him to stop by the clinic. She'd written, "*Or come to dinner if your afternoon is full. I have news.*" Tennant could have postponed the interview with Lady Styles and gone to Whitechapel. But a whisky with Dr. Lewis, an excellent meal, and a chance to spend a few hours with Julia? He'd sent a runner to the clinic to accept her dinner invitation. *But first, Lady Styles.*

The cab made a slow right turn from Marlborough Road, and Tennant registered an enhanced presence at the gate. Four ghostly soldiers stood guard in the fog, their scarlet tunics and lofty black hats appearing out of the mist as the cab drew closer and stopped. Tennant held out his warrant card. The sentry scrutinized it, stepped back sharply, and saluted. In addition to the soldiers, Sir Richard had assigned additional teams of constables to patrol the grounds' perimeter.

The footman at the front door recognized Tennant and ushered him to the familiar sitting room to wait for Lady Styles. She arrived promptly, offering her hand and a seat.

"You have news, Inspector?"

"A few developments, but nothing that brings me closer to a resolution. I'm hoping you can assist in a winnowing process."

"I will, if I can."

"Thank you. I have two questions. One goes back to Osborne House on the afternoon Lizzie was murdered. I understand the day was fine. Did you leave the house that day? You or perhaps Princess Louise?"

"As you say, you are taking me back." Lady Styles smoothed her skirts. When she looked up, the inspector thought, *Buying time? And was that wariness in her eyes?*

"I thought perhaps a walk around the estate?" Tennant said. "Major FitzGerald claims he rode on Osborne's grounds that day. It would be helpful if someone provided independent confirmation."

"Yes, I see." Lady Styles folded her hands. "Now that you mention it, Princess Louise and I left the house and rode in a pony cart around the park. I don't remember seeing Major FitzGerald on the grounds, but I was at the stables when he returned his horse."

"Perhaps Princess Louise might recall—"

"She's resting," Lady Styles said quickly. "The princess is plagued by frequent headaches that only repose will ease. Shall I ask her and get back to you?"

"Thank you. The police rely on frank and cooperative witnesses."

She dropped her gaze. "Of course. You . . . you had a second question?"

"Yes. The day you expected Brigid Dowling, was anyone here for luncheon?"

Lady Styles considered. "Princess Louise and Alexandra.

Harriet FitzGerald—no, that was another day. And two other ladies of the household."

"I wondered about Captain Montgomery. As a royal equerry and a friend of the princess, was he here that day?"

Susan shook her head. "No. It was just the five ladies at the table. The two princesses, Alexandra's two maids of honor, and me. We talked of Miss Dowling's impending visit, wondering at it."

"I'll have to question Captain Montgomery about that afternoon and the evening of the fire."

"He's here now, waiting for Alexandra to come downstairs. Shall I ask him to see you?"

"Thank you."

Five minutes later, the captain appeared. All pretense of geniality was over. His eyes were steely, and his voice clipped. Tennant thought, *Here's the natural man. A nasty piece of work?*

"What is it now, Inspector?"

"I have a few questions about your movements."

"I thought we went over this at Osborne House."

"About the afternoon of Brigid Dowling's murder in London. I believe you said you were in town that day. Where in London, Captain?"

"I do not recollect precisely. I seem to recall working at home on correspondence for the prince."

"And the morning of the fire. You arrived rather quickly."

"That's a statement, but I'll answer your implied question. The prince sent for me."

"Please account for your movements that night."

Montgomery's jaw tightened. "This is no longer amusing, Tennant."

"I imagine the Dowling sisters would agree. So, the night of the fire, where were you?"

"At my club, all evening. The Army and Navy."

"Did you see Captain Locock there?"

"Yes, we left together as it happens. Parted at the front door around one."

"Captain Locock walked to his residence. Did you take a cab?"

"My house is on St. James Square, a few minutes' walk on foot."

"Did a servant let you in?"

"I have a latchkey. Make of that what you will, Inspector."

Tennant hailed a cab outside Marlborough House and got in. He rubbed his sleeve against the hackney's window and squinted into the mist. *I hope the cabbie has a better view.*

Had the inspector wasted his time? Montgomery's answers got him nowhere, and Lady Styles couldn't supply an alibi for Peter FitzGerald. Tennant smiled grimly. *Sir Lionel will be pleased about that.* He shifted in his seat, exasperated by the state of his aching leg in the foggy weather and by the results of his interviews. One thing struck him: his questions had made Lady Styles uneasy. *There's something there,* he thought. *Something about the afternoon of Lizzy's death.*

Julia's cab had crawled through the streets, halting at almost every intersection by bobbies waving lanterns. She arrived home just as Inspector Tennant paid off his cab. He opened her door.

"Perfect timing," Julia said, handing her driver some coins. "But that was a dreadful ride from Whitechapel."

Inside, Mrs. Ogilvie took Tennant's coat and hat. "Doctor Lewis is just back," she said. "He'll not change for dinner. Just out of his boots and into his smoking jacket."

"Good. I'll eat as I am," Julia said, handing Kate her cape and medical bag. "Come into the library, Richard, and I'll pour you a drink."

Julia turned up the oil lamp on the console table and gave

Tennant an appraising glance, not liking what she saw. His face was thinner than ever with deeper lines etched his cheeks. He'd labored up the steps behind her, concealing his efforts as best he could.

"You look tired," she said. "Are you getting enough sleep?"

"Oh, the usual."

"Hmm . . . I'm not sure that's an answer."

"It's been a bloody awful day."

He rarely swore, at least not in front of her. "Tell me about it."

"I made a man relive his worst memory." He told her about the former constable at the pub.

"Have you considered . . ." *In for a penny,* Julia thought. "It helps to talk about past pain. Bottling it up doesn't work. Remember, you told me that once."

"Easier to give advice," he said lightly. Then he walked to the fire, raised his hands, and rubbed them.

Not ready yet. Julia had shared her most aching memory, the guilt and remorse she felt over Helen's suicide in medical school. She'd caught glimpses of Tennant's pain in his father's public disgrace, entangled as he was in a financial scandal. And from Aunt Caroline, she'd heard about a broken romance. But he had shared little about himself with her.

Julia poured a whisky and carried it to him. "Consider this a doctor's prescription." But when he reached for the glass, she set it on the mantel instead. She took his right hand and turned it over.

"The wound has healed," she said, frowning. "But it's difficult to know what's happening inside with the muscles and tendons. Push against my palm with your fingers, one at a time." He followed her instructions. "Do you feel any weakness?"

When he didn't answer, Julia looked up. She stood there, holding his hand while he looked at her. Warmth crept past her shoulders and up her neck.

"Nothing to speak of." A slight smile warmed his eyes.

She felt the color creep into her face, released his hand, and looked away. "Well . . . that's good."

Julia stood awkwardly for a moment before retrieving his glass and passing it to him. Then she retreated to the drinks cabinet to pour herself a sherry, spilling a little onto the foot of the glass.

Mrs. Ogilvie entered the room with a dish of olives. "Doctor Lewis is in the cellar, looking for a special bottle of claret. Is there anything else you need, Doctor Julie?"

"No, I don't think . . . Wait, yes. I left a cable for the inspector in my medical bag."

"I'll ask Kate to find it."

After Mrs. Ogilvie left, Tennant said, "A cable? Intriguing. Is that what you want to discuss?"

Julia had initiated a line of inquiry without consulting him, and it had been a contentious issue in the past. She knew she occupied vulnerable ground. She decided to go on the offensive.

Julia set her sherry down and crossed her arms. "Have you ever hired a domestic servant, Richard?"

"No." He shrugged. "Hannah manages everything in Kent. I supposed you'd say I inherited my London housekeeper. Mrs. Markham came with my grandmother's house."

"So, you've never interviewed a skivvy or a parlor maid?"

"The housekeepers take care of all that." He set his glass on the table. "Julia, what is this about?"

"Another reason why the Yard should hire female coppers."

"Not that, again. For heaven's sake—"

"Hear me out. There is something odd about an Irish country girl working for the Queen of England and acting as a lady's maid for Princess Louise."

"Well, I suppose that may be true."

"There's no 'suppose' about it, as any woman who hires servants will tell you. The details of Lizzie's employment may have nothing to do with her tragedy. But the question of how she came to serve Her Majesty needed to be asked. So, I did."

"Good God." He looked up at the ceiling. "Please don't tell me you wrote a letter to the queen's private secretary."

"Of course not. I wrote to Lady Styles, who asked Princess Louise, who sent a cable to Princess Alice in Germany, who sent one back."

Tennant rolled his eyes. "All in the house that Jack built."

"Or, in this case, Jill."

"Amusing."

"Richard, you have a murdered girl whose hiring was unusual, and—"

"Two facts must have a causal link to be relevant. I wake up in the morning, and the sun rises. It has nothing to do with me."

"But when the sun rises, you wake up. Perhaps because a chink of light came through your window curtains. You must admit that the connection between two singular events warrants investigation."

Tennant sighed. "I'm running out of rabbit holes, so I might as well explore yours."

"If it proves to be a treasure hole, I'll expect some gratitude."

"Fair enough." He smiled.

Julia picked up her sherry and sipped it, regarding him over the rim. "You should do it more often, you know."

"What should the inspector do more often?" Her grandfather closed the library door behind him.

"Smile. It's good for the insides."

"As a doctor, I agree. Good evening, Richard." Dr. Lewis shook Tennant's hand. "Happy you're able to join us."

"Aside from the pleasures of your company and kitchen, Julia promises revelations in the case. In a cable from Germany, no less."

"Indeed?" Dr. Lewis said. "The investigation has gone far afield."

"Not exactly, Grandfather. And whether revelations follow . . . well, we shall see."

Julia's maid entered with a cable. "Mrs. Ogilvie said you're wanting this from your bag."

"Thank you." Julia held up the telegram. "Kate is my expert witness. We agree that Lizzie's employment was unusual."

Dr. Lewis said, "You were right about her death, Kate."

"A stopped clock is right twice, but that was murder at any hour," she said, closing the door behind her.

"Kate is O'Malley's match at a turn of phrase," Tennant said. "I'm happy to concede *her* expertise, but what does an English princess living in Germany know that we don't know?"

"Lizzie arrived at a difficult time," Julia said. "Prince Albert had just died, and the royal family was in disarray. Princess Alice was the eldest daughter living at home, so she took charge of the household for her mother."

Tennant asked, "Would she remember the hiring of a young maid? Seems unlikely."

"Princess Louise offered to write to Princess Alice to find out. Then, impatient for a reply, Louise sent a cable to her sister. She sent this in return." Julia passed it to Tennant.

He read it and looked up. "Who is Lady Middlebury, and where do I find her?"

Dr. Lewis stopped with his glass halfway to his lips. "Lady Middlebury?"

"Do you know her, Grandfather?"

"Knew her, yes. But you're too late. Her death notice appeared in the paper yesterday."

The following morning, Tennant sat across the desk from the head of Windsor Borough's police force. At first, Superintendent Eager was reluctant to act on Tennant's theory.

"Lady Middlebury was an old woman," Eager said. "The doctor's verdict was probable heart failure."

Tennant asked, "Did he perform a postmortem?"

"Well, no, given the lady's advanced years and the state of her health."

"Bear with me, Superintendent, while I lay out the links that connect three murders." When Tennant finished, he said, "I was on the point of interviewing Lady Middlebury when I heard of her sudden death."

Eager sighed. "Our mayor and his son found the body on Sunday. William Harris and his older boy were riding in Windsor Great Park when they found the lady slumped on a bench."

"This is Thursday. Where is the body now?"

"On its way to Ireland for burial in a family crypt in Kildare. Yesterday, a service was held at St. George's Chapel, attended by the queen."

"When did the body leave Windsor?"

"This morning." Eager checked his wall clock. "It's on a train halfway to Bristol by now."

"I'll send a telegram to the superintendent there. Then I must speak to the county coroner about a postmortem."

Eager rang a bell. "His office is in the Guildhall. A constable will escort you."

"And I need to see the medical report."

At seven that evening, Inspector Tennant rang the bell at number 17 Finsbury Circus. He had a doctor's report tucked into his breast pocket.

Mrs. Ogilvie opened the door. "Dinner is in a quarter of an hour. I'll lay another plate."

"Thank you, but I ate at the station. Are the doctors in?"

"They're in the library." He followed her into the room.

Julia said, "We wondered if it were you."

"I must see Sir Richard this evening, so I have a cab waiting."

"You found something?" Dr. Lewis said.

"Yes." At the end of his narrative, he said, "The magistrate ordered the body's return to Windsor." He reached into his breast pocket. "Will you give me your opinions on this report before I see the commissioner?"

The document wasn't long, and Julia read it in two minutes. "The description of her eyes . . ." She passed the report to her grandfather. "What does this 'eye infection' sound like to you? In the last paragraph."

He read and returned it to Julia. "Red spots in the whites and on the insides of the lids? Sounds very like 'Tardieu's spots' to me."

"I agree."

Tennant said, "Tell me what it means."

"It means murder, most likely," Julia said. "I saw a case my first year out of medical school."

"August Tardieu is France's leading authority on forensic medicine," Dr. Lewis said. "He first wrote about this condition nearly ten years ago."

"It's the rare English doctor who keeps up with professional developments outside of Britain," Julia said.

"True enough, my dear. Tardieu identified those spots as a sign of asphyxia. Often the result of strangulation or smothering."

Julia held up the report. "There's no mention of marks on her neck. But it's winter, and they found her outdoors. Perhaps a scarf pressed to her nose and mouth?"

"The magistrate ordered a postmortem for tomorrow," Tennant said. "I asked if a Yard consultant could be present to assist."

Dr. Lewis asked, "Have you any private patients tomorrow morning, my dear?" Julia shook her head. "An afternoon in the clinic won't exhaust this old duffer."

"Thank you, Grandfather." Julia kissed him on the forehead.

"My occasional substitutions are hardly taxing." Dr. Lewis shrugged. "Nurse Clemmie seats me with a cup of tea and does most of the work."

"They've scheduled the postmortem for eleven in the morning," Tennant said. "And I'll be surprised if you don't turn up evidence of murder."

CHAPTER 12

Inspector Tennant and Sir Lionel waited outside the county coroner's examining room for the postmortem to conclude. For once, Dermott was in no mood for jokes. He sat forward, head down, with his hands hanging between his knees.

"My God, Tennant, an old woman. The man is a monster," Dermott said.

"A careful and audacious one. It takes nerve to smother a victim in the open air in the middle of the day."

"And in Windsor Great Park, by God."

"Not getting caught required planning."

Sir Lionel rubbed his forehead. "It will be my unhappy duty to inform Her Majesty. What are your next steps?"

"Superintendent Eager is waiting for the autopsy's results. If it's murder, it happened on his patch, so he's in charge at this end. He's preparing to canvass the immediate area and the Windsor railway station."

"The logical mode of travel."

"It won't be easy," Tennant said. "Eager tells me that Eton's Lent term began on Monday. On Sunday, the station overflowed with schoolboys and their parents."

"Almighty Christ! Nothing is easy with this case."

"I've recommended that Superintendent Eager widen his calendar," Tennant said. "The killer must have surveilled his prey. He wouldn't count on stumbling on the old lady by accident."

"So, he kept his eye on her."

"It's probable."

"When will the superintendent release the body?"

"Immediately. Lady Middlebury resumes her final journey to Ireland tomorrow, accompanied by one of Superintendent Eager's most reliable sergeants."

"Is there someone at the other end?" Dermott asked. "I understand she had no children."

"Eager says a great-nephew travels to Dublin from Cork to take charge of the burial. The sergeant will ask what, if anything, he knew about his aunt."

"Living on separate islands two generations apart." Dermott shook his head. "I wouldn't count on his knowing much."

A young constable with a pillow in his hand strode past them and into the examination room.

"Something's turned up," Tennant said. "Perhaps the murder weapon."

"Thank Christ," Dermott said. "If I must tell the queen that someone murdered her old friend, I'll need more than spots on her eyes."

"Princess Louise believes the queen remembers nothing about Lizzie Dowling's employment. She may be wrong."

Dermott sighed. "You want me to question Her Majesty?"

"Would you like me to do it? I could delay my return to London."

"No. I'll do it and take a Saturday morning train."

The door opened, and a wiry, beak-nosed doctor with flaming hair and a thick Scottish burr waved them into the examining room. Two attendants lifted a tiny, shrouded corpse and returned it to its oak coffin. Julia dried her hands at the sink.

"Aye, it's murder. There's no doubt," Dr. McAllister said. "I'll testify to that at the inquest. Wee hemorrhages in the eyes tell the tale, and Doctor Lewis found bits of the murder weapon."

McAllister squeezed the sides of an envelope, opening a gap, and extracted a feather with a pair of tweezers.

"From her windpipe," Julia said, carrying a cushion over to Tennant. "You can see the rip in the center. The goose feathers inside are a match."

"May I?" Tennant borrowed the tweezers and pulled one out, comparing it to the one in the envelope.

"The killer smothered Lady Middlebury with her pillow," Julia said.

At breakfast on Saturday morning, Dr. Andrew Lewis said, "So, Tardieu's spots after all?"

"Yes," Julia said, cracking her eggshell. "The poor woman was murdered with her seat cushion. In the shadow of Windsor Castle."

"The coldness of it. And the brazenness. Julie, my dear . . ."

The quaver in his voice stopped her. Julia set aside her half-peeled egg and laid her hand on his. "You needn't worry, Grandfather. This killer isn't concerned with me."

"Pray God it stays that way."

She patted his hand and returned her attention to her egg. "You said you had something to discuss?"

"Yes," he said. "A collaboration. You've given me an idea for next month's presentation to the young doctors at the London Hospital. I'll open with a lecture on Tardieu's spots. You conclude with a case study. Lady Middlebury's autopsy."

"Will Uncle Max play along?"

"Why not? He gets two Doctors Lewis for the price of one."

"The price being . . ." Julia drew three circles in the air with her index finger.

"Ah, but the experience of the lecture hall. Priceless."

"And irresistible . . . so long as you keep my participation a surprise." Julia grinned. "I'll enjoy the looks on those young men's faces when I walk from the wings to the podium."

Mrs. Ogilvie entered with a note for Julia. "The coachman from Kensington Palace is waiting."

Tennant spent the first hour of his Saturday morning in the commissioner's office with Sir Richard and the Irish department chief. The death of Lady Middlebury, with her roots in Ireland, triggered Colonel Fielding's inclusion in the meeting. The murder hardly dented the colonel's stubborn doubts about the relevance of Lizzie's murder to the Irish threat.

On his way to his office, the inspector passed a smoldering Chief Inspector Clark. The commissioner had insulated Tennant from his chief's oversight, and Clark resented the second-hand reports that kept him minimally informed. The commissioner's only explanation had been "Too many damned cooks in this Irish stew."

Clark called after him, "Running in place, are we?"

Tennant stopped. "Incremental progress, sir."

Clark hadn't the wit to conceal his resentment. He radiated fury and contempt. "That's what we're calling it these days? I suppose crawling is better than nothing."

"That's right, sir. Small steps leading the way." Tennant turned into his office and nearly ran into O'Malley lurking inside the doorway.

The sergeant cocked his thumb and muttered, "Should we be worrying about that one?"

"Sir Richard and the colonel understand we're turning every stone."

"While you were away, one puzzle piece fell into place," O'Malley said. "We've found where the milkman met his end.

St. James's Gardens. The groundskeeper is after finding four empty paraffin tins in the garden's bushes."

"Have the constable on the beat question every cart driver, cabbie, and knocker-upper who drives or walks by St. James's Gardens between the hours of three and five."

O'Malley smoothed his wiry mustache. "Sure, it's how things happen, sometimes. Between coppers here and in Dublin, cables from the commissioner, and a princess in Germany—first, it's a drought. Then the rains lash down."

"I hope you're right, Paddy." Tennant shrugged into his coat.

When Tennant arrived at Marlborough House, he found Sir Lionel Dermott in the foyer. Gone were the man's high color and mobile features. His face had the hue and quality of stiff parchment. The inspector had come to inform the household about Lady Middlebury's murder. The two princesses and Lady Styles knew about the tragedy.

"The Prince of Wales got wind of the story while he was out last night," Dermott said. "He greeted Alix with the news this morning, leaving Susan to cope with her flood of tears. His wife's illness and distress are Bertie's cues to head for his club or a ride in the park."

"Callous but well-informed," Tennant said. "How, I wonder?"

Dermott shrugged. "Susan sent for Doctor Lewis, and she's with Alix now. Christ, what a bloody awful business."

"You left Windsor early. Have you slept?"

"I couldn't, so I hopped on the milk train. Last night, having to tell Her Majesty about her old friend's death . . ."

"It's about as grim a task as I know."

"I imagine so, in your line of work." Dermott sighed and said, "Come, I'll take you to Alix's sitting room."

Tennant followed Dermott into the room, but it took the inspector a moment to locate the chamber's occupants amid the clutter. The princess followed the fashion of dressing a room from floor to ceiling. Paintings crowded the walls. Vases, bowls, and statuettes covered every surface. Lady Styles sat on a sofa by the fire, holding Louise's hand. The princess rested her head on Susan's shoulder.

An inner door opened, and Julia entered the sitting room.

Louise lifted her head. "Alix?"

"Princess Alexandra is calmer now," Julia said. "She's drifting off."

Louise's voice shook when she said, "You examined Lady Middlebury. I . . . I suppose there's no doubt?"

"I've seen it before, Princess. The signs were there."

"Good God." Louise hung her head. "I was a troublesome child, but Lady Middlebury was kind to me. Other ladies-in-waiting . . ."

Susan asked, "Is there anything else you can tell us, Inspector?"

"Only what you already know. Inquiries are underway, here and in Ireland."

"The queen was deeply shocked," Dermott said. "But Her Majesty's memory isn't entirely a blank. Lady Middlebury brought Lizzie Dowling to Osborne when the lady entered royal service shortly after Prince Albert's death."

Lady Styles frowned. "That's very odd. Royal attendants don't bring along personal servants."

Tenant asked, "Your Royal Highness, may I ask if you've had a letter from Princess Alice?"

"No." Louise stood, putting her hand on the armrest to steady herself. "You'll have it as soon as it arrives." She stopped at the door and turned. "But I don't understand why Lizzie . . ." Louise looked at Tennant like a lost child. "Why Lizzie never mentioned Lady Middlebury or told me how she came to Osborne."

Downstairs, Tennant waited while the footman helped Julia

with her coat. They headed for the taxi stand on Marlborough Road.

"The queen's fragmentary memory confirms a link between the lady and the maid," Tennant said.

"Raising new questions," Julia said, pulling on her gloves.

A chilly fog had lingered for another day. Tennant signaled to a passing hackney, saying, "It's too cold for an open hansom," and opened the door for her.

"If you're heading back to the Yard, I'll drop you on my way to the clinic."

Tennant climbed in after her. They rocked along silently, with Julia looking out the window. He studied her profile: her high cheekbones, firm chin, and chestnut hair pinned back beneath her hat. Just then, she looked like a young version of Lady Aldridge. He thought, *I know what she'll look like when we're old and gray. She'll still be a handsome woman, just like her aunt.* Julia turned her head and looked at him.

He asked, "What were you thinking just now?"

"Secrets," Julia said. "I suppose all families have them. Lady Middlebury and Lizzie Dowling. There's a mystery there. The two princesses have their troubles, as well." Julia sighed. "And Susan worries about them all."

"Lady Styles is 'a woman who lives in other people's houses.' She said that once to me. The lady leads a strange life, and I doubt her salary is large enough to make their problems hers. Yet, she does." Tennant smiled. "And now there's you, drawn into their orbit."

"Oh, I'm a very minor moon of Jupiter," Julia said lightly as the carriage slowed and stopped at the back entrance to the Yard.

"No. You're just the same." Tennant climbed out of the cab. "You're never 'in for a penny.' It's always a pound." Before he closed the door, he said, "I wouldn't have you any other way at any price."

* * *

On Monday morning, Susan, Princess Louise, and Sir Lionel, accompanied by a groom, rode on horseback from Marlborough House to Hyde Park. Susan had suggested the ride to Lionel as a distraction for Louise.

They entered at Hyde Park Corner and turned their mounts toward Rotten Row, the park's oddly named bridle path. Princess Louise lasted five minutes on the sedate stretch where London's fashionable riders went to see and be seen.

"I'm going for a canter along the North Ride," the princess said. "I'll meet you at the far end of the row." She pulled away and headed toward the Serpentine Road, the groom trailing her.

"I didn't think she'd last long at this leisurely pace," Susan said. "A gallop will be good for her."

Ahead, a crowd had gathered at a section of the low fence that separated the bridle path from the footpath. Most onlookers were there to see Catherine Walters. "Skittles" was London's most famous courtesan and was a superb horsewoman. Her riding costumes, tailored by Henry Poole of Savile Row, clung to her like a seal's skin. That morning, Skittles wore a jet jacket and skirt with snowy lace at the cuffs and throat. She'd massed her dark curls at the back of her head. A top hat tipped forward at an acute angle shaded her eyes from the morning sun. A creamy ribbon streamed from its crown.

"Miss Walters hasn't disappointed," Susan said. "The curious have turned out to see what she's wearing. But I had read she was in Paris."

"Skittles is back from the City of Light, having bowled over a finance minister and the French emperor, if the rumors are true. But I'm surprised that Susan, the Dowager Lady Styles, follows her dubious career."

"'Dowager' makes me feel in my dotage, Lionel."

"Nonsense, my dear. Ah . . . what have we here? FitzGerald

and another fellow have reined their horses, and the major has tipped his hat to the lady. What do you suppose FitzGerald is about? Some 'sleight of hand,' perhaps?' "

"What do you mean?"

" 'Sleight of eye' might be more apt. Rumor has it that Skittles is 'entertaining' the major, so logic dictates they'd avoid public encounters. And nothing is more public than Catherine Walters riding in Rotten Row. Therefore . . ."

"Therefore, what?"

"Meetings in the park telegraph that there aren't private rendezvous behind closed doors . . ." Dermott waggled his brows. "A neat double bluff."

"Lionel, your brain is overactive."

"I'll remind you of this conversation when Harriet sues for divorce. It's the second time I've spotted FitzGerald and Skittles riding together. Both times, he's been in the company of that chap as chaperone. More window dressing?"

"He's the major's groom and coachman. Harriet doesn't enjoy riding, so the groom keeps her horse exercised."

"Hmm . . . perhaps. There must be some reason for dragging the fellow along. Perhaps he knows his horseflesh and keeps his eye on FitzGerald's racehorse."

"He owns one?"

"Yes. He named the beast 'Marmalade' in honor of his father-in-law's jam." Dermott shook his head. "If FitzGerald thought the gesture would make the old chap sweet on the deal . . ."

"You think not?"

"Fitz doesn't understand the merchant class. Sensibly, they believe in earning their money, not risking it on something as chancy as horse racing." Lionel cocked his head and looked down at her with a slight smile. "Speaking of taking chances . . . There's a solution, Lady Styles, if you're interested."

"A solution to what?"

"Ditching the 'dowager' in your title. You could—oh, blast."

"What is it?"

"Greaves," Dermott said. "Gathorne-Hardy's private secretary. I'll wager he's looking for me. He's walking along the footpath, bobbing his head like an inquisitive goose."

Dermott turned his horse and headed to the edge of the bridle path. "Mister Greaves?"

"You're wanted at the Home Office, Sir Lionel. The French rifles have turned up."

Lionel had expected to find an exultant gathering in Gathorne-Hardy's conference room. Instead, the faces of Commissioner Mayne and Inspector Tennant matched the home secretary's habitual gloomy expression.

"Nine hundred French guns turned up in Waterford, Ireland, on Saturday," Sir Richard said bitterly.

Dermott looked around the table. "But that's good news."

"Aside from the missing hundred rifles," Tennant said.

"Who found them?" Lionel asked.

"The local Irish coastguard," the home secretary said. "They caught a band of Irish Americans offloading the crates near Waterford."

"Well, the French will be delighted to have the lion's share of their weapons back," Dermott said. "And so should we. The threat is reduced by ninety percent. Why the long faces?"

Sir Richard slammed his fist. "Because it's a complete cock-up on our side."

Tennant said, "Evidence seized tells us that the guns landed in Southampton, but slipped through the port inspection undetected. And those missing hundred rifles may have remained behind in Britain."

On Wednesday morning, Julia returned to Marlborough House to attend the Princess of Wales. She'd finished her examination and found Susan Styles pacing outside Alix's sitting room door.

Julia said, "You can rest easy. The princess is calmer this morning, and she managed to sleep the last two nights."

Susan shook her head. "It's something else. Can you come to my sitting room? Something confounding has happened, and I was about to write a note to Inspector Tennant."

Julia followed her into a bright, ivory-painted room with well-stocked bookcases and a writing desk. An unfolded map lay across it. They sat in the claret wing chairs by the fireplace.

"It's about Hackett, the prince's valet. The butler and Elsie came to see me this morning. She's the long-serving head laundress at Marlborough House, and she strikes me as a shrewd and sensible person. What Elsie told me . . . well, it's been going on for months."

Susan explained that items in the prince's wardrobe were disappearing. At first, Elsie attributed their absence to Bertie's changing tastes. But the laundress checked his wardrobe and found that recently acquired items were missing, too.

"Twice since the family returned from the Isle of Wight, Elsie noticed something odd," Susan said. "She saw Hackett leave with a bulging carpetbag on his half day off. Yesterday, it happened a third time. But Witcombe, the butler, was waiting and followed Hackett's taxicab."

Julia raised her eyebrows. "Playing detective, was he?"

"And enjoying himself thoroughly. He loathes Hackett."

"Is he loathsome?"

Susan considered. "Oily."

"Still, I'm not sure Inspector Tennant is the one to consult about household theft. Maybe the local police?"

Susan stood. "Come, look at this map." Julia followed her to the desk. Susan drew her finger down from St. Paul's Cathedral, pointing to a spot near the river. "There," she said. "That's where Hackett got out of his cab and continued on foot to a warehouse."

Julia's eyes widened. "Trig Wharf. But that's—"

Susan nodded. "Just off Trig Lane, where they found Brigid Dowling's body. They named the street in the newspapers."

"That certainly changes things. Write your note to the inspector, and I'll carry it to Scotland Yard on my way to the clinic."

Late in the afternoon, Tennant returned to the Yard and found Susan's note. "Paddy," he called to his sergeant. O'Malley appeared in the doorway. "Fetch four constables and a police wagon. We're heading back to the river."

On Upper Thames Street, a hackney cab and a police wagon rolled to a stop at the top of Trig Wharf. On foot, Tennant and his officers started down the darkening canyon of brick warehouses. Mist rose from the cooling river, and the slapping water against creaking pilings sounded eerie in the fog. The inspector counted down three warehouses on the left. The butler had spotted Hackett unlocking its door. Tennant saw lights and movement by the building and signaled his officers to stop.

A man in a dark cap and peacoat fumbled at the lock. As the door swung open, Tennant sent two constables forward, and they grabbed him under the arms.

A second man had been waiting by a wagon. He scrambled away, dashing around the corner to Trig Lane. Tennant dispatched the second pair of constables after the man. Five minutes later, they frog-marched him back to the inspector.

"Heading for a dinghy tied up at the bottom of the steps," the taller copper said. "Couldn't see it in the fog, but a steamboat fired its engine and chugged off."

"What's all this then?" O'Malley shone his bull's-eye lantern into the wagon. The light illuminated four wooden crates marked MARTELL V.S.O.P COGNAC. The shipping labels read OSBORNE HOUSE.

Tennant said, "Let's have a look inside the warehouse, Paddy."

The sergeant found four bundles stashed inside two seaman's bags. He tore the wrappings off one and pulled out two silk shirts and a paisley cravat. "Prince Bertie would like these back, I'm guessing."

They found eight additional crates of expensive cognac hidden under a tarp. All had shipping labels for Osborne House. Then O'Malley raked the beam of his bull's-eye lantern across the back of the warehouse, illuminating a bulky pile hidden by an oilcloth. He pulled away the covering, unearthing a stack of wooden boxes with markings Tennant recognized from the Waterford Police report.

"Well, well, Paddy. Our missing French rifles."

Sir Lionel entered the smoking room of the Army and Navy Club. He spotted Frederick Locock sunk in a leather armchair. Dermott was about to clap him on the shoulder when he stopped. Locock looked like a sailboat that had been through rough seas, mainsail sagging, and lines in a tangle. An untouched glass of port sat at his elbow, and an open newspaper tented his knee.

Lionel took the chair next to him. "Freddie, old man," he said. "Haven't seen you since Alix's ball. Were you in London for Christmas?"

Locock roused himself and sat up. "We spent it on the Isle of Wight with my father."

"And your lady-wife and the little chap, how are they? Thriving?"

"Yes, although Mary is apt to fuss."

"Ah, women. And you, Freddie. How are you?"

"I'm well." Locock looked away, making a business of folding the paper and setting it aside.

Dermott waited. "Forgive me, old friend, but you don't look well. Still, if you'd rather not talk about it, there's always boxing or the weather."

Locock ran his hand through his hair. "It's this investigation.

Father tells me that constables on the Isle of Wight are asking questions. And Tennant came to see me the other day, demanding an account of my movements."

"Did your answers satisfy him?"

"I lied and said I was out walking."

"Thin. May one ask why you didn't tell Tennant the truth?"

"I can't . . . honor forbids me to speak."

So soon? Dermott thought. Locock had only been married six months. "As a gentleman, you can't supply a name. I understand that. But Tennant strikes me as a man of the world. You could be, ah, explicit about your activities without mentioning the lady's name."

Locock shook his head. "That's just what I cannot do."

Dermott sat back, eyeing Locock under half-closed lids. "I shouldn't worry too much. You're one name on a long list that includes mine. And I'm somewhere nearer the top, I fancy."

Locock picked up his glass. "I want to be crossed off it, Lionel."

"Drink up, and I'll get the next round." Dermott signaled the waiter.

Oliver Montgomery strolled in, intercepting one of two glasses of port on their way to Dermott.

"I just left Marlborough House," Montgomery said, "and you won't believe it."

"Let me guess. Bertie is having a quiet evening by the fireside with Alix?"

"Don't be an ass, Lionel. No, the police arrested Stanley Hackett, the prince's valet. The chap's been pilfering Bertie's . . ." Montgomery futtered his left hand at his chest. "His shirts, cravats, and whatnots."

"I always thought Hackett was a slippery sod," Locock said.

"Uriah Heep in a well-tailored suit." A waiter offered Dermott a note on a silver tray. He read the home secretary's message: *Ninety French rifles found in a London warehouse. Ten still missing. Come at once. G-H.*

Thirty minutes later, Lionel said to the home secretary, "No Colonel Fielding?" He swiveled his head and pretended to peer under the table. "Where is our resident Irish expert?"

Gathorne-Hardy waved impatiently. "I'll inform the colonel tomorrow. Tell Lionel what you found, Inspector Tennant."

"Nine crates of guns at Trig Wharf."

"Trig Wharf?" Dermott said, startled. "Surely, that's where—"

"Brigid Dowling was murdered. And there's more. The crates had their original shipping labels for Southampton still attached."

Lionel shrugged. "We knew that they came through the port."

"We didn't know they were sent to Her Majesty as the recipient," Tennant said.

Lionel whistled softly. "Who takes charge of shipments to Osborne House?"

"According to the queen's private secretary, the house steward, Michael Bolger," Tennant said.

"Dear, dear." Lionel tut-tutted. "We have a conspiracy on our hands after all. Of royal household rogues pilfering stolen linen and the queen's brandy. Toss in French rifles and murdered Irish serving girls. Colonel Fielding won't be pleased."

On the way to the Yard, Tennant sent a cable to the Isle of Wight, asking the chief constable to arrest Michael Bolger. Two hours later, he got a response. *Bolger dead in Southampton harbor. Sending police report and autopsy results by special messenger.*

"Damnation," Tennant said, handing the telegram to O'Malley.

The reports from Southampton's chief constable arrived in the morning. Two days earlier, the harbor police had fished a body from the waters near Moonraker's Tavern. Osborne House's head groom identified the dead man as Michael Bolger. The mortal injury was a single penetrating stab to the base of Bolger's throat.

"'Tis as plain as a signature," O'Malley said.

"Still, let's have Dr. Lewis take a look." Tennant handed him the autopsy. "Send it with a constable. And let's get someone onto the Trig Wharf warehouse records. What's his name?" Tennant snapped his fingers. "The human ferret."

"Constable Williams."

"Have him search the City of London property records for a name. Someone owns or leases that warehouse."

"Will you be wanting him to follow up if he finds a name?"

"Yes. Our murderer leaves no loose ends or tongues," Tennant said. "Maybe there's still one left that's eager to wag."

The two men arrested at Trig Wharf had been willing to talk but knew little. They were down-and-out Southampton dock men hired by Michael Bolger to ferry shipments to the London warehouse. They gave up the name of the boatman and the vessel that moved the goods between the coast and the capital. The Southampton police were looking for him.

That left the prince's valet.

Tennant took a cab to Newgate Prison. A guard brought a shuffling, shackled Stanley Hackett into the prison's exercise yard. High stone walls barely thirty paces apart and topped with iron spikes enclosed the oppressive space. *It's not going to take much*, Tennant thought. Two days in a cell had rubbed the shine off the sleek valet. He wore a rough, gray shirt over loose, baggy trousers and boots that looked two sizes too large for his feet.

Tennant's gaze wandered up the walls as if he were estimating their height. Then he looked at Hackett. "For the next ten years, you'll enjoy this courtyard as an hour's escape from your crowded, lice-ridden cell."

The man shook. He wiped tears using the rough canvas of his sleeve.

"Unless . . ." Tennant shrugged.

"Unless what?" Hackett said, his voice ragged. "Tell me, please."

"Cooperation can shave a few years and win you better living arrangements."

"Anything," the valet said, gulping convulsively. "Anything you want to know."

Tennant called over to the guard. "Bring out a chair for Mister Hackett." The inspector pulled some coins from his pocket and handed the guard five shillings. "That will buy you clean bedding and keep you out of Newgate's moldy basement cells for the present."

Tennant calculated. Would telling Hackett that Bolger was dead loosen his tongue or lubricate the lying? He decided to say nothing.

"Tell me about Michael Bolger. What were you and the house steward discussing when I saw you at Osborne House in December?"

"Bolger sought me out. He wanted to know what you asked me about the girl, Lizzie Dowling."

"What was his interest in her?"

"I've no idea. Still don't. It was the first time her name came up."

"And the stealing?" Tennant said. "How was that arranged?"

Hackett said the scheme was Michael Bolger's brainchild. He'd recruited the valet for a plan of profitable pilfering.

"We started small, just Bolger and me. A few shirts here, a case of brandy there. I'd double-order the prince's linen. We've been doing it for years. Then some army chap from Bolger's Crimea days showed up and persuaded him that if you can steal small, you can loot big. If you're smart about it."

"What was his name?

"I don't know. Bolger said I didn't want to know."

"Why?"

"Said the fellow was a nasty piece of work. But I saw him once, waiting on the docks in Southampton. That's where the wine shipments came in."

"Describe him."

"Tall and thin. Well-dressed in a topcoat and bowler. I didn't see him close-up."

"You'd better not be lying to me," Tennant said. "Where did the stolen wine end up?"

"Gentlemen's clubs on Pall Mall and a few hotel restaurants in London," Bolger said.

"Which ones?"

"Honest, I don't know. If it would get me out of here one day quicker, I'd name them all."

"And what about the rifles?"

Hackett's eyes widened. "Rifles?" Despite the cold, sweat beaded on his brow. "What are you talking about?"

"We found nearly a hundred stolen rifles in the back of the warehouse."

"I swear to you, I had nothing to do with any guns."

Either Hackett was a consummate actor, or the man knew nothing about the weapons. The inspector told the guard to take the man away.

Tennant exited the prison and walked into the filtered light of Old Bailey Street. A pale, noon sun shone dimly in the ochre-gray haze, a combination of fog and coal smoke that hung in the air, acrid and sulfurous. The inspector hitched his shoulders and brushed his sleeve as if shedding Newgate Prison's contagion. He hailed a hansom and gave the cabbie the address of Julia's clinic on Fieldgate Street.

Julia set aside the autopsy report. "In position, width, and depth of penetration, I'd say Bolger's wound is identical. The man's a precise killer."

"And a practiced one," Tennant said. "May I ask a favor?"

"Of course."

"You've seen the medical reports. Will you write up your assessment of all the wounds? I have a stubborn colonel on my hands who refuses to admit the connections among victims."

"Send the other reports back to me. I'll take a second look and have my summary to you by Monday."

Julia stirred her tea and took a sip, studying him over the rim. Tennant shifted in his seat, his jaw muscles clenching as he uncrossed his legs. The strain she'd observed since his return from France hadn't gone away. She'd often noticed the weather-triggered stiffness in his gait. His walk across the clinic's foyer had seemed unusually labored.

"Tell me," she said.

"Tell you what?"

"What's wrong."

"Trains and steamers and too little sleep." He shrugged. "It's caught up with me."

She'd allowed him to deflect too often. *Not today.* "Something more, I think." Julia waited.

He leaned forward, returning his cup to the saucer on her desk. "There are . . . times when I loathe my job. Probably a good thing. Days when . . ." He shook his head.

"What happened today?'

Haltingly, he told her about his morning at the prison. Julia listened, thinking how unpracticed he was at sharing his thoughts and fears. *First the army, then Scotland Yard. No, it begins much earlier*. Boys were schooled in stoicism and reserve. He'd learned those lessons too well.

"I know coppers who enjoy making men squirm," he said. "A hazard of the job."

Julia rounded her desk and sat on the edge. "You'll never be that man, Richard. Never."

"You're surer than I am." He looked at her. "What about

you? Are there times when you question"—he spread his hands—"this path you've taken?"

She slid off the desk and picked up a wooden stethoscope, spinning it between her fingers. It was an antique, used by her grandfather early in his career, a souvenir. "Aunt Caroline tried her best to dissuade me. Just before I left for medical school."

"Why?"

Julia smiled. "You haven't the time for *all* her reasons. But she was wrong about one thing. It wasn't to fill the void of my father's death. To fulfill Grandfather's dream of the Doctors Lewis practicing medicine together."

"No?"

"No. I did it for me . . . a strange ambition for a woman, in the minds of most people."

"Not strange to the patients in your wards . . . or to me."

"Ah, but once upon a time." She waggled the wooden horn. "Come clean, Inspector."

Tennant stood. He took the instrument from her and returned it to its desk stand. "Strange, now, that there was *ever* a time when . . ." He held her hand for a long moment before releasing it, smiling into her eyes. "I wouldn't change a thing."

Sir Lionel arrived at the Yard ten minutes after Tennant's return, bearing two reports.

"This one is from the authorities in Ireland." Dermot handed the document to Tennant. "They nabbed all the gunrunners except one. A surly mountain of a man folded under questioning and gave up the name. Patrick McGrath. Sound familiar, Inspector?"

"The man the French warned us about."

"He fled to Liverpool on his way to London."

O'Malley smoothed his mustache, considering. "Is he coming for a purpose or to lose himself in a crowd? Why am I thinking he's here for a reason?"

Sir Lionel Dermott nodded. "I fear your supposition is correct, Sergeant."

" 'Tis a case where I'd rather be wrong."

Sir Lionel held up a second document and passed it to Tennant. "The Home Office report on Patrick McGrath." He ticked off his fingers. "Born in Naas, Kildare, joined the British Army, served in the Crimea, won a battlefield promotion to sergeant, and lived for a time in Liverpool. Oh, and he served in the same Irish Guards' regiment as Peter FitzGerald."

"I suppose you'd like me to see that as suspicious," Tennant said.

"Not really, but I couldn't resist. Even I can't propose a Fenian FitzGerald with a straight face. As McGrath is a Kildare man, the major's regiment was a logical choice."

"Happy to hear you're keeping an open mind."

"More to the point, McGrath emigrated to America and fought in the Civil War. He joined the Fenian brotherhood in 1866, and he's a crack shot, renowned for his prowess as a sniper."

"Mother of God," O'Malley muttered. "We recovered ninety of the last hundred guns. That leaves ten French rifles and a sniper in the wind."

Tennant said, "Chabert, the French colonel, thought McGrath might be the 'man in square-toed boots' who bought the guns from Romilly."

Sir Lionel tapped the report in Tennant's hand. "McGrath's description is at the bottom of the first page."

The inspector read, " 'Average height, solidly built. In his early forties. Dark, curly hair and gray eyes.' We'll get this into circulation."

O'Malley said, "Those stab wounds to the neck are making me think of bayonet jabs. McGrath's soldier, but not tall enough to be our killer."

"A soldier . . ." Tennant said. "It's a thought, Paddy."

Dermott said, "In addition to being too short, our report places him in France when the Dowling sisters were killed."

"Patrick McGrath . . . a man on a mission?" Tennant said.

Dermott shrugged. "You don't need an arsenal for localized bloodshed. A few guns will do the job. Well, I'll let you gentlemen get on with it."

Dermott stopped at the door and spun on his heels. "I've just remembered. Peter FitzGerald's ancestor, Lord *Edward* FitzGerald, was in the thick of the Irish uprising of '98."

Tennant said, "We'll bear it in mind."

"Treason could be in the blood." Dermott winked, gave a two-fingered salute, and strode out the door.

"Fancies himself a comedian, Sir Lionel," O'Malley said.

"What's not amusing is McGrath. We may have a sniper on the loose in London."

CHAPTER 13

On Sunday afternoon, Julia's coachman nosed the horses toward Hyde Park Corner through light traffic. Two inches of snow had fallen overnight, although wheels and hooves had churned and stamped most of it into slushy puddles. But it was cold enough for the flakes to linger on the park's trees, frosting the branches like tea cakes.

Lady Styles had written in her luncheon invitation, "You'll be my first guest. I've only had two cookery lessons, so don't expect too much." Julia smiled, remembering Mrs. Ogilvie's efforts before she left for medical school. "You'll not leave for Philadelphia without knowing how to boil an egg," her housekeeper had said.

The coachman turned left from Knightsbridge Road, stopping the carriage at a row of three-story houses. Glossy black doors and shutters shone against the white Portland stone, and Julia saw the curtains twitch in the window of number 6 Trevor Place. Lady Styles opened the front door before Julia's knock.

"You found me," she said.

"Easily, Lady Styles."

"High time you called me Susan, Julia."

"High time, Susan." Julia smiled, stepping over the threshold. "What a marvelous location. A five-minute walk to the park."

"It's my second favorite thing about the flat."

"What do you like best?"

"That it's all mine." Susan sighed happily. "Well, at least the ground floor belongs to me."

She gestured toward the inner door, and Julia walked into a bright, high-ceilinged room, a combination sitting-and-dining space, fully furnished, the table already set for luncheon.

"You've been busy." Julia presented a box. "I hope you have room for a crystal bowl."

"It's lovely," Susan said, peeking under the lid. "How generous everyone has been. The table setting is Alexandra's gift, and Sir Lionel—"

As if on cue, he emerged from the kitchen. "I tasted the sauce and complimented the chef." He clicked his heels. "Doctor Lewis, always a pleasure to see you."

"I was about to say that the lovely decanter and glasses are your gift. I've tried to persuade Lionel to join us to no avail."

"Alas," he said, pulling on his gloves, "duty calls in the form of a luncheon invitation from Mrs. Gathorne-Hardy. And a gloomy affair it's bound to be."

When Sir Lionel raised Susan's hand to his lips, Julia read a gesture beyond common politeness. She remembered Susan's consultation and thought, *Perhaps she does have a particular gentleman in mind.*

After Sir Lionel left, Susan opened the door to the kitchen. "And Princess Louise—"

"Is busy in the kitchen," the princess said, suspending a wooden spoon over a saucepan. "My gift. Pots and pans."

"And cooking lessons, although I'm a backward pupil."

"Nonsense," Princess Louise said, dipping the spoon into

the pot. "Dearest Papa insisted we children learn, so anyone can. We're dining this afternoon on the consommé I prepared at Marlborough House, cutlets in white wine sauce, and my oyster pâté. What could be easier?"

Susan smiled and said, "Do you remember the French ambassador?"

"My shining moment," the princess said, ladling the broth into a tureen.

"The ambassador complimented the pâté and was agog when Princess Louise thanked him and explained her recipe."

"The French think they alone understand food," Princess Louise said, reaching behind her to untie her apron. She breezed past them, carrying the consommé into the dining room.

When they finished the last course of cheese, pears, and dried figs, Julia complimented the cook and thanked her hostess.

"The pleasure is all mine. It's a delight to share a first meal in my new home."

Princess Louise sighed. "How lucky you are to have rooms of your own."

"Lady Quarles said the same thing to me."

"She married one of my brother's courtiers," Princess Louise said to Julia.

"Lady Quarles declared that she would rent a flat if she could sign a lease," Susan said. "I'd forgotten married women can't. The law allows widows and single ladies to do so."

"But not unmarried princesses," Louise said.

Julia said, "I signed the lease for my building and arranged sundry contracts for services to the clinic. All that would be impossible if I married."

"Not if you married the right person." Susan smiled. "Someone who would sign without question."

"Hmm . . . perhaps." Julia glanced up at the clock on the mantel. "I wondered. Is there a cabstand nearby? I told Mister Ogilvie I wouldn't need him to return with our carriage."

"*Mister* Ogilvie?" Princess Louise said. "How democratic."

"Blame my American grandmother. 'Servants' were 'staff.' And when I was a child, she expected me to use surnames and titles for adults. So, he'll always be Mister Ogilvie to me."

"I like that," the princess said.

Susan raised an eyebrow. "Will you 'mister' John Brown from now on? Please tell me when you'll begin so I can sell tickets."

"Odious, odious man. And *his* brother, who looks after *my* brother Leopold, is worse. But the queen will hear nothing against the Browns. Walter tried—"

Susan knocked over the pepper shaker. "Clumsy of me. Thank goodness it wasn't the salt. That would be an unlucky end to my first luncheon party." She stood. "Shall we move to more comfortable chairs? Princess Louise has news for you, Doctor. A letter came from Germany."

Deftly done, Julia thought, wondering, *Who is Walter?*

"My sister apologizes for the delay," Princess Louise said. "She nursed the little princesses through colds and then wrote reams of family news."

"I've extracted the information about Lizzy Dowling and Lady Middlebury," Susan said, handing Julia a piece of paper. "After Prince Albert's death, the question of who should surround the queen became—"

"To be blunt, Mama, in her misery, found it hard to bear the happiness of others. Lady Middlebury was a recent widow, so she was the ideal companion for the queen."

"The lady had been left with limited means," Susan said. "She wrote to Princess Alice, accepting the position of lady-in-waiting. But there was a problem. A young servant, a local girl who'd fallen on hard times, had come under her wing."

"My sister remembers Lady Middlebury writing of a promise she made to look after the girl," Louise said. "So, a place was found at Osborne House for her 'little Kildare bird.' Lady Middlebury's family seat was at Kilcullen in Kildare, and the girl came from a nearby village."

"Princess Alice remembers a younger sister was settled somewhere in Ireland." Susan sighed. "Brigid Dowling, one supposes."

Princess Louise asked, "Will any of this be useful to Inspector Tennant?"

"Two things are interesting," Julia said. "Lizzie Dowling attracted a surprising number of influential friends, including you, Princess. What was it about the girl?"

Louise considered. "It's hard to put into words, and if you asked for an instance, I'm not sure." She shrugged, at a loss. "I suppose I felt a kindness in her toward me. Oh, not because I was a royal and she a servant. She was sensitive to moods and needs. Most of all, I believed I could trust her with my . . . with any troubles. And when she spoke of her younger sister, I thought she would do anything for that girl."

"Brigid Dowling said something like that in her last letter, poor girl," Lady Styles said. "But you said two things, Julia."

"Princess Alice names a location. The Dowling sisters came from a village near Kilcullen in Kildare. It's a place to start."

That night, at her dressing table, Julia realized Kate was no longer brushing her hair. Her maid looked back at her in the mirror, smiling.

"You've something on your mind, Doctor Julie, or you'd have stopped me five minutes ago." Kate lifted Julia's hair and spread it across her back. "You should wear it loose and lovely, like Princess Louise in the picture card you gave me."

"I can see Nurse Clemmie's face. She'd frown and hand me a set of hairpins."

"Still," Kate said, pointing the brush in the mirror. "You've got color in your cheeks and a sparkle in your eye. More than you had all those weeks when the inspector was away."

Julia took the brush and set it aside. "I was thinking about Lizzie Dowling. Something I learned today."

"Is that all?" Kate sighed. "And what might that be?"

"Before she served the queen, she worked in Ireland in the household of Lady Middlebury."

"From a high place to a higher one."

"Lizzie came from a village somewhere in Kildare." Julia swung her legs around and faced her maid. "How does it work, Kate? I imagine people leaving Ireland might settle together in London or Liverpool neighborhoods. Yes?"

" 'Tis like a daisy chain, one following the other. An older brother makes a few pounds and sends for the younger. That man knows of a job on the docks and an empty room in his boardinghouse, so he writes to a cousin. *He* travels with his friend who lives in the cottage down the lane."

"So, with a little digging, you could discover where people from a particular part of Kildare cluster."

"Are you wanting me to ask around about the Dowling sisters?"

"No, Kate, not you. There's a dangerous man out there. Sergeant O'Malley, on the other hand, is just the person. Speaking of the sergeant . . . did I see him walking from the tradesmen's entrance the other day, eating a scone?"

"He was after dropping off those reports from the inspector. He stopped for a civil word and a bite."

"I see," Julia said, her smile widening. "A civil word and drawn by Cook's baking. Nothing else?"

"As to that, I couldn't say." A pink-faced Kate put her hand on the wooden handle of the copper bed warmer. "Should I take it out, or will you?"

"I'll take care of it."

"Don't be staying awake 'til all hours when you're up with the birds."

"Good night, Kate," Julia called as her maid closed the door.

But Julia wasn't sleepy. She sat at her window seat, drawing her woolen wrap around her. *Sergeant O'Malley* . . . Why not? The man deserved a good wife, and there was none better than Kate. *Matchmaking.* Julia smiled wryly. Aunt Caroline would tell her to stick to one heart at a time. *Starting with my own.*

In June, when she'd packed a bag and shown up at Richard's house in Kent, she never really intended to spend the night alone in a Dover hotel. But over the months of separation . . . *Cold feet?* She looked down at her slippers and smiled. *They feel warmer now.*

Julia parted the starched white curtains. A full moon lit the circular sweep of Finsbury Circus, the bare trees black silhouettes against the paler sky. She sat, leaning on her elbow. *Is Kate right about the sparkle in my eye?*

Julia threw off the covers each morning, happier than she'd been for months, eager for the day. But her nights . . . most nights felt longer and lonelier. Her grandfather nodded off most evenings, retiring early, leaving empty hours until bedtime. She'd look up from a book, listening, hoping for a late knock, disappointed when the ticking clock and the whoosh of falling fireplace ash were the only sounds.

Julia roused herself when a bank of thin clouds drifted, veiling the moon. She removed the warmer from between the sheets, tipped the hot embers from the pan, and leaned the long handle against the fireplace. Julia turned back the blanket and looked down at the bed. She hovered her hand, feeling the rising heat against her palm. A smile played on her lips. She wondered, *What would it be like*? To share a bed with someone who warmed the sheets.

On Monday morning, Tennant's day at the Yard began with a report from Liverpool: confirmation that McGrath had taken a steamer from Cork, landed, and moved on to London. But there, the trail ended. He smiled when the knock that interrupted him was Julia's.

"Just the person I wanted to see," Tennant said, rounding his desk and pulling out a chair.

"That's always pleasant to hear." She sat, peeling off her gloves.

"I'm eager for your summary about our corpses."

"Hmm . . . not so delightful." Julia handed him her report. "There's no doubt a single killer is at work. Any rational person—"

"Rational. That's the rub. Well, the colonel will believe what he will, but this will convince the commissioner."

Tennant brought her up to date on the recent developments.

"So, you have servants stealing from the queen," Julia said, "using royal service to cover up a smuggling enterprise. Is it your theory that Lizzie stumbled on the scheme?"

"It seems reasonable . . ."

"But?"

"Brigid Dowling's murder doesn't fit. Our gentlemen suspects, not the servants, knew about her travels. And they had the leisure and means to move around, not Bolger, the Osborne House steward."

"There's what's his name," Julia said. "The valet to the Prince of Wales in London."

"Stanley Hackett's a low-level crook and a scared rabbit," Tennant said. "No, first things first, Julia. How often I've gotten it wrong by losing track of that simple principle."

"Meaning?"

"It starts with the murder of Lizzy Dowling. For some reason, she had to die. Why?"

"I have something for you on that score. It's the second reason I'm here." Julia extracted a sheet of paper from her medical bag. "Faithfully transcribed by Lady Styles from Princess Alice's letter, sparing you pages of royal family news."

"About time," Tennant said, scanning the paper. "Well, it clears up part of a mystery—how Lizzie got to Osborne House. Still, an intriguing question mark remains about Lady Middlebury's interest in the girl."

"And Princess Alice names a location for you. A village near Kilcullen."

"Kilcullen?" O'Malley said, entering the room. "'Tis wild country thereabouts."

The inspector rummaged in his drawer, found a map of Ireland, and unfolded it across his desk. O'Malley pointed to a spot.

"Hmm . . . only a scattering of villages," Tennant said. "Most of the area seems taken up by the great plain of the Curragh and the British army base."

O'Malley said, "More soldiers and sheep than locals."

Julia looked at the sergeant. "What do they think about a British military base in their midst?"

O'Malley smoothed his mustache, considering. "'Tis a bit of a mix. Not much love lost, but plenty of Irishmen 'take the queen's shilling' and serve in the army."

Tennant folded the map back to the rectangle that showed Kilcullen. "Make a list of the villages, Paddy. Then we'll send a message to the Kilcullen constabulary. Someone must know the Dowling family."

O'Malley grinned. "Sure, it will give those sleepy coppers something to do."

Julia said, "Perhaps if you ask around London's Irish neighborhoods for people from Kildare. Kate said emigrants tend to cluster."

Tennant said, "We're looking for someone else from Kildare." He explained the hunt for McGrath, the sniper.

"Paddy, can we identify some likely neighborhoods?"

"There was a flood of famine emigration from Kildare and other Leinster counties, so it'll be hard to find just one or two."

Tennant picked up a box of red-tipped pins and turned to his wall map of London. The inspector stuck markers as O'Malley rattled off place names, and Julia added some Irish neighborhoods in Whitechapel.

Tennant stood back from the map. "We'll start by alerting these divisional inspectors to look out for an Irishman in 'square-toed boots.' "

Two days later, they received a report of a sighting, so Tennant, O'Malley, and a pair of constables headed to a Whitechapel pub.

The Blue Anchor's barman dragged a mop cloth from his shoulder and wiped a few circles around the smooth oak surface. He'd had crossed anchors inked into the webbing of his left hand, and his fingers were stamped "H-O-L-D" and "F-A-S-T," one letter per knuckle.

Tennant held up his warrant card.

The barman peered at it and said, "The copper on this beat said to keep an eye out, so I reported a bloke wearing square-toed boots. He's a new face around here and looked and sounded like a typical Mick."

"And where will we be finding this typical Mick?" O'Malley asked in his broadest brogue.

"Sorry, mate. Meant no offense. Said he was lodging at Cohen's rooming house. Down the street, over the butcher shop."

A five-minute walk brought them there. The shop bell's tinkle summoned the butcher from the back, wiping his hands on a bloody rag. He said he'd seen the "upstairs Irishman" mounting the stairs thirty minutes earlier.

Tennant asked, "Any other exit besides the side staircase?"

"Not unless you take a flying leap out the back window," the butcher said.

O'Malley asked, "Will the lock be giving us trouble if we force the door?"

"No worries, Sarge." The butcher tapped the side of his nose. "I got a key from old Cohen. Likes me to keep an eye on things."

Tennant assigned the two constables to watch the back window. "All right, Paddy. Let's move."

Tennant unlocked the door and pushed it open with a bang. The crash sent a man leaping from a wooden chair, knocking it backward. He had taken off his boots and jacket and had been reading a newspaper. O'Malley grabbed him under an armpit.

"What the fecking hell?" he said, struggling to free himself from the sergeant's grip.

"Name?" Tennant said.

"Who wants to know?"

"Scotland Yard." The inspector held up his warrant card. "Answer my question. Your name?"

The man stopped squirming. He blinked nervously and said, "Willie Hood. William Hood. Why are you here? I've done nothing wrong."

"He's not from Kildare," O'Malley said. "The fella's an Ulsterman. And he looks ten years too young."

"Have you ever been to America?" Tennant asked.

"That I haven't."

Tennant picked up his square-toed boots. "Where did you get these?"

Willie Hood pulled his arm out of the constable's grip and cocked his thumb. "A stall on Rosemary Lane. An old woman sold them to me at the rag fair."

Tennant tossed the boots at his feet. "Put them on and take us to her."

It was getting late, but traders in secondhand goods, mostly women, still lined one side of Rosemary Lane, hawking patched shirts, threadbare coats, and battered bowlers. They found the old boot seller packing her boxes for the night, a wizened woman in a tattered gray shawl with a face as creased as a walnut shell. When she confirmed Willie Hood's story, the inspector let him go. Then he asked her about the boots.

"Bloke gave 'em to me last week—a long drink of water, he was."

"English or Irish?" Tennant asked.

"English, but not an East Ender. He gave them boots to me, not asking a penny."

"Did he say why?"

She shrugged. "Said his Irish friend didn't need them, and if anyone came calling . . ." She screwed up her face. "He said to tell them it'll be harder to find him than tracking a pair of old boots. Pitched me a shilling to repeat it back. Then he pulled his ginger beard. Phony, but you'd never guess. Snapped it, like, and winked."

"Mother of God," O'Malley muttered. "He's playing games with us now."

Tennant sent O'Malley home and took a cab from Rosemary Lane, returning to the Yard under a snow-gray sky. When he arrived, the first fat flakes had changed to rain. He passed through the deserted lobby, the duty sergeant alerting him to a pair of reports left on his desk. The inspector took the stairs as fast as his leg allowed. It had been a long day, and his thigh ached. He slung his overcoat and hat on the rack, added some coals to the grate, and lit the oil lamp on his desk. Then he snatched up the report from Superintendent Eager of Windsor Borough Police. Tennant eased into his chair and read it.

The sergeant accompanying Lady Middlebury's body to Ireland interviewed the great-nephew, Sir Hugo Browne of Lansdowne House in County Cork. Tennant instantly recognized the name from the first report from Ireland about Brigid Dowling. He read on. *Sir Hugo's connection to two murders as-*

tounded him. Brigid Dowling had been a lady's maid and companion to his grandmother, continuing to work for the family after her death. The elder Lady Browne and Lady Middlebury were sisters.

It all made sense. Princess Alice's letter said that Lady Middlebury took charge of Lizzie and "a sister had been settled as well." Lady Middlebury had turned to *her* sister to employ Brigid Dowling.

Tennant considered sending O'Malley to Ireland but decided he couldn't spare him. Instead, he drafted a cable to the divisional inspector in Dublin, asking him to dispatch an able man to Lansdowne House to interview the other servants and the family. A local copper had been there in December, but the Dublin man would do a more thorough job of it.

Chief Constable Phillips on the Isle of Wight had sent the second report. He'd worked with the Southampton police to compare shipping records at the port to the inventories at Osborne House. What they uncovered was a lucrative plot to defraud the queen. Michael Bolger had diverted scores of cases of expensive cognac and claret as well as vintage port, sherry, and Madeira. Bolger had reshipped them to the warehouse on Trig Pier in London, telling the Southampton officials they were destined for distribution at Buckingham Palace and Windsor Castle. The London receiving agent listed in the records was the valet, Stanley Hackett, now a guest of Her Majesty's in Newgate Prison.

Phillips concluded the report by noting that the port officials never thought to question Michael Bolger's instructions. He'd served for a decade as the queen's trusted house steward.

Tennant set aside the reports and considered the murderer and the message he'd left with the shoe seller. Was he throwing down a marker for some purpose or simply hurling a silly taunt? The man's action was confounding, like an actor who steps out of the scene and speaks to the audience. *Boots belonging to an Irish friend—was the original owner McGrath?*

Was McGrath in England at the murderer's behest? If so, why? The tall man was a ruthless, proficient killer. Why would he need the specialized skills of a sniper?

Tennant tipped his chair and contemplated the cracks in the plaster ceiling. He knew them well, but they were hard to follow in the evening's flickering lamplight. He thought about the first inspector he'd worked with at the Yard. He would have said that a criminal sending messages to the police wanted to be caught. Tennant wasn't sure, but he had worked on such a case in his first collaboration with Julia.

Julia . . . he wished she were there to talk the day through, to pick holes in his theories, to help him weave the strands into a pattern. He closed his eyes, thinking about her. Then he roused himself and turned down the lamp's burner, wishing he were going home to her.

In the morning, Sergeant O'Malley entered Tennant's office, waving a paper.

"Our human ferret has come up with the goods. Constable Williams found the name and address of the Trig Wharf warehouse owners. Big fellas who own half the dockside between Blackfriars and Southwark bridges."

"Good man. Did Williams follow up with the owners?"

"That he did," O'Malley said, handing over the sheet. "Look at the name of the warehouse renter. The last line."

Tennant read and looked up. "Osborne Bros. Imports."

"The cheek of it. After lifting the goods from the queen's own house, he's using the name."

"More games. It cheers me, Paddy. The man thinks he's as slippery as a greasy pole. Overconfidence breeds mistakes."

"We're needing a trip-up."

"Constable Williams's description from the company clerk is halfway there. Tall and thin, but he's abandoned the ginger beard. Hmm . . . and something else. He describes the man's eyes as pale. An almost colorless blue."

"I'll be adding it to the description." O'Malley smoothed his bushy mustache and stroked his chin.

"What is it, Paddy?" Tennant said.

"This tall, pale-eyed killer . . . The boot seller is saying he's English, not Irish."

"Gunrunning for money rather than the cause?"

"I'm thinking how many of our suspects are Irish," O'Malley said. "There's Michael Bolger, the house steward, although he seems to have been born in England. Even the toffs serving the crown are Anglo-Irish."

"There's Major FitzGerald, most obviously," Tennant said.

"And Sir Lionel *Dermott.* Not to mention Captain Oliver Montgomery. Montgomery's an Ulster name that you'll find all over County Down."

"It leaves Captain Frederick Locock as the odd Englishman out."

"They all took the queen's shilling," O'Malley said, "but I'd not be giving tuppence for any of them, save Sir Lionel. He's value for the money."

Tennant held up Constable Williams's report. "Our ferret has given us a company name and a description of the agent. It's time to find out where all that Osborne alcohol wound up."

Tennant spent the rest of the day making the rounds of London's exclusive hotels and Pall Mall's gentlemen's clubs. The hotel managers and the club secretaries gave strikingly similar descriptions of the agent representing Osborne Brothers. The man gave his name as "Albert Schmidt." *Another joke?* Tennant thought. *A German last name and the first name of the queen's German-born husband?* The witnesses described him as a well-dressed Englishman, tall and thin, with pale blue eyes and fair hair, wearing a dark tweed coat and bowler hat. As Tennant walked west along Pall Mall and the gaslights winked on in the late afternoon, he found himself eyeing every tall man he passed on the street.

If the inspector had lingered in the area another twelve hours, stayed until just before daybreak, and walked the short distance to the road between Buckingham Palace's gardens and Green Park, he might have spotted the man he sought.

The driver glanced down at his fidgety passenger and said, "I told you, mate. London never sleeps—even long after midnight. Not tucked up in bed like most of County Kildare. We've plenty of company."

McGrath had told the driver he was mad to venture out at that hour, conspicuous, driving the streets before dawn. But the man with the reins knew they would be invisible. Piccadilly teemed at night, lit by lamplight and alive with traffic moving by wheel and on foot, even at five in the morning. He steered the wagon between the street sellers rumbling their barrows at the curbside and carters clopping down the road. Women staggered at crossings, setting down baskets of oranges, stopping at the coffee stalls on the corners, drawn by glowing braziers and the scent of the brew.

"Mother of God," McGrath muttered. "You'd be thinking it was the middle of the day."

The driver turned off Piccadilly just before they reached Hyde Park Corner. The coal wagon they'd "borrowed" rattled onto Constitution Hill, the road between Green Park and Buckingham Palace's grounds. The night was moonless. Dark, leafless trees rose in silhouette on either side.

"Jesus," McGrath muttered after they rolled under a gaslight, passing a bobbie on his beat. He twisted around, checking that the long, narrow object wrapped in oilcloth was still hidden under its thin black layer. "What if he stopped us?"

The driver laughed. "Never. London runs on coal, so we're a

familiar sight. No worries, mate." He'd given the copper a two-fingered salute as they passed him.

McGrath cocked his thumb at Buckingham Palace. "Thought I'd be seeing more soldiers."

"Nah," the driver said. "The palace walls are high, and the queen's soldiers stick to the gates. When the guard changes, they march around in their silly fur hats. Stop fretting, boy-o."

They passed under another gaslight, nearing the halfway point down the hill.

"We're sure she'll be here tomorrow?"

"Oh yes. Information received from high places."

"I'll be needing a clear day at that distance."

"Barometer's rising. Now, forget tomorrow and get yourself ready."

McGrath reached around, pulled a sooty bundle from the back of the cart, and waited for the slowing wagon to stop. The Irishman jumped and ran toward the tree line. Then the driver gave his horse a touch of the whip and rumbled on. Five minutes later, McGrath caught up with him at the bottom of the hill.

"Find a good spot?" he asked when a sweating McGrath hauled himself into the cart. "You'll be able to find it easy tomorrow?"

"Now who's fretting, boy-o?" the Irishman said.

The driver snapped the reins, and the horse clopped on. They skirted the palace forecourt, avoiding the gates and the soldiers of the Queen's Guards. As they drove through a pool of lamplight, the driver fixed his pale blue eyes on McGrath and winked. "Piece of cake, mate."

They disappeared into the darkness.

CHAPTER 14

Susan Styles stopped on the landing between the first and ground floors and peered at the face of a brass-and-oak barometer. She tapped the glass and smiled. The black hand pointed reassuringly to a spot between FAIR and VERY DRY. The servants had drawn back the burgundy drapes, and sunlight streamed through the southeast windows, slanting bright rectangles across the floor's Persian carpets.

Susan caught the butler as he crossed the entrance hall. "Did the footman catch Mrs. Locock before she left?" She'd sent a note to Mary about their morning walk.

"Yes, my lady. And William was grateful for the half crown. He's a good lad with an elderly mother to keep. And being out on a morning like this wasn't a chore."

She smiled. "Today is a reminder that winter isn't a life sentence."

Susan hadn't been away from the house and grounds in days. Princess Alexandra's knee had been bothering her. Louise had holed up in her room, producing sketches and clay models for a new project. When Mary Locock sent an invitation to stroll in Green Park with her baby, Lady Styles accepted with pleasure. Susan's note would prepare Mary for two unexpected additions to their walking party: Harriet FitzGerald and Princess Louise.

At Marlborough House the evening before, dinner conversation had wandered down the oft-visited topic of the weather. Susan had read the prince's boredom as easily as a child's picture book, wondering if he would ever grow up. Bertie's gaze had drifted over Alix's head and fixed on the mantel clock. *He's calculating when he can slip away to the Midnight Club.* The prince wasn't the only one who found the evening dull, so Lady Styles amused herself by conducting a small experiment.

Susan turned to Oliver Montgomery, seated at her left. "I'm meeting Mary Locock in Green Park tomorrow morning. That is if the sun shines and it's not too cold." She glanced across the table at a bored Harriet FitzGerald. Then she asked, "Princess Louise, are you still planning to join us?"

When Louise said yes, Harriet had brightened at once. "Oh, I adore Green Park. And walks are just the thing to shake off the winter doldrums."

"Why don't you come?" Susan had said. "We arranged to meet at eleven at the Queen's Walk."

As Susan waited for Princess Louise to come down in the morning, she thought, *I shouldn't have baited Harriet last night.* Still, she couldn't help smiling. At least Harriet would be rewarded with a morning spent in her idol's company.

Princess Louise called from the first-floor landing, "Do I need my muff?"

"I think not. Gloves are enough."

"Good." She handed it to a footman and descended. "Harriet is meeting us at the park?"

"Yes."

The princess waved away the waiting carriage as Susan guessed she would, and they walked the short stretch from

Marlborough House to Green Park. "Cantered" was a better word, and Susan fell behind after twenty paces.

"Come along, Susan. With all this waiting on Alix, you've lost a step or two."

"Perhaps if Their Royal Highnesses would make up their minds—decide on the time they wished to go out—there would be less sitting involved in waiting."

Princess Louise laughed. "Guilty as charged. Still, your early mornings are predictable. Nothing much happens before eleven. I cannot understand how Alix lazes away the best part of the day. She was still in bed, picking at her breakfast tray, when I looked in to say goodbye."

Susan stole a look at Louise's profile. It had been their liveliest exchange in days, and her moodiness and preoccupation had lifted. Still, Lady Styles wondered about the outing. But she buried her misgivings, thinking, *Perhaps it's a good idea after all.*

Susan said, "You'll have to slow the pace when we arrive at the park. A stroll with a baby carriage isn't a race."

They reached the end of the Mall and turned right onto the Queen's Walk. Louise waved, spotting Harriet FitzGerald and Mary Locock strolling in their direction, Mary pushing a perambulator. Then the four set off to traverse Green Park along the main path that cut across the lawn like the hypotenuse of a triangle. Louise walked beside Mrs. Locock; Harriet and Susan fell in place behind them.

Nursery maids pushed most of the baby carriages they passed, but Susan knew that Mary Locock delighted in every small act of motherhood.

"Your youngest must still be in his perambulator, Harriet," Mary said. She leaned into the carriage, adjusting little Henry's blankets. "Why didn't you bring him along?"

Harriet waved away the question. "Oh, I never interfere

with the workings of the nursery. Nanny and the maids have their schedules."

Princess Louise caught Susan's eye and looked away.

They walked along, four ladies and a baby, the infant nestled in a three-wheeled, rattan perambulator. They'd nearly reached the center of the triangular park where they would turn and make the circuit back to the Queen's Walk. A tittering, tweeting chorus serenaded them as they passed a thick planting of trees.

"Redwings, I think," Susan said.

"They've woken the baby." Princess Louise bent forward over the carriage.

A loud, sharp crack sent the flock of frantic birds flapping from the branches.

"Damn it, another dead end," Tennant said, dropping the report from Kilcullen on his desk.

The chief constable of Kildare's Royal Irish Constabulary had forwarded their report on the Dowling family. They'd traced them to a small village west of Kilcullen, but the trail ended there.

"The hamlet lost its church years ago," Tennant said to O'Malley, "but the copper from Kilcullen found an old priest in the next town who remembered the family. After the husband died, his wife and children were forced off the farm. Margaret Dowling and her daughters, Elizabeth and Brigid."

"'Tis an old story in Ireland, packing up after generations in a place but with nowhere to go. Is the priest remembering where they headed?"

"To Naas Workhouse," Tennant said. "The local removing officer wrote up the order, so we have a date: September 1856."

O'Malley shook his head. "Poor lasses."

"Here's the mystery, Paddy. Naas Workhouse has no record of them."

"'Tis a puzzle. We have Lizzie Dowling, an ordinary Irish lass living in Kildare. She never arrives at the workhouse but starts working for Lady Middlebury."

Tennant nodded. "The Middleburys' estate is eight miles east of Kilcullen, not far from the Dowlings' village. Then Lizzie crosses the sea to work for the queen and is murdered."

"And the little sister, Brigid Dowling, travels far to the south in County Cork to work for Lady Middlebury's sister. Then Brigid is murdered in London, and Lady Middlebury in Windsor Great Park."

"Neither of the sisters ended up at Naas Workhouse," Tennant said. "Nor did their mother, Margaret Dowling."

"What happened to their mam, I'm wondering?"

"Unknown." Tennant handed the report to O'Malley. "One last riddle. Take a look at the final paragraph. According to the old priest, someone else was looking for the Dowlings."

The sergeant read it and looked up. "A soldier, showing up a year or two later."

"Pity this Father Flynn's eyesight and memory are half gone."

O'Malley twisted around in his seat at the sound of raised voices and boots pounding down the corridor.

"Sir"—a panting constable took a deep breath—"there's been a shooting in Green Park."

He watched her fall. Then he dropped the rifle among the black poplars, the cover from where he aimed and fired. The bullet struck higher and farther to the right than an ideal kill shot, and he smiled. *Couldn't be better,* he thought. He knew not to run and draw attention to himself. He walked twenty yards parallel to the line of trees, then calmly cut across the verge, joining the foot traffic along Constitution Hill.

Passersby along the street had heard nothing over the din of carriage traffic, their gazes turned away from Green Park, intent on Buckingham Palace, looking to see if the Royal Standard flew from the flagpole. It waved from it rarely, and the pole was empty that day. The queen was elsewhere.

He headed up the hill toward Piccadilly, one dark-haired man of average height lost in the late-morning throng.

Sir Richard stopped Tennant and O'Malley at the end of the corridor. "Three ladies were taken to Westminster Hospital."

"Three?"

"Princess Louise is reported to be among them. The first report identified her as the victim, but a second says she wasn't injured. I don't trust either account, given all the confusion. You and the sergeant go to the hospital and sort it out."

Tennant asked, "Who's taking charge of the investigation in the park?"

"The local divisional inspector, for now. You take command when you finish at the hospital."

"Yes, sir," Tennant said, turning away.

A hansom waited at the back entrance to the Yard. The driver applied his whip when Tennant said, "Westminster Hospital. As quickly as you can." As they rattled down Whitehall, passing Downing Street and the Home Office building, Tennant wondered if Sir Lionel Dermott knew about the shooting. He got his answer when the cab swung right, passing Westminster Abbey on the left, and rolled to a stop behind a hansom. Dermott looked over his shoulder as he paid off the cabbie.

"You've heard," Sir Lionel said.

"Our information is that Princess Louise was among the party but is uninjured, Tennant said. "I'm here to confirm that report."

"And Susan? Lady Styles. Was she—"

Tennant took his arm. "There's only one way to find out."

They climbed the steps of a castle-like building, entering

through the center bay of its triple-arched portico. A row of crystal chandeliers was an inadequate light source for the vast waiting room. Its luxuriousness was at odds with the ragged, coughing sick who waited on the wooden benches that lined the space.

A pair of harried nurses moved from one sick patient to the next. The more senior of them snapped, "Admittance window," in answer to Tennant's request for information. He showed his warrant card to the porter on duty, who released an unseen catch, and the adjacent door popped open.

"This way, guv." The porter led them down a short hallway and opened the door to a waiting room.

Susan and Princess Louise looked like they'd exited a battlefield or a butcher's shop. Blood stained the skirts of their gowns. Two pairs of gory gloves sat crumpled and discarded on a table, curling and hardening in the cold room. Someone had given them blankets. Susan stood; it slipped from her shoulders, uncovering her bloodied sleeves.

"My dear." When Dermott took her hands, Tennant noticed rusty stains around her fingernails. Lionel seated her again, replacing the blanket around her shoulders, and bowed to the princess.

"The surgeon is with Harriet," Princess Louise said.

"A parkkeeper and a constable carried her to a hackney," Susan said. "The princess knew what to do, and we did our best."

"Padding and pressure on the wound," Louise said. "I've seen the doctors attend to my brother, Leopold, who bleeds easily. The parkkeeper had a knife, so we cut strips from our underskirts and took turns."

"Mrs. FitzGerald owes her chances to your quick thinking, Princess," Tennant said. "Now, tell me what happened at the park. First, did you see the shooter?"

"No," Susan said. "The shot came from a distance as the four of us reached the intersecting paths at the park's center."

"Four of you?"

"Mrs. Locock was with us. And her baby," Susan said. "We sent her home."

Tennant said, "Will you describe how you arranged yourselves as you walked?"

"I'll show you if you have a paper and pencil," Princess Louise said.

"Sergeant?"

O'Malley handed the princess his notepad and pencil. With confident strokes, she sketched four women walking in pairs, one pushing a baby carriage. Louise had labeled the figures, but he recognized Lady Styles and the princess even in her rough drawing.

"Thank you, Your Royal Highness. Could either of you tell from what direction the shot came?"

"I'm not sure." Susan looked at the princess, who shook her head. "Except . . ."

"What is it, Lady Styles?" Tennant said. "Even an impression may be helpful."

"I'd just commented on some birds singing in a grove. They were to the left of the paths' intersection on the Buckingham Palace side of the park. The shot sent them flying in all directions."

"Was that your impression as well, Princess?"

"I'd just bent over the baby carriage at that instant, so I'm unsure."

Tennant glanced at the sketch. He looked up and saw Lady Styles's startled expression. *She's just realized Louise may have been the target, not Harriet.*

"Sergeant O'Malley, give the divisional inspector my compliments and ask him to assign some constables to search that grove immediately."

A nurse entered as O'Malley exited. "Sir Godfrey is leaving the operating theater for his office."

"And Harriet?" Dermott asked.

"Stable. Are you the lady's husband?"

"No," Sir Lionel said. "He's at Windsor. The Home Office informed him by telegram."

"I see," the nurse said. "If you gentlemen will follow me?"

Tennant and Dermott found the blood-spattered surgeon in his office. Sir Godfrey Fellows turned his back to the nurse, and she slid a gore-encrusted frock coat off his shoulders and hung it on a peg behind his door. Then she helped him shrug into a pristine one.

He adjusted his cuffs and said, "The bullet went through her chest well above the heart and toward the shoulder, exiting her back. It nicked no major arteries but did its damage all the same."

"You're saying it struck her in the front and not at the side?"

"That is correct, Inspector."

Dermott asked the surgeon, "What are Mrs. FitzGerald's chances for recovery?"

"I'm not going to quote odds. Surgery is not a game of chance. Her husband is the queen's equerry, I understand."

"That is correct," Dermott said.

"She's being moved into a private room instead of the general ward. My assistant in surgery, Doctor Rennie, will keep an eye on her. Infection is the danger now, but only time will tell."

When Sir Godfrey opened the door for them, the surgeon's filthy frock coat slipped from its hook. The inspector picked it up and rehung it.

Tennant remembered a conversation with Julia's grandfather about an article in *The Lancet.* The medical journal described patients who remained free of infection when the surgeon and his assistants washed their hands and instruments, wore clean surgical aprons, and treated wounds with a special solution.

The doctor you draw, Tennant thought. *Surgery is a game of chance, after all.*

Dermott stopped Tennant outside the office. "You think Princess Louise was the gunman's target, don't you?"

"It's probable. And I believe Lady Styles thinks so, too."

Lionel said, "I'll speak to the home secretary. All the royal residences in London must have their guards increased."

"Will you escort the ladies to Marlborough House?" Tennant asked. "And explain the danger to the princess? We need to ascertain the whereabouts of the Prince of Wales."

"I'll see to it."

"One more thing. Can you get a written order from the home secretary to admit Doctor Julia Lewis to Mrs. FitzGerald's recovery room?"

"I'm not sure Gathorne-Hardy will think it's . . ."

"Press him. Mrs. FitzGerald is the wife of the queen's equerry."

"Very well. If you think it's necessary."

"I do. I'll send Doctor Lewis a note explaining my reasons."

At Green Park, O'Malley handed Tennant a rifle. Stamped into the side of the gun's metal receiver were the markings C 1867 and SAINT-ÉTIENNE.

"One of our missing French weapons," Tennant said.

"Coppers found it among the trees." The sergeant pointed to a stand of black poplars. "Lady Styles was right about the direction of the shot."

"Did they find anything else?"

"Some scuff marks. And this." O'Malley signaled to a constable, who handed him an oilcloth bag covered in coal dust. He measured it to the rifle. " 'Tis a perfect fit."

"Show me where you found them."

They walked through the trees. "Here," O'Malley said.

"He had a clear view of the convergence of the paths." A short walk brought them through the trees and within yards of the foot and carriage traffic on Constitution Hill.

"I'd be guessing he took off up the hill," O'Malley said. "Then he's got a choice. Right along Piccadilly or left on Knightsbridge to melt into the crowds."

"We'll ask the divisional inspector to—" Tennant looked around. "Where is he?"

"He's thinking along the same lines, taking some coppers up the hill, looking for witnesses. And there's a cabstand there, as well."

"I'll ask him to keep his officers on the streets until evening. People are creatures of habit. We might get lucky when they return home by the same route."

They didn't get lucky. No one saw a man with a long, dusty bag walking in the park or along Constitution Hill.

When Julia got Tennant's note, she packed gauze and gloves into her medical bag and waited for Nurse Clemmie to return. Her head nurse entered the office with two bottles of carbolic solution and added them to the bag.

"I've sent a message to Doctor Franklin at the London Hospital," Julia said. "If something too complicated to treat arises, send the patient there."

"A rifle wound to the chest. That sounds grim." Clemmie shook her head.

Julia's nurse was right, and she hoped to find the patient alive when her carriage reached Westminster Hospital. The porter ushered her into Mrs. FitzGerald's room and then vanished. A young doctor with flaming, wiry hair looked up briefly from what he was doing.

"Who the blazes let ye in?" he said in a thick Scots accent. "We're having no visitors. Nurse Howland, show her the door." He continued to spray a mist from a metal contraption the size of a teakettle. A bottle of carbolic solution stood on the table by the bed.

"I'm Doctor Julia Lewis." She walked forward, waving the home secretary's note. "And I've brought replenishments." She opened the bag containing carbolic solution for him to see.

"Woman, yer a godsend. Nurse Howland, bundle the carbolic away from prying eyes." He put the sprayer aside. "I'm Doctor Rennie. Why is the Home Office sending a lady doctor to us, bearing gifts?"

After Julia explained the circumstances, Rennie said, "A copper who reads *The Lancet?*"

Julia smiled. "Not exactly. Inspector Tennant heard about Doctor Lister's experiments from my grandfather, Doctor Andrew Lewis."

"That's more than I can say for the likes of Sir Godfrey Fellows. And I left all six of Lister's articles on the man's desk."

Julia moved to the bed. "How is Mrs. FitzGerald?"

"Early days. Early hours, but I'm hopeful. We're doing our best, Nurse Howland and I." Rennie gave the girl a friendly wink. "We're fellow conspirators, soaking the instruments in the surgical theater before the great man arrives and spraying the place down."

"We've changed the bandages once," the nurse said.

"And we're following Lister's wound treatment methods to the letter." Dr. Rennie felt Harriet's forehead and nodded. "If the lass lives, she can thank Nurse Howland's care and her friends' quick thinking for saving her life. They ripped their petticoats and held them fast to the wound."

"One of them was Princess Louise," Nurse Howland said.

"Now that's strange," Rennie said, cupping his palms as the nurse poured carbolic solution onto his hands.

"What is?" Julia asked.

"The victim." Rennie rubbed his hands vigorously. "Why shoot this lady and let the princess be? It's the royals these lunatics are after. Think of all the attacks on the queen. Did the gunman make a mistake?"

Julia looked down at the fair-haired Harriet. *There is a resemblance.* She wondered if Tennant had ever met Mrs. FitzGerald.

In the morning, Commissioner Mayne summoned Tennant and Sir Lionel to a meeting with the Fenian Department's chief. Colonel Fielding looked pointedly at his watch. Sir Lionel Dermott was late.

"Let's begin," Sir Richard said. "Inspector?"

"I think the stolen French rifle all but settles the matter," Tennant said. "We must consider that the shooter is Patrick McGrath, and his real target was Princess Louise, not Mrs. FitzGerald."

"By God, I want action." Sir Richard banged the conference table, rattling the French rifle lying in the middle. "It's time the gloves came off."

The door opened. "Apologies, gentleman." Sir Lionel took his seat. "A cable from Karachi arrived at the Colonial Office. The message was sent there by mail steamer from Australia. Five days ago, an assailant in Sydney shot Prince Alfred in the back."

The commissioner groaned. "Christ, Almighty. And the prince?"

"Expected to recover."

"What else do we know about the attack?"

"The shooter is in police custody," Dermott said. "His name is Henry O'Farrell, born in Dublin, and a suspected Fenian."

"Worse and worse," the commissioner muttered. "What in Hades was the prince doing in Australia?"

"His Royal Highness is on a round-the-world voyage," Dermott said. "The HMS *Galatea* isn't due back for several months."

"It's hard enough to protect the royals at home, damn it,"

Colonel Fielding grumbled. “Never mind on the other side of the world.”

“And half the royal princesses are married to bloody Germans,” Sir Richard said. “Is the Prince of Wales under lock and key?”

“Yes. Bertie called it house arrest,” Dermott said. “But he’s agreed to remain at Marlborough House if only to avoid Princess Louise’s fate.”

“Which is?” Sir Richard asked.

“The queen ordered her back to Windsor. The remaining royal offspring in England are at the castle now.”

“Good,” Colonel Fielding said. “Safest place for them.”

“Bollocks, Fielding!” Sir Richard shouted. “No place is safe.”

“I agree,” Tennant said. “Lady Middlebury was murdered in Windsor Great Park.”

“The number of soldiers patrolling the castle will double,” Dermott said. “The commander has given the Home Office that assurance.”

“Good,” Sir Richard said. “London is the Yard’s responsibility. I want constables out in force in Irish neighborhoods. Inspector Tennant, see to it.”

Sir Lionel asked, “What intelligence do we have from the Fenian Department, Colonel? Anything at all, or have all your ‘eyes and ears’ gone blind and deaf?”

Fielding pushed back his seat; the leg caught on the carpet and fell with a thud. “You’re a smug bastard, Dermott.” The colonel stalked out and slammed the door.

“Dear me,” Lionel said, getting up and righting the chair.

“You are a smug bastard, Sir Lionel.” Sir Richard’s smile flickered. “But I had the same question.” He waved Tennant and Dermott out of his office. “You have my orders, Inspector. Carry on.”

Outside, Tennant asked Lionel, "Any word on Mrs. FitzGerald?"

"I came directly from the hospital. She's holding her own, thank God. The surgeon's assistant, Doctor Rennie, seems a sensible chap."

"That's a relief. Sir Godfrey struck me as a—"

"Pompous blowhard?" Dermott said. "I understand Doctor Lewis was there yesterday and returned in the morning."

"And Major FitzGerald?"

"Bowled over, poor fellow. You'll hear no more jokes from me."

"Turning over a new leaf?"

"Well . . ." Dermott pulled on his gloves and drew his walking stick from under his arm. "At least until Harriet is out of the woods. As for the two heroines of the hour, Princess Louise and Lady Styles leave for Windsor this afternoon. The queen asked her to accompany the princess."

"What about their escort to the castle?"

"A detachment of the Queen's Household Guards. Now, I must run. I'm collecting Susan at her flat and taking her to the station to catch the royal train."

"And I must crack the whip at Sir Richard's command."

"About this show of force in Irish neighborhoods . . . Useful?"

Tennant shrugged. "My guess? We'll do more harm than good and learn nothing."

Tennant and O'Malley took charge of the raids on the two Irish neighborhoods closest to the scene of the shooting. As for the others, Tennant relayed his recommendations to the divisional inspectors and was forced to rely on the common sense and restraint of sergeants he didn't know.

Sergeant O'Malley and six constables headed to St. Giles

while Tennant and a squad of coppers traveled to Kensington. The inspector's destination was one of London's most squalid Irish rookeries: the collection of backcourt houses known as the Jennings Rents, located just beyond the gates of Kensington Palace.

The inspector shared his cab with a Kensington constable and a sergeant. Tennant rapped the cab's roof, and the hackney slowed to a stop near "the Grandy," the Marquis of Grandy public house on the High Street. A second cab carrying four other constables rolled up behind them.

Tennant and the young sergeant took a quick look behind the pub. Ramshackle wooden houses with rotting clapboards and missing roof tiles ringed the courtyard.

"Must be hell in the cold and wet," the copper muttered. "The pigs on my uncle's farm live better than this."

"There's a back door from the Grandy into the court, Sergeant. We'll need to cover the exit." They headed back to the waiting officers.

Tennant gathered them. "Before we go into the pub, remember. It's information I want. Cracking heads and turning over tables is the surest way *not* to get it. Your sergeant agrees with me, I know."

"Yes, sir," he said.

Tennant assigned the sergeant and two coppers to the backcourt to "grab any bolters." He gestured to the others to follow him. When the inspector and three uniformed constables walked through the front entrance, half the drinkers froze. The others scrambled out the back door. Tennant delivered his message and then made his way to the building's rear.

Two men sat with their backs against the Grandy's rear wall. A third twisted and squirmed in the sergeant's grip.

Tennant said, "Stop resisting, or the officer will apply his truncheon to your head. Which will it be?"

The man's shoulders went slack. When the sergeant released

him, he slid to a sitting position at the base of the wall and glared.

Tennant looked around the backcourt at the careworn women with soiled aprons knotted over tattered gray dresses, their faces as colorless as their clothing. They stared, looking up from basins, pots of peeled potatoes, and piles of washing. The inspector hoped his message might register with them.

"I am Detective Inspector Tennant, and I'll tell you what I told them inside the Grandy. The Yard is looking for two men. One is English, tall and thin, fair-haired, and with pale blue eyes. The second is a Kildare man named Patrick McGrath, dark-haired and of middling height. In his early forties. He served in the Crimea and has been to America. I'm offering five pounds for useful information. No questions asked."

No one spoke, but Tennant hadn't expected them to inform before an audience.

"You know the bobbie on this beat. A quiet word to him, and he will pass it on to me."

Tennant didn't know it, but he had driven by the house where his quarry hid. McGrath was a world away from the squalor of the Jennings Rents but closer than the inspector imagined, holed up in comfortable quarters. He stretched out on a hay bed and eased off his new boots. The narrower toes pinched a bit.

McGrath waited for his "host" to return, knowing he'd worn out his welcome. The man was desperate to get him out of his carriage house loft. McGrath had reminded him that coppers would swarm the rail stations and ports at Dover and the south. He'd head west to Bristol, where he had friends. But McGrath had to wait until the storm blew over and proposed to hide in the last place on earth anyone would expect to find him.

His host's first reaction had been, "You're mad." But McGrath saw the calculation in his eyes: the scheme might work, no matter how unlikely. He'd looked McGrath up and down and said, "Can you sound like something other than a bog-trotting Irishman?"

"Don't get yer cob on, mon. Lived a few years in Liverpool," he said in a Merseyside accent.

The man left, and McGrath waited. Then he heard the scrape of boots on the ladder's rough wood, followed by the sounds of a second man who handed McGrath a sheet of paper. It was a letter addressed to the head groom and signed with a flourish.

"He's given you an English-sounding name, Marcus York." The man's smile didn't touch his pale blue eyes.

"How do I get there?"

"No worries, boy-o," the thin man said. "I'm old mates with the head groom." Then he dropped to his knees by a wooden crate, lifted the lid, and sighed. "Shame, that."

McGrath said, "What is?"

"These." He pulled out a rifle and fixed its bayonet. "They're worth the better part of a hundred quid, but it's too risky to flog the last lot now."

After the men left, McGrath lit a Havana, a luxury he hadn't indulged in since his time in the States. He blew smoke ring after smoke ring, watching them rise, blue halos that wobbled and vanished as they drifted toward the ceiling. McGrath thought through his final moves on a chessboard in his head. The knight was nearing his last jump. As for the pawn, the newly christened Marcus York had an endgame in mind for him, too.

Susan heard the crunch of carriage wheels. A moment later, she opened the street door.

"I'm early, I know." Sir Lionel angled his shoulders and pointed his walking stick at the pavement. "I could circle for twenty minutes."

"No need. I'm nearly ready. Come in, take off your coat, and have a seat."

He did as she instructed and searched her face. "How are you today? After that appalling experience."

"Better. Better after talking to Doctor Lewis at the hospital this morning. Harriet is . . . well, she's holding her own."

"I must have just missed you."

"I've . . ." Susan looked away. "I've felt guilty about Harriet."

"Why on earth? Doctor Lewis said you and the princess saved her life."

"I only mentioned the walk to see if she'd accept, knowing Princess Louise was among the party." She closed her eyes for a moment. "A heartless, private amusement that ended in a shooting. And Harriet is a harmless creature, really."

"Well, this is a confessional afternoon. I've had similar regrets about FitzGerald. I've had a running joke for weeks with Inspector Tennant about his probable guilt in all this business."

"You don't believe he— "

Lionel shook his head. "He's certainly no Fenian. All those lesser FitzGeralds in the Leinster clan would be poor as church mice if the Irish nationalists clawed back their land. No, it was a harmless joke about a man I dislike. Now, it seems callous."

"Why don't you like him?"

"Let us say that I have my reasons. Did you see him at the hospital?"

"Yes. He'd taken the afternoon train from Windsor and was there all night. He was still at Harriet's bedside this morning."

FitzGerald's face had looked like bleached driftwood washed up on a strand: stiff, white, with lines deeply etched. Peter had followed Susan out the door and then stood silent, searching for words. "I've not been good to her." He touched her arm. "Nor to you. Have you forgiven me?"

"Of course. It was a long time ago." When he took his hand

away, Susan realized she'd felt nothing for him but compassion.

At the end of a slight pause, Lionel looked around the room and said, "I like the way you've arranged things."

Susan smiled wryly. "My sister-in-law asked if I would be more comfortable with the furniture from my old rooms. When I accepted, it arrived with almost indecent haste."

"Ah. And was she right?"

"Yes, as it happens."

"And shall you enjoy living on your own?"

"It's strange, but I've felt less alone here than amongst the multitudes in other people's houses. I think my nature is solitary."

"Hmm . . . not much chance of solitude at Windsor Castle. Why has the queen sent you a summons, do you know?"

Susan shrugged. "I'll find out. I have a five o'clock audience with Her Majesty."

"How long will you be away?"

"I wish I knew. My waiting for Alix is nearly over—next week, the end of January. Another lady-in-waiting shuttles in on the first day of February."

"You certainly got more than you bargained for, but never mind the calendar. If Her Majesty commands, you wait," Lionel said.

"While *you* wait, let me pour you a sherry in one of your beautiful glasses."

Susan went to the drinks cabinet, set out a glass, and struggled with the seal on the bottle's neck. She froze when she felt hands on her shoulders, trying to turn her. Susan jerked away, smashing the bottle into a glass and breaking its bowl.

Lionel stepped back instantly. Crimson surged into his face. "Forgive me," he said stiffly.

"I'm sorry. I'm sorry, Lionel. It's . . . it's not you. Not your fault." She covered her face with her hands, her shoulders shaking. She looked up. "If only I could explain."

"Come," he said, standing carefully to one side, touching only her elbow. He led her to a chair, and she sat. "I won't press you. But if you'd like to tell me, please know that you can trust me."

"Yes. Yes, I know that." She looked up with streaming eyes. Lionel fished out his handkerchief, and she wiped away her tears.

He said quietly, "Tell me."

"You see, I didn't hear you come up behind me. I . . . didn't realize you were there." She took a deep breath and let it out slowly. "Last Saturday . . . Oh, I'm starting in the wrong place. Telling this badly."

"Take your time. Shall I pour another sherry?" He glanced at the cabinet and said, "I see five glasses are still intact." She returned his smile tremulously and nodded. He poured a sherry and handed it to her.

Susan took a sip and set it aside. She knitted her fingers, looking down as the silence stretched out.

"It's humiliating to put into words," she said huskily. "But I want you to understand." Susan breathed a shuddering sigh. "It's an older story, but I'll start with the Prince of Wales. He stopped by on Saturday, knowing I was alone for the afternoon. After nearly three years, I'd forgotten what it felt like to be . . . cornered. The horror came back. And the disgust. Augustus, my husband, would . . ." She looked away.

"I think I understand."

"There was no tenderness, you see. Only pain. No intimacy, only his taking what he wanted. And always from . . . he never . . ." Susan looked away. "It was as if he didn't want to look into my face, my eyes, to see *me*. So, when you came up behind me . . ." She covered her face with his handkerchief.

"Susan."

Her hands dropped to her lap. "After a particularly . . . brutal night, I sought advice from our family lawyer—my family's, not my husband's. I thought the changes to the marriage laws . . . It was an excruciating conversation."

"I can guess what he said."

"He said I had no hope in law and quoted some jurist from the last century. A husband's right to his wife's body for . . . marital relations is absolute. Aside from him, I've never told this to another living soul."

"It's past time you did." He watched her trembling fingers fold his handkerchief into a neat square and set it aside. He pulled a dining chair beside hers and took her hand. "Things fester when you don't speak of them."

"I think you are right." She smiled tremulously. "Thank you, Lionel."

"Susan, my dear . . ." He released her hand. "Perhaps this isn't an ideal time . . ." He stood. "Will you allow me to say what I came early to ask?"

Susan looked up at him, her eyes luminous.

"Surely, you have some inkling . . . you've guessed my feelings." He laid his hand on his breast and asked, "May I speak?"

She nodded.

He offered her his hands; she grasped them and rose. "Dearest Susan, will you marry me? Please don't say the past is in the way. Please let me try to wash away every painful memory."

"I won't say it," she said softly. Then more confidently, "Because it isn't true. In all this terrible business, you are the one good thing." Her eyes filled, and she blinked at her tears. "I fell in love with you."

Lionel took a step forward and touched his lips to hers. When she slid her hands across his shoulders and around his neck, he kissed her again, lingeringly. Then his lips slid across her cheek, and he whispered, "Susan. My lovely, lovely Susan."

She pulled back and looked into his eyes, smiling. "Your Susan." And they kissed again.

After a while, Lionel held her at arm's length. "I believe I could stay here all afternoon. Longer. But the royal train and Windsor await."

"Goodness," Susan said, startled. "I'd forgotten."

"I shouldn't crow, but not every man can say he drove an appointment with the Queen of England out of a young woman's head."

Lionel drew Susan to him and kissed her again.

CHAPTER 15

Susan's efforts to cheer Princess Louise on the ninety-minute train ride from London to Windsor Station failed.

Lady Styles couldn't blame her. Exchanging Marlborough House's gilded halls for the queen's gloomy court was a poor bargain. Yet, sympathy was an effort, given Susan's happiness. She had been discreet with Lionel at the station, thinking, *Joy can be vexing when others are miserable*. So, she listened patiently to Louise's string of complaints, ending with two familiar ones.

"The queen's demands will be endless. Helena is busy with her baby, so my sister is relieved of her duties as Mama's secretary. Now, *I* will become the queen's indentured servant."

Susan murmured soothing sympathy as Louise moved to her second grievance.

"If only Mama would allow a studio at Windsor. *She* may sketch and paint wherever it pleases her, but one cannot *sculpt* in the corner of a sitting room!"

On the short ride from Windsor Station to the castle, Susan finally thought of something to distract the princess from her miseries. "Prince Leopold will be pleased you're back."

Louise brightened at once. "Dearest Leo. How he misses me." Then her smile faded. "He sounds miserable in his letters. Oh, that odious brute, Archie Brown. Why Mama ever made that man Leo's personal servant . . ."

They knew why. He was John Brown's brother, and the queen would not hear a word against either of her Highland servants.

"You will cheer the prince. You always do."

"Leopold must be my object. His terrible bleeding . . . I wish I understood it better. I must ask Doctor Lewis the next time I see her."

For all of Louise's self-absorbed misery, she threw herself into schemes of happiness for those she loved. The princess spent the rest of the ride listing them: sketching with Prince Leopold, challenging him to backgammon, riding around Windsor Great Park, and playing duets at the piano.

"Leopold always feels better when I'm near."

Susan knew it was true. He loved her best among his siblings. Princess Louise often read aloud his letters addressed to "My dearest Loo."

The carriage reached the top of Castle Hill, rolled through the twin-towered gateway, and stopped. They parted at the doorway, Louise to her apartment near the queen's chambers. Susan followed a footman to her guest room in Lancaster Tower.

"The queen will receive you in Her Majesty's private study at five, my lady," the footman said.

"Thank you. I know the way." Susan glanced at the mantel clock. *An hour.*

At ten minutes to five, Lady Styles headed down the Grand Corridor. Two hundred feet of crimson carpet separated her chamber from the apartments in the Queen's Tower. The busts of kings, generals, and statesmen stared down from their plinths, looking haughty and disapproving. Susan knew the castle well enough to have exchanged her open-knit gloves for a kidskin pair and to wear her warmest shawl. Still, she shivered.

She was curious about Victoria's summons to her private study. Susan's fluttery insides felt as if she'd swooped down on a high swing. She touched the nape of her neck and smiled. *A few centuries ago, I'd worry about my head.*

The imposing, scowling John Brown waited at the curve of the corridor. Susan nodded. "Good evening."

"Aye, that's as may be." He cocked his thumb. "She's in her study. Don't make her wait."

Charming as ever, Susan thought.

Brown turned on his heels, led her down a short hallway, and opened the door. "Lady Styles to see ye."

The queen sat at her desk. She closed the notebook she'd propped against a large inkstand's base and set aside a silver-nibbed pen. Victoria picked up an ivory fan, twisting awkwardly to face her visitor. Brown strode forward. He lifted the ebony-and-gilt chair by its armrests and turned it forty-five degrees. Although the room was frigid and Brown had done all the work, the queen's beet-colored face glistened, and she fanned herself rapidly.

"Woosh, woman, yer an armful."

The queen laughed coquettishly, a light musical sound at odds with her solid bulk. "Thank you, my good Brown. That will be all."

"As ye say." Brown closed the door behind him.

"Majesty." Susan made a deep curtsy.

The queen regarded Susan from a round, unsmiling face, her light blue eyes slightly hooded. "The queen understands that Lady Styles accompanied the Princess of Wales to the offices of a doctor *not* on the list of royal physicians. A female person."

Good lord, her spies are everywhere, Susan thought. "Your Majesty is correct. Her name is—"

"The queen knows her name," Victoria said, snapping her fan shut.

Whatever happened next, Susan thought, her days as a courtier were numbered in any case. *Thanks to Lionel.*

Julia climbed the stairs from her ground-floor office and reached the landing as the knocker clanged. Mrs. Ogilvie opened the front door to Inspector Tennant.

"I'm not interrupting the doctors' dinner?"

"The doctors are having drinks in the library." Julia waved a copy of *The Lancet* medical journal. "If you stay to dinner, we'll happily postpone our discussion of head wounds." She felt a pinch of disappointment when he said he had a cab waiting.

"Sir Richard expects me. I have two questions, and he'll press me for the answers."

"Of course," Julia opened the library door, and Dr. Lewis twisted around in his armchair. "Richard's come for a consultation, Grandfather." Julia perched on the armrest. "Fire away."

"Will Mrs. FitzGerald recover? I asked the surgeon, not expecting an ironclad guarantee," Tennant said. "But Sir Godfrey Fellows refused to hazard any sort of answer."

As Julia considered, her grandfather said, "We're a cautious lot. Doctors with knighthoods are the worst."

"One can't be certain, of course," Julia said, "but I'm optimistic."

"May I give Sir Richard a reason?"

"Infection is the greatest danger, and the doctor and nurse charged with her care took every precaution. When I arrived, I found Doctor Rennie spraying down the room with carbolic solution."

"Thank you for a straightforward answer."

"What's your second question?"

"Can you confirm the location of Mrs. FitzGerald's wound?"

"Yes, I watched the nurse dress it. The bullet struck the upper front of her left shoulder."

"That's what Sir Godfrey said, but I must be certain. It's surprising, given the position of the shooter."

"Do you know where the gunman stood?"

Tennant nodded and handed her Louise's sketch. "He fired from a point forward of the walkers and to the right."

Julia studied the drawing. "The shot looks impossible. Princess Louise is blocking it."

"The princess bent over the baby carriage just as the sniper fired."

"Then Mrs. FitzGerald may not have been the shooter's target. I'd wondered."

Dr. Lewis asked, "Have you any news about the gunman?"

"We believe his name is Patrick McGrath."

"An Irishman," Doctor Lewis said.

"And a Fenian."

Julia sighed. "More flames to fan."

"Something else will be in all the morning newspapers to add to the fire," Tennant said. "Earlier in the week, a gunman in Australia shot Prince Alfred."

"Good God," Dr. Lewis said.

"Not fatally, but the shooter is an Irish nationalist." Tennant pulled out his watch. "Now, I'll let you get back to head wounds and *The Lancet*."

Julia followed him to the front door. "I spoke to Susan Styles at the hospital. Thank goodness she and Princess Louise took quick action."

"They kept cool heads in the crisis."

"I'm not surprised. On Sunday, I had lunch with Susan at her new flat. I had hoped to return the invitation and ask her to Grandfather's Wednesday dinner party. But she's been called to Windsor Castle." Julia shrugged. "Just as well, perhaps."

"Why do you say that?"

"I had thought of asking Sir Lionel, as well. But the man is so charming that it's easy to forget he's a suspect. Mixing friendship with murder is probably a mistake."

Tennant said with a trace of bitterness, "An error I made."

"Richard, that was thoughtless of me. I didn't mean—"

"I know you didn't. Still, it's true."

"No one could have imagined . . . in the end, you saw it all."

"In the end."

Julia touched his sleeve. "I had a similar experience, just out of medical school. Someone I liked and trusted." She searched his face. "But we shouldn't live with hardened hearts, closed off and suspicious."

He looked away. "A hazard of my profession, I fear."

Julia heard the sadness and saw the twist in his half smile. He was a step away, so close that she could count his dark lashes and see the fine lines etched around his eyes. A lock of dark hair had fallen across his forehead. One sweep of her hand, one step forward, and she could close the gap between them.

Julia started at the sound of two loud knocks. She opened the front door, and a boy from the telegraph office handed her a message. She opened it and read the heading: HANDED IN AT WINDSOR.

Julia looked up. "It's from Susan Styles."

Patrick McGrath, posing as Marcus York, arrived at Windsor Castle a few hours after Princess Louise and Lady Styles. He'd driven the carriage into the castle grounds about an hour before dusk. Before he left London, he'd sent a telegraph to Windsor's head groom, so he was expected. He'd also mailed a letter to his London "host" that would arrive in the morning post. Last, he'd paid a sweeper lad a half crown to deliver a message to Scotland Yard.

"Tomorrow," McGrath had said to the boy. "One o'clock sharp. Listen for the bells. And mind you, not a minute sooner or later." He ruffled the sweeper's unruly hair. "Deliver the message on time, and a steady stream of half crowns will come your way. I'll know if you don't."

McGrath drove the familiar coach up to the gray stone gate

of the Royal Mews, smiling, remembering why the driver was unavailable. Heavy oak doors swung open to admit him after he showed the man the paper with its recognizable signature.

"So, you're Marcus York," the head groom said.

"That's right," McGrath said. "Where should I stow my guvnor's carriage?"

The head groom led the horses to the last bay. McGrath jumped from the coachman's seat and pulled a carpetbag and rifle from the back.

"The guv heard you're expecting trouble. He'll arrive by train in a day or two, but he thought you could use an extra hand on the spot."

"He's right about that. Stow your gear in the loft." The head groom eyed the rifle. "You're handy with that gun?"

"You could say that."

"More soldiers are on the way from the barracks, but another man with a rifle is welcome."

"Barracks?"

"The Coldstream Guardsmen quartered in town. They're changing the guard in an hour. I'll introduce you to the major in charge."

"Dead right, mate," McGrath said, grinning. "Don't want 'em shooting *me* dead by mistake."

An hour later, a sergeant major drew three concentric chalk circles into the brick wall of an outbuilding. Then he marched "Marcus York" fifty paces away.

"Take three shots," the sergeant major ordered.

The light was fading, but McGrath didn't need the third. His first two bullets shattered the brick in the center circle.

"That's enough, York," the sergeant major said, grinning. "You'll do."

* * *

Dr. Andrew Lewis drove to the railway station with Julia. She would catch a midmorning train. He handed her down from the carriage while Mr. Ogilvie signaled to a porter.

"Now, Grandfather, you know you can depend on Clemmie to do most things," Julia said.

"I plan on it," he said, smiling. "I brought the morning newspapers with me. Just the odd consultation in a pinch."

"Doctor Barnes will relieve you at three."

"Stop fussing, my dear. Go, or you'll miss your train."

Julia kissed her grandfather's cheek and followed the porter to the platform. She settled in her seat, grateful to occupy an empty first-class compartment. She had an uninterrupted ninety minutes to wonder what the day would bring. Susan's three-line telegram had said, "*HRM QV requests consultation. If able, take 9:20 a.m. from Waterloo for overnight stay. Bring dark dress for dinner.*"

Julia had handed the message to Tennant. He'd read it, frowning. "I wish you weren't going."

"To Windsor Castle? Is there a safer place?"

"People keep saying that. There are enough soldiers to repel a small army, but the killer got past the Marlborough House guards disguised as a milkman."

"Well, it's only for one night. Packing for an audience with the queen will have Kate in a flutter."

Tennant hadn't returned her smile. "I'll see you in two days," he said gravely. He took her hand and raised it halfway to his lips. Then he released it abruptly and bowed.

Julia had closed the door behind him and watched through the sidelight window. She'd raised her hand, but he had ducked into the cab without a backward glance.

Julia looked out the train window, wondering about their recent encounters. Sometimes, they left her exhilarated; other times, flattened. She sighed and pulled out a copy of *The Lancet*.

* * *

Lady Styles and a porter were waiting for Julia on the Windsor Station platform. In the carriage, Susan said, "First, let me say that I have no idea what the queen wants of you. I am as astonished as you must be."

"How did it come about?"

"Lord only knows. Only God and the queen. Somehow, she heard about Alix's visit to you. I thought I was about to get a royal dressing-down. Or sent packing. Instead, she asked me to telegraph you."

A short carriage ride brought them up Castle Hill, past the looming Round Tower, and through the double-towered entrance near the visitors' apartments.

"Your bedroom is two doors down from mine," Susan said as they mounted the stairs. "The footman will follow with your case." At the bedroom door, she glanced at the doctor's medical bag. "You have everything you need?"

"Yes, thank you."

Susan opened the door. "I'll come back for you in half an hour."

Thirty minutes later, Julia and Susan walked past the glaring "absurd Scotsman in a kilt." The doctor straightened her shoulders and followed Susan into the queen's private sitting room, trailed by John Brown. Julia hadn't much practice curtsying, but she acquitted herself reasonably well. Then the queen dismissed Susan and Brown. Silence followed as the queen surveyed her.

"Pray, be seated, Doctor."

After some skirt-smoothing and rapid fanning, a perspiring Victoria explained her problem. What ailed the queen was simple: the change of life, coupled with a lack of sympathy from her male doctors. Victoria had all the classic symptoms of approaching menopause, a newfangled term that made a natural phase in a woman's life sound like a disease.

"I trust the royal doctors are not telling the queen that Her Majesty imagines things?"

"That is precisely what they imply. The queen 'exaggerates.' The queen needs to 'calm herself.' The queen is experiencing 'climacteric syndrome,' never explaining what that means. One doctor used the term 'hysteria' for my . . ." The queen fluttered her hand. "For my unruly emotions."

"The queen's feelings are real and natural." Julia thought for a moment. "I wonder if Your Majesty recalls late girlhood, the time on the brink of womanhood and just after. Perhaps the queen remembers those changeable emotions?"

"Yes. I was a trial to my governess. Poor Lehzen," the queen said sadly. "How I plagued her, yet she loved me all the same."

Julia smiled. "I remember being quite impossible when I was about thirteen. The two phases are rather like bookends."

"Are there remedies? Treatments that might ease the discomfort?"

"Sadly, Ma'am, I know none that are effective," Julia said. "Patent remedies are plentiful but worthless. But the queen may command that windows stay open and order her subjects to don extra layers if they are cold. Keep the bedroom cool at night and put aside heavy bedclothes. Avoid overly seasoned foods. As for clothing, less constricting—"

"You are advising the queen to dress like Princess Louise?"

"Well, looser gowns might give relief. If I may be blunt, ma'am, tight corseting will not help the queen feel less heated. But symptoms ease with time. Until then, women endure a trying period."

The queen sighed. "Well, one's mind is eased by information. And to be listened to without condescension is a relief, even if there is no ready cure."

Julia nodded to John Brown, guarding the queen's door, took Susan's arm, and walked her beyond the Scotsman's earshot.

"I won't ask you to betray professional secrets," Susan said, "but your smile tells me it went well."

"I think I was able to reassure Her Majesty."

"What a relief," Susan said.

"The queen mentioned luncheon. I brought an evening dress, but . . ." Julia spread her skirt.

"You're fine as you are. We'll sit down at one o'clock with the three princesses and Prince Leopold."

"Dining with the royals." Julia smiled. "You're an old hand at it."

Susan patted Julia's arm. "It should be lively today with Louise back. And Henry Ponsonby is always amusing company at the table. He's rumored to be next in line as the queen's private secretary. I'll give you a few minutes and come back for you."

Twenty minutes later, Julia waited inside the dining room for Her Majesty's arrival. She stood between Colonel Henry Ponsonby and Lady Sarah Winthrop, a lady of the bedchamber. Lady Sarah surprised Julia with a connection.

"I knew your great-aunt quite well when we were young," she said. "Once upon a time. Caroline and I had tea last spring and reminisced, as the ancient are apt to do."

"Ancient? Never. I won't hear of it," Colonel Ponsonby said.

"My aunt seems ageless to me. And redoubtable." Julia smiled. "She's never shy about giving me good advice, although I don't always admit it. What was she like as a young woman?"

Lady Sarah laughed. "Much the same, and with a wicked sense of humor. She had me in disgraceful stitches at a wedding, whispering about the hideous hats on the bride's side of the family." Then Lady Sarah frowned. "But I'm forgetting."

"Forgetting what?" Henry Ponsonby asked.

"I was thinking of poor Lady Middlebury's wedding. Caroline and I were attendants." She sighed. "My, those two Fitz-Maurice girls were lovely. The sisters were the beauties of their seasons. They hadn't a farthing between them, but they were well connected. Cousins to the Duke of Leinster, if I remember."

Ponsonby said, "The Duke of Leinster?" Then he launched into a story about the duke, His Grace's second cousin, a horse, and a well-known fountain in central London. In telling the anecdote, Ponsonby used the duke's and his cousin's full names.

"I apologize, but you must excuse me," Julia said, turning away. She gripped Susan's arm and said, "May I speak to you? Quickly, before the queen arrives?"

Susan walked Julia to the door. "What is it? What's wrong?"

"I must send a telegram at once."

Just before noon, Sir Lionel strolled into the smoking room of the Army and Navy Club, looking for a drink before luncheon. He cursed his luck and nearly turned on his heels, but he'd been spotted. The club's biggest bore—and resident sot—weaved his unsteady way toward Dermott.

"Lionel, old chap. Just the fellow. Crimean comrades-in-arms and all that. We were refighting the Battle of Inkerman before you arrived." He saluted unsteadily. "Come along. I'm buying."

At least the fellow signed for his share of drinks. Lionel gave him credit for that. He nodded his thanks, and they moved to chairs by the fireside.

"Speaking of the Crimea reminded me. Saw a fellow on the street the other day. Thought he'd be hanged by now. Do you remember . . . no, you were in the Blues, so you wouldn't know the chap."

That didn't stop the man from boring him with several stories attached to an unfamiliar name. Someone he called the Pale

Assassin. While Dermott waited to sign for a second round, he idly asked, "Why was he called the Pale Assassin?"

"Chap looked like a cadaver. Like he had no blood running through him. Beanpole of a man, but strong, with a grip of iron."

"Really?" Lionel took a sip and a discreet peek at the mantel clock.

"The fellow had a signature way of handling the Ivans. He'd smash a Russian to the ground with the butt of his rifle and drive the bayonet into his throat, just under the chin. Carved notches on the butt of his rifle. And he had the coldest, palest blue eyes you ever saw. Got a field promotion to sergeant."

Dermott spilled his drink and mopped his lapels. "What's his name?"

"The Pale Assassin."

"His real name. Damn it, man. Think."

He screwed up his face and then snapped his fingers. "Flood. Sergeant Simon Flood. That's the chappie."

Lionel dashed out the door, passing the waiter without signing for the second round of drinks.

CHAPTER 16

O'Malley often said that a troublesome case was like a drought's end: parched until it poured. "And when the rains come lashing down, the air clears at last."

Tennant's day began with a visit to Westminster Hospital, where Dr. Rennie gave him an encouraging report. After three days, Mrs. FitzGerald's wound showed no signs of infection.

"She's a strong lassie, that one."

Tennant looked around. "Is Major FitzGerald here?"

"Not yet," Dr. Rennie said. "I told him to come back at noon. He did himself and his wife no favors, fretting by her bedside all day. And I want the lady to rest in the morning. His wife rewarded him yesterday with a few words and a squeeze of his hand."

Divisional reports on the incursions into London's Irish neighborhoods took up the rest of the inspector's morning. They were as Tennant expected. "Next to nothing exaggerates their usefulness," he told O'Malley.

Then before noon, a courier arrived from Ireland, carrying a packet sent by the chief inspector of Dublin's Fenian division. O'Malley cut the string and opened it.

"'Tis a letter and a notebook." The sergeant handed them to Tennant.

"The chief inspector writes, 'Lady Browne searched Brigid Dowling's room several weeks ago when asked to do so by the local constable. As you know, she found no letters or personal papers in her bedchamber. But we sent a sergeant to Lansdowne House at your request. When he questioned the servants, the housekeeper remembered something. A year ago, the girl asked if she could keep a box in the storeroom. The sergeant found the enclosed notebook among her things.'"

Tennant set the letter aside and opened the marbled cover of a schoolchild's composition book. It started with a date in the top right corner of the first page: 26 December 1865.

"Boxing Day," Tennant said. "I wonder if she'd been given the notebook as a Christmas gift."

"Like as not," his sergeant said. "What does the poor girl tell us from beyond the grave?"

Tennant turned up the oil lamp. "She writes, 'I have a tale to tell and a longing inside me to shape it into a story. Our story. Lizzie's and mine.'" Tennant looked at O'Malley and continued reading.

"'In the time that came after, when all was lost, and we'd left our village, the women of the nests told fairy tales around the fire, waiting for the dark to fall. But night never fell over the Curragh. It rose, swallowing the valleys, the hedges, and then the hills, the light lingering in the sky. Women and wide-eyed children sat in a double ring, listening, firelight kindling their eyes. The storytellers told tales of the banshee's wail, announcing the death of a loved one, and the changeling fairy-child wandering the hills.

"'But Lizzie never joined in with fairy stories. She would smooth my curls, rock me, and tell the tales of our history, reminding me we were happy once. She whispered, telling me about Daddy and Mam, Granny and me. She'd pass me a pencil and a ratty old pad and have me practice my letters as the flames danced and my lids drooped. I'd write about a cottage with blue shutters and the cow in our field until the rent was overdue and the auction man tying a rope and leading her away.

"'Granny passed on the year I turned five, but I saw her circle the holy well in Lizzie's telling of it. I pictured Mam of a Monday, bending over the washtub, twisting Daddy's Sunday shirt dry, her hands raw and her arms corded. I saw my father's slow, stooping walk, him using his shovel like a crutch, swinging it in time with his stiff right leg. And I'd fall asleep by the fire. Soon after, I'd feel Lizzie shift under me and her gentle shake. I'd open my eyes and find the women gone, then Lizzie would lead me away.

"'That terrible day—the day the unraveling began—I'd waited for Daddy, watching for him, the rain's blur smearing the windowpane. But he never came. In the weeks after, Mam sat with her back to the rough stone wall. " 'Tis God's will," the cottage women told her. "He's gone to a better place." But she sat, looking across the fields. Even the clouds massing and bursting wouldn't budge her. Not until Lizzie and I ran with shawls tented over our heads, rousing her, recalling her to a life that still needed living. We raised her and walked her into the warmth. I didn't sleep that night, listening to my mother's rattling cough.

"'In the morning, the priest carried the letter from Kilcullen. "I think you know what it'll be saying, Maggie. They're wanting the land for the sheep."

"'Eviction. It was the word I'd heard whispered, muttered, and shouted after the men returned, drunk on the stout at Mister Makin's wake. "What's eviction, Da?" I asked after they'd gone. 'Hush now, 'tis nothing, my Brigeen," he'd said, brushing the curls from my forehead. "It won't be happening here."

"'Now, Father Flynn was saying, " 'Tis happening all

around these parts, Maggie. Yer man should have left with the others. Taken you to England to work the hops, at least." I wanted to say it was no use telling us now. The priest asked Mam, "Haven't you a brother?" She said, "Padraig. He went soldiering." The priest asked if she'd heard from him at all. Mam hung her head. "That I haven't," she said in a whisper. "He went off to the Crimea, but he was never a hand for writing."

"'The priest said, "Your Lizzie's gone seventeen. Old enough to be on her own. The Poor Law guardians might pay one fare to Liverpool." But Lizzie said in a flash, "I'll not be going without Mam and Brigid." And that was that.

"'The priest shrugged. "Then 'tis Naas Workhouse for you and yours, missus, as you've nowhere else to go." He raised his hand, and the three of us bowed our heads for his blessing. But Father Flynn had given Mam an idea.

"'We packed two baskets with all we owned and a smaller bag for me to carry. Then we waited in the morning for the removing officer to come. He handed Mam a signed warrant admitting us to the workhouse and counted out three shillings, a parting gift from the guardians of the poor. He said it would pay our omnibus fare to Naas and spare us miles of walking. "You can catch it at Kilcullen Bridge at noon. Good luck to you, missus." And that was that.'"

Tennant looked up from the notebook. O'Malley said, "'Tis a tale told ten thousand times and more all across poor Ireland."

"The first part ends with a twist, Paddy. Brigid writes, 'Instead of heading east toward Kilcullen, we walked west across the Curragh plain.'"

Tennant turned the page. "'An officer on horseback appeared at the crest of the hill, his scarlet coat blazing against the blue sky. We drew nearly abreast, with Lizzy a little behind, and his eyes were on her. And no wonder. I turned and saw her copper hair set fire by the sun and her skirts bunched in her hands as she swung up the hill, breathing hard as she climbed. The basket's straps strained against her shoulders, and I saw something of what he saw. But not all.

"'We trudged on until we crested another mound and came upon a cluster of furze bushes at the bottom of the hill. Beautiful they were, studded with yellow blooms and purple heather growing in between. I didn't notice the spiny shoots and needle thorns that would dig and tear, leaving their mark.

"'At first, the wrens of the Curragh stared at us, silent and hollow-eyed. Dirty, ragged children hung back behind their mothers' tattered skirts. But the shilling Mam offered for a place to stay warmed the women's grudging welcome a degree or two. "Just for a short while, mind," Mam said. "While I seek news at the encampment about my brother." But I'd heard her confess to Lizzie that it might be weeks before she heard about Uncle Padraig if they'd tell her anything at all.

"'A black-haired woman smoking a clay pipe said, "You can have Bridie's nest. She'll not be coming back." She pointed the stem at a tiny opening at the bottom of a hedge. It was crawling we'd be doing, in and out of our new home. Mam eyed the linens drying on the bushes. "My girls can do the washing to earn our keep, and our Lizzie's a fair hand at making a stew." She looked around the circle of women sitting around the fire. "But that's all the work they'll be doing." The pipe-smoking woman leaned back on her elbow and puffed. Maeve O'Connor was her name. "'Tis well enough . . . for now."

"'We saw the officer on the third day, Lizzie and me. We were hauling pails of water from the stream to pour into the washing tub. Lizzie put her burdens down as he drew abreast, and she dragged the back of one hand across her brow, the other resting on her hip. The red-coated captain smiled, saluted her with his riding crop, and trotted on. After that, we saw him on most fine days. He'd offer Lizzie a flower; the next time, it was a bow for her hair. Then he'd be stopping by the stream before we arrived. And he'd take our pails, smiling, climbing down, dipping them in the water, and dumping them into the tub. And they'd walk off a little way, the soldier and Lizzie. Turn a corner and disappear for a while.

"'After he rode away, Lizzie said, "You've clouds in your face, Brigeen. 'Tis nothing more than a kiss, but don't be telling Mam, now." I wouldn't add to my mother's worries as she coughed and trudged to the encampment's gates. That last night, she lay by the fire, feverish and shivering. "She's looking bad," Maeve said. "Keep her warm." Then the women plucked their clean clothes from the bushes and disappeared into their nests. They crawled out when the sky purpled and the sun set. The women walked toward the encampment, pairing off with waiting soldiers.

"'Mam died that night. In the morning, Maeve said, "No priest will be coming to this place to bless her. So, we'll pray over your mother, and you'll make your goodbyes. The soldiers will take her away to lie in a pauper's grave." One woman wrapped Mam's blanket around her and closed it with loose stitches, folding one end to expose her face. The other women formed a circle, holding our hands, as Lizzie prayed the Hail Mary. She tucked sprigs of yellow furze and purple heather into her shroud. We kissed Mam's still, white face for the last time before they stitched the blanket closed. Aggie, who had a kind and gentle way about her, led me away and brewed some tea.

"Maeve went off to report the death, and Lizzie slipped away, too. Then Maeve returned with soldiers and a cart, and they drove Mam across the Curragh. I watched her go until she disappeared over the hill. Maeve puffed on her pipe and looked at me. "From here on, your sister will do more than the washing. If you want to stay, that is. We wrens work to feather our nest, share one, share all. We can't be caring for those who don't bring in a shilling or two each week. You're a little young now, but you'll be old enough in a year or two."

"'Lizzie appeared, hands on her hips and chin high. "That she will not, Maeve O'Connor. That my Brigid will never do." We packed one basket and left the rest of our poor things as payment for our stay. I held one handle, Lizzie took the other, and we were off. "Where are we heading, Lizzie?" I asked. "Is it the workhouse at Naas for us, at last?" My sister smiled. "Never."

"'When we crested the hill, there he was, sitting on the coachman's bench, blazing scarlet, his black boots shining like dark mirrors. Lizzie set the basket down and shaded her eyes. The officer gave the horse a touch of the whip and drove the carriage to where we waited.

"'I looked at my sister. She said, "Peter is taking us to Newbridge and a room of our own. Captain FitzGerald will look after us now." And so we left with him.'" Tennant looked up from the notebook.

"Mother of God," O'Malley whispered, stunned. "He knew the girl of old."

"There are twenty pages more, but we've read enough." He looked at the clock. "FitzGerald should be at the hospital now. Paddy, ask the duty sergeant to have two officers ready and waiting in five minutes. And flag a four-wheeler while I inform Sir Richard."

The constables and O'Malley had assembled by the time Tennant came down. "The commissioner has ordered Major FitzGerald's arrest." He looked at his watch. "He'll be at the hospital by now. Let's go."

"Inspector Tennant," Sir Lionel called, pushing through the lobby doors. "Inspector, I have a name for you. Simon Flood is your man."

"And I have a name for you, Sir Lionel."

* * *

O'Malley peered out the cab window as it swung into the curve of the Old Sanctuary road. "Still following in his hansom," the sergeant said. "Our comedian was right about the major all along. Shocked, he was, despite his jokes."

"Sir Lionel had better be as good as his word and stay out of our way," Tennant said as the cab rolled to a stop in front of Westminster Hospital.

The doctor had expected Major FitzGerald at noon, but it was nearly one, and he hadn't appeared.

Tennant asked Sir Lionel, "Do you know FitzGerald's address in town?"

"He has a house on Kensington Road, on the corner of Prince's Gate."

"Get in the carriage with us and point it out. Constables, follow in Sir Lionel's cab.

When they arrived, FitzGerald's butler informed them that the major was not at home.

Tennant showed the man his warrant card. "Where is he?"

"Well . . ." The butler adjusted his tie nervously.

"Listen carefully and answer my questions truthfully, or you risk a charge as an accessory to capital crimes. Where is Major FitzGerald?"

The butler swallowed hard. "The major packed a carpetbag and left by hansom cab."

"What happened to make him pack up and leave?"

"Something in his morning post. As I poured a second cup of tea, he uttered an oath, crumpled the letter, and ran out of the house. Through the window, I saw him exit the carriage house minutes later. "Staggered out is a better word."

"Take a look," Tennant told one of the constables. "What did the major do then?"

"He asked me to hail a cab. Then he packed a carpetbag and

left. He instructed the cabbie to bring him to Charing Cross Station."

"Charing Cross," O'Malley said. "Heading for Dover, like as not."

Tennant asked, "What time did the major leave?"

"Some time before noon. He had a late start this morning."

"What was he wearing?"

"Ah . . . a bowler, dark gray Chesterfield overcoat."

"Paddy, take that down. Add Arrest Major Peter FitzGerald. Tall, dark-haired, carrying a carpetbag."

"Don't forget the scar on his cheek," Sir Lionel said.

"Thank you." Tennant sent the second constable to the telegraph office on Pall Mall with orders to send it to Dover, Portsmouth, Southampton, Bristol, and Liverpool.

"Sir?" A flushed copper had returned from the carriage house. He jerked his thumb over his shoulder. "There's a dead bloke inside."

They rounded the house and entered the stables through its flung-open doors. Just inside lay the body of a man with a bayonet driven into his throat, a rifle at his side. His staring, milky eyes shaded to light blue at the edges of the irises.

"Simon Flood," Dermott said. "The Pale Assassin, by the color of those eyes."

"Someone's turned the tables on him." O'Malley rounded the body. "There's something . . ." He bent over the corpse. "It looks like a letter folded into his hand."

"Retrieve it, Sergeant." Tennant said. "Constable, search the hayloft."

Tennant opened the letter and turned it over to look at the signature. "It's from McGrath." He read, " 'This is a deathbed confession because I won't be surviving the week. I know that, and I am prepared to die a martyr's death for Ireland. But I believe in God and a reckoning in the hereafter, so I testify to this as true. I contracted with Peter FitzGerald to smuggle the rifles to aid our holy cause. Not his cause. He did it for the lion's share of ten thousand pounds to settle his debts. But when that money wasn't enough, and there was none more to be had from the smuggling, he hired me to shoot his wife. In return, he was to help me escape, so he thought. Her death makes him guardian to his two sons and puts his wife's fortune into his hands, at last. I aimed for the lady's shoulder and hope she recovers. I went along because I needed his help to achieve a last great aim. FitzGerald is unaware of my intentions.

"'As for that piece of horse dung with the bayonet in his throat, Simon Flood and I served as sergeants in the Crimea with the major. FitzGerald was our company captain then. Like me, Flood was a Kildare man. When he was a child, his people farmed FitzGerald lands before hard times and eviction sent them to England. Flood enlisted in FitzGerald's regiment, making the most of the family connection. Now that I think of it, Flood did all the man's killing. FitzGerald got his scar from a Russian saber, but it was Flood who knocked the Ivan off his horse and ran him through the throat.

"'When Flood and I met up again in London, he was FitzGerald's head groom. When he was in his cups, Flood bragged about a smuggling scheme. Later, it gave me the idea for getting the guns into the country with no questions asked. Truth be told, I was surprised FitzGerald played along. But gambling debts made him desperate for money.

"'Flood murdered Lizzie, persuading FitzGerald that the girl was a mortal threat if word of her condition reached the queen and his wife. The other deaths followed the first. Flood bragged about it a week ago, not knowing I was Maggie Dowling's brother. No reason he should. I was in France and Ireland when he murdered my nieces. But never has the hand of Providence been so clear to me, His instrument. My one regret is that I returned to Ireland too late to save my kin from destitution. I tried. I looked for them, but the trail ran cold at Naas.

"'The truth of this, I swear on my mother's grave. I sent Fitz-

Gerald a warning in his morning post, and he'll head straight to Dover. But the message I sent to the Yard that brought you here—'"

O'Malley grunted. "What message, I'd like to know. The creature might escape us yet."

Tennant continued. "'You'll catch him before he gets away. He thinks he has more time than I gave him. It pleases me to have the major on the run for a bit, hunted like an animal. Like the red-coated officers galloping across the Curragh, slaughtering foxes, caring about nothing around them. You'll trap him at Dover and drag him back to London in disgrace. I'm sorry I won't see it. I'm sorry I won't watch him hang. Now, I have one last act of devotion to carry out.

"'God save Ireland,

Padraig McGrath, Patriot.'"

"Sir?" the constable called down from the hayloft. "I found a crate of seven rifles up here."

"Mother of God." O'Malley looked around the empty coach house. "FitzGerald took a cab, the butler's saying. Where is his carriage?"

"And why warn him," Sir Lionel asked, "if McGrath wants him caught?"

"Not just for the fun of a chase," Tennant said. "He wants to divert us. 'One last act of devotion.' My guess? The missing carriage is on its way to Marlborough House or Windsor Castle with McGrath and a rifle inside. He wants us chasing FitzGerald to Dover."

Twenty miles away in Windsor, "Marcus York" patrolled the castle's grounds with a white handkerchief tied to his sleeve. The other armed grooms and groundmen mustering with the uniformed soldiers wore them, too.

"Don't want some jittery private shooting you, York," the head groom had said, tying the knot.

He'd been assigned with four other stablemen to make the

rounds of the castle's perimeter. McGrath felt strangely calm, but tension thrummed in shouted orders, rifles at the ready, and in the soldiers' eyes, scanning the distance. Six Coldstream Guardsmen stood at each gateway into the inner courtyards. From time to time, a tall, burly Scotsman in a kilt and tweed cap appeared at a gate and stood with his arms folded over his barrel chest, watching. Five Guards detachments patrolled Windsor Great Park and guarded Castle Hill, the road leading from the town to the castle's gates.

At one o'clock, replacements relieved McGrath and his companions for a meal and an hour's rest. The other stablemen wandered back to the mews while he stayed behind, talking to the sergeant in charge at the William IV Gate.

McGrath looked up at Windsor Castle's towers. "Which one is the Queen's Tower?"

The sergeant grinned. "All of them, I'd say."

"I mean the one with her rooms."

"That one," he said, pointing. "On the corner."

"Right. I'll get on with my meal. Be back at two."

On his way down Castle Hill, a woman in a carriage passed him at speed.

Thirty minutes later, the officer in charge listened to Marcus York and liked what he heard.

"You're a crack shot, the sergeant major here tells me. One of the best he's seen."

"And I'm a handy fellow with this, as well," McGrath pulled a pistol from under his jacket. "Bought it from a Liverpool gunsmith."

"You won't need it. No one will get close enough for you to use it."

"Right, then. I'll put it away." McGrath holstered the gun in his belt.

"I'll pair you with our best man. The two of you atop the

Queen's Tower will give us a vantage over the entire grounds. Sergeant Major?"

"Sir."

"Find Private Sylvester. Then, locate the Scotsman, Brown. Have him show York and Sylvester the way to the Queen's Tower roof."

They found Brown at the twin-tower entrance with his trunk-like legs planted wide, glowering as he listened to the sergeant major explain his orders.

Brown pointed to Private Sylvester. "Yon uniform tells me who he be. But that man . . . I've never set eyes on him afore now."

"This is . . ." The sergeant major turned to McGrath. "What's your name again?"

"Marcus York, groom to Major FitzGerald, and sent from London to help protect the queen. He's still at his wife's bedside, poor lady."

"Aye, I know Major FitzGerald. Follow me." Brown turned and headed through the gate. "Rifles on the roof . . . 'tis a good plan." And the three of them, Brown, Padraig McGrath, and Private Sylvester, headed up a stone staircase. The Scotsman led them down the ornate hallway past the private apartments in the Queen's Tower. At the turn, they heard laughter from behind a door.

"Eating the woman out of house and home." Brown jerked his head to the right. "The queen's rooms are over there. We'll not be letting anyone close."

McGrath patted the butt of his rifle. "You can count on this."

Tennant left a constable guarding the Pale Assassin's corpse and drove to the Pall Mall telegraph office with Sergeant O'Malley. The inspector sent this message to the Windsor police: YARD ORDERED ARREST OF MAJOR PETER FITZGERALD. SUSPECTED SNIPER WITH RIFLE AT WINDSOR. Then he directed the cabbie to Marlborough House and informed the captain in charge of the guard. Sir Lionel drove on to the Home Office to inform the home secretary.

"We'll brief the commissioner, Paddy. Explain the steps we've taken. Then I'm catching the next train to Windsor."

But Sir Richard had other plans for Tennant. "I want you on the train for Dover. The boat to Calais doesn't leave until six. Plenty of time to bag our bird."

"With respect, sir—"

"Windsor Castle and its grounds are crawling with soldiers. You're not needed there. Go to Dover and be sure the local coppers don't cock up the arrest. I want FitzGerald in Newgate Prison tonight."

"Yes, sir."

O'Malley was waiting outside. "What are our orders?"

"It's Dover for us, damn it."

"This arrived thirty minutes ago." The sergeant handed the inspector Julia's telegram: LEARNED MAJOR FITZGERALD IS RELATED TO LADY MIDDLEBURY.

"Well, now we know why Lady Middlebury had to die," Tennant said.

"And a sweeper lad dropped this with the duty sergeant at one o'clock. 'Tis the note from McGrath, sending us to FitzGerald's house."

"All right, Paddy. Let's bring the bastard back."

Julia arrived outside the queen's dining room just as John Brown rounded the bend.

"The queen was asking for ye. What were ye thinking, woman, running out on her?"

"I'll apologize to Her Majesty, of course."

"It's bedlam hereabouts. Soldiers, marching, a gunman sent by Major FitzGerald stationed on the roof . . ."

Julia swung around. "Sent by Major FitzGerald?"

"Aye. Are ye deaf, woman?" Brown barked, just as two footmen opened the dining room's double doors. Luncheon was over. The queen rose, and everyone at the table stood.

Julia grabbed Brown's arm. "Major FitzGerald will be arrested today. You must get Her Majesty away. Quickly."

Brown shook off her hand and headed for his queen. Julia followed him inside. She called out, "May I have your attention? For your safety, please follow Mister Brown's instructions."

But they weren't looking at her. The two footmen at the door brushed by her. Julia turned. A man stood in the doorway with a pistol in his hand. He pointed the gun at Julia and jerked the barrel.

"You. To the side."

Julia backed away. Everyone else in the room froze in position. Brown stood by the queen, and Louise had her hand on Prince Leopold's shoulder. The rest of the royal family and the courtiers stared in shock. Only the queen looked composed. She waited with her hands folded, staring at the gunman, her lips compressed and her chin up.

"You know why I'm here," the gunman said to her. "Atonement. Centuries of British boots at the neck and the crack of the whip. Millions starved or driven from our land."

When a young courtier shifted his position, inching closer to the door, the intruder shouted, "Move again, and you're a dead man."

The gunman's gaze circled the table. Princess Helena had her arms wrapped around a shaking Beatrice, the youngest of the queen's children. She'd buried her head in her sister's shoulder, whimpering.

The gunman said to the queen, "You won't be hard to miss, but like many a starving mother in Ireland, you'll see your children die first."

Prince Leopold lost his grip on his cane and fell back into his chair. The gunman swung the barrel away from Victoria and pointed it at the prince.

"I'll start with this scrawny fellow." He fired a split second after Princess Louise lunged in front of her brother. She crumpled, falling at his feet.

Brown sprang, bellowing. He jerked the gunman's arm, and the next shot hit the chandelier, sending a cascade of shattered crystals pinging around the room. The Scotsman and the intruder struggled for the weapon. One of the young courtiers rushed forward, but the gunman kicked him away. But it was just the distraction Brown needed. He reached down and pulled his *skene-dhu* from the scabbard in his sock. The gunman gasped as the Scotsman thrust once, then again, and twisted. The intruder fell with a sliver-handled knife protruding from under his ribs.

Julia scrambled to Louise's side. Firmly but gently, she moved the sobbing Leopold away from his sister. "Please help us, sir," she said to the boy. "The footmen will carry the princess to her bedroom. I will follow and treat her wound."

The young prince nodded, wiping his eyes with his sleeve. Julia instructed two footmen to lift the princess into a dining chair and carry her to her room. Then she asked Susan to fetch her medical bag from the guest room.

The queen looked from her daughter to the doctor. Voice shaking, she said, "Save my darling Loosy." She turned to her private secretary. "General Grey, see that Doctor Lewis has everything she needs." Reluctantly, the queen allowed Brown to lead her away as the footmen carried her daughter away in a chair.

General Grey asked, "What can I do, Doctor?"

"Send two more footmen and a housemaid to Prince Louise's room."

The shots had finally brought soldiers pounding down the Grand Corridor. "We did yer job for ye," Brown said, jerking his head. "He's on the floor. Look on the roof, and you'll find one of yours. Dead, I'm guessing."

Two additional footmen and a housemaid followed Julia into Princess Louise's room. The doctor ordered the male servants to shift the table in the center of the room and move the single bed away from the wall to the window.

"I need as much light as possible, so push back the drapes and curtains. Shift that mirror stand to the table. Now, one of you fetch a stack of freshly laundered table napkins."

When the bed was in place, Julia pulled off the bedcoverings, and the footmen moved the princess. A red stain had soaked through the right side of her gown.

Julia told a housemaid, "Move all those candlesticks from the mantel to the table. Set them in front of the mirror. General Grey, have you a box of matches?" When the queen's secretary nodded, Julia said, "Light the candles, please." She stopped a footman as he backed away from the bed. "Move the washing stand next to the table."

Susan arrived with Julia's medical bag.

"I need two more washbowls. Send the housemaid to fetch them. And fresh water to fill them." Julia opened her medical bag. "Now, the gentlemen may leave us."

She took out a lancet and cut away Louise's dress and petticoat. She unhooked her corset. When Julia lifted and turned the princess by her shoulders, she saw no wound on her back. The chemise was the final gory layer to remove. Julia cut it away and exposed the bleeding wound, a small, dark ruby circle.

A knock brought the housemaids with napkins, a water jug, and two more washbowls. Susan moved the items to the table and asked the servants to wait in the hallway.

Julia poured carbolic solution on her hands and rubbed them. "I must remove the bullet."

After a few minutes of careful probing, she found it. Julia

cleaned the area around the wound with carbolic and bandaged it.

"The stays in her thick corset slowed and diverted the bullet," Julia said. "Otherwise, it might have passed through and struck Prince Leopold, as well."

"Thank God," Susan said. "The prince bleeds easily."

Julia wrung a wet napkin and wiped away the excess blood from the wound. Lines appeared on Louise's lower abdomen, jagged, pink, and white. Significant weight loss was a possible explanation, but the princess had always been one of Victoria's more slender daughters. That left one cause. Julia covered the princess with a clean sheet and a warm blanket. Then she stepped back from the bed. Lady Styles had been watching her closely.

"Aside from Sir Charles Locock and his son," Susan said, "you are the only person outside the innermost royal circle who knows that Princess Louise bore a child."

CHAPTER 17

Tennant and O'Malley arrived at Dover's train station with over an hour to spare. From there, it was a short walk to the ferry pier. They approached cautiously, Tennant scanning the streets ahead.

"No sign of him," the inspector said.

"He has time. He'll not be hanging about and making himself conspicuous."

"Let's hope so, Paddy."

"Too many coppers at the pier, I'm thinking," the sergeant grumbled.

"I'll have a word."

They located the officer in charge and persuaded him to withdraw most of his force. The ticket takers had been alerted, and the inspector reminded them of the telltale scar on the man's cheek. Then Tennant, O'Malley, and two Dover constables withdrew to the harbormaster's shed and waited.

Thirty minutes passed, and Tennant pulled out his watch. "If FitzGerald doesn't turn up soon, we've wasted our time." He seethed with frustration, knowing it would be hours before he heard news from Windsor.

Fifteen minutes later, Tennant spotted FitzGerald. He joined the ticket line, looking over his shoulder, his gaze shifting left to right. The major's eyes focused on the lone constable at the ferry dock. Tennant had ordered the officer to ignore the queue. The constable yawned, ambled to the railing, and stared out to the sea, doing a first-rate imitation of a man bored by a routine job. FitzGerald stepped forward and offered his ticket, his moment of maximum tension, Tennant guessed. The taker looked at it, said something to FitzGerald, and the major laughed.

"Good man," the inspector murmured.

FitzGerald walked on, his step looking a little lighter. "He thinks he's home free." Tennant clapped O'Malley's shoulder. "Let's move."

FitzGerald stopped at the bottom of the gangway and set his carpetbag at his feet, waiting for the passengers to move forward. Tennant and O'Malley came up behind him.

"Major FitzGerald?"

He turned reflexively. O'Malley seized him by his right arm and shoulder, and a constable grabbed him on the left.

"Taking a little trip, are we?" Tennant asked, picking up his carpetbag and bouncing its weight. He opened it and rummaged under a shirt. "Well, well." The inspector pulled out a wad of banknotes.

"Blood money," O'Malley said.

"Major Peter FitzGerald, I arrest you in the queen's name," Tennant said, "The charges are conspiracy, treason, murder, and attempted murder for hire." Passengers on the line gasped.

A Dover constable produced a pair of handcuffs and passed them to O'Malley.

"Clap on the Darbies, Sergeant," Tennant said. "Then lead the way."

Two constables followed O'Malley, who dragged the manacled Major FitzGerald through a gaping crowd.

* * *

The queen spent twenty minutes at her sleeping daughter's bedside. Victoria stood and looked at Julia. "I trust that Princess Louise may consult you as her physician from time to time."

"Of course, Your Majesty," Julia said. "It is an honor." The seal of doctor-patient confidentiality was thus assured, and the queen allowed Susan to walk her back to her apartments.

Their departure gave Julia a few moments to look around the room. Pictures crowded the walls, including watercolors by the queen, Prince Albert, and Princess Louise. Her collection included oil paintings by Landseer, Grant, and other celebrated artists of the day. But most revealing was the worktable in a window bay. Sketches of a baby boy littered the tabletop. And a clay model of a seated, curly-haired child, his arm extended for something just behind his reach, waited for the sculptor's final touches. Julia turned at the sound of the door closing.

"The queen agreed," Susan said. "You alone shall look after the princess until she is out of danger. I told her about Harriet's Scottish doctor. The one who washes his hands and changes his coat. I explained that you follow his practices."

"It's a relief not to worry about butting heads." Julia smiled wryly. "A female physician half the age of doctors knighted by the queen? It's an uneven playing field."

Susan walked to the bed and smoothed a strand of Louise's fair hair.

"I'm optimistic," Julia said. "Cautiously, of course, like all doctors."

"She *would* throw herself in front of Prince Leopold. Louise can be impossibly selfish. Impossible, in general. But she's impulsively generous and warm-hearted."

"I've felt that, even in our short acquaintance."

Susan said, "Shall we sit?"

They took seats by the fire. After a pause, Julia said, "No explanations are necessary."

"I know that, but . . ." Susan sighed. "A sympathetic lady-in-waiting once told me that Louise fell through the cracks. She was the fourth daughter and as eager as a puppy in the company of anyone who paid her a little attention. And she doted on Prince Leopold's handsome tutor."

"Is he still— "

"No. The queen dismissed Walter after he complained about Archie Brown's rough treatment of Leopold. Knowledge of the pregnancy came later. The tutor has no idea."

"And the baby . . . you mentioned the Lococks. Frederick Locock adopted the child?"

"Yes. But even Mary Locock doesn't know the mother's identity. Sir Charles Locock delivered Louise's baby. The palace released the story that the princess was traveling on the continent, visiting her sisters. But for three months in the spring, she and Lizzie Dowling lived in a cottage near Osborne House."

"That explains Princess Louise's attachment to the girl."

Susan nodded. "Frederick Locock has an alibi for the day Lizzie died. Louise and I were with him at the cottage for a last goodbye. Sir Charles had arranged for a wet nurse who cared for the baby until his son took the baby away."

"But he couldn't explain."

"There was a need for absolute secrecy. None of Louise's sisters know, only the Prince and Princess of Wales. I extended my waiting into the fall and winter to assist."

"It's a small circle, then."

"And the queen decreed nothing would be written down. No birth or baptismal record or written agreement of adoption." After a pause, Susan said, "I know that Louise has questions about the marks on her body. After she marries, her husband . . ."

"I wouldn't worry. The lines are comparatively faint, and men tend to be in the dark about such things."

Lionel was still in the dark about events inside the castle. He'd taken the first train from Waterloo Station and arrived at the William IV gate in time to watch a pair of privates carry out a body on a stretcher. When they tilted it down a short flight of steps, a soldier's scarlet arm slipped from underneath the blanket.

Lionel took the tower steps two at a time in search of Susan. A footman told him of the shooting and that Lady Styles was assisting Dr. Lewis in Princess Louise's bedroom. He asked for General Grey, but the queen's private secretary was busy with Her Majesty. Lionel paced the hallway with seething impatience. At one point, Lionel stopped at the dining room doorway. He stared at the shattered chandelier and the remains of a luncheon party. He thought, *Susan sat at that table*. Princess Louise's shooting, terrible enough, might have been so much worse.

Then Susan closed a door in the hallway of royal apartments and looked up, smiling as Lionel strode toward her. He didn't care if the queen and the entire household were there to witness. He took her in his arms and kissed her.

Then he held her away and looked at her. "You are uninjured? Nothing—"

"Nothing is wrong with me." She looked to the left and right, kissed him again, and took his hand. "Come. I'll tell you what happened." She led him into the dining room and closed the door.

Lionel pulled two chairs forward and listened to the story. At the end, Susan said, "Julia tried to give us a few minutes' warning."

"Doctor Lewis?"

"Something Lady Sarah Winthrop and Henry Ponsonby

said before luncheon. Julia realized it was Peter. She dashed out of the dining room before the queen arrived and telegraphed Inspector Tennant."

Lionel chuckled. "Did she, now?" His smile faded. "And the princess? How is she?"

"Julia says she's 'cautiously optimistic.' I think it means Louise will recover. She's young and strong."

Lionel nodded. "All that vigorous walking and riding."

"I'll never again complain about her 'forced marches' through the park."

"You realize she saved Prince Leopold," Lionel said. "He would never have survived a gunshot wound." He looked at her. "You know it's not simply a matter of a little bleeding. His condition is far graver than that."

"Yes," Susan said. "The royals know, too. Louise included. But they don't like to name it."

"This may be treason, but Louise would make a better heir to the throne than her feckless brother."

"She has twice Bertie's spirit and three times his heart."

Lionel grasped her hands, and they stood. He took her in his arms, and Susan felt his laughing breath tickle her ear. "It just occurred to me."

She pulled away and looked at him curiously. "What?"

"John Brown, Louise's 'absurd man in a kilt,' is the hero of the hour." Lionel smiled his slow grin. "He'll be utterly insufferable now."

At ten at night at Charing Cross Station, a phalanx of constables transferred the shackled Peter FitzGerald from a railway car to a waiting police wagon for the short journey across central London. Tennant and O'Malley followed in a cab.

Despite the late hour, Newgate Prison's front yard blazed. Workmen toiled by torchlight to finish the construction of a wooden platform. It lifted a scaffold high above the street to give the expected crowd a proper view of the public hanging scheduled two days hence.

News of the hunt for the queen's equerry had made late editions of the evening papers, and rumors swirled. But the precise charges were not yet public. Somehow, a curious crowd had gotten word of the prisoner's imminent arrival. They were rewarded when a handcuffed FitzGerald exited the police wagon just as the joiners fitted the gallows beam. The major looked away from the gibbet, shuddering. It was the first sign of emotion Tennant had glimpsed in FitzGerald since his arrest.

Two lines of grave-faced policemen flanked the prison entrance. Sir Richard Mayne and Mr. Gathorne-Hardy stood sentinel as well. The commissioner was there because he had vowed it. The home secretary attended to report to the prime minister on FitzGerald's arrest and transfer to Newgate. The major passed them, his face as stony as the prison walls. He ascended four steps to a recessed iron door. It clanged behind him, metal bolts scraping and iron keys rattling in the lock.

Sir Richard held the carriage door as the home secretary climbed in. The commissioner turned to Tennant and O'Malley. "McGrath is dead. He killed a soldier and wounded Princess Louise. Doctor Lewis is treating her by the queen's command and is hopeful of her full recovery."

"Thank you for telling us, sir," the inspector said.

The commissioner nodded. "Good work in a bad business." He climbed in, and the carriage rolled away.

From their vantage on the corner of Old Bailey Street, Tennant and his sergeant looked up at St. Paul's dome, ghostly in the moonlight.

O'Malley said, " 'Tis only a few hundred yards from there to Trig Lane, where we found poor Brigid Dowling. Are the sisters resting easier this night, are we thinking?"

"I'd like to think so, Paddy."

* * *

The following evening, Tennant and Lady Aldridge were the only guests at Dr. Lewis's Wednesday dinner party. Julia's grandfather and great-aunt had too many questions that couldn't be answered in front of others. Julia was still away at the castle, attending Princess Louise.

They dined and settled into the library's comfortable fireside chairs. Dr. Lewis looked into his glass. "A toast seems wrong after so much tragedy."

"Perhaps we might drink to the truth's discovery," Lady Aldridge said. "And to justice for those whose lives ended so cruelly."

"Just right, my dear." Dr. Lewis raised his glass. "And to averting an unimaginable tragedy."

Tennant said, "You'll have to wait for Julia's return to hear about that. I know only the broad outlines of the events at Windsor."

Lady Aldridge asked, "Did Major FitzGerald know about the assassination plan?"

"No, according to McGrath's testament. But to supply lethal weapons to a sworn enemy of the crown is enough to condemn him for high treason."

She sighed. "And my old friend, Lady Middlebury. Why did she die?"

"She befriended the Dowling girls at FitzGerald's request, exposing him to questions about his relationship with Lizzie. They met ten years ago in Ireland and had a brief affair. It resumed on the Isle of Wight."

Dr. Lewis said, "It's hard to imagine his elderly cousin agreeing to employ a former mistress."

"FitzGerald made up a story about orphaned daughters of an Irish brother-at-arms who died in the Crimea. In her diary, Brigid confessed to feeling guilty about the lie, but she was glad to be saved from a life on the Curragh."

Lady Aldridge shook her head sadly. "My kindhearted old friend would have been easily persuaded. I wonder about the girl, Lizzy. Was she really a danger to Major FitzGerald?"

"I wonder, too," Tennant said. "She was uncommonly close to Princess Louise. Perhaps he feared Lizzy might confide in her."

"It's strange . . ." Dr. Lewis struck a match and drew on his pipe stem until the bowl glowed red.

His sister looked at him curiously. "What is, Andrew?"

"FitzGerald made good on his early promises to Lizzy, finding a place for her and her sister." He shook his head. "People are a strange mix of things, even the worst of us."

Lady Aldridge said, "To contract for the murders of your lover, unborn child, and elderly cousin, and the attempted murder of your wife . . . He *is* 'the worst of us.' It was a tragedy that FitzGerald ever crossed paths with the Dowling sisters."

"Brigid's diary is a long record of tragedies," Tennant said. "One Irish family's sorrows. When I reached her narrative's halfway point, Paddy O'Malley said to me . . ." Tennant looked away and into the fire.

Lady Aldridge said, "What did my friend, the sergeant, say?"

"He said it was 'a tale told ten thousand times' across Ireland, a story of poverty, eviction, and displacement."

"Like 'wild geese set loose on the winds,'" Lady Aldridge said softly.

Dr. Lewis looked at his sister quizzically. "Caroline?"

"That's how the sergeant once described leaving Ireland," Lady Aldridge said. "Julia told me, and the poetic phrase has lingered in my mind."

"He's a man of parts, Sergeant O'Malley," Dr. Lewis said.

Lady Aldridge nodded. "His parents died during the Hunger. Julia said he brought his siblings to England when he was little more than a boy himself."

Tennant looked at her. "I didn't know that. But Julia would."

She smiled. "Yes."

Lady Aldridge planned to stay with her brother until Julia's return, so she walked Tennant to the door. She planted the point of her ebony walking stick, placed both hands on its ivory crown, and faced him. Like Julia, she was a tall woman, erect despite her years.

"You haven't been to Windsor to see Julia?"

Tennant shook his head. "Meetings all day, tying up loose ends. Tomorrow morning, there's another conference scheduled at the Home Office. And then . . ."

And then, he thought bitterly, seething with frustration. Sir Richard ordered him to leave for the Isle of Wight the following afternoon. The queen insisted that a new coroner's jury be convened immediately to change the open verdict in Lizzy Dowling's death to one of murder.

Lady Aldridge raised her eyebrow. "What then, Richard?"

"I travel to Cowes tomorrow afternoon to give evidence on Friday morning. At the command of Sir Richard Mayne and the queen."

"Julia knows this?"

Tennant nodded. "We . . . we've exchanged telegrams." *Christ, how pathetic it sounds.*

Lady Aldridge offered her hand. "Don't let it drag on too long, Richard . . . and I don't mean your trip to the Isle of Wight."

The following morning, the home secretary rapped his conference table for attention.

Mr. Gathorne-Hardy eyed the three men at the table. "What I want to know is this: is the evidence strong enough to send that blackguard to the gallows?"

"Yes," Sir Richard Mayne said.

"Tell me."

The commissioner looked at Tennant. "Inspector, your summary, please."

"We have FitzGerald's signed note to the Windsor head

groom, offering the services of 'Marcus York.' Then there are the stolen French rifles found on his property and his attempted flight with a carpetbag filled with thousands of pounds in unexplained banknotes. I'd say it's damning."

Sir Richard smiled grimly. "FitzGerald will have his appointment with the hangman."

Lionel Dermott said, "And there is McGrath's 'last testament.' Juries find deathbed statements persuasive. An Irishman who swears on his mother's grave? The prosecution will read that in court to full effect."

"McGrath's letter explained that FitzGerald killed by proxy," Tennant said. "Simon Flood murdered at the major's command. FitzGerald counted on McGrath's sniper skills to put Harriet in her grave and her fortune in his hands."

"Happily, the lady lived," Dermott said. "There are a few additional twists and turns—"

Gathorne-Hardy raised his hands. "I've heard enough. More than enough to measure FitzGerald for a rope. We're done here, gentlemen."

Tennant walked with Dermott to the corner of Downing Street, eyeing the sleeve of hothouse roses in Lionel's hand.

Dermott caught his glance. "Susan is on the 2:10 leaving from Windsor."

"I see."

"I imagine you do. No one pulls the wool over the eyes of 'Tennant of the Yard,' or so says the *Illustrated London News*. No one except . . ." Lionel's lazy grin spread. "Except Tennant himself?"

"Meaning?"

"I understand Dr. Lewis returns tomorrow. Give her my regards."

"Unfortunately, I will be on the Isle of Wight." The inspector nodded curtly and crossed Downing Street.

"Tennant." The inspector turned at Dermott's call. "Then see her the next day, man. Stop dithering, you bloody fool. She might not wait forever."

Just before noon, Princess Louise took her first walk down the corridor to the queen's dining room. Louise eyed the shattered chandelier without comment and turned.

"Short walks like this one, Your Royal Highness," Julia said, watching Louise lean on Susan's arm as she retraced her steps to the bedroom. "Today and tomorrow, twice a day. After that, you can extend the distance. But not too much at first."

Susan looked at Louise. "I leave today. I trust the princess won't overdo it."

"And I'll say goodbye tomorrow," Julia said.

Louise shook her head. "Only farewell, Doctor. Mama placed me in your care, and when the queen commands . . ." Her smile trembled, and she said, "I'm grateful to you. If ever I should require . . ."

"Her Royal Highness need only summon. A note will bring me."

"Thank you, Julia. For everything."

An hour later, Julia and Susan took a last turn around the castle's Upper Ward courtyard.

A footman approached. "The carriage for the station will be at the gate at half past the hour. Does Your Ladyship require a telegram sent to arrange a coach in London?"

Susan said, "Thank you, that won't be necessary." After he bowed and strode away, she said to Julia, "Lionel is meeting me at the station."

"Ah . . . Like that, is it? I thought so," Julia said, smiling.

"Yes, but I've said nothing to Alix, so keep it under your bonnet. She'll be surprised. *I'm* surprised, after two terrible choices . . ."

"Two?"

They'd reached the halfway point along the graveled walkway surrounding the Upper Ward's emerald lawn. Susan stopped and turned to Julia.

"Years ago, I expected a marriage proposal from Peter FitzGerald." Susan shuddered. "Horrible to think of it now, but I was . . . besotted. Then he met Harriet."

Julia squeezed her arm. "A lucky escape, although I'm sure it didn't seem so at the time."

"No. And then I rushed into my disastrous marriage to Augustus."

Julia kissed her cheek. "I wish you every happiness, though you don't need me to cheer you on. I suspect life with Lionel Dermott will be a delightful adventure."

"Bless you for that, Julia." Susan looked up at the looming towers and the windows of the guest wing. "Royal service and a tiny legacy . . . I could live in modest independence. There was a time when I thought that would make me happy. But when you meet a person—someone whose absence leaves a hole in your life and heart—what you *thought* goes out the window."

"Yes," Julia said, and they walked on. They'd reached the gateway before she felt Susan's gaze.

"Tell me, Julia. Was that a polite 'yes' or a 'yes' with conviction? I rather think the latter. I imagine Inspector Tennant hopes so, too."

Julia's smile spread slowly. "Aunt Caroline would say I've taken far too long to figure it out. But yes, with conviction. Both of you are absolutely right."

CHAPTER 18

On Saturday, the first day of February, Susan Styles stood at her window, watching the gray-white mist curl across Marlborough House's great lawn.

Fog veiled the distant trees, and she wouldn't be back to see them bud. That morning, Susan had waited on the princess one final time. It was the last morning she'd live in another person's house. A tap brought her to the door, and four footmen carried her buckled bags and trunks downstairs.

Susan took a last look around. She'd raised her window an inch and smiled at the sound of a rattling carriage. Then she closed the door and walked to the top of the staircase.

Lionel had arrived at Marlborough House ten minutes before his appointed time. For a change, he wasn't wearing Home Office iron gray and black. Susan wondered if he'd dressed to match his mood. He wore a dove-gray cutaway coat over a creamy double-breasted waistcoat, a red-and-gold paisley tie, and a matching pocket square. He'd pinned a white carnation to his lapel to crown it all.

Lionel bounded up the steps two at a time and met Susan on

the landing. Then he took her hands, kissing them one by one. He tucked her arm under his and said, "Time to break the happy news to Alix."

When they finished their audience with the Princess of Wales, Lionel grabbed Susan's hand and raced her down the "God-awful" battlefield staircase. At the bottom, he took her in his arms and waltzed her across the Blenheim Saloon's checkerboard floor, passing two astonished footmen and a gaping housemaid. Lionel threw back his head and laughed.

At the front door, he said, "Let's be off, my darling. We're going to have a deliriously happy life!"

That same misty Saturday, Julia walked to All Hallows, carrying a small vase with six pink carnations. She loved the simplicity of the familiar brick church with its white stone tower, although the belfry was barely visible that morning.

Julia escaped the fog by slipping through the west front doors. She entered the nave and looked up. The ceiling's barrel vault arched over white plaster walls and golden oak pews, the plain glass windows letting in the misty day's meager sunlight. Julia crossed to a side aisle, her clicking heels echoing along the north wall.

She stopped at a spot between the first two windows and found the plaque she sought. It read, WILLIAM AND SUSANNAH LEWIS, 1841, LOST AT SEA ON THE SS *PRESIDENT*. THEIR GRAVES ARE KNOWN ONLY TO GOD. Fate had decreed that Julia never knew her parents. But her grandparents had built a foundation of love and security as solid as the Roman stones beneath the church. She bent and placed her bouquet at the base of the wall. The first of February was her mother's birthday; she would have been fifty-four that day.

Julia wondered what her mother would say if she could speak. Perhaps, "Life is a precious gift. Don't waste the time you're given." The church bells rang the hour, a reminder of time's passage. Julia would be twenty-nine on her next birthday. "Seize the day," her grandfather had said, referring to Richard Tennant.

She thought of him and smiled. His attraction was undeniable. She felt its pull each time they met. *One of these days, he may speak.* What would she say? Julia had wondered if she could be happy with such a guarded man. Some people married, thinking their partners would change. Julia neither expected nor wanted a different Richard.

She walked toward the altar and looked up at the half-domed apse. So many had kneeled beneath it, praying for guidance, strength, or the gift of acceptance, "Thy will be done."

What of *her* will? It had been a journey. At last, Julia understood what she wanted. She loved him. And as for the world's opinions? She wouldn't let its narrow views about marriage rule her. So, if Richard walked into the church, took her in his arms, and asked her to marry him, she knew what she would say. She closed her eyes and imagined him drawing near, his embrace, his kiss.

Julia exited the building and walked along the churchyard path, wondering if Richard caught a morning train to London. She calculated the hours, thinking, *Perhaps I'll see him this evening.* Then there he was, walking out of the mist, moving with a slight hitch in his step, his unbuttoned overcoat flapping. Julia's heart lifted.

"Richard." She extended her hands, smiling. "You're back. I didn't expect—"

"I caught the milk train." He tucked her arm under his elbow, and they walked along the path. "Mrs. Ogilvie told me you were here."

"And the coroner's jury?"

"A verdict of murder, as expected, although they'll try FitzGerald for treason in London. It trumps all other charges."

Julia shook her head. "Each time I see a newspaper headline,

I think of his poor wife and sons, wondering how they will survive it."

"The world won't soon forget his treachery. Still, the Yard's work is finished, and I left my report on the commissioner's desk. I was halfway to the clinic when I remembered today was Doctor Barnes's Saturday."

"We're truants, both of us. Do you . . . have you plans for the day?" Julia felt a twinge of disappointment when he hesitated. "Can you come to luncheon at least? Aunt Caroline will be there."

He released her arm and turned. "It depends."

"On what?"

Tennant looked over her shoulder. "Is it too cold to sit on that bench?"

"Not at all. The fog is lifting. I think we're in for a lovely day."

After a fleeting smile, he said, "Perhaps."

The sun remained a pale, veiled disk, but filtered streaks sliced through the mist, picking out shrubs and stones like footlights on a stage. They walked through the dappled light and sat beneath a sprawling yew's green needles and red berries.

Tennant removed his hat and leaned forward, sliding the brim through his fingers as it hung between his knees. Julia recognized the habit and waited for him to gather his thoughts.

He laid his hat on the bench. "Do you visit here often?"

"Yes, it's our parish church. My grandparents were married here, and there's a memorial to my parents inside." Julia smiled. "When I was a little girl and feeling sorry for myself, I'd stare at it, brooding. Not that I had much to complain about. No grandparents could have been more loving."

"You were lucky."

Julia waited for more. Then she said, "My grandparents said *they* were the lucky ones. They'd lost their only child, but God had gifted them another, although I'm not sure I was always much of a present."

"My mother . . . well, let's say she was nothing like your grandmother. That's why . . . perhaps it explains . . ." He cleared his throat. "Julia, you've tried to draw me out many times. But it's . . . difficult to break a lifetime's habit of reticence. I'm sorry."

His labored admission wrung her heart. "Well, you're making a start."

"More than you know." Then he stood, raking his fingers through his dark hair.

Julia rose from the bench and touched his arm. "Tell me."

"Your grandfather. His welcome. Including me in the family circle. And your aunt. Lady Aldridge has a kindly interest in me, always."

Julia smiled. "More than *you* know."

He took a step closer. He took her hand and pressed it above his heart. She felt hers race.

"Before we met, my life was empty. I never want to live that way again."

Her eyes filled, and she blinked at tears. He turned her hand over and raised her palm to his lips. The sensation thrummed through her like a cello's deep chord. Her lips parted, and she took a shaky breath.

"I love you, Julia. Say you'll marry me."

Doubts? They vanished like the mist. He released her hand, and Julia touched his cheek with her fingertips. "Yes. Oh yes."

He cupped her face, and she closed her eyes. His lips found hers, and he kissed her lightly, then deeply, then lingeringly. When he finally pulled back, she felt like a diver after a plunge, swimming, breaking the surface, taking a first deep breath. She slipped her arms under his overcoat and around his waist and laid her cheek against the rough tweed of his shoulder.

An hour later, they walked arm and arm around Finsbury Circus and mounted the steps of number 17. He put out his hand to stop her as she inserted the latchkey.

"Wait."

"What is it?"

"Suddenly, I feel oddly nervous about speaking to your grandfather," he said, bemused.

"Truly? Well, I know what Aunt Caroline will say." She turned the key and pushed the door.

"You're certain?"

"About everything." Julia took his hands and backed over the threshold, pulling him with her.

"Dearest Richard. Welcome home."

AUTHOR'S NOTE

In the late eighteenth and nineteenth centuries, events in the wider world spawned a new violent phase in England's overlordship of Ireland. Revolutions and surging nationalism helped fuel Irish risings in 1798, 1848, and 1867, the year *Murder by Moonrise* opens. All failed to rally the populace. The novel foreshadows the shift from armed uprisings to the terror tactics employed two decades later. The "dynamite campaign" of the 1880s targeted British military, government, and civilian sites. Readers can find a balanced and readable survey of Ireland by the Irish historian John Gibney in *A Short History of Ireland: 1500–2000.*

Two attacks carried out by Irish republicans—the Manchester and Clerkenwell "outrages"—happened as I describe. Young Willie Abbott is a fictional patient treated at Julia's clinic. The little sister he sought among the survivors was Clerkenwell's youngest victim: eight-year-old Minnie Abbott. Of the eight men initially charged in the bombing, only Michael Barrett was found guilty. His hanging outside Newgate Prison in 1868 was the last public execution in Britain.

The threats to the queen at Balmoral Castle and Osborne House—false alarms—did scramble a police and military response that irritated the queen. Irish émigré Henry James O'Farrell did shoot Prince Alfred during his tour of Australia, the first visit to the Antipodes by a royal family member. (It happened a little later than in my story: in March, rather than January, 1868.) While Victoria's second son survived, the Australians hanged O'Farrell, and the attack triggered a wave of anti-Irish sentiment. As for the arson at Marlborough House and the assassination attempt at Windsor Castle, they are my inventions, although the queen survived eight attempts on her life during her long reign. The theft of the French rifles is fictional, too, but gun smuggling and Irish plots to gather weapons kept the Home Office awake at night. The "pike upon your shoulder" celebrated in the Irish ballad "The Rising of the Moon" was replaced by rifles, revolvers, and dynamite in the 1800s.

Like many historical novels, *Murder by Moonrise* mixes real and fictional characters. Scotland Yard Commissioner Sir Richard Mayne, Home Secretary Gathorne-Hardy, and the Fenian Branch director, Lt. Colonel William Fielding, are historical figures who struggled to contain the Irish threat. The Yard's failures damaged Mayne's reputation and sparked calls for his removal. He survived only to die in office in 1868 after nearly forty years as commissioner. Fielding's Fenian division perished in the same year. In the 1880s, Scotland Yard organized a new Irish department in response to the wave of bombings. It evolved into the Yard's famed "Special Branch," tasked with investigating politically sensitive cases and those involving national security.

The geography and locations described in *Murder by Moonrise* are largely accurate, with one exception: the site of the holy well at Quarr Abbey's ruins. I first read about the well ritual in *Exiles of Erin* (1979), Lynn Hollen Lees' study of Irish immigration to Britain. The Isle of Wight has several holy wells, including one dedicated to St. Lawrence. It's located on the Whitwell Pilgrim Path near Ventnor, on the southeast coast. I moved the well to Quarr's spot near Fishbourne, an easier trip for Lizzie Dowling to manage on her half day off.

By 1867, Victoria's Albert had been dead six years, and the widowed queen rarely appeared in public. Her "Highland Servant," John Brown, was her chief emotional support. The relationship provoked gossip, bemusement, and a measure of disgust. Members of the royal household called him the "Queen's Stallion" and referred to her as "Mrs. Brown." Most historians dismiss rumors of a sexual relationship or a secret marriage. But the queen's emotional dependency on Brown is beyond dispute, and his open familiarity—addressing the queen as "woman"—shocked onlookers (including my fictional Inspector Tennant). Victoria's children felt displaced by Brown and loathed the Highlander. He showed them scant respect and often restricted access to their mother.

Mrs. Brown, the 1997 film starring Judi Dench, gets the story mostly right. But some biographers of the queen's children are critical of the film's portrayal of Brown. Lucinda Hawksley (a biographer of Princess Louise) charges that it romanticizes a "deeply unpleasant" bully. In *Prince Leopold* (1998), Charlotte Zeevpat argues that Victoria's blindness about Brown extended to his brother Archie. He served as an abusive personal attendant to the vulnerable, hemophiliac Prince Leopold, endangering his life. Jane Ridley, the award-winning biographer of Prince Bertie (*The Heir Apparent*, 2014), writes that Brown "terrorized the household" and that the royal children "came to dread holidays at Balmoral, where Brown reigned supreme."

As to Princess Louise's illegitimate child, historians acknowledge the extraordinary pregnancy rumors that circulated and persist. Elizabeth Longford, editor of Louise's letters (*Darling Loosy*, 1991), dismisses the story. But in *Queen Victoria's Mysterious Daughter* (2015), Lucinda Hawksley makes an intriguing case that Louise was the mother of Frederick Locock's adopted child. Viewers can stream the 2018 documentary *Queen Victoria and Her Nine Children* on Prime Video, BBC Select. In episode two, Hawksley presents her evidence.

(The episode also explores the queen's relationship with John Brown.)

All three episodes in the series are absorbing explorations of Victoria as a mother, as well as her fraught and complicated relationship with her children. "You cannot deny that Queen Victoria was a very, very difficult mother," one writer says. She was no modern "*mea culpa*" mom "beating herself up," comments another. Victoria was their queen *and* their mother, and they'd jolly well better knuckle under. In *Murder by Moonrise*, the fictional Susan Styles observes that the queen's children are her subjects, and daughters are more subject than sons.

For additional reading, Julia Baird's *Victoria the Queen* (2016) is a graceful, galloping biography that blends scholarship with readability. A book that looks at Victoria from a different angle—that of her courtiers and attendants—is Kate Hubbard's *Serving Victoria* (2013). It details the daily duties and rituals that "waiting" on royalty entailed.